THE EXECUTIONER'S APPRENTICE

THE EXECUTIONER'S SONG BOOK 2

D.K. HOLMBERG

ASH
PUBLISHING

CHAPTER ONE

The steady tolling of the Shisen Bell rang out as Finn Jagger followed Master Meyer through the street. He looked up to the tower in the distance, noting the massive spire rising over the city, casting a faint shadow along everything. He counted off the number of times the bell rang, and when he neared ten, he glanced over to Master Meyer.

"Do you think we should hurry?" Finn asked.

Master Meyer didn't look over at him, though his wrinkled face was lined with worry. "They will not start without us."

"Are you sure?"

Master Meyer was dressed in his more formal leathers, his brown shirt and matching pants more befitting a merchant than an executioner.

"They require our testimony in order for them to carry

out the sentencing," Master Meyer said. "They will not proceed without us."

Finn just nodded. He was nervous, but his nervousness stemmed not from coming to present to the jurors the findings he and Master Meyer had discovered during their questioning of the accused; this was the first time that he had presented himself before the jurors—and Bellut—since realizing the truth about Bellut.

"I'm not sure I can do it."

Master Meyer glanced over to him, shaking his head. His flat blue eyes watched Finn, the wrinkles on his brow furrowing more deeply than usual. Sweat beaded along the corner of Meyer's close-cropped forehead, running down his cheek, completely ignored by Master Meyer. "You can, and you will. You will not say anything beyond what is asked of you. Do I make myself clear?"

Finn nodded, surprised. "I'm sorry; it's just that I—"

"I know your hesitation, Finn. I understand your fear."

"It's not fear," Finn muttered.

"It *is* fear. You fear you won't be able to remain impartial when you present yourself before the jurors."

Finn looked around the street. They headed through the Theiry section, making their way to City Hall, and they passed by people oblivious to their presence. The only time anyone paid any attention to Master Meyer and Finn was when they were accused of some crime. That, and during the Blood Court. People throughout the city came to the Gallows Festival to watch the condemned proceed through the streets, celebrating the sentencing.

"I can be impartial. And it's not fear. I just want them to know the truth."

"What truth is that?" Meyer asked him.

"The truth of what he's done."

Meyer stopped, crossing his arms over his chest. He was a large man, muscular, which had surprised Finn when he had first trained with him. He hadn't realized the physicality of the job, but having worked with Master Meyer as much as he had over the last year, Finn had grown stronger as well. Training with the sword, along with his hurried pace through the streets, had given him a different physique.

"The truth comes out when you have information, Finn. Otherwise, it's your opinion."

"I know what happened. I know what I saw and heard."

"And we will have to prove it."

Finn took a deep breath, letting it out slowly. He appreciated that Meyer intended to work with him in order to prove what happened, but it wasn't happening nearly as quickly as how he wanted. Bellut, the man Finn now knew to be the Client, had planned an attack on the kingdom. And gotten away with it.

"He instigated an attack on the king," Finn said softly. He looked along the street before holding Meyer's gaze. "Aren't we meant to protect him?"

A slight smile quirked Meyer's mouth. "The Executioners' Guild does not need to protect the king. We serve as his arm of justice. I thought you'd learned that by now."

"I get that," Finn said.

"Then you should understand that the Archers, along

with his personal guards, provide the king with a layer of protection we cannot."

"If we serve as the king's justice, then shouldn't we want to find justice against those who have wronged him?"

"Wronged him, or wronged his people?"

"Isn't it the same?"

Meyer frowned, and he turned away from Finn, heading along the street. "There are differences. We serve the people of Verendal. We serve at the king's behest. I as the master executioner, and you as my apprentice. In time, when you progress to journeyman, you can serve him more directly, but until that time, you serve as I demand."

"Which means—"

"Which means we will present ourselves to the jurors and the magister, and you will say nothing."

"Bellut thinks he got away with it." And Finn didn't know who he'd been working with, but he couldn't have been acting alone.

"If he is guilty"—Meyer glanced over at Finn, holding his gaze—"*if*, I say, then eventually we'll uncover the truth. Those involved will face the king's judgment. For now, focus on the case at hand. We don't have enough information to press charges against Bellut yet, so we will continue operating as if everything is normal, we will continue to bring justice elsewhere, and when the time is right, we will deal with Bellut. But don't let his case force you to make mistakes on others."

They continued onward toward City Hall, and Meyer said nothing more. Finn knew better than to argue with him about this, but it didn't change his feelings. He wanted to bring justice to Bellut and to the magister, though there was a part of him—the part of him that Meyer had been training—that questioned whether it was justice or vengeance Finn wanted.

Couldn't it be both?

Many of the sentences they carried out were a mixture of vengeance for those wronged along with justice for the king. He'd not been a part of some of the more brutal sentences, but what were those other than vengeance for those who had been wronged by the condemned?

As they neared City Hall, Meyer slowed, glancing over to Finn again. He didn't say anything, but there was a hint of worry in his pale blue eyes. This was the first time he'd permitted Finn to come and present to the jurors since Finn had discovered Bellut's role in what had happened to him. Otherwise, Meyer had been the only one coming and presenting. He claimed it was because he needed Finn performing the other aspects of his duties, whether that was running errands, continuing his studies, or even simpler things like cleaning or practicing with the sword Justice so he could ensure he had an accurate strike when he used the blade for the first time, but Finn knew better.

"I'm not going to say anything."

Meyer inhaled deeply before letting out. "I'm not asking you for silence. I'm asking you for self-control."

Finn swallowed, turning his attention to City Hall. It was an older building, but large, occupying much of the block. The stone was well maintained, and the overly large steps leading up to the entrance gave an air of authority that the two Archers standing on either side of the door augmented. They were dressed in leathers and chainmail, and both carried short swords, though Finn knew that the Archers within the city were not nearly as well-trained or deadly as the palace Archers.

Meyer strode up the steps, nodding to the Archers, and pushed open the doors. Finn lagged behind, his mind racing as he knew he needed to get control. Were it up to Bellut, he would have hanged. Someone else had been complicit, ranking high enough that it left Finn wondering if it might be the viscount himself, though Finn had not even learned that until much later. Both of them had been tied into some plot on the throne, but it was the matter of proving it that had become challenging.

Finn would prove it. Somehow.

The problem for him was that the people who might be able to offer the testimony needed to convict both Bellut and his accomplice had disappeared. The only one who remained was him—and his friend Oscar. Oscar would never testify, and seeing as how he had escaped without any stain upon him, there was no reason for him to do so. That left finding Wolf or Rock, but both had been banished from the city.

Meyer glanced back at him. "Come."

Finn hurried into City Hall. The entrance gave off a grand feel. The marble tile gleamed, and portraits of the king, along with kings of the past, hung along the walls in the entrance. King Porman's portrait hung in a prominent location with a painting of the viscount just below him.

Meyer didn't linger. He had likely been there hundreds upon hundreds of times.

Meyer stopped at the door leading into the juror chambers. "Say only what you're asked to say," Meyer said.

"I will."

"Do not draw attention to yourself," Meyer said.

"I won't."

Meyer shot him a look. "And speak confidently. You are here on behalf of the king, not on behalf of the jurors. You do not serve them."

"We don't?"

"We serve independently. The Executioner's Guild sits outside of the authority of the jurors. We make recommendations, and we are subject to their sentencing, but we are not beholden to them."

There was something within what Master Meyer told him that struck Finn, but he didn't have the chance to process what it was.

Meyer pushed open the door and stepped inside.

Finn followed, moving carefully, watching Master Meyer more than anything else. The juror chamber was draped in the colors of the king along with his crest—a massive wolf head over crossed swords—along with markers for the kingdom, making it an official-looking room. Rows of benches took up the back half of the room, though they were empty today. A man stood in shackles near the front of the room, one of the Archers standing alongside, making sure he couldn't run.

Finn knew Ralston as well as he could. He had attended the questioning with Master Meyer, facilitating the interrogation. He was a heavyset man, and of average height, with wild hair that had grown even wilder in the time he'd been imprisoned in Declan. His cheeks were ruddy, looking like he had already drank several pints of ale, and he leaned forward with a slight stoop to his back.

The magister sat at one end of the bench. Finn didn't know much about him. He was the legal expert within the city, had trained at the university, and led the jurors in their deliberation, guiding them, purportedly to serve the king's justice. The magister had short, graying hair and the pudgy face of a scholar. His thick glasses hung down his nose as he stared at a stack of papers in front of him, ignoring the fact that Meyer and Finn had approached.

The other jurors were arranged along the bench. Bellut sat near the center. Finn couldn't read his expression, though there was a darkness to his gaze. He was not much older than Finn and wore his crimson cloak, his blond hair looped back with a crimson ribbon, as if to play at his service to the king, and he had bright blue eyes that stared at Finn. Finn refused to look away from Bellut. Regardless of what Meyer taught, Finn was determined to get vengeance.

When Meyer reached the front of the juror chamber, he glanced over to the Archer, nodding. Ralston glared at Meyer.

"You're late," the magister said without looking up.

"My duties are extensive," Master Meyer said. "And I'm here only a moment after ten bells. I apologize for my delay, but it was inconsequential."

The magister looked up, folding his hands together and leaning forward. "Well?"

Meyer glanced over to Finn. "My apprentice will present the details of the crime to you."

"We don't need your apprentice to report anything," Bellut sneered.

Meyer looked over to him, an unreadable expression on his face. "Tradition dictates that the apprentice executioners are permitted to speak before the jurors. If you would like that changed, perhaps you could petition the executioner court, along with the king. Otherwise, we will proceed based on tradition."

Bellut sat back, crossing his arms. Finn wished he could have accused him, bringing him before the jurors, but Meyer claimed they didn't have enough evidence. The other jurors looked out at Finn, waiting.

There were seven sitting in front of him, all told. Six jurors, plus the magister. Two of the women were older with dark graying hair. One of them, Isabel, had a sharp nose and thin lips. She still looked at him with the same suspicion that she'd looked at him with when he had come before the jurors as one of the condemned. The other woman had a round face and rosy cheeks, and constantly dabbed a handkerchief across her brow and at her nose. The men were dressed in dark clothes, formal attire, and one even wore a wide-brimmed hat that tipped to the side, almost hitting Isabel every time he turned his head.

Meyer coughed softly.

Finn took a step forward. "I present to you Ralston Jol. Accused of many crimes, but primarily of rape. During our questioning of Mr. Jol, he admitted to five episodes, with four different women."

"He admitted to this?" the magister asked.

Finn looked over to him, trying to keep his face neutral. This was what Master Meyer wanted from him. Describing these crimes was more difficult than he'd expected, and a man like Ralston deserved what would come for him.

"He admitted to these crimes. We have corroborated his admission with those he violated."

The jurors tore their gazes away from Finn, all but Bellut, and turned them upon Ralston.

"What do the victims request?" Isabel asked.

Finn shook his head. "The victims seek justice."

"What measure of justice?" a heavyset man near the end of the bench asked. Finn knew him to be Alor Hostal, a somewhat wealthy merchant from the center of the city. He served several different merchant sections that elected him as juror and had found him to be relatively impartial most of the time.

"They did not specify," Finn said.

"They didn't specify, or you didn't ask?" Bellut asked.

Finn took a deep breath, letting it out slowly as he held his gaze on Bellut. "We assured the victims, along with their families, that the king's justice would be served, as it always is."

Next to him, Finn could feel Meyer stiffen.

He needed to be careful. He wasn't trying to anger Meyer.

"Of course," the magister said, waving his hand and

drawing the rest of the jurors' attention to him. "The king's justice will always be served. That is our responsibility. We are here on his behalf." He leaned forward, watching Ralston. "Do you have anything to say for yourself?"

It was unusual for the condemned to have the opportunity to speak on their behalf, so Finn wondered why they would permit it now.

Ralston was a mason, a man of some training and skill, but not someone who would warrant careful consideration on behalf of the jurors. It was the reason Meyer had wanted to ensure that they had all the details of his crime as carefully constructed as possible. If they made a mistake, it was possible that Ralston would hang even if he were innocent.

"I don't have anything to say to you," he spat.

"Then unfortunately, you will face the king's justice," the magister said.

"Seems to me you've already decided. You always already decide. There is no justice here."

The magister stared at him before leaning back and motioning to the other jurors. They whispered softly amongst themselves before the magister nodded and looked to Ralston, his eyes narrowed. "Ralston Jol, you have been accused of the crime of rape, attacking four women in the city, and you have not denied the allegations. Given the nature of the accusation, you will hereby be sentenced to the king's justice, and we sentence you to death by hanging."

Ralston just grunted.

The magister turned to Meyer. "Make preparations. We expect this to be carried out within the next two days."

"Of course," Master Meyer said.

He elbowed Finn, and they turned, heading out of the room.

Once they reached the door, Finn paused, glancing behind him to look to Bellut, though the juror paid little attention to him. Finn glowered at him, but only for a moment, then he had to hurry back out into the street after Master Meyer.

Once there, Meyer turned to him. "I saw what you were doing," Meyer said. "If you cannot keep your emotions in check—"

"I kept my emotions in check."

"You glared at him. Perhaps I'm the only one who noticed it, but if you want to find the justice you claim, you must be patient."

"Patient? That one," he said, motioning to City Hall, "was nearly the reason I hanged."

"And now you have an opportunity to ensure that the king's justice is carried out. Is that not what you want?"

Finn squeezed his eyes shut and then settled his irritation. He needed to find that calm center within him. "That's what I want."

"Good. Now, seeing as how we have a sentencing to prepare for, I expect you to inspect the gallows, ensure that it is intact, and prepare the Stone." Meyer watched him. "Can I count on you to do that?"

"I can do it," Finn said.

Meyer nodded. "Good. Meet me back at the house

later. We will make sure you remember how to tie the rope. You will be the one to carry out this execution, especially as you were the one to lead the questioning."

Meyer started off, leaving Finn alone in the street.

He had been giving Finn more and more responsibility, letting Finn lead questions during their interrogation of prisoners, though even as he did that, Finn still had not questioned any prisoners on his own. Not yet. He worked under the guidance of Master Meyer, and though he felt like he was ready to take the next challenge, to begin working on his own, it all depended upon when Meyer felt confident in Finn.

Which meant he needed to be careful with his agitation. He might be irritated with Bellut, but he did need to keep those emotions in check. It was no different from how he had needed to act when he was on the crew. You just didn't show your anger with the leader of the crew. You might be frustrated, and you might not care for what role they gave, but you had to smile, take the shit they offered, and hope the next time you were given more responsibility.

He hurried through the city, making his way to the Teller Gate and then beyond. The gate was an enormous structure made out of wood and iron, and could be pulled open with levers from the massive wall surrounding the city. Named after one of the city architects, the Teller Gate was identifiable throughout the city, and easily spotted from the road beyond.

He needed to work quickly. If there was an issue with the gallows, they would need to repair it before the sentencing. As he stepped out of the gate, the open road leading up to the city spread before him. It wound beyond Verendal and headed to Vur, and then farther to the east, all the way to the capital. A dense forest lined the road, though there was no danger of the Alainsith out of that forest. That was farther to the north. Finn had never seen any of the Alainsith, though he had seen their artifacts when he'd broken into the palace, and he knew that the king continued to work with them to ensure stability between their people. Off to his left, the hegen section of the city pressed up against the outside walls. It was chaotic but vibrant. Most of the buildings were painted in bright colors, as the people in the hegen section cared for maintaining their homes, however much like shacks they might be.

None of that was what brought him out there. It was the Raven Stone, and he hurried over to it. It was a towering white stone, flat-topped, though the surface of the stone had been stained with blood over generations of sentences that had been carried out there. The stone itself was said to have always been situated outside of the wall of Verendal, though it looked out of place, as if one of the gods had simply taken an enormous rock and set it down, leaving it amidst a field of grasses.

The last execution had been two weeks before, long enough that Finn needed to ensure the stability of the gallows. It wouldn't do for someone to be sentenced only to have the rope snap, or one of the timbers supporting the gallows to collapse.

He climbed the steps leading up to the Stone and stood

on it for a moment. He had been a part of two dozen executions in the time that he'd served Master Meyer, and had been directly involved in many of them.

Finn made quick work of inspecting the timbers, checking the connections, testing for any sign of damage or cracking, anything that would imply that the gallows needed work before the next festival, but he found nothing. Finn moved on to testing the rope. Meyer preferred to tie a new knot each time and typically used a fresh rope with each condemned, but he also liked to have one hanging for show.

When he was done, he turned away from the gallows and sighted a figure standing near the edge of the hegen section.

He'd hesitated to return to Esmerelda. He still had the card he'd been given by the hegen in his pocket, and he carried it with him everywhere. Finn slipped his hand into his pocket, fingering the thick paper of the card, tracing his thumb along the edge and then along the surface. He had memorized the gold crown on the surface of the card long since, but he didn't know what it meant. He glanced back at the city, and when he turned his attention to the hegen section again, the figure was gone.

Finn climbed down the steps of the Raven Stone. As he headed into the city, a dark cloud drifted overhead. It bloomed over the city, billowing up from some place just inside of the wall, and continued rising with an ominous plume of dark smoke.

He passed through the gate, and the smoke continued billowing up, getting thicker and darker than it had been.

This was not just smoke. This was a fire.

A fire in the city could be dangerous and devastating. Most were put out by the fire brigade, but not all. Having the Vinlen River run through the city gave a fire brigade an opportunity to extinguish most fires quickly, but Finn had seen entire homes burned within minutes. Lives destroyed.

He followed the smoke.

It didn't take him long to find it.

The fire was situated in the Jorend section. It was a more run-down part of the city, similar to where he had grown up, and the homes were built close together and all made of wood. Massive flames crackled along the length of the street, running on either side. People scurried along the street, many of them racing free of the fire, but some ran back toward burning buildings. The fire brigade had already responded and worked to pump water through their hoses at the flames, but the fire burned hot and furious.

Somebody shouldered past him, and Finn looked over to see a dark-haired man racing away. Soot coated his face, and he covered his mouth with his arm, coughing.

A scream caught his attention, and he darted forward. The sound had come from a home consumed by smoke. Everyone around him ran away from the fire.

He raced toward the home and headed inside.

Smoke billowed around him, thick and oppressive.

Where had the sound come from?

Another scream, this time softer, but he could get a sense of direction.

Up.

Finn searched for the staircase. He had to fight through the smoke, coughing, and pulled his shirt up over his nose and mouth to keep from breathing too much smoke. His studies had taught him just how dangerous fire could be, and he knew better than to linger here too long.

He found the stairs. He staggered up them.

At the top of the stairs, he found a body. Smoke made it difficult to see much of anything else. The child was small, curled into a ball, coughing weakly.

As he lifted them, they cried out again, though softer this time.

Finn ran, darting down the stairs, cradling the child carefully. Outside, he carried the child along the street. There had to be someone with this child.

"Nels!"

A panicked shout caught his attention over the crackling of the flames and the groaning of buildings as they collapsed.

Finn turned toward it.

A woman approached. Her face was covered in soot and smoke, tears streaming down her face.

"Nels?" She saw Finn and sprinted. "That's my son!"

Finn handed the child over to her, coughing and unable to say anything.

He heard another cry for help. It was on the opposite side of the street where the flames were worse. The crowd around him was all trying to run away from the fire, but someone had to help.

He followed the shout. Another building consumed by smoke.

He started inside, ignoring the smoke, coughing to clear his lungs, and a burst of flame pushed him back.

Finn covered his face with his arm, trying to shield himself from the burning building, but he struggled. The smoke made it difficult to see anything, but he knew what he'd heard.

When the scream came again, he tried to push forward, but the flames were too much.

The heat was too much.

Someone grabbed him, dragging him back.

"Get out of there!" the man shouted.

Finn looked over. The man was dressed in wax leathers. He recognized the crest of the fire brigade.

"Someone is in there," Finn said, coughing.

The sound of the scream inside of the home lingered in his mind.

"Can't get in with the flame. Not without killing yourself. Get back."

The man shoved him.

Finn staggered.

He couldn't do anything to help the person he'd heard.

After all of the time that he had spent questioning people, he would've expected a scream wouldn't have bothered him quite so much, but it stayed with him.

He watched as the fire brigade began to work, dragging their hoses, all connected to pumps and stretching to the river, and began to extinguish the fire.

Finn couldn't help. All he could do was watch.

The flames grew, and something crackled, heat and energy building until it was too much for him to withstand. One of the fire brigade pushed him back as they approached to spray a nearby building.

There was no purpose in him staying there any longer.

The scream lingered with him, almost as if he could hear the person burning to death.

Despite being an executioner, it was a horrible sound.

CHAPTER TWO

The kitchen was quiet. Many times Finn came to the kitchen early in the morning to find his sister Lena was already cooking—but not today. Finn pulled out the pan, set it on the stove, and got it heated, melting some grease in it. When it was crackling with heat, he threw in some sausages, along with a couple eggs, getting breakfast ready.

He coughed. His lungs still burned from running into the fire the day before.

"It's you."

Finn glanced over to Meyer, nodding. "I don't know where Lena is this morning, but she's probably busy with my mother." Finn's mother had started to come around. She still didn't get out of bed, but she was alert. That was a positive change.

Meyer sniffed. "That's too bad. Lena makes breakfast better than you do."

"You can cook for yourself, if you would prefer." He coughed again.

Making breakfast had been one of the first chores he'd taken upon himself when he'd moved in with Meyer.

Meyer took a seat at the table, resting his elbows and looking over at Finn. He offered a hint of a smile, more like a smirk, but with Master Meyer it was difficult to tell. "Are you prepared for the day?"

Finn stared at the bubbling grease, moving the sausages around and flipping them to make sure they were heated evenly. He needed to tell Meyer about Jorend, but he wanted to talk about work. "I think I'm as ready as I can be."

"You've gone through this a few times now."

Finn just nodded. It didn't make it much easier. He tried to push away the nerves, but he had never managed to shake them entirely. Finn didn't know if he ever would and didn't know if he ever wanted to.

"He deserves it," he said. He pulled one of the sausages off, slipping it onto a plate and handing it over to Meyer. "If anybody deserves what's coming to them, it's Ralston Jol."

He flipped the eggs and waited until they were done cooking before using the spatula and handing one to Meyer. Finn scooped the other egg and the other sausage for himself.

Meyer had trained him not to eat too much on the morning of an execution. He needed to find a balance those mornings between settling his stomach with just enough food and not overeating so that he didn't get sick while carrying out the execution. It wouldn't look good for the executioner to vomit all over the top of the Raven Stone.

"We work on more than just what he deserves. We need to ensure we're carrying out justice." Meyer settled his elbows down on the table, looking across at Finn. "This is not about vengeance. I feel like I've been having this conversation with you too often these days, but perhaps a reminder is necessary."

"You don't need to remind me," Finn said.

"You look at what we're doing as if this is something to satisfy our needs." Meyer shook his head. "When the jurors asked the question about what the families requested of us, it's not an unusual request. There was a time when families helped decide the sentencing." He took a bite of his sausage, chewing slowly. "It was a darker time, and one I'm thankful that we've moved past. It's unnecessary for us to carry out the sentencing families request of us. That is not the reason we do this."

"The people Ralston wronged need to know that the king understands their need for justice."

"That is true," Meyer said, taking another bite of his sausage.

Finn looked down at his plate, scooping up the egg and chewing slowly, working through it. "We carry out sentencing for the king, but we also carry it out to ensure that others will see it and be deterred."

"Also true."

"And the families of those he's hurt are offered a little bit of retribution."

"They are," Master Meyer said, settling his arms down on the table. "What do you think they would do if they were given the chance to request their own justice?"

Finn shrugged. "I don't know. They'd probably want to hang him themselves."

Meyer grunted, and he finished the rest of his sausage as he chewed slowly. "I had been an apprentice back when the tradition still held that families of the wronged could request specific sentencing. A time when we dealt with a rapist like Ralston, and the family wanted vengeance during the sentencing. Do you know what they requested?"

"I don't."

"A broomstick."

Finn frowned. "They wanted to beat him to death with a broomstick?"

"No. They wanted to shove the broomstick inside him, to recreate the trauma their loved one experienced."

A wave of nausea worked through him. What would happen if he were asked to do something like that? "What happened?"

"My master executioner at the time, a man by the name of Wilhem Vorges, was forced to carry it out." Meyer closed his eyes, shaking his head. "I have seen some horrific things in my time serving the king, but that stands among the worst." He shook his head again. "They strapped him down, bending him over, and he was forced to slam the broomstick inside him until his intestines exploded."

Finn swallowed. "That wouldn't kill him straight away."

"No. And I knew the same. That was the challenge, though. Those who requested the sentencing had no idea. They sought only a way to torment him in the time before his dying. They certainly accomplished that. He was tormented, but his death was slow and painful."

"I imagine they approved of that."

"They approved, but was that justice? Or was it simply vengeance?"

"Was it not both?"

Meyer took a deep breath, letting it out slowly. "It's a question I find myself pondering from time to time." He looked up, holding Finn's gaze. "It's a question all who pursue this work struggle with. As an executioner, we're tasked with carrying out the sentence the jurors demand. While we can make recommendations, we are often overruled. The challenge is knowing when to step in and to be more forceful with our recommendations, and when to stand aside and let justice border on vengeance."

"The jurors permitted Ralston to hang."

"They did. And to their credit." Meyer got to his feet, carrying his plate to the washbasin. "The alternative was worse. I could imagine them sentencing him to be quartered, but that was not the request."

"What would you have done if they had?"

Meyer glanced back at Finn. "I would have done it. His crimes warranted the sentence offered, but they could've warranted a more severe sentence."

Finn finished eating, chewing slowly until he was done

there and then set his plate into the washbasin next to Meyer's. "Are you telling me this because you want me to be prepared for whatever sentence befalls Bellut?"

"I'm telling you this so that you understand there are times when the vengeance you seek is not available. You must find satisfaction in the king's justice, whatever that might be. I can't tell you what that will be for you, and I can't tell you what that justice might look like, only that you have to find it for yourself." Meyer regarded him a moment. "How many crimes do you think are committed within the city every day?"

"Probably quite a few," Finn said.

"How many of those crimes draw the attention of the Archers?"

Finn had some experience with that. When working jobs with his crew, he had gotten away with quite a few crimes and had never gotten caught. "Not many."

"How many people have been wronged by those crimes?"

"I suppose all of them at some point."

"Exactly. Every single one of those people want the same vengeance as you want."

"It's not vengeance, but people getting punished who deserve it," Finn said.

Meyer chuckled. "You can call it whatever you want, but it *is* vengeance. If you get your vengeance, what comes next? What will you sacrifice on behalf of your search?"

"I see what you're trying to tell me."

"I hope so. Now, I trust you can make the final preparations for the day?"

"I can."

"Good. I have a few things that I need to do before we meet Ralston at Declan."

"Is there anything I can help with?"

Meyer shook his head. "Not with this. I wanted to take a look at the fire in Jorend."

"I was there." Finn shook his head, coughing again. "I've never seen anything quite like it before. Saved a kid. I wasn't able to save another..." He swallowed, ignoring the way Meyer looked at him. "The fire was so hot, it forced me back. As far as I know, it burned much of that section to the ground. An entire street was devastated. I could help you look into it." If there *was* anything for them to investigate, Finn wanted to be a part of it.

Meyer shook his head. "That won't be necessary. Besides, your tasks will keep you here. Finish whatever you need to do this morning, make arrangements for the sentencing, and be prepared."

Finn just nodded.

When he finished up in the kitchen, he had still expected his sister to have come down, though Lena did not. He didn't know why she had still not gotten up for the day. He paused in his small room, glancing to the desk pushed up against one wall and the stack of books. Now wasn't the time for him to study. Now was the time for him to focus on getting himself ready for the sentencing.

His gaze lingered on the hegen card he'd left on the desk. Finn picked up the card, flipping it over. The gold ink on it was slightly raised, and he traced his finger along the surface of the card.

Finn stepped out of his room, closing the door, and reached into the closet outside, pulling out the sword Justice. It was a long blade, standing almost up to his chest if he were to rest the flat point on the ground. It took two hands to wield, and there was a weight behind it, enough that when he was to swing it, it would carry enough energy through.

He carried the sword out into the front courtyard of Meyer's home. A small stone wall encircled the home, high enough to prevent anyone from seeing inside, but not so high as to keep Master Meyer from looking beyond it. A tidy garden inside the wall had flowers and vegetables growing throughout. At this time of the year, the tomatoes were ripe and in bloom, but he had seen beds filled with carrots and potatoes and beans off to one side of the house. The flowers in the garden gave off a pleasing fragrance, as if to mask the type of work Meyer did.

Finn found a stack of pumpkins near one end of the garden, and he carried them to where he worked. He stacked them up and focused, swinging the blade quickly. It sliced directly through the pumpkin.

Finn worked through them, carving pumpkin after pumpkin, ensuring that his aim was accurate. He struck directly where he intended each time. When he had carved through a dozen pumpkins, Finn finally stopped. He grabbed the rag that he'd brought out and wiped off the blade, cleaning it before sticking it back in the sheath and replacing it in the closet. He looked down the hall but still didn't see any sign of his sister. He was tempted to go and check on her, but he didn't think anything had happened to her.

Instead, he went back into the garden, cleaned pumpkin off the path, and paused when the sound of bells in the distance caught his attention.

Finn looked down. He was dressed in his typical festival clothing, prepared for the Gallows Festival, wearing the gray leathers Meyer had purchased for him. The pumpkin splatter cleaned up easily off the leathers, and he straightened, gathering the rope he'd brought out, along with a few other supplies they might need, and stuffed them into a pouch before heading along the street toward Declan Prison.

The crowd had already started to gather.

There was always an energy in the air when it came to the Gallows Festival, and there was a time when Finn would have been equally as excited. Not quite as excited as during Fallow Fest, a celebration of the harvest, or Ordol's Order, where the city still celebrated the end of the war with the Alainsith—something few in Verendal even remembered—or any of the other celebrations recognized by the churches, but the Gallows Festivals were more common. When he was working with his crew, the festival gave them a chance to move unencumbered, unmindful of the dangers of the Archers. Most people wanted to see the condemned and an opportunity to watch the sentencing carried out. Having a crowd to hide out in had always helped their jobs.

Now he had a different feeling about it. Not excitement, but nervousness.

Anxiety burrowed in his belly, and his stomach roiled a little bit, though he tried to ignore it. Thankfully, he'd eaten enough to settle his belly, but he didn't want to ignore that feeling altogether. He figured it was normal and natural for someone to feel like that before carrying out the king's justice.

As he approached Declan Prison, he slowed. The prison was an enormous building, all of dark stone. It had a forbidding appearance. The entrance door was solid oak with crisscrossing bars of iron. Most people worried about others breaking out of prison, but having been inside of Declan as both a prisoner and as an executioner, Finn knew the issue wasn't only in breaking out but also breaking in. Either would look poorly upon Master Meyer.

He found Meyer standing outside of the prison, waiting.

When he joined him, Meyer nodded. "It won't be long," Meyer said.

He fell silent. The streets grew steadily busier the longer they stood there. Carts were moved into place to line the road, and hawkers prepared to sell food and crafts and other items, turning what was the last day of a man's life into an opportunity for those who remained. The crowds pushed toward the street, though it wasn't quite as pronounced near Declan as it was closer to the Teller Gate. Most people wanted to see the actual execution, and few wanted to watch the condemned emerge from the prison, though some did.

Finn noticed an older man standing off to the side, his

eyes drawn and watching the prison door. Finn motioned to Meyer and said, "Who do you think that is?"

"Perhaps one of the victims' families," Master Meyer said.

"Should we try to move him out of the way?"

"The Archers will take care of that," Meyer said.

"If he's injured before we have a chance to sentence him..."

"The Archers will take care of that," Meyer said again.

Finn just sighed. There was no point in saying too much. Meyer was right. The Archers would protect against it, and he didn't need to get involved.

Finally, the door to Declan came open, and a balding priest of Heleth emerged, dressed in his brown robes of office, and guided Ralston out. The priest had the book of Heleth propped open his arms and was speaking softly. Finn had been through this procession enough times he recognized the words the priest might say, the passage that he might read from the Book, and wondered how Ralston reacted. Many of the condemned found religion, even if they hadn't done so before.

"Did you visit with him earlier today?" Finn asked.

"Briefly," Meyer said.

"What did he say?"

"He remained unrepentant," Meyer said.

Committing a crime was bad enough, but not feeling remorse for the crime, or making amends for what was done, was a greater crime according to Master Meyer.

The priest guided Ralston forward, and there were a pair of Archers on either side of him to ensure that he marched along with them. Ralston had been dressed in the grays of the condemned; the Sinner's Cloth. Finn still had his own Sinner's Cloth. He never took it out of the closet, though he hadn't gotten rid of it. He used it as a reminder for where he'd been and what he still might face.

When the priest neared Meyer, he nodded to him. Though already balding, he was a younger man, one whom Finn had met a few times. Dedicated to Heleth, Garrett was devoted, but also had a way with the condemned. He always managed to sound as if he were truly sympathetic to their plight; as if he wanted nothing more than to help them find salvation.

They started forward, moving through the street. The crowd lining the street watched, and occasionally food would get thrown at Ralston. It was more frequent with a rapist than it was with murderers or thieves, and Finn had learned which of the vegetables hurt the most. By the time they reached Teller Gate, Finn was murmuring the words of Heleth along with Garrett and keeping his gaze fixed straight ahead.

The Raven Stone rose up in front of them, and like most prisoners, as soon as Ralston saw it, his demeanor shifted. His shoulders slumped, and his steps faltered. He began speaking the words of Heleth along with Garrett, joining in with Finn.

Meyer glanced over to Finn, nodding, and they took up a position on either side of Ralston, moving the Archers out of the way. They guided him forward, reaching the Raven Stone and the gathered jurors along with the magister. Even the viscount had come out, which wasn't always the case with these criminals. The priest guided Ralston up the steps of the Raven Stone before standing and praying with him.

Meyer stepped forward, speaking quietly to the magister before turning and nodding to Finn. "Are you ready?" Meyer asked softly.

"I've done this before."

"You have, but that doesn't change the question. Are you ready?"

Finn took a deep breath, pushing down the nerves that threatened to unseat him. It wasn't that he couldn't do this, even. Finn knew what was expected of him, and he was ready to do anything to complete this sentencing. Besides, Ralston deserved it.

It was just the conversation he'd had with Meyer kept going through his head. He had to move past the idea that somebody *deserved* anything, and simply carry out the king's justice.

At the top of the stairs, Meyer standing alongside him, Finn approached Ralston.

"Ralston Jol, I, Finn Jagger, executioner for the king, will carry out your sentencing. Do you have any final words?"

Ralston looked up at him, his eyes wide, and then he swept his gaze out over the crowd before turning back to Finn. "It was worth it."

Finn took a deep breath. That made it easier for him.

He pulled the rope out of his pouch, tested the knot, and climbed over to the gallows, situating the rope. Once it was secured, he took Ralston by the arm. He tried to fight, but Finn held firmly, forcing him up the small ladder leading to the gallows. Once he had climbed up, Finn placed the noose around the condemned man's neck, securing it tightly.

"Do you enjoy this?" Ralston hissed at him.

"You're getting what you deserve."

Ralston grunted. "I deserved more women."

Finn took a deep breath, climbed down the platform, and then looked out over the gathered jurors and magister. His gaze lingered the longest on Bellut, and then Finn kicked, sending the platform out and Ralston dropping. His neck snapped, and he stopped breathing immediately.

Finn never took his gaze off of Bellut.

In the distance, he could see the hegen standing at the edge of their section, and one among them stood more prominently, as if watching, waiting for their prize.

CHAPTER THREE

The narrow streets of this section were unfamiliar to Finn. He knew most of the streets in Verendal but none in the hegen section, where the paths often twisted suddenly, or the buildings looked as if they would topple onto his head. The people there often cast him a side-eyed stare, but he had learned long since to ignore such looks when sneaking through the city, so he wasn't about to pay any attention to them now that he had no reason to hide his presence.

A younger man wearing the vibrant colors of the hegen jostled past Finn. Dark hair hung loose around his shoulders, and nothing more than a sliver of his black eyes was visible beneath the hair hanging down. Finn still felt a strange stirring, as if he had somehow irritated the man.

He paused at a street corner. Most of the streets in the

hegen section were difficult to navigate, and when one ended, it flowed into the next. It was easy to see why the others passing him would be irritated by his presence. He was the only non-hegen there. Few from within the city ever traveled to the hegen section, and then only when they had reason to do so. They often found that the cost was more than they were willing to bear.

Finn flipped the card he carried in hand.

The card was his marker that something would be asked, but he still didn't know what that might be. The only thing he had was the card, the symbol of the crown, and a small trail of painted blood along the card that left Finn wondering what else the hegen might know.

The fading sunlight caught the card, making the ink appear alive.

The crown *had* changed in the time that he'd had the card. Most of the time, it looked only a little different from when he'd first been given it. Other times, though, it looked almost as if the ink had smeared along the edges of the card, leaving it trailing down the face.

He started forward again. Finn had a better idea of where he needed to travel in the section, but that didn't mean he didn't get a little disoriented coming into it. The streets looked as if they were designed to confuse and make it difficult to pass through, probably so that he'd be forced to ask someone for directions and incur additional cost with the hegen. Finn refused. He already felt as if he were in deep enough with them.

The red door of Esmerelda's house appeared in the

distance. In the fading daylight, it looked painted in blood. Considering the kind of magic they used, that wouldn't be altogether surprising. When he'd passed the Raven Stone on his way to this section, he'd seen the shadowy movement of figures behind the rock, though hadn't seen any of the hegen. The last execution had been yesterday, which meant the hegen would have had plenty of time to have picked over the body for whatever prizes they wanted from it.

Finn looked at the card again before stuffing it into his pocket.

As he approached the door, three hegen started down the street toward him. They were younger, though with the hegen, Finn had learned it was difficult to know for sure. Some of the hegen like Esmerelda looked older at first, but he had come to think she wasn't quite as mature as he had first believed.

"What are you doing here?" a blond boy said as he started toward Finn. "You don't belong in this section. This is for our—"

The girl walking next to him elbowed him in the side, turning to smile at Finn. "Don't mind Danior. He's just jealous."

Finn looked around him. He hadn't expected any trouble by coming to the hegen section, and certainly had never had any trouble when he'd come before, but he hadn't been as fully established as Meyer's apprentice then. He'd still been trying to build his place. Now there was no doubt about how he served Meyer, which might mean that the hegen were less interested in having him around. There certainly were others in the city who felt that way.

"I came to visit Esmerelda," Finn said, nodding to her door.

"She's not here," Danior said quickly. "So, you might as well leave."

"Would you *stop*?" The girl turned to Finn, flipping her pale hair over one shoulder and flashing a quick smile. "She can be tricky. Just be careful."

"I know," Finn said.

"Don't you know who that is?" the third person asked, leaning closer to the girl.

"He looks to be a young man who's come to find a love potion, Elian."

Elian held his gaze on Finn, something in his expression darkening. Finn had thought that Danior might be the one to be concerned about, but Elian reminded him of some of the bruisers who worked the crews in the rest of the city.

"Not a love potion," Finn said. "I just have a few questions for her."

"She's not the kind to answer too many questions," the girl said.

"He said he knows," Danior said.

"What was that?" she asked.

Danior tipped his head toward Finn. "He said he knows, Kezia."

Kezia grinned at him. "That means you've been here before. Why haven't I seen you?"

"Because of *her*," Danior said, looking back toward

Esmerelda's home. "That's why he's here."

"What's the executioner doing here meeting with *her*?" Elian asked.

"Executioner?" Kezia turned toward Finn, and some of the happiness in her face slipped. Only a little, then she forced a renewed smile. "Is that what you are?"

"I'm an apprentice," Finn said. Standing there and talking to the hegen felt strange. He was constantly aware of the possibility of hegen magic.

"How long have you been an apprentice?" Kezia asked.

"Kezia!" Danior snapped. "Don't you know that we're supposed to leave him alone?"

"Why can't I ask questions?"

"You know the reason."

Finn frowned. Why were they supposed to leave him alone?

"Come along," Danior said. "Just leave him be."

He took her arm, dragging Kezia with him. Elian followed more slowly, casting a long look over his shoulder every so often until they disappeared around the corner, leaving Finn once more alone in the hegen streets. Somewhere distant, music drifted toward him, a different rhythm from what was found in the rest of Verendal. It was almost boisterous, though a steady drumbeat felt as if it were meant to carry him forward, guiding him along with the rhythm.

Finn pulled the card back out of his pocket, eyeing it again. The golden crown hadn't changed, though he wasn't sure why he expected it would.

Sunlight had faded even more, and he hurried forward

to Esmerelda's door before it got any later. He wasn't necessarily the superstitious type, but he didn't want to be in the hegen section much after dark if he could help it. He may have learned the hegen weren't what he'd feared for so long, but that didn't mean they were harmless. If anything, he knew the opposite. He'd seen confirmation of their magic.

After knocking, he took a step back and waited.

There was no answer. Maybe she *was* gone like they'd said.

Finn knocked again, staring at the card while waiting.

What might the crown mean?

Finn believed it was the king, but he'd already helped the king. Maybe Finn was supposed to ensure Bellut faced his own sentencing. With Bellut's service to the viscount, along with Meyer's feelings about vengeance, that proved difficult.

Though he *thought* he knew what the card represented, there was a possibility he was wrong.

What else might the hegen want with a crown? Perhaps it was the gold of the crown that was significant. Maybe they wanted the king's wealth? The palace held the king's jewels, so it could be that, though the hegen *had* wanted to stop the attack. Maybe there was another crown Finn needed to find, though in his service to Verendal, it would be difficult for him to leave and search for this other crown.

Finn felt like he'd been standing in the doorway waiting on her for far too long. There hadn't been any others coming along the street, but he wouldn't expect that to be the case for much longer. If Kezia and the others returned, maybe he could have them get word to Esmerelda that he'd tried to find her.

It was time to head back. He'd had a little free time in the evening—Meyer often gave him stretches of freedom for him to explore on his own—but that didn't mean he could abandon his studies. Though he might have been promoted to apprentice, there remained a considerable amount that he needed to learn. He didn't know if he would ever reach the depth of knowledge Meyer possessed, but that was the expectation of him. As he turned to make his way back, someone called his name.

"Finn Jagger."

Finn turned to see Esmerelda coming down the street. She was tall, with raven black hair and full lips, and wearing a simple bright yellow gown. Finn found himself staring. She was lovely.

Esmerelda was also dangerous.

"I heard you came looking for me," she said.

Finn flicked his gaze past her, though didn't see anyone else. Kezia and the other two hegen had gone the opposite direction. Hadn't they?

"I thought it was time I had answers about this." He pulled the card from his pocket and offered it to Esmerelda.

She eyed it for a moment before lifting her gaze to him, as if sizing him up in the process. It was strange— and oddly seductive. "That is for you alone, Finn Jagger."

He flipped the card over, curious whether it had changed. He didn't think that it had, but when it came to Esmerelda and the way that she could use her magic, he didn't know. "What does the crown mean?"

"I'm afraid I don't understand."

He looked around the street before turning back to her. "The crown. What does it mean?"

She smiled slightly. "Is it not obvious to you?"

"I thought maybe it had to do with the king—"

"From what I understand, you sentenced the King."

"Not him. The *king*. King Porman."

"I'm afraid I don't know him."

She toyed with him. The soft amusement in her eyes suggested how much she enjoyed it. "Were you telling me that I'd have to do something to the king? Now that I'm apprenticed to Master Meyer, I serve the king."

"I am well aware of the service required of you, Finn Jagger."

She kept saying his name as if repeating it bound him to her. Which he had to wonder if it might. What if that was the way her magic worked?

"What do you want me to do?"

Esmerelda tilted her head to the left before motioning to the door. "Why don't you come in and we can discuss?"

"Will I have to serve you more?"

"Not everything has a cost, Finn Jagger," she said softly.

She reached her door and stepped off to the side. Finn debated whether to go in or whether he should return to the city. There were other errands he had to run and more that he needed to study, but this *was* the reason that he'd come.

Finn glanced over to her for a moment. "If you have other things you need to be doing, I don't need to intrude."

She smiled at him, the light catching off her full lips. "I have nothing more I need to be doing other than speaking to you, Finn Jagger."

He stepped into her home and swept his gaze around it. Last time he was there, he had noticed shelves containing strange items, including the bowl that had been stolen during one of the jobs he had been a part of. An Alainsith bowl, as far as he knew. He used the opportunity to look around the inside of her home for any other magical artifacts she might have, but other than shelves filled with books, a few ceramic sculptures, and a couple paintings, he didn't see anything unusual. Even the books weren't necessarily out of place. It was more the bindings that caught his attention, thick spines that carried silver and gold inlay, along with lettering that he couldn't read.

Esmerelda brushed past him, glancing up at him. "May I offer you a drink? Perhaps a mug of tea?"

"That would be fine," he said.

Everything with the hegen incurred a cost, though he had no idea what costs he might incur by simply accepting a mug of tea from her. Maybe none. Besides, he did have questions for her.

She made her way to the kitchen, where she set a teapot on her cookstove and turned back to him, clasping her hands in front of her. "I expected to see you before now," she said.

"Because of the card?"

She hesitated before answering, and Finn tried reading the expression on her face but found it more difficult than he expected. If there was one thing he had learned from Master Meyer, it was how to read people.

"Perhaps because of the card."

"Meyer knows you tried to keep Bellut and his crew from gathering the Alainsith bowls." Finn couldn't remember how to say the name she'd called them, the word too foreign to stick with him.

She turned back to the kitchen, stirring together several different powders before tapping them into the teapot. "I'm not concerned about whether you would share with Master Meyer. He and I have known each other long enough, I do not fear him learning of what's asked of you."

"Did you force him to claim me?" Meyer, like Oscar, had owed a debt. Finn didn't know *what* he owed, though.

"Force him?"

"Is that why he exerted his right?"

After what she had told Finn about the connection she shared with Master Meyer, he had started to wonder. What if the hegen were the only reason that he still lived? It would tie him to them far more than what he had believed.

"Henry Meyer makes his own choices, Finn Jagger. Much like you make your own choices."

"You *have* tried to guide things, though."

She shrugged. "I will not deny that I have interest in seeing my people succeed in the city. We have struggled in other places, so we would like to have an opportunity here we cannot have in others." She tipped her head to Finn. "Don't you have the same interest? That is why you came to me the first place, is it not?"

"That was about my family, not my people."

"My people are my family, Finn Jagger."

She grabbed a mug from a cupboard and poured some of the steaming liquid into it before taking a scoop full of powder and stirring it into the steaming water. When she was done, she handed the mug to Finn. He took it carefully, holding onto it, then waited while she poured another for herself. Only when Esmerelda took a drink did he take his own.

She smiled at him. "I thought the two of us might get to know each other better, especially now that you are an apprentice executioner. It is an important role within the city." She motioned to a faded wooden table. Streaks of color remained in the solidly constructed surface. Finn took a seat, setting the mug on the table in front of him, waiting for her to sit across from him. "Have you come to understand the responsibilities required of you?"

"I don't know all that will be required of me," Finn admitted. "To be honest, when I first apprenticed with Master Meyer, I thought most of it would be hanging and torturing people."

"And it's not."

Finn shook his head. "Most of it is studying and healing and preparing," he said.

"Does that disappoint you?"

It was almost as if she were interrogating him, which considering he had come to her place, maybe she was. "It's not a disappointment. It's an adjustment in thinking."

"How do you feel about the work asked of you?"

"Surprisingly better than I thought," he said.

"Surprisingly?"

"I enjoy the healing side," he said.

"I imagine he has you studying with an apothecary, perhaps even one of the surgeons."

"He tells me I need to spend more time with the apothecary Wella."

Esmerelda lifted her tea, inhaling deeply and smiling. "You would do well to listen to her. Any advice she offers should be heeded."

"You know her?"

"Oh, yes. I know her."

"All of the medicines are complicated." Learning the names of each one she carried, along with their purpose, wasn't the most difficult thing. What was more complicated for Finn had been learning how to mix them and compound them. He hadn't spent enough time with the apothecary to master that, though he had come to appreciate the knowledge and skills she possessed.

"You may relax and drink, Finn Jagger. It is not unsafe for you."

Finn regarded the tea for a moment before lifting it and taking a deep breath, much like Esmerelda had. The steaming tea helped clear his mind, and as he breathed it in, he found his thoughts starting to clarify. He took another sip. It had a bit of a minty flavor to it, though it was not unpleasant.

"What is this?"

"That is tea."

He shook his head. "That's not what I meant. What did you mix together?"

"That would be a secret of the hegen. Perhaps if you joined the people, you might learn."

"Someone could join the hegen? I thought you had to be born to it."

"Did you have to be born to your role as an executioner?"

"That was sort of forced on me."

Esmerelda smiled. "Perhaps the same could be said about the hegen for you one day."

He had the sense she said it as a joke, but there was something unsettling about it as well.

"That's not really why I am here."

"You are here to have me explain the card to you. Unfortunately, I cannot."

"You cannot, or you will not?"

Esmerelda sipped at her tea, watching him.

"I see," he said.

"You look for answers where none are necessary. Time will reveal what must be done, Finn Jagger. Much like the cards reveal their intentions in time."

"The last card you gave me didn't reveal anything."

"The last card? What is it you think was asked of you?"

There had been a picture of a bloody hand on the last card, and Finn had thought she had wanted him to somehow betray his friend Oscar, but that wasn't what she'd wanted of him. Oscar had served the hegen as well. "I just want to ensure that you aren't going to ask anything of me that will be too onerous. I've done what you needed so far."

She smiled tightly. "So far? I'm afraid I didn't realize I demanded so much from you."

"That's not it; it's just that—"

"You don't need to fear, Finn Jagger." She held out her hand, resting it on the table. He reached into his pocket again, pulling out the crown card and sliding it across the table to her. Esmerelda took it, flipping it several times, and the crown began to shift, the face of the card turning blank. "Is that better?" She slid the card back to him.

Now that it was blank, Finn wasn't sure if it was any better. It might've been safer for him to have the crown card rather than a blank card. At least with the crown, he had an idea of what might be asked of him.

"If that means you're taking back what's asked of me, I suppose it would be better."

"This is not a sentence such as you have served, Finn Jagger."

"What is it?"

"I would think it would be something of a friendship." She smiled, leaning forward and taking another sip of her drink. "We didn't have much of a relationship with your predecessor. I have been hopeful that you wouldn't reject the opportunity to develop a relationship with the people."

"The same relationship Master Meyer has with you?"

Maybe he could turn this, and learn a few things from her, regardless of how much she might try to keep from him. Esmerelda was difficult to know, and skilled at turning the conversation in her favor. It was easy to wonder just how difficult questioning her under a formal interrogation might be.

"I would never presume to have the same relationship with you as Henry Meyer has with us."

"What is his relationship with you?"

"That is a question you should ask of Henry Meyer."

"Why didn't you have any relationship with my predecessor?"

Master Meyer rarely spoke of the Lion, the apprentice who had served before Finn, though Finn wondered if that was because he knew how he'd tormented Finn, or whether it was simply because Master Meyer himself had never had much of a relationship with him. As far as Finn had learned, that had been forced by the Executioner Court.

"He came to the city as a journeyman, assigned by the Executioner Court since Master Meyer had not claimed an apprentice. I don't know the details, so that is something you will have to ask Henry Meyer about, but I did know he was displeased to work with him."

"That's what he's told me, as well."

"I am surprised," Esmerelda said. "He's usually too

professional to speak poorly about someone he's asked to work with."

"He didn't say it outright," Finn said. "It was more how he alluded to it."

Esmerelda regarded him while taking another drink. "I see. You gleaned that from conversation with him. You're picking up on your responsibilities quite quickly. I imagine Henry Meyer is pleased with that."

"I'm doing my best to learn what's asked of me."

"Have you given any thought to leaving the city?"

"Why would I leave the city?"

"I believe you had contemplated it before."

Finn froze. How much of him did she really know? He had considered running, but that was when he still had a sentence lingering over his head. He no longer did, and no longer had a reason to run. More than that, now his mother and sister were with Master Meyer.

Could that be what she attempted to get at? That he might not have the same fear of what would happen to him, but he still had to worry about what would happen to his mother and sister were he to leave?

"I contemplated it before, when I didn't know what I wanted."

"Do you know that now?"

It was a seemingly simple question, but it was one that didn't have any easy answer. What *did* he want?

The answer that came to him surprised him.

"I want Bellut to face sentencing for what he did," he said.

"Sentencing or vengeance?"

That she would ask the same question as Meyer left a chill working through him. How much had they shared about him?

He chose his words carefully. "Sentencing. I want him to face the king's justice."

She smiled at him and glanced down at the table.

The card shimmered, and once again a gold crown appeared on the surface.

CHAPTER FOUR

The streets of the Reval section were quiet, though that wasn't uncommon. They weren't in one of the more expensive sections of the city, but having the master executioner live in this section meant there was a bit less activity than in some places. Streetlights provided enough light for him to make his way toward Meyer's home, but when he had a feeling that someone was following him, Finn ducked back into a nearby alley.

Old habits were hard to move past, even if his skill in them had faded.

He had sentenced the King, but there were others from the old crew he still hadn't dealt with. Finn didn't worry about Rock—he didn't know if they were still friends, but doubted Rock would do anything to him—but he *did* worry about Wolf. There was a darkness within him, along with a craftiness the King hadn't had. The King might have run the crew, but the Wolf was the one to have organized much of the planning. As far as Finn knew, Wolf was the one to have coordinated with the Client.

But both Wolf and Rock had been banished from the city. It was for the best.

When convinced there wasn't anyone following him, Finn started back along the street. It was dark, and a full moon threatened to peek out from the clouds. Distant thunder rumbled, though there hadn't been any rain yet. The air had turned colder, and it wouldn't be long before the first snowflakes began to fall. For the first time in years, he didn't have to worry about having enough heat when winter came.

Wind whispered along the street, much colder now that the sun had gone down. Another rumble of thunder rolled from the east, a promise of a coming storm. At least he had a place he could go and safety he would know.

When he reached Meyer's home, he glanced along the street again. There remained the strange sensation that he'd been followed, though he hadn't seen anyone along the street after him. Ever since his time in the hegen section, he'd felt like there was something there. He was jumpy. That was it. Finn could imagine Oscar teasing him about it, the old thief wanting to taunt him for how quickly he let himself get spooked these days, though Finn hadn't had the chance to visit with Oscar in a long time. Ever since the job had failed and he'd confronted Esmerelda about what she'd wanted of him, he hadn't seen Oscar.

Could it be Oscar?

It had troubled Finn that Oscar would suddenly have

disappeared from his life. Though he might have left the crew and moved off to something different, losing Oscar felt like losing his father all over again.

Nothing else moved in the growing night, and he stepped through the gate to Meyer's home, hurried up the path through the small garden, and reached the door. Master Meyer had a large and solidly made home, typical for this section of the city. Finn had initially felt as if the home should belong to some wealthy merchant rather than the executioner, though he had changed his opinion after learning just how often Meyer would treat injuries in the evenings.

A small lantern in the kitchen gave off enough light for Finn to see once inside the front door. He glanced over to the closet in the entryway to check if Meyer's cloak was there, and saw that it was. He was there.

"Finn?"

Lena poked her head out of the kitchen. She was a few years younger than him, though she'd aged in the time since they'd lost their father. Now she wore a weary expression almost constantly, one of worry she'd earned while caring for their mother. Finn had never earned the same worry lines as his sister, though he thought that his time working in the crew should have given him some.

"It's just me." He took his cloak off and hung it on the hook in his room right off the entrance. It was a small room, with little more than a bed and a desk, but the bed was comfortable and the desk afforded him all the space he needed for his studies. "Is Meyer—"

"In his study. With someone."

Finn nodded, making his way to the kitchen to join Lena. Her auburn hair hung loose around her shoulders, though it seemed to have slipped free from a pale yellow ribbon that had fallen onto her back. The one slice of color Lena afforded herself. Her dress and shoes were both a dark brown.

"Can I get you anything? You didn't eat."

The mention of food set his stomach to rumbling. "Now that you mention it, I suppose I could use something to eat."

"Unless you're supposed to be with him?" Her gaze drifted toward the closed door at the end of the hall. It was stout enough that Finn couldn't hear anything from the other side.

"If he wanted me with him for the session, he would have let me know."

"I don't want you to abandon your responsibilities."

Finn took a seat at the table and pulled the hegen card from his pocket while leaning back and staring at it. The lantern glowed with a soft orange light on the table, just enough for him to make out the raised surface of the crown on it.

"I'm not. I've plenty of studying to do before I'm ready to assist him there."

Lena brought a tray of bread and cheese and set it in front of him. "Do you like it?"

He shrugged. "I find the study more enjoyable than I would have thought, though I don't have much practice."

She poured herself a mug of tea, then one for Finn, and took a seat across from him. The black tea was nothing like the herbal mint that Esmerelda had given him, but Lena knew how he preferred it, and he took a long sip before picking at the lump of bread.

"I borrowed one of your books," she said.

Finn laughed softly. "What would you do that for?"

Lena's eyes darkened. "You don't have to make fun of me, Finn."

He put down the bread. "That wasn't what I intended. I just wouldn't have expected you to want to borrow one of the books he lent me."

"Not one on *that*." Lena had never talked much about the darker aspects of Finn's job, though he never had a feeling from her that she disapproved, only that she found it distasteful. "One on anatomy. I've never seen anything like it. It surprised me, is all."

"That the executioner would know about anatomy?"

"That he would know about all of these things." She settled her hands on the table and stared at the mug of tea in front of her. "I had this image of the city executioner in my head that has been all wrong. He's nothing like I thought he would be."

Finn took another bite of the bread, chewing slowly. "What did you think he would be?"

"I guess a brute."

Finn chuckled. "When I first got to know Master Meyer, I didn't know what to make of him either. He was always something of a mythical person in the city, you know. This stoic man who would bring people up to face sentencing atop the Raven Stone, and slip a noose around a neck, or use the sword Justice to..." Finn looked up, shaking his head. "I'm sorry, Lena. I don't need to go through that with you."

"That's fine, Finn. If you need to talk about it, you can tell me what is on your mind."

"That's just it, though. I don't even know if I need to talk about it. It's just what I need to do."

They fell into a silence for a while, both of them focusing on the food and drink in front of them. Finn took a sip of his tea before picking up the bread and chewing slowly.

"Mother continues to improve," Lena said. "I think she's getting some color back."

He nodded slowly. "That's good."

"Master Meyer tells me that we need to keep feeding her. He tells me food is medicine at this point for her."

"Then she's in good hands," Finn said.

"I don't know about that. I just tried to do everything I could to help her, but I don't know."

Finn smiled. "She wouldn't be here were it not for you," he said. He meant it, too. Had Lena not done all that she had for their mother, she wouldn't have survived. She had suffered the way it was, and whatever strange wasting illness had taken her had continued eating away at her, taking her mind, her awareness, and finally taking her strength.

"Have you ever asked him about Father?"

Finn looked up, meeting his sister's gaze. "I don't know that Master Meyer knows anything about what happened to our father."

"You're in charge of all the prisons, aren't you? It seems to me you'd be able to learn what happened to him."

Finn stared at the lump of bread in his hand. "I don't know where our father ended up, but it's not in the city."

He'd looked at the prison records once he had gotten established enough that he didn't worry about Master Meyer getting upset with him for doing so. Unfortunately for them, there had been no record of what happened to their father. It was unusual, which meant that whatever crime he'd done had been a peculiar one.

"How can that be? Why would he have been captured here but in prison somewhere else?"

Finn shook his head. "I'm still learning these things, Lena. I'm barely an apprentice, and certainly not far enough along in my responsibilities that I can question Master Meyer about such topics."

"He's our father, Finn."

"I know who he is," Finn said, more abruptly than he intended.

Lena sat back, frowning. "I should go check on Mother."

"Lena—"

She got to her feet and shook her head. "I need to be more like you, I think. I need to be thankful for what we've been given and not question it. I suppose I should keep these thoughts to myself."

"That wasn't what I was getting at," Finn said.

"I know that's not what you were getting at." She glanced over to Meyer's office, shaking her head. "He's been kind to us. I don't want to do anything that would disrupt that kindness."

Would Meyer keep working with Finn if he started questioning, digging into what happened to his father?

"I can ask him," Finn said.

"Not if you don't think it's safe to do."

"I'm sure he wouldn't mind." He took a sip of his tea and set it down near the hegen card. It seemed as if the colors had shifted just a little bit, though that might be the reflection off of the lantern. As Finn picked up the card, he rubbed his thumb across the surface of it, but the ink didn't change.

"I didn't realize you still had one of those." Lena frowned at him. "If you owe them something, you need to take care of that before you get in too deep. I know they helped you, much like they helped me, but they will take and take from you, until you are so caught up in the hegen schemes, you have no choice but to serve."

He just nodded.

"I'm going to check on Mother," Lena said again.

Finn just nodded. When she left him, he sat quietly, chewing at the bread, before moving on to the cheeses. Meyer always had enough food, and had so far not asked for anything in return for housing Lena and Finn's mother, which made him a little uncertain. At what point would that change? At what point would Master Meyer begin to demand something more from Finn?

Maybe he was no different from the hegen.

For that matter, how did Finn know that Master Meyer wasn't bound up with the hegen as well? He'd heard Esmerelda say that he had been a part of some plan, and though he didn't know what that plan was, or how he'd been bound to the hegen, Finn suspected it had something to do with him. Should he be concerned someone else seemed to have a plan for him?

At least they wanted him.

He finished the food Lena had given him and brought the tray to the washbasin, setting it inside and scrubbing it. When finished, he moved on to the other dishes, getting them clean and then dry, and had started toward his room to study when he heard the door to Meyer's office open.

He turned to see Meyer standing in the doorway. A shadowed light shifted across his face as he turned, making the wrinkles on his face deeper than they normally appeared. "You're back late," Meyer said.

"I just had to check on something."

Meyer grunted softly. "You went to the hegen section."

Finn swallowed. "You knew?"

"I still receive reports from the Archers on your comings and goings."

So much for the autonomy that he thought he had. Finn had thought that by passing the Executioner Court trials, he'd have been trusted more. He'd given Meyer no reason not to trust him since executing the King.

"I didn't go to do anything to dishonor you."

Meyer frowned, then motioned for Finn to join him.

He stepped into Meyer's study. The room was comfortable and cozy, the better for those who came to visit to feel as if they were seeing a traditional healer rather than an executioner. A long, padded cot rested near one wall, and he had a desk near another wall. Bookshelves behind the desk were filled with texts on healing, anatomy, medicines, and the like. Meyer had made the expectation clear to Finn that he would read through most of the books before he could be trusted to heal anyone.

Meyer nodded to the chair resting across from the desk, and Finn took a seat. It wasn't common for him to come into the office, so when Meyer invited him in, he knew better than to refuse.

Taking a seat across from Finn, Meyer rested his elbows on the desk and regarded him. "Did you think I feared you would discredit me?"

"I just wanted you to know that I wouldn't do anything like that."

"I believe you, Finn."

"I went to the hegen to try to—"

"Understand the card you have." When Finn nodded, Meyer asked, "What is on it?"

Finn held it up and Meyer frowned at it.

"What is it?"

Finn glanced at the card. "I see a golden crown. Do you see the same?"

"Ah. And you wondered what they might ask of you and whether it would have you harm the king." Meyer smiled tightly. "I don't think the hegen have any interest in harming the king."

"I don't think so either, but they have their own motivations for the things they do."

"Of that there is no doubt, but the hegen are treated well. At least, as well as they can be, given the kind of magic they employ. It's not quite witchcraft, a dangerous sort of power, but some feel it's dangerous enough. Hedge magic, of a sort, though the kind of magic the king has permitted."

It was interesting to hear Meyer talk about it so matter-of-factly. That hadn't been Finn's typical experience with him. Most of the time, Meyer had been quiet when it came to talking about and dealing with magic, so for him to speak of the hegen magic, and what it meant not only for the city but for the kingdom...

"I didn't think you liked to acknowledge magic."

"Wanting to deal in it and acknowledging its existence are different matters. How can I deny what I've seen with my own eyes?"

"Have you?" Finn leaned forward. Would Meyer reveal what he'd done to gain the hegen's attention? If so, it was a story he wanted to hear.

"There have been hegen living on the outskirts of Verendal for as long as I remember. Not all of them have been accessible, though these days, they have come to appreciate a different relationship with the city."

"Why is that?"

Meyer looked down at his desk, opening a book and jotting down a note. "Perhaps if you ask her, she will tell you."

"I doubt Esmerelda will tell me anything that doesn't serve her purpose."

Meyer looked up, holding Finn's gaze. "Is that any different than the prisoners you've interrogated?"

Finn frowned. Strangely, that had been what he'd felt about it as well. When he'd been talking with Esmerelda, it had felt like a questioning session, only one where he had been the target. Perhaps when it came to the hegen, he had to view things in a different manner.

"I suppose it's not."

"You can learn to speak with the hegen and not position yourself into a corner. I would suggest it's good practice for some of the criminals you might visit."

"That's probably true."

Meyer nodded absently and continued writing in the book. Finn had never seen Meyer's notes. Of all the books that he had in his study, his personal notes were kept private. Finn knew better than to try to sneak a peek at them, though he *was* curious about what Meyer might be writing down. He often took notes while talking to Finn. Did he keep records of their conversations?

"We have an early start in the morning. A man was brought in who the magister would like us to question."

"What did he do?"

"He's an arsonist."

"The Jorend fire?"

Meyer nodded. "The same."

The scream he'd heard—the person he hadn't been able to help—echoed in his mind. "Has he admitted it?"

"No. Which is why we have to question him. The magister believes in his guilt, partly because the warden has sent word of it."

"I didn't realize the wardens had any role in that."

"Generally, they do not, though if a prisoner makes a claim within the prison, the warden can report to the magister." Meyer's brow darkened for a moment. "Typically, they report it to me, and I get word to the magister, but only after I have taken an opportunity to question further. After we talk with him, I think this is a good opportunity for you to take the lead."

Finn stared at Master Meyer for a moment. "The lead?"

"Eventually, you will progress to journeyman status, and in order to do that you need to be comfortable and confident in not only leading investigations but also leading sentencing if appropriate. In this case, I would have you pursue your investigation, the questioning of the prisoner, and ultimately present your findings to the magister and the jurors. Do you think you can do that?"

Having something like that to focus on would give him an opportunity to be out in the city a little bit, and it might even give him an opportunity to look into Bellut. Going before the jurors would definitely give him that opportunity. That was what he wanted more than anything else.

"I can do it," he said.

Meyer nodded. "You need to remember that you are acting on my behalf. You remain my apprentice, which means that you and your work are reflective upon me."

"I won't do anything that will dishonor you," Finn said.

"I don't think that you will," Meyer agreed.

He turned his attention back to the book resting in front of him, scratching out another note.

He said nothing more, and after a while, Finn got to his feet, closing the door to the study behind him. Finn made his way to his room, where he took a seat at the desk and pulled out a book. He might have responsibilities in the morning, but for now, he needed to focus on continuing his studies. If he truly wasn't going to dishonor Master Meyer, he needed to keep working.

The hegen card resting on the desk drew his attention every so often, the gold crown glittering on the surface catching his eye. Regardless of what he might do for Master Meyer, Finn needed to learn what the hegen wanted of him, and he was going to have to figure out some way of investigating Bellut. He still needed to pay for what he had done. Finn was determined to find whoever Bellut had worked with and prove the guilt of both parties.

CHAPTER FIVE

The outside of Declan Prison was dark, and it stank of rot and shit. It was all too familiar to Finn. He'd been there many times in the months since he had apprenticed to Master Meyer, and he had still never quite adjusted to the stench that surrounded the prison. It came from this section of the city, but it also seemed to emanate from the prison itself, a stench that grew worse the more time he spent inside. It was one of filth, that of shit and piss and sweat, but it was also one of fear and a strange odor of the condemned.

Master Meyer had been silent during their walk over to Declan. Now that they were there, he paused in the street, sweeping his gaze around them before glancing over to Finn. The early morning sunlight seemed to reflect off his graying hair, making it appear almost silver. "Many in the city feel that arsonists are the worst criminals," Master Meyer said. "The jurors and the magister would prefer we get to the bottom of this investigation as quickly as possible. They don't want us leaving an arsonist out in the city, especially if this man is not guilty."

"I thought you said they believed in his guilt."

"They believe it, but there always is the possibility we have the wrong man. When it comes to an arsonist, time can be critical. Once someone gets a taste for starting fires and watching the destruction of the city, they are unlikely to stop."

"I would have thought murderers were the worst."

"Murderers end one life and disrupt several, including the family of those they killed Arsonists disrupt many lives and often kill just as many, though much more indiscriminately."

There was something about the way that Master Meyer spoke about arson that left Finn questioning whether he believed something more.

"And if this man didn't do it?"

"If this man didn't do it, then it is incumbent upon us to learn who did. We must work quickly, Finn. That is the expectation of us as lead investigators within the city. I trust you recognize the danger?"

There hadn't been too many fires during Finn's time in the city. Most of them were confined to a single house. Having the river flowing through the city allowed the fire brigade to put most fires out before they spread too far. This one had been different. Finn had been there.

He nodded to Master Meyer. They moved forward and Master Meyer unlocked the door, swinging it open and waiting for Finn to step inside.

There was always a moment of adjustment after entering Declan Prison. It took his mind a moment to clear, but it also took his nostrils a moment to adjust to the air. It was still, humid, and the stench within the prison lingered far more than Finn thought natural.

Meyer closed the door, locking it. There were times where Finn felt like he became a prisoner again, despite being able to move freely, and despite the fact that he didn't have to fear the prison guards; the iron masters.

Meyer watched him. "It hasn't gotten better?"

"I'm fine."

"There is no shame in acknowledging that you struggle with what you encountered."

"I'm not trying to get your pity."

"And you won't have it. I'm simply telling you that there is no shame in acknowledging the feelings you have coming here. This place changed you. It changed the course of your life. Either you embrace it and recognize that it is more than just what you experienced when captured here, or you will continue to struggle each time you come. This is an essential responsibility as my apprentice. We supervise the prison system, including Declan, and that involves supervising the wardens and all of the iron masters here."

Finn nodded. "I am fine."

"As you should be. You're my apprentice now, so you have every right to be here. More than most."

"Why do you say that?"

"We supervise the prisons, Finn. Yes, even you. Eventually, you're going to have to build those relationships."

"With the warden?"

"Wardens. Yes. All the prisons in the city are under our supervision. The wardens might as well get used to your presence and the fact that you're acting on my behalf." He glanced along the hallway. "Eventually, you'll take on greater responsibilities, and it won't seem quite as—"

"Strange?"

"I would have said *uncomfortable*, but perhaps you find it strange. That might be the case for you. Regardless, your duty is to serve."

Finn nodded. He didn't need a reminder of his duty, though it seemed to him Meyer felt like he needed it. Maybe he worried Finn would abandon his duty in order to get vengeance.

"What about the iron masters?" Finn asked.

"They serve under the warden. You need to get them to respect you to be able to work with them. They can be allies, or they can make your job much more difficult."

"How do I make them allies?"

"That will be up to you. They're not so different than the man you had been before taking up your apprentice-ship. Once you understand that, you might find it easier to know how to interact with them." Meyer watched him for another moment before nodding. He strode off along the hall, heading toward the stair at the end. "Gather the prisoner. I will meet you in the chapel."

"What's his name?"

"David Sweth. One of the iron masters can lead you to him."

Finn had enough experience within Declan to know

that the iron masters would and could lead him to the prisoner. Perhaps it was simply his unsettled nature that had made this more difficult today than it usually was. When he'd questioned other prisoners, Finn hadn't struggled as much, though he had done so under Meyer's supervision. From the way Meyer had spoken last night, Finn would be the one responsible for looking into this case. That involved serving as the primary questioner.

He headed down the stairs into the depths of the prison. When he reached the first set of iron masters standing guard, he nodded to them. "Meyer would like to question the prisoner Sweth."

The dark-haired man turned to Finn. He had a hooked nose and a prominent forehead. "That bastard needs to pay for what he did. You make sure the hangman knows."

"He *is* the hangman, Gord," the other iron master said.

"He's just the 'prentice. I'm talking about the old one." Gord looked at Finn. "I got family in the Jorend section. Lost half their house because of Sweth. If I get a chance to be alone with him…"

Finn needed to assert control. "He will face questioning and sentencing if he's guilty."

"If?" Gord practically spat it at Finn.

"All men are questioned before they're brought to the magister for sentencing."

"We know he's guilty. He's in here, ain't he?"

The other iron master started to chuckle. "He's got you there, Jags."

Finn frowned at the iron master. "Jags?"

The iron master shrugged. He was solid enough that

Finn doubted he had trouble with too many of the prisoners. "We got to have a name for you. Figured that was a good one. Better than what they called you in the street."

"What was that?" Gord asked.

"Aw, we don't want to mess with Jags, now, Gord. Don't need to remind him how they called him Shuffles."

Finn clenched his jaw. He'd been careful to try to keep his old life from the new one, but he *had* been a prisoner there, so it wasn't terribly surprising that the iron masters would learn about him.

"*Finn* is fine. Now, if you don't mind, I would like the prisoner brought to the chapel so I can question him to determine his guilt." He turned to Gord. "I expect him to be intact. If he's guilty"—Finn said it more harshly than he intended, but then again, given that the iron masters had decided to bring up his past, he figured they deserved it—"he must be unharmed going into his sentencing. The gods demand that of us."

Gord glared at Finn but stomped down the stairs while pulling out a keyring and jingling it.

"Time to bring the heat! The fires will surge. The gods look to eat! It's our lives they purge." A long-haired, thin man cackled from one of the cells while pressing his face up against the bars.

"Shut it, Hector!" Gord shouted, slamming the keys against one of the cells.

Finn smiled to himself. More than anything, having Hector in the prison left things with a sense of normalcy.

He didn't have to wait long before Gord returned,

dragging a shackled man with him. He was young, with bright eyes and short hair. He was clean-shaven and could have passed as a merchant. Certainly not someone Finn would have expected to come out of Jorend—or to be responsible for starting fires in the section. One lesson that Finn had learned from Meyer was that he couldn't assume anything about prisoners. Men who looked like filthy men from the streets could be the most honest workers, while others who looked to be the most upstanding citizens would often be guiltier than any others.

Finn stood to the side while Gord dragged Sweth to the stairs and then up.

"Gotta get you up to the chapel, Sweth. Looks like Shuffles needs to have a chat with you."

"Who's Shuffles?" Sweth asked, his voice catching with the question.

Gord glanced over his shoulder, casting a wide grin at Finn before dragging him up the steps and away. Finn didn't get the chance to hear what he answered.

"Don't mind him," the other iron master said. "We got to take the piss out of you a little. Brings you down to our level."

Finn turned to him. "What level is that?"

The iron master held Finn's gaze for a moment before shaking his head. "Didn't mean nothin' by it."

Finn suppressed a sigh. This was the sort of thing that Meyer had wanted him to work on. He needed for Finn to find a way to work with the iron masters. Not only so that he could learn what they might know about the prisoners but also because he would have to work with them on a regular basis.

"I don't really like the nickname Shuffles," he said. The iron master looked up at him. "The man who gave it to me tried to get me killed. You've probably heard the story." A hint of a smile spread on the iron master's mouth. "So, I'd rather it be anything *but* Shuffles, if you know what I mean."

The man nodded slowly. "I got you. My older brother used to call me Shits. Never cared for that name either. Took me the better part of my youth to get past it. Still get called it when I go back around home."

Finn grinned. "I'd say that's worse, but I got Shuffles when I joined my crew."

"You really *were* in a crew?"

Finn nodded. "Most have heard the stories. Got pinched breaking into the viscount's manor. Ended up here. Sentenced to hang. You could ask Hector, if you doubt it. I suspect he'll remember me."

The iron master whistled. "I've heard the stories, but you never really know, you know? Not the kind of thing most men would talk about."

It wasn't something Finn wanted to talk about, either, but maybe Meyer was right that he somehow had to get through to the iron masters. And it wasn't like Finn had an assortment of friends. These days, he didn't even know if he could count Oscar as his friend. He had his family, Meyer, and... that was about it.

"It's not a bad story," Finn said, "as stories go."

The iron master chuckled. "Maybe you want to join

me for ale some night and share it. That's got to be a drinking story."

"I'd like that." He looked up the stairs where Gord had taken Sweth. "Time to get to work."

"See you next time, Jags." When Finn arched a brow at him, he shrugged. "Don't like that one? We can find you something better in time."

"What about you? What do they call you these days?"

"Around here they call me Shiner."

"Do I want to know why?"

Shiner grinned, and Finn realized he was missing a tooth. "Nah. Probably best you don't, Jags. Can't tell you until I know if you're going to run off and share with the warden. I'm too new here, you know. Gotta wait until I get my feet settled before you hear the good stuff."

Finn laughed as he made his way up the stairs. When he reached the next level, the amusement faded while he headed toward the chapel. He came often enough that he no longer felt uncomfortable in the chapel, but there was still something about it that left him unsettled. This was where he would question the prisoners and where he'd use the various techniques Meyer had to gather information.

Now this was where he would have to take the lead.

Finn took a deep breath and entered.

Light streamed down into the inside of the chapel from a stained glass window high overhead, leaving the room awash in different colors, swirls of yellow and red and a hint of orange. It caught his attention, and more than that, it was enough that he didn't need a lantern in there while working.

Gord crouched in front of Sweth, securing him into the chair. When he stood, Finn nodded to him, noticing Meyer standing in the doorway. "We've got the prisoner. When we're done, we'll bring him down to you and Shiner."

Gord tipped his head slightly as he regarded Finn. "You sure about that, Shu... I mean Jags?"

"I'm sure about it. We're just going to ask him a few questions. You secured him?"

Gord nodded. "Got him plenty bound up for you. The bastard isn't going nowhere."

He headed out of the chapel and closed the door behind him. He didn't lock it. Sweth couldn't go anywhere.

He looked over to Meyer, meeting his gaze for a moment. Meyer took a position on the far side of the room, leaning back against the wall.

This was going to be Finn's time to question.

Which meant he had to prove himself.

Finn took a moment, barely more than that, and stepped in front of the prisoner. "What's your name?" he asked softly.

The man looked up at him. "You're Shuffles?"

Finn clenched his jaw. This was what Meyer meant about the iron masters making his life harder than it needed to be. That was the very thing that he wanted to avoid if at all possible.

"I'm Finn Jagger, apprentice executioner." He let the words settle for a moment. "What's your name?"

"Sweth. David Sweth. Listen—I didn't do what they're claiming I did. I didn't light no fires. I was just in the wrong place and I—"

"We'll get to that," Finn said.

He grabbed the stool from the far side of the room near the bench holding the instruments of questioning. He didn't think he needed any of them just yet. Maybe this was all part of the test with Meyer, to see if Finn had the stomach to use them on a stranger. It was one thing using them on a bastard like Rock, but another using them on a man like Sweth who had already started to babble.

Pulling the stool over to sit in front of Sweth, Finn made certain he was close enough to catch small changes in his expressions but not so close that Sweth could reach him. There was a bit of a balance in doing it. "Why don't you tell me a little bit about yourself?" Finn said.

"Will that help?" Sweth tried to look behind himself, as if he knew Meyer was still there.

He probably did. Meyer would have been there when Sweth had been dragged in by Gord. If he recognized Meyer, it might change how he reacted. That might be another part of Meyer's test. As far as Finn knew, this was all some sort of evaluation for him.

"I'm here to find as much about you as I can. The more you're willing to share, the easier this will be for both of us."

Sweth looked up, holding Finn's gaze. For a moment, there was a hint of anger that flashed in his eyes, but then it passed, leaving him with the same beaten expression that Finn had seen from him when he'd first been dragged out of the cell.

"I'm not the man you're looking for."

"Why don't you tell me what kind of man you are?"

He ignored the look he got from Meyer. This wasn't the way that Meyer would run an interrogation, but that didn't mean it wouldn't work.

"I've been working as a scribe under Master Johan. It's good work, but now…"

A scribe required training and a level of literacy that he wouldn't have expected from a criminal. "Where is Master Johan's shop?"

"He's in the Grindle section."

"Not Jorend?"

"That's where I live. Lived. My home burned during the last fire. I tried to go in and get some of my belongings, along with the paper and inks Johan lent me, but couldn't get in there before the fires claimed everything. Now it's all lost."

Finn regarded Sweth, looking for any of the telltale signs that he might be lying to him. There wasn't anything. As far as Finn could tell, the man told the truth. That didn't mean he *did*. Finn knew he wasn't going to be the same judge of character as Meyer, but he'd started getting a feel for people. In this case, when he looked at Sweth, he had a sense that the man was exactly who he claimed.

It would be an easy thing to investigate. All Finn would

need to do would be to track down Johan and ask him about his apprentice.

"Was it lost before you ran in?" Finn asked.

"What was that?"

"The fire. Was it blazing through your home before you ran in?"

The memory of the smoke billowing came back to him. No one would have been able to get in for anything through that. Not for inks and paper.

Sweth stared at him for a moment. "I... I don't remember." He closed his eyes, lowering his head. "The fires burned so hot. All I could think about was getting inside and getting to the inks and papers. Johan would *kill* me were I to lose them, then he'd take it out of my pay. I'd never be able to move out on my own."

"I understand," Finn said.

Sweth looked up. "You do?"

Finn had to be careful.

He *did* understand, though. Having been there gave him a greater understanding than he would have were he just investigating any other crime.

Finn glanced to Meyer, who remained unreadable. That left Finn wondering if he had missed something. He turned his attention back to Sweth, trying to see if there was something that he might have overlooked, but couldn't tell. As far as he could determine, Sweth had been honest with them.

"What do you remember about that day?" Finn asked.

"The flames," he said, his eyes going wide. "They

burned so bright. I remember the heat. The people screaming."

The scream echoed in Finn's mind, and he paused for only a moment.

"Did you try to help them?"

Sweth looked up. "Did I what?"

"Help the people screaming? Did you try to do anything to help them?"

"There wasn't anything I could do. The fire brigade had already started to come, and by that time, they were going to be able to do more than I could have done, anyway."

"So, you went into your home after ink and paper."

He nodded.

"While others burned."

Finn glanced to Meyer. That was what this was about, more than the fire. People had burned. Meyer hadn't said how many, but Finn could tell that it had to have been more than just a couple. There would have to be a reason that Meyer had come with him to question. This kind of crime wasn't one that Meyer would necessarily get involved in otherwise.

"I didn't know they were burning. As I said to you—"

"You were concerned about your inks," Finn said.

Sweth swallowed. "It's not a crime to try to save my belongings. The others have to be responsible for themselves."

There, Finn had almost let himself get sucked in by the possibility that Sweth had been innocent. Maybe he still was innocent of the crime that he was imprisoned for, but that didn't mean he was innocent of everything.

"We'll see," Finn said.

He reached down and unbuckled the straps holding Sweth's ankles to the chair, then did the same with his wrists, before pulling him by the arm and forcing him to stand.

"Is that it?" Sweth asked.

"We're done for today."

"You mean—"

"I mean we're done for today." Finn guided him to the door and found Shiner waiting for him.

The taller iron master winked at Finn. "Figured you'd need someone to escort him back. Let me take him for you, Jags."

"Thanks."

Shiner jerked on Sweth's arm, forcing the prisoner along with him. Sweth stumbled and nearly fell, but Shiner grabbed him. That was probably for the best. They didn't need him getting injured if he *was* guilty of something.

Finn turned back to Meyer, who now stood at the counter, moving some of the instruments across the table.

"You didn't feel you needed to ask more questions?" He didn't turn to Finn as he spoke.

"That wasn't the point."

Meyer glanced back, and Finn shrugged.

"I could have used your interrogation techniques, but at this point, I figured it was probably for the best that I take a look at what burned before proceeding with anything else. That and I visit with Johan."

Meyer nodded. "Very well."

"You don't disagree?"

"This is your investigation, Finn. I will observe."

"That's all you're going to do?"

Meyer sniffed. "If you think you need me to walk you through all aspects of your responsibilities, then I will. I merely thought you might be ready for something more."

"I am."

"Good." He turned and looked around the inside of the chapel. "This was once a place of worship. Strange we've converted it to this use."

"It was?" Finn hadn't known that, though it did make a certain sort of sense. It *was* called the chapel, after all.

"Long ago. There was a time when prisoners were offered a chance to pray for forgiveness. The chapel afforded that chance. Now they pray, but for different reasons."

He looked to the window and the figure of Heleth, the mother, worked into the glass. The way the light shone through the window made her look as if she were glowing, holding out a hand as if to offer her support to those who would come to celebrate her. Heleth had always been favored by the condemned, mostly because she was the one to offer the chance at salvation in the afterlife. The other gods chose different tactics.

"What about the prison?"

"The prison has been in Verendal for hundreds of

years. You can't have a city this size without a place to hold those who would try to violate the king's laws."

"Not all are held."

"No," Meyer said, turning to him.

"And not all are held here. Or even in the city."

Finn bordered on pushing too much with Meyer, but he wanted to know what had happened to his father. If he couldn't learn from the master executioner, there might not be anyone he *could* learn that answer from.

"Not all," Meyer agreed. "There are some crimes that must be sentenced differently. Some criminals who must be sent elsewhere."

Finn frowned. "Why? Declan handles the dangerous criminals in the city."

"This is a different kind of danger," he said.

"What different kind of danger?"

How different could it be from housing those who would rape or kill or destroy?

"The only kind that really matters to the king. The kind that challenges his power. The kind that means treason."

CHAPTER SIX

The Jorend section of the city wasn't all that far from Meyer's home. Finn followed the stench of smoke to the burned street. Buildings on either side of the road had been turned into little more than smoldering ash, leaving the homes in ruins.

Finn lingered at the end of the road for a moment, simply taking it in. Others picked their way along the street, most of them gawkers, before moving on. Toward the middle of the burned section, a woman picked through the broken boards and remains of what had once been a home or a shop or even both.

How many had been lost there?

He knew of one, but that couldn't have been the only loss.

The memory of that day lingered for him. Finn dealt with torment. That was one of the harder aspects of his new responsibilities. Burning someone alive was a kind of torment he simply couldn't fathom.

He started along the road. The fires had been out for several days, but the stink of ash still hung in the air. Finn could almost taste it. Knowing how much had been lost there made it difficult for him to breathe, and he covered his mouth and nose with his sleeve to keep from inhaling it all.

There wasn't much he thought he'd find, coming there. It was more about having a chance to see for himself what had happened, but now that he *was* there, he wanted to take a moment and appreciate all that had been lost. The people of Jorend might not be his section, but they were still people in the city, and he would have wanted the same were it his section that had burned.

When he reached the woman he'd seen, he found her kneeling inside of the home, bent forward and sobbing softly. Who had she lost?

He continued onward.

The farther he went along the street, the more he started to see buildings that hadn't collapsed completely. A few more people were there, picking through the buildings. Hopefully, they only picked through their own belongings and didn't try to steal from those who had lost so much. It wasn't until he reached the end of the street that the buildings were mostly still intact. Even those had been heavily damaged with ash and char along the sides of them.

Finn turned and looked back along the street. A shadowed figure at the end of the street disappeared.

Was someone watching him?

Finn frowned before heading back along the street. There was a time when he would have been concerned about the idea of someone trailing after him, but now he didn't fear Archers. This was *his* investigation. If Meyer were there, Finn knew what the master executioner would do. He'd make sure that he took the time to investigate anything strange that happened around him.

Which was what Finn needed to do now.

He had to be careful, though. While he wasn't convinced Sweth was responsible for the fire, that didn't mean that whoever *was* responsible had disappeared. It was likely that if someone else had done this, they might still be around.

When he neared the end of the street, he didn't find anyone. A few curious stragglers, though that hadn't been uncommon in the time that he'd been there. Very few had actually gone along the street, as if they didn't want to get tainted by the fire. There were superstitions all throughout the city, especially in some of these outer sections, so it wasn't surprising that someone would be wary of coming there, especially if they blamed one of the gods.

Finn wouldn't find anything there. The street was too quiet and most of the buildings too burned. Which meant he'd have to go and find Johan. Meyer had given him a little help there, which Finn appreciated. He didn't have to wander through the Grindle section to find him.

Reaching Grindle took some time. As a scribe, it didn't surprise Finn that he'd been situated in a nicer section of the city, but Grindle was across the river and much more central to many of the merchant sections than to any of the outer sections. As he crossed the bridge, he felt a bit out of place, the way he often did, but he continued along, moving as quickly as he felt comfortable. Finn looked around him, watching the people who *did* feel comfortable there.

Most were obviously merchants, or they had shops that catered to the people in this section. A few were dressed in the dark robes of the priests, and Finn passed a pair of black-robed priests of Fell heading toward their church.

The Church of Fell welcomed only a select group within Verendal. Those who attended had to have an invitation. Though he was now more honorable than he had been when a thief, Finn didn't think they would welcome him. Probably not Meyer, either, though knowing what he did of Meyer, he doubted the man would care. Finn still had yet to decide if Meyer celebrated any of the gods, or if he had lost his faith after working as an executioner. Finn had never really had it to begin with—at least, that was what he'd always told himself—but when he'd been marched toward the Raven Stone, he had found himself praying along to Heleth no differently from any of the Poor Bastards Finn had been with in the time that he'd served Meyer.

After passing a massive building advertising a construction business, he stepped into the Grindle section. The buildings were older, many of them still quite formal, though they were smaller. The detail of their construction was different from those in even the sections nearby, but there was a certain charm to Grindle that some of the other sections didn't have. The streets were narrower as well, giving a more intimate feel than he'd had when walking through nearby sections. The air had a floral fragrance to it that came from a few gardens situated in the middle of the street, narrowing the road and forcing him to loop out and around.

There weren't as many people in the streets, but when he passed those who were out, none of them paid any attention to him. That wasn't surprising. One of the things Meyer had wanted for Finn was to have him dressed in clothing that would blend in almost anywhere. With the kind of work they had to do and places they had to travel, anywhere from outside of the Teller Gate to the palace itself, he had to be dressed so that he could fit in throughout the city.

Johan's business took Finn a while to find. The building was near the end of the main street leading into the section, close to another building with a tall, slanted roof. That was all that Meyer had been able to uncover for him. Finn wasn't surprised when he came across it easily. Meyer had probably known how to find it without asking. For all Finn knew, Meyer had already visited.

That was a troubling thought, but he wouldn't put it past Meyer. Master Meyer might trust that Finn would do the work asked of him, but all of this was an apprenticeship as well, so there was an element of testing involved. Finn couldn't take offense to that. He had to understand

Meyer would need to ensure the job was done as he expected.

That was why Finn had to be as careful as possible and make certain he did what Meyer would want done. This *was* his apprenticeship, and though he might never have thought that he would want to be an executioner, it beat the alternative for him.

When he stopped at Johan's shop, he studied the sign outside. It was a simple wooden sign hanging from a metal pole, with a marking that depicted a scroll and a feather pen. It suited a scribe.

He paused in front of the door, looking at the buildings on either side of it. A candlemaker was to the left, while a seamstress was on the right. When Finn stepped into the shop, a bell tinkled, announcing his presence.

To Finn's surprise, the interior was dimly lit. A single lantern resting on a table in the center of the room was the only source of light other than what drifted in through the windows, which was less than Finn would have expected.

An older, gray-haired man stepped out of the back and eyed Finn for a moment. "May I help you?"

Finn must have passed the initial test about whether he could afford the scribe's services. The man hadn't been subtle about it at all in looking him over. "I came to ask you a few questions."

The man frowned, pushing a pair of wire-framed glasses up onto his nose, wrinkling his brow at Finn. "I'm afraid I don't have time for questions. If you want to hire my services, you should know I've got a week delay. Not as much as some, but there aren't many who can scribe as quickly. I do require a deposit—"

"I'm not here to question your services." A deposit? He must be doing well if he could charge a deposit. "I came to ask you a few questions about a man under your employ by the name of David Sweth."

The scribe's eyes widened slightly. "I have released him from his duties. I don't need anyone like *that* working in my shop."

"Even if he's not responsible?"

"How can he not be responsible? I heard what happened."

Heard about, not seen. Finn doubted a man like this would ever even cross the river if he could help it, and when he did, he probably stayed on Porman's Path through the city, wanting to take the way the king would take, never venturing off on any side streets.

"That is why I'm here."

Johan regarded Finn again. "You don't look like an Archer."

"My name is Finn Jagger, king's executioner."

That elicited the most reaction out of Johan. "So, he *did* do it. That stupid bastard. What was he thinking?"

"Do you have some place we could sit and talk?"

"Must we do it here?"

"If you'd rather come visit him in Declan, I'm sure I could question you there. I thought you'd be more comfortable here."

"I've done nothing that would make you need to bring me to Declan Prison."

"I didn't say you did. I was offering an alternative."

Johan pulled an ornately curved wooden chair away from the wall and slid it toward the table, motioning for Finn to sit. Then he pulled another out and took a seat. Finn followed. He looked at Johan, studying him while settling into the chair and trying to gauge what kind of man he was. Older and thin, there was something almost delicate about Johan, though he stared at Finn with a heated intensity, almost as if he didn't care for him.

Finn had been used to that. Growing up as he did in the Brinder section, there had been plenty of times when he'd been viewed as less than those from the more central sections of the city. Even after coming to work with Meyer, there were plenty of people who viewed him as beneath them.

"What can you tell me about Sweth?" Finn asked.

The scribe sighed. "What's there to tell? I needed a man to assist me. He took the job. Now I will have to find another."

"Did he do good work?"

There was a hesitation. "It was adequate."

"What does that mean?"

He started to smirk. "Do you need for me to define the word *adequate*?"

Finn sat upright. "Your answers to me have been less than adequate. I'm looking for clarity and detail. If you think it would be easier to answer these questions elsewhere—"

Johan shook his head quickly. "That is not necessary. I meant no disrespect. I don't know your education, Mr.

Jagger. The work of a scribe is about efficiency and legibility. David Sweth managed both adequately."

"Why is that?"

"He was not the most efficient with his time. With the backlog of customers, I need someone who can help expedite requests. Now it's only going to get worse."

"And his legibility?"

"If you would permit me a moment?"

Finn shrugged. Johan got up and headed to a shelf near him, where he pulled off a few stacks of papers before returning and sitting in front of Finn. He set the pages down, creating two stacks. Finn scanned each top page. They looked to be inventory lists from a general store, nothing all that exciting.

"What would you like me to see?" Finn asked. "You were hired to record the inventory of a shop, I presume?"

Johan blinked a moment before nodding.

Could he really have thought Finn wouldn't be able to read it?

"The one on your left is the work of a master scribe. As you can see, the work is quite legible. The work on the right was done by Mr. Sweth."

Finn struggled to see much of a difference, though suspected that was mostly because he hadn't been trained to see anything different between the two.

"It looks like Sweth did adequate work," Finn said.

Johan nodded. "He wanted me to move him along, but he wasn't ready. There are many aspects to learning how to scribe. Unfortunately, he hadn't taken the time to master some of the earliest parts of what I asked of him. He was too eager to move on."

"I see."

"That's not to say Mr. Sweth wouldn't have eventually progressed beyond his current state. I had given him suggestions on how to improve. He seemed to take them to heart, which is all one can ask of their apprentice, I suppose."

Finn sat for a moment, staring at the pages, still struggling to understand if there was anything to the difference. Were he to have been given both documents, he would actually have believed they were done by the same person.

"What can you tell me about his character?"

"His character?"

Finn looked up, meeting Johan's eyes. "Was he reliable? Trustworthy? Did you fear sending him on assignment? Would you leave him alone in your shop? Would you—"

"I understand the question, Mr. Jagger. As to Mr. Sweth, he was *mostly* reliable. He didn't come from the nicest part of the city, and you know how that kind can be."

"I'm afraid I don't."

"They often have deficits that must be corrected before they're useful, and Mr. Sweth was no different. Like so many others I've hired from those sections over the years, I found that he struggled with what was asked of him. A little slow, but I've always enjoyed the opportunity to help others move ahead in the world, so I've taken chances."

Finn sniffed. "By that, you mean you've enjoyed underpaying what you would offer someone else who might have apprenticed to you."

"I wouldn't—"

"Do you know if Mr. Sweth had any family in his section?"

Johan shook his head slightly. "I'm afraid I didn't ask." He gathered the stacks of papers and got to his feet, carrying them back to the shelves. "It wasn't necessary for the kind of work that we did."

Finn watched as Johan moved around this section of the shop. Maybe he really didn't concern himself with learning anything about Sweth, though Finn thought that unlikely. Johan had brought Sweth in, and he had trained him, which meant that he had thought that the apprentice could be useful, even if it wasn't as useful as a master scribe.

Johan was hiding something from Finn.

"Can you tell me a little about the type of clients you work for?" Finn asked.

Johan turned to him, tensing slightly. "Most of my clients ask for simple documentation. You saw the inventory list."

"Is that all you do?"

"There are others who ask that we scribe letters or sometimes longer works."

"Who do you generally work for?"

There was something there. Finn could feel it, even if he couldn't tell what that might be. It was a matter of digging and asking just the right questions. He knew that Meyer would probably not have any trouble getting someone like Johan to talk, but Finn wasn't the master executioner. He would have to find his own way forward.

"I am known as one of the most skilled scribes in the city. I have clients throughout the city that can attest to it."

One of the most skilled. That meant there were others who were more skilled. That might be where Finn would need to go. Figure out more about the scribes, then maybe he could better understand what else there was for him to be considering.

"But you have a backlog of clients you haven't managed to get to."

"There is always more work than there are skilled scribes, Mr. Jagger. It is why I was so hopeful that Mr. Sweth would have been useful. Unfortunately…"

The possibility that Johan didn't want the competition with an up-and-coming Sweth had been something that Finn had started to consider. If there really *was* enough work, then it wouldn't matter. There were some industries like that. The skills took time to master, and there was never a shortage of work, so those who possessed them could not only charge often exorbitant amounts for their work, but they didn't fear the competition among others in the same field.

It reminded him of the physicians. There were only a few fully trained physicians in Verendal. The training took years, and the perceived skill so impressive, that there was never a shortage for their healing, though there were others in the city who offered comparable—and in the case of Master Meyer, often quite similar—level of skill.

"What will you do if he's released?" Finn asked.

"I didn't think that was even a possibility. From what I have heard, he burned half of his section to the ground. Lives were lost. Homes were destroyed. A crime like that must be punished, Mr. Jagger."

"A crime like that must be punished," Finn agreed, "but what if Mr. Sweth is innocent? Would you take him back?"

Johan leaned on one of the shelves. "I suppose I could use the help. My clients will now be forced to wait for many weeks. Some of them will undoubtedly go elsewhere, though I can't say I mind. More work will come. It always does."

Finn got to his feet, sweeping his gaze briefly around the inside of the scribe's shop, before looking to Mr. Johan. "Thank you for your time. It has been most helpful."

Johan bobbed his head in a nod. "Of course. I am, of course, eager to help your investigation in whatever way I can."

Finn stepped through the shop then back out into the street, straightening his jacket once outside. He lingered a moment. There was still something Johan was keeping from him, but the problem was that Finn didn't know if it was anything to be concerned about. Meyer had made a point of telling him that even honest men kept things to themselves. The real challenge was trying to determine who was honest and merely striving for a level of privacy, and who intentionally misled and concealed. Finn just couldn't get a read on Johan, so didn't know where the scribe fit.

He headed through the streets, taking in more of Jorend section. He found himself drawn toward the Heshian Palace in the distance, where it sat upon a small rise within the city. When he reached it, he circled around the street outside, nodding to the Archers patrolling. Palace Archers were different from the city Archers. They watched everything with a darkness in their eyes, and even Finn didn't avoid their attention. This time. He smiled to himself, knowing that he *had* managed to sneak into the palace despite their patrols.

The king hadn't visited the city in quite some time. That wasn't uncommon. His visits were infrequent. When he did come, he rarely spent much time there.

Finn moved beyond the palace and headed toward the viscount's manor. It was not far from the palace, and while an impressive structure, it paled in comparison to the palace. The low stone wall that surrounded the viscount's manor did not carry the same menace as the palace walls.

The main gate leading into the manor home opened as Finn approached. He stepped back, moving toward the shadows on the far side of the street, looking toward the viscount's home. The last time he'd seen the viscount had been during the most recent execution a week before, and that only from a distance. He didn't get too close to the Blood Court and certainly didn't seem to enjoy the proceedings. As far as Finn could tell, he only attended so he could make the claim to the king that he attended during his sentences to assure his justice was carried out.

The man who exited caught Finn's attention. Bellut

served the viscount. That was partly what offered him a layer of protection once Finn had discovered Bellut's involvement in the plot against the king. More than that, Finn had been unable to actually prove anything. Seeing him at the viscount's manor irritated Finn.

Finn hadn't the opportunity to chase Bellut in the time since he'd learned that Bellut was responsible for what had happened. Not that he hadn't tried, only that it was difficult to get close to him and know whether there was anything more that he might learn about Bellut.

He'd tried going to Bellut's house, but Finn hadn't been willing to break in. A crime like that would be added to his others. Finn had little doubt as to what would happen to him then. He would face his full sentencing, and there would be no pardon this time. There would be no offer of a right, which meant that he would hang.

Bellut would probably love it. That was even more reason for him to be careful. He didn't want to do anything that Bellut would approve of.

Then there was his curiosity about what else Bellut was involved in. Bellut couldn't be the only one responsible for what had happened, which meant there was a great plot taking place in the city, though it was one that even Meyer didn't want to get involved in, despite knowing that Finn had gotten caught up in it.

Bellut didn't see him as he headed along the street.

Finn lingered, considering whether he should follow. When Bellut headed the opposite direction, to his home, Finn decided to trail him.

CHAPTER SEVEN

Skulking through the streets was a skill Finn had gained when still working with his former crew. All the time that Oscar had worked with him, trying to get him better at moving in silence and darkness, had been wasted when Finn had been captured.

Thankfully, Bellut didn't move with all that much discretion either. That was probably because he had nothing to fear. Finn tried to be as careful as he could, slipping along the streets and moving in the darkness of alleys.

He headed toward the outer sections—toward the Meldran section, Finn noticed. There wasn't much in that part of the city. Mostly slums, it was home to those who had to work in the slaughterhouses or often outside of the city on the farms. A few loggers lived in the section, but even they were generally much better off than that.

Finn slowed as Bellut neared the section.

Everything about this was suspicious. There wasn't any reason for him to venture into this part of the city unless he were after something. Bellut stopped in one alley and handed something to a shadowed figure before moving on. He did that several times before Finn drifted back, not wanting to follow too closely. He couldn't tell what Bellut had handed him, only that they seemed to be fairly large bundles.

There was an almost distinct demarcation for this part of the city. The rows of buildings transitioned from taller into more sloped roofs, some that looked as if they'd been hastily strapped to the house, making Finn think they'd blow off at the first sign of a severe storm. He hadn't spent much time in this section even when he'd been a thief. There wasn't much for him there. Since working with Meyer, there hadn't been reason to come to this section, either.

Finn slipped forward, nose wrinkled. The streets had a foul odor to them, though it wasn't necessarily that of refuse. Just a stench he couldn't quite place. Something awful, but also something that suggested rot.

Bellut rounded a corner, and Finn tried to keep up with him.

A shadow slipped by in the distance as well, moving quickly. They had a practiced step, as if not concerned that they might be caught, and Finn noticed how this other person turned from side to side, looking all around as if keeping watch for anyone who might follow.

Or for Archers.

There wouldn't be many Archers in this section.

Finn trailed after the figure, having lost sight of Bellut. There was something about them that reminded him of Wolf.

Rounding a corner, he saw the street was now empty. There was no point in staying in this section of the city any longer than he needed. If he couldn't figure out what Bellut was after, then he didn't need to remain any longer.

He saw Bellut again.

He passed a beggar child, and shoved him hard enough that he fell.

Tension filled Finn.

Bellut turned, heading out of the Meldran section.

Finn reached the edge of the section and turned, sweeping his gaze over the streets. There was no sign of any movement. The city was surprisingly quiet, and Finn wondered why that might be.

It was late enough that he should return to Master Meyer's home, continue his studies, and at least report in on what he had seen.

He took a roundabout way back to the Reval section and Master Meyer's home. He found himself heading through the Olin section and even passed close to the Wenderwolf. There were times when he felt compelled to enter the tavern, to sit with the crew once again, and to visit with them the way that he once had, but Finn didn't know if he even could.

It wasn't so much Oscar that he worried about. He feared Annie and her reaction. She had been close to the King, and having been the one to have sentenced him, Finn suspected she might hold more than a grudge with him. He turned away and hurried back toward Meyer's home, not stopping until he reached it.

Once inside, he heard his sister's voice, along with that of Helda, her oldest friend.

Finn hung his cloak in the closet before making his way to the kitchen where his sister and Helda sat at the table.

Helda was a lovely woman, with long brown hair, deep brown eyes, and a pretty face. She always had a sour expression when she looked at him. There had been a time when he'd had a crush on her, though that had faded. Finn tipped his head politely to her before nodding to his sister.

"Finn," Lena said, getting to her feet. "You can have a seat."

"I don't want to disrupt your conversation. Besides, I need to have a word with Master Meyer."

Lena glanced in the direction of Meyer's office before shaking her head slightly. "He has someone in there with him tonight," she said.

Finn arched a brow, and Helda scowled at him.

"Not like that," Lena said hurriedly, and Finn was surprised to see her glare at Helda. "Just somebody he's been working with for the last few weeks. He never lets me see, so I can't say who it is, but I have a feeling they are someone of importance within the city."

"Why would somebody of importance come to the executioner?" Helda asked. "If they have wealth, they could afford any physician in the city."

"Sometimes it's not about wealth but about knowledge," Finn said. He pulled out a chair, taking a seat at the table. "Master Meyer has studied for decades. He's not only a master executioner, but he's a master of various healing techniques."

"That's what Lena keeps telling me."

"More than a few people come to him for healing," Lena said, sitting again. She glanced over to Finn, though he couldn't tell whether she was annoyed with him or whether she wanted to talk with him. "He has me cleaning up after him. Since I keep getting turned away elsewhere—"

"Jobs are hard to come by," Helda offered.

"This feels more than that." She glanced in Finn's direction. Was it because of him that she couldn't find another job? "At least cleaning up after Meyer is something."

"You said that," Helda said, "but he has to want something from you."

"I don't think so," Lena said. "He has his apprentice, and…"

"And what?" Finn said.

"And he has encouraged me to read," she said.

Finn smiled, not at all surprised by his sister's interest in Meyer's books. Lena had always enjoyed studying, though she had never had the opportunity to do so. Living in the Brinder section made it difficult for anyone to get much of an education, let alone the children of thieves.

"What else does he want from you?" Helda asked.

Finn glanced from Lena to Helda, before laughing. "Do you really think that Meyer is trying to seduce my sister?"

Helda frowned. "He wouldn't be the first man of some age to try something like that."

"Then you don't know Master Meyer," Finn said.

"He's an executioner. What's there to know?"

"Quite a bit." Finn got to his feet and nodded to his sister. "I'm going to check on Mother. If Master Meyer comes out, let him know that I'm back."

Lena nodded.

He stepped out of the kitchen, pausing long enough to hear Helda making another comment about executioners, but Lena defended him.

Finn smiled to himself as he headed up the stairs. At the top of the stairs, there were several rooms. Master Meyer took one of them for his own personal sleeping quarters, and another was shared by Lena and Finn's mother. He didn't know much about the previous occupant, though the stuffed animals, along with the decorations, had been removed as Lena and Finn's mother had settled in. Meyer never spoke about his life before Finn had arrived.

He tapped on the door before pushing it open.

His mother sat up in bed, a lantern glowing on the table next to her and a book propped in her lap. Her long, brown hair had gone mostly gray, and her blue eyes were flat, though she looked at him with a little bit of vibrancy in her gaze.

"Finn. What time is it?"

"It's getting late," he said.

"Has Master Meyer sent you to check on me?"

Finn smiled. "No. I thought that I would see if you needed anything."

"I don't. Lena was in earlier, and she made sure that I had food, and anything else that I might need, but then again, Henry ensures the same."

He kept waiting for Master Meyer to tell him what more he wanted for providing for Finn's mother and sister, but Meyer had not asked for anything. Finn was accustomed to people asking for something in return.

"How are you feeling?"

"I'm feeling about as well as I could expect," she said. She shifted on the bed, letting the book fall closed, and glanced down at it, staring at her hands. "I'm not used to being the one cared for."

"You have cared for us enough over the years. It is time Lena and I did the same for you."

"Lena needs to find herself a husband and get married," she said.

Finn sniffed. "I don't have a feeling that Lena is altogether motivated by that."

"What sort of life does she expect to live if she doesn't get married? She doesn't have any skills."

"I'm sure Lena appreciates your concern," Finn said.

"It's a wonder that you ended up here." She looked around. This was the most alert that Finn had seen his mother in weeks. Even though Meyer and the hegen had healed her, there was still enough residual effect from what she had gone through that left her *off* a bit. "You never really told me how you ended up apprenticed to

Master Meyer." She smiled slightly. "I still can't believe my son is the executioner."

Finn didn't know how she felt about it. "I'm not *the* executioner, and it's a long story. All that matters is that he was willing to take me in. It's better than the alternative."

"Your father would be pleased. You know how he wanted so much for you and your sister."

"I know," Finn said.

She clasped her thin hands in her lap. "You're still angry with him."

"I'm not," Finn said.

"There is no reason for you to be angry with your father. He was only doing what he thought necessary to provide for you and your sister."

Finn took a seat on the end of the bed, looking at his mother. "I know." He never admitted that he had done the same thing. He worried about how his mother would take it if she learned that he had taken up stealing to provide for her. "I've been trying to find what happened to him."

Her brow furrowed and her eyes darkened. "I don't think it matters."

"You're not worried about what happened to Father?"

"I know what happened to him," she said. "I warned him. I tried to get him to stop, and that if he were to keep with it, eventually he would end up jailed or worse."

"Master Meyer didn't hang him," Finn said.

His mother looked up. "I know. I asked."

Finn hadn't been aware of that, though he could easily imagine his mother and Master Meyer having a conversation about what had happened to Finn's father. Knowing Master Meyer, he would have been blunt but probably managed to be delicate at the same time. Finn had found the contrast within Master Meyer intriguing and struggled to know if he could act the same way.

"That's more than I've done," Finn said.

"He earned his fate, Finn. Everything he did was to help us, but at the same time, he had other opportunities but didn't take them."

"What other opportunities?"

"He could have taken more respectable jobs," she said.

"He was working with the cartwright—"

"That wasn't going anywhere, and we both knew it."

Growing up, Finn had assumed his father would one day be more than an apprentice. Obviously, his parents hadn't shared that view. "He didn't have any other skills, and there aren't too many people who are willing to hire somebody like him from our section of the city." It reminded Finn of the conversation he had with Master Johan. What would David Sweth have felt like? Probably the same as Finn's father.

But then, he had been given an opportunity. He had apprenticed with Master Johan, and he would have no reason to have committed any crime.

"I'm not going to have the same argument with you that I had with him all those years ago," she said. "I tried. I failed. And now here we are."

Finn nodded. "Here we are."

"You don't have to stay with me," she said.

"I want to. I wanted to see how you were doing."

"I'm here, aren't I? I don't have any choice otherwise."

"What's that supposed to mean?"

"It means I can't get up even if I wanted to. I'm stuck here in this bed. I'm dependent upon you and your sister and Master Meyer all helping me. I can't get out of bed, and I can't go anywhere, and I can't do any damn thing for myself. Heleth has cursed me."

Finn regarded his mother for a moment, wishing he knew the right thing to say. There wasn't anything, though. His mother had been sick for a long time now, and even though her mind had seemingly recovered, the rest of her had not. She still suffered.

What would he do were the situation reversed? Would he want to sit in bed all day, waiting on the hope that he might have someone come and help him or would he want to get up and move?

Finn knew the answer.

"What can I do to help you?" he asked.

His mother looked down, keeping her gaze away. "It doesn't matter anymore."

"It does."

She looked up at him. "Let me go." The words hung in the air. "If I get sick again, just let me go. Your father is gone. You've started a new life and don't need me around. Even Lena has started to have her own life. Neither of you need me."

"We *do* need you. You're our mother."

"Not like this, I'm not. I can't do the things I once did for you. Gods, I don't even know the things you did for me. I just…" She turned away, and tears started streaming down haggard cheeks.

Finn sat alongside her, saying nothing, not knowing the right words to say. That had always been Lena's gift with their mother. It was the reason that he'd been willing to join Oscar. There had to be something that he could offer, which was why he had stolen.

When she drifted off to sleep, he stood and turned to see Master Meyer standing in the doorway. His eyes were dark, and he looked past Finn to Finn's mother, watching her.

"She has recovered as much as she can," Meyer said.

"I know."

"There's only so much the hegen healing can accomplish."

Finn squeezed his eyes shut. He'd lost his father and didn't want to lose his mother. Not like this when it seemed like everything should have gone well for them. When it seemed like his mother should have the chance to recover and thrive. They didn't deserve it.

"There has to be more. I can go back to Esmerelda and can see if she—"

"There's only so much that can be done."

Finn locked eyes with Meyer, and then he saw it. Something that he'd missed before but shouldn't have. He understood that Meyer had lost something. Maybe everything. "What happened to them?"

Meyer turned to Finn then shook his head. "It doesn't matter."

"You went to the hegen. They tied you to them." Meyer didn't deny it. "Is that why you helped me?"

There had to be some answer why Meyer had rescued him. It might even be the hegen.

"I helped you because it was my right." He spoke softly so as to not wake Finn's mother.

"What about your family?" Finn turned to look at the room. "I remember when you brought mine here. The room looked like it had just been used."

"It hadn't been used in many years," Meyer whispered.

"What happened to them?" He wanted to know, though with Meyer, Finn didn't know if he would be given the chance. It was possible that he wouldn't share anything more with Finn.

"I couldn't save them. Neither could the hegen." He looked to Finn's mother. "Take the time you have with her and cherish it. I fear she won't be here long."

Meyer turned and headed down the stairs.

Finn inhaled deeply, this time smelling something of the room that he'd missed before. There was the medicinal odor in the room, that of the various compounds Meyer mixed, each of them used for some healing process, but underneath it all, a hint of sickness.

No.

She had been healed. The hegen had saved her. Meyer had given her what he could to help. Finn had seen it.

His mother's words came back to him.

If I get sick again, just let me go.

What did she know?

He looked toward the doorway and down the stairs. If

he strained, he could just make out Lena's voice as she spoke to Helda. It was soft, comfortable, the way she had been ever since coming to Meyer's home.

What would happen to Lena if they lost their mother?

Finn didn't want to think about that, but he thought she deserved to know. If there was anything that he could do to help...

Maybe he could help his mother.

He didn't have Meyer's knowledge, neither did he have the apothecary Wella's, but that didn't mean he couldn't study and try to learn. Meyer expected him to study and learn. Trying to find a way to help his mother would be a part of what Meyer would have asked of him. Why couldn't he apply his studies to something that mattered?

As Finn had looked at his mother, knowing that she didn't want him to save her, he didn't know if he could do anything else. Either he would find something from one of Meyer's texts, a way to understand what he might do to help her, or he would return to the hegen and Esmerelda.

His mother stirred briefly, opening her eyes just halfway and looked at him. The slight smile that formed told Finn everything he needed. This *was* something he had to do.

His mother would have to understand.

CHAPTER EIGHT

The apothecary shop was located in a quiet part of the Olin section. Finn had visited there a few times since becoming Meyer's apprentice, and each time he visited, the ancient apothecary provided him with more than just the items that Meyer required of him. There was always an element of advice in what she said to him.

The painted sign outside of the shop had a staff with a circle around it, the symbol of the apothecaries. Wella was not only knowledgeable, something Finn had come to appreciate the more that he had come to visit, but she had stocks of supplies that were fresher and purer than any other place.

He stepped inside, taking a deep breath. The inside of the shop had a strangely pungent smell to it, though it was not unpleasant. He detected a floral hint, maybe rose or lilac, along with several different medicines that had a slightly minty aroma. Different smells mingled, making it difficult for him to identify one underlying theme to all of it.

Rows of shelves filled the inside of the apothecary, and on them were stacks of various powders or oils or other strange items. Finn had come to learn that Wella was one of the few who stocked human remains following executions. He found that strange the first time that he had seen it, but had come to learn that the hegen weren't the only people who believed in the power of life and death.

Wella tottered out from the back of her shop, the stoop to her back a little more pronounced today than it had been even two weeks before. She wore the same striped shawl over her shoulders that she always did, clutching it in each fist.

"Mr. Jagger. I wasn't expecting to see you today." She stepped forward, tapping on the floor with her cane.

"I'm still trying to learn as much as I can. Master Meyer wants me to continue my studies of all of the apothecary medicine you can teach me."

She laughed, the sound a mixture of a rustle of leaves and a deep throated cackle. "Is that right? Henry never does anything half-assed, does he?"

"What does that mean?"

She tapped her cane on the ground again and leaned close to Finn. "It means that I'm not surprised he wants you to learn as much as possible." She smiled at Finn. "What does he want you to learn from me today?"

Eventually, word of Finn coming to Wella would reach

Master Meyer, so he would have to present something that would be believable, and something that Meyer wouldn't be able to deny. It wasn't as if Master Meyer didn't want Finn to learn as much as possible, anyway.

"I've been studying a book on herbs. It's a bit dense, but I've been trying to work through it. I was curious if you might be able to help me understand some of it."

Wella arched one brow as she leaned toward him. "Let me guess. He has you reading Gisles?"

"That's right."

"Henry always preferred some of the older books. There are some newer works that are a little easier to work through, but he's not wrong in having you study Gisles."

"Why does he prefer the older books?"

"It was from a time before the university opened and all apothecaries thought they should abandon the ancient teachings as they studied. Not that any of the ancient teachings were wrong, mind you. They were simply different. Perhaps not studied quite as rigorously as the fools in the university might study, but that isn't to say that what the apothecaries of old know is wrong."

"You don't care much for physicians?"

"Some of them are fine," she said, tapping her cane yet again. "But some of them think that their title means more than experience. I can show you many apothecaries, even wise women, who know far more than the physicians do about basic ailments. Not everything needs a complicated solution, Mr. Jagger."

Finn chuckled. "What about when it does need a complicated solution?"

"There are some illnesses that can't be easily cured. As you will learn as you read through Gisles's work, some of the concoctions are incredibly complex. I doubt you will find any physician capable of mixing those. They don't have the patience, you see. Still, those old techniques are quite effective. All you have to do is ask any of the people who've been cured by them."

"What about how that compares to the hegen technique?"

Wella waved her hand, *tsk*ing softly. "You can't compare what I do with the kind of magic they practice. They are complementary in many ways. I suppose if you ask any of the hegen practitioners, they would share with you that they incorporate aspects of the natural world in what they do, which makes them similar to an apothecary, though the depth of their knowledge is probably not the same."

"They incorporate body parts," Finn said.

"And is that not part of the natural world?"

"I suppose it is. It's just that it—"

"Makes you uncomfortable. I can see it in your face. You question their methods."

"Not when they work."

Wella grinned at him. "Do you have firsthand experience in that?" She leaned forward, watching him. "You do. Interesting. I wouldn't have expected Henry to have pulled you into the hegen quite so soon. It's a bit dangerous, you know."

"I know."

She cackled. "What did they ask of you?"

Finn debated how much to share with her. Wella had an inquisitive mind, and he suspected she would learn regardless of what he wanted to share with her. If he didn't tell her anything, then she would learn from Meyer.

"They didn't really tell me what they asked of me."

"They always tell you what they want, though it's not always the way you think they will." She watched him. "I suppose you know that."

"I have seen it."

Wella cackled again. "That's an important lesson in its own right, especially when you're taking on the responsibilities you have. It's good for you to realize others will ask something in return. What you promise might be more than what you can give."

"I didn't promise anything to the hegen."

"Then perhaps they don't have you quite under their thumb as they would like. You should be careful, Mr. Jagger. They will keep working on you. You're too valuable to them."

"Why?"

"Because you have access to what they need, of course." She laughed. "Now. What can we talk about today?" She stepped out from around the counter, tapping the cane as she walked. "The last time you were here, we discussed several different local leaves, many of which have some qualities you can use. I suspect you've found that information helpful?"

"I find all the information you've shared with me helpful."

Wella stopped in front of a strange wooden carving. It was shaped something like a wolf, though larger, and with an enormous head. Dark eyes practically watched Finn.

"What's this?"

"Ah. This is something from before Verendal was ever much more than a village. An old find, and a talisman that has served to make me comfortable, though I don't think that's its purpose."

He studied it. There was something about it that reminded him of some of the hegen items he'd seen with Esmerelda. Maybe even Alainsith.

"What is its purpose?" Finn reached for it.

Wella tapped his arm with her cane and shook her head. "It watches over us. The hegen would probably call it protective, and given that I've had my shop here for decades and have come to no harm, perhaps it is protective at that. The king would probably call it an item of the Alainsith, one which he would love to claim so that he could further the treaty with them." She shrugged. "Either way, it's staying put."

"I wondered if it was Alainsith." Finn knew so little about the Alainsith, though he had seen many different items of theirs. The Alainsith had magic—real magic, not the kind like the hegen used—and lived beyond the trees surrounding Verendal. The kingdom had a peace with them, though it had been tested over the years. "I've never seen anything like it."

"There are other Alainsith relics in the city."

"There are, but most of them are old and faded." The strange sculpture was anything but that. Not faded, and it didn't even look old. Finn could imagine that it had just been sculpted.

"Old and faded because those in the city have failed to care for them. We might come to wish we had done otherwise."

"Why?"

Wella shrugged. "Like this talisman, they are supposed to offer protection. Wouldn't we want protection, especially out here on the outskirts of the kingdom?"

"Protection from what?"

Wella's face soured, wrinkles around the corners of her mouth growing deeper. "From what? There are many things to fear in the world, Mr. Jagger. Witches. Spirits. The Alainsith. Even the gods."

Finn started to smile, but he had a sense that she wasn't joking with him. "The hegen are witches, so you're saying we need to protect against them? They've lived outside the city for as long as I know."

"The hegen aren't the kind of witches we need protection from."

Finn frowned, but she didn't elaborate. "What about the Alainsith? They wouldn't hide from their own creations." He wasn't going to challenge her on the belief in spirits. There were too many people in Verendal who believed in spirits. The gods... they might be real, and they might not be, but either way, he didn't think they were all too concerned with what happened to mankind.

"You would be surprised." She looked at the talisman for a long moment before moving on. "Why don't we discuss the various oils and liniments we have here?" She stopped in front of another cabinet and reached for a jar of a dark liquid. "Now, most of the time, you'll be the one creating the liniment to ensure its purity, but there may come times when you aren't able to concoct it on your own. Any fool can mix a few things together into a lotion and call it medicine. In your position, you will need to know whether it will be effective."

Wella tipped the jar to the side, and the oil flowed, but it did so very slowly. "There are other times when you might need to determine what someone has been given by another. This requires you have knowledge of the oils and various concoctions in order for you to pick apart what someone else may have thought to use." She turned and looked at Finn. "Not all apothecaries have the same skill set, as you have likely seen. Not all surgeons know how to mix an appropriate healing compound. Even the wise women, thinking to help, are often misguided."

She pulled the stopper off the jar, and a terrible stench drifted out.

"What is that?"

"This will be one of your frequent bases used."

Finn stared at it, thinking about what he'd read in some of the books that Meyer had lent him, and he thought that he recognized it. Druzen oil had been described as a dark oil, thicker than blood, that was incredibly sticky. "Is that druzen?"

She smiled. "Very good, Mr. Jagger. This is druzen oil.

Collecting it from the tree is complicated. It's much harder than you think that it would be. More than simply boring into it like when acquiring maple sap, or even oak and elm. The druzen trees are hidden deep within the forest surrounding Verendal, and in order to reach them, it takes knowledge and skill."

"If it's just into the forest, why does it take all that knowledge and skill?"

She shrugged. "I only purchase it, and do not collect it on my own. I know better than to try to fetch my own supplies. I did that once and found the purity wasn't quite what I intended. I find it easier to simply acquire what I need."

Finn chuckled. "I can only imagine the kind of people you have bringing you supplies."

"That is another lesson you will one day need to learn, Mr. Jagger. Eventually, you'll want to know who you can trust as you acquire supplies. Some will know more than others, and some will be skilled at their acquisition, while others..."

"What about others?"

"Others might think they have acquired one thing when they have gathered another. If you're not careful, they'll mislabel it, and if you follow their labeling, you may mix something unintentionally."

"What about your shop?"

She frowned at him. "Nothing in my shop is mislabeled."

Finn grinned at her. "Should I test it?"

"Of course. You should believe I know my way around

my apothecary, but you should also question it. I believe Henry does the same. He recognizes he must test everything he acquires, mostly to ensure it is exactly what he intended to acquire in the first place."

Wella set the jar of oil down and grabbed a ceramic bowl with a top on it. She pulled the sky-blue painted top off the jar and dipped a finger in a white paste before pulling it out and bringing it to her nose. "This is a particularly nasty liniment. If you find that you need to use this, the person that you have worked with would have been infected with a significant illness." She turned to him. "Can you tell me what it is?"

Finn shook his head. "How can I tell what it is just by looking at it?"

"Looking? I didn't ask you to simply look at it."

He took the jar from her when she offered it, and he dipped his finger into it the way that she did. Bringing the finger to his nose, Finn took a deep breath and immediately wished that he hadn't. It was bitter, almost stinging his nostrils, though there was an undercurrent of something almost minty to it. A hint of a floral edge mixed alongside it, though maybe that was his imagination and something that he wished were present. He couldn't tell based on what he smelled.

Finn looked over to Wella. "Is it safe to taste?"

"Do you think that will help you better understand what is in it?"

"It might. It depends upon what is inside the concoction."

Wella smiled tightly. "Nothing in this liniment is fatal.

I doubt you will find anything in any of the liniments you will work with that are fatal."

He touched his tongue to it, and it went numb.

His whole mouth went numb.

His eyes widened, and Wella started cackling.

"It's not fatal, but I warned you that some things are not quite what they seem. And I also warned you this one was a particularly nasty liniment."

"What is it?"

Finn could barely get the words out, and when they did come, his tongue felt thick, as if he'd been drinking heavily the night before.

Wella handed him a towel off the counter, and he wiped his finger before handing the jar back to her. "This is a mixture of several different compounds I suspect you are familiar with. Henry would have worked with you on them." She put the top back on the jar and set it on the counter, shifting it around with the others. "It has a base of meren oil, that's what gives it the white consistency, and mixed in with meren oil are holar wort, neverthorn, and cinzel berries." She turned, smiling at him. "So simple, and so few ingredients, but quite effective. As I suspect you've discovered, it does lead to a little bit of numbness."

"A little bit?" Finn tried to get out.

"A little. There are other compounds that can lead to longer-lasting numbness. This one gives you an opportunity to numb the skin before you attempt to incise and drain an infection." She cackled and looked up at him. "The fools from the university don't think it's of much use, and they would prefer just to have their patients bite down on a leather strap. Torment, if you ask me. I would much rather take the time to apply the appropriate medicines before tormenting my clients."

His tongue started to get feeling back into it. It surprised Finn just how quickly the liniment had worked.

"The challenge, as in all things, is in knowing what might work and not overdoing it. You can mix the most complicated compound, but if you don't target the right aspect of the illness, even a complicated compound is going to be of no use." She tapped her cane on the ground. "That is something Gisles never seems to mention in the entirety of the work, but which, in my opinion, needs to be clarified."

Finn swallowed. Finally, his throat was starting to feel a bit more normal. There was a reason he had come there today, and he wondered if he might be able to convince Wella to answer his questions, or if perhaps she was unwilling.

"Do you remember when I first came with Master Meyer to your shop?"

She glanced over, nodding. "Of course."

"What was that concoction?"

Wella regarded him, arching a brow. "What do you remember of that concoction?"

"I don't remember all that much. I was a bit distracted at the time."

"You were still trying to learn your way. Henry can be a bit intense."

"A bit."

"What can you tell me about what you came for that time?"

Finn remembered the compound well, though he didn't have all the ingredients memorized. He'd struggled to know what Meyer had wanted from him and had tried to do everything the executioner had asked of him.

"There were a few things that he wanted. Thistledown. Jasper berry." Finn closed his eyes. He usually had a good memory, and when it came to the various items that he'd used with Meyer, he had done a good job of keeping that with him, but this had to do with Finn's mother. "I think he had wanted crispon leaves and thender bark."

"You're missing something, but you've got the gist of it. What does that concoction tell you?"

Finn had studied most of the elements that had gone into the concoction in the time that he'd been working with Meyer. There shouldn't be anything in it that would be terribly difficult for him to determine. "The crispon leaves are for alertness."

"Only in the right quantity. You can overdo it, much like I've told you about many things."

Finn nodded. Knowing what he did of Master Meyer and his skill, he had a hard time thinking he would have overdone it. Master Meyer had more skill than almost anybody else Finn had met in the time that he been working with him, and there was a level of detail to his work that mattered.

"The thender bark is little bit more complicated. I'm

not sure what purpose that would have." Finn frowned as he thought through it. "Thistledown is just a binding, used to bring the other ingredients together. The jasper berry would probably just add a little bit of flavor, more than anything else."

Wella nodded. "Very good. You're starting to piece it together.

"But you say I'm missing something."

"A bit of fennel, though as you can imagine, it's unlikely that was the key ingredient."

"The thender bark."

She nodded. "Very well."

"What does it do?"

She cackled. "I think that you need to uncover that on your own. I can't tell you everything. Sometimes, studying makes a difference."

"Even for this?"

"Especially for this," she said, laughing again.

Finn realized she must know exactly why he was asking.

The door to the shop opened, and an older woman came in. She glanced from Finn to Wella, nodding politely as she wandered around the back of the shop.

"I have another customer, Mr. Jagger. If you would like to discuss Gisles's volume later, I am more than happy to offer my corrections."

"I would like that."

Finn swept his gaze around the inside of the shop again before sighing and heading out.

He needed answers, but it seemed as if answers for his mother would come back to studying, trying to understand just what the thender bark component had done for his mother. He might be able to ask Master Meyer, but Finn wondered if he would even share that with him.

As he made his way down the street, the Teller Gate came into view. Wella's shop was near the edge of the city, close enough to the gate leading outside, and close to the Raven Stone, which was probably how she acquired so many of her human remains.

He had spent enough time on his own needs, and now it was time for him to get back to his pursuit of whether or not Sweth was guilty of the fire. Not only did he need to study, but Finn needed to dig more into that piece. If he failed, he could imagine Master Meyer's disappointment.

He turned and saw a familiar figure hurrying along one of the side streets.

Finn hesitated a moment before deciding to dart after it.

There was no mistaking Oscar. The man known as the Hand was tall and lean, and moved with a strange sort of lumbering grace that had always made him easy to spot but difficult to catch.

Finn hadn't seen Oscar much since executing the King. It was not for lack of looking, though. Oscar was Finn's oldest friend, so far as friends went. He didn't have many people he was close to, and Oscar had been the one who had helped him the most after losing his father, bringing him into the crew and giving Finn a little bit of meaning and purpose to his life. Without Oscar, Finn wasn't sure what he would've become.

He hurried forward, trying to catch up to him but also alert and curious.

Oscar had a way of looking around him at all times, a careful and measured manner of surveying the street all around him, as if he were always aware of the Archers who might be patrolling him at any given time.

He turned a corner, trailing after Oscar, and saw him duck into a shop in the distance. Finn slowed, keeping the shop in view as he headed toward it, nodding politely to people on either side of him.

All he had to do was wait.

"You've gotten stale," Oscar said.

Finn spun, taking a step back. "Dammit, Oscar."

"You were obvious the moment you stepped out of the apothecary back there," Oscar said, tipping his head toward Wella's shop. "I probably saw you before you even saw me."

"Maybe," Finn said. It wouldn't surprise him to learn that Oscar had, but at the same time, he thought that he had caught sight of him as soon as he had emerged onto the street. "How are you?"

Oscar flashed a wide smile. "I haven't seen you in the better part of a few months, and that's your first question?"

"Is there a better one?"

Oscar chuckled. "I suppose not. What are you doing right now?"

"Running a few errands."

"That's what he has you doing these days? Errand boy?"

"It's a little more complicated than that," Finn said.

"Just a little?"

Finn glanced back to Wella's shop. "It's quite a bit more complicated than that. Is that what you wanted to know?"

Oscar grinned at him. "You know they've asked about you at the Wenderwolf."

"Have they?" Finn said carefully.

"Not who you might be afraid of. I haven't seen the Wolf or Rock around in quite some time. Of course, the Mistress would make sure of that."

"They were both banished, Oscar," Finn said, and Oscar shrugged. "Annie?"

Oscar shook his head. "Not her. Another. Runs things in the city. Does a damn good job of it, too, keeping most of the crews from fighting for jobs." He shrugged. "Annie wonders how you're doing, though."

Finn smiled tightly. "I'm sure she just wants to know how to get revenge for what happened to the King."

Oscar's face darkened for a moment. "Leon got what was coming to him. Don't you forget about that, Finn." He looked along the street for a moment before turning back to Finn. "You might've gotten off the streets, but there is no way you can deny justice was served in that case. The bastard tried to double-cross us."

"I know," Finn said. He debated how much to mention what he knew of the hegen, but realized Oscar wouldn't say anything about his role in that. He'd paid his debt.

What Finn wanted to know was *why* Oscar had owed

the hegen. That would be a worthy story—and likely another the Hand wouldn't reveal.

Oscar smiled tightly. "I suppose you do. You were the one he targeted, after all."

"It wasn't just me. He intended Rock to get pinched."

It was strange for Finn to have this conversation after all the time that had gone by. Stranger that he had moved past everything that had happened and no longer worried the way that he once had. Finn no longer cared. The only thing that he cared about was having lost his friends. He missed Oscar and Rock.

"Yeah," Oscar said, flicking his gaze in either direction. He tensed just a little bit, enough that it told Finn he had seen something. "Leon had gotten himself involved in something more dangerous than I think he intended."

It was the most Oscar had admitted to what he knew. "I'm sure." Finn resisted the urge to reach into his pocket for the hegen card. "Would you like to catch up?" Finn asked.

It wasn't the way that he should be using his time, but at the same time, Finn did want to sit with Oscar, ask him a few questions, and he needed to know a little bit more about what happened with Wolf after he had gotten away. More than that, Finn needed to know more about Bellut. He might not be able to investigate who he worked with, but that didn't mean Oscar couldn't.

Oscar watched him, and Finn had an unsettling feeling that he knew exactly what Finn intended. "Where would you have us go?"

"Not the Wenderwolf." When Oscar arched a brow,

Finn shrugged. "I don't feel like I'm going to be welcomed there."

"You might be surprised. But if you're not comfortable going there, then we can go someplace else. I know just the place."

CHAPTER NINE

The Brinder section of the city was one of the oldest, run-down with narrow streets covered in filth, children running along the alleys, chasing each other and shouting. The few people who were wandering along the street all had heads tipped forward, shoulders slumped, and were dressed in tattered and dirty clothing.

"Your father and I used to frequent a place over here," Oscar said. "He was the one who wanted us to stay local, but I always wanted to push. It was my fault we kept taking bigger jobs, you see."

It was strange for Oscar to elaborate on all the jobs that he and Finn's father had taken.

"I'm sure he didn't mind. He loved working with you."

Oscar paused with his hand on the door to a narrow building. A faded sign hung overhead, though Finn couldn't make out the details on it. There were quite a few places like this in Brinder. Most of them had once been thriving businesses, or had some history to them, but time had turned them into these run-down establishments.

"He would never have worked with me if he didn't have to," Oscar said.

He stepped inside and Finn followed. The tavern was dark, with a single lantern hanging from a pole in the center of the tavern. The hard-planked flooring was clean, unlike so many of the poorer establishments. A dozen or so tables were scattered around the inside of the tavern, and there weren't many people at this time of the day. Smells of roasting meat and fresh bread drifted from a kitchen somewhere nearby.

"This isn't what I expected."

Oscar sniffed. "You getting so classy you forget what your section was like?"

Finn frowned. Was that what this was about? Did Oscar want to remind Finn about who he'd been and where he came from? Finn didn't need those reminders. He was all too aware of where he'd come from. "It's not a matter of getting too classy. It's just I didn't know there were places like this in Brinder."

"There are places like this all over the city. You just have to know how to find them." Oscar took a seat at a table along one wall, positioned so he could look toward the door. Finn just smiled at the precaution. It wasn't surprising, coming from Oscar. "I haven't been here in a long time, but it don't look much different than it did then. They always made a point of keeping it clean. Food is pretty good too." Oscar nodded to an older man with a dirty apron on who came to the table. "Food and ale, if you don't mind."

The man glanced from Oscar to Finn. "You need to pay up front."

"How long that been the case, Jimmel?"

Jimmel frowned and leaned close to Oscar. "That you, Hand? Damn, but it's been a minute since I've seen you around. You working this section again?"

"Not this section, so you don't have to worry."

"Nah. Not worried about the Thirsty Flute. You and the Goat never caused much trouble for me. Brought in a bit of business, too." Jimmel leaned back, clasping his hands across his belly. "Haven't seen the Goat in a while, neither. He doing all right?"

Oscar glanced to Finn. "He got himself pinched."

"Aw, that's not what I wanted to hear."

"I'll give him your regards when I see him next."

"You do that." He wrapped a knuckle on the table. "I'll get you boys some drinks. Looks like you've got a new employer, Hand, so don't want to offend him."

He hurried off, and Finn watched him leave. "New employer?"

Oscar chuckled. "Dressed the way you are, I can see how he'd think that."

"I don't think I could pass as an employer."

"You'd be surprised. Men change quickly."

Finn leaned back in the chair and looked around the inside of the tavern. "He knew my father."

Oscar sighed. "A lot of men in this section knew your father. He was a good man."

"Is," Finn said.

Oscar's brow darkened, but he nodded. "Sure, Finn. Is."

"I didn't know he was called the Goat."

Oscar smiled. It was a real smile, not one that looked forced. He shook his head slightly as he leaned back against the wall, resting his hands on the table, tapping his fingers in a steady rhythm while he did. "He had a bit of a reputation."

"As what?"

Oscar shrugged. "Stubborn. Like a goat. Got him places he probably wouldn't have gotten otherwise. Got both of us places, if I'm honest."

Oscar's voice had taken on a wistful quality. "You sound like he was the reason you did some of your jobs." Finn had always thought that Oscar had been the one to have brought his father into the difficult jobs. That it had been Oscar who'd guided Finn's father down the road into working for a crew. Maybe that had been a mistake.

"He had an eye, Finn. Not too many like him anymore. Not just an eye, but he was good man, you see. Someone you could trust. Someone like that…"

"Did he give you the nickname the Hand?" Finn had never heard the story, and Oscar had never offered it. It was better than Shuffles.

"It's not anything exciting. I was pulling my first job when I'd finally gotten onto a crew, and it involved grabbing a few things from a shop in the Rester section." He shook his head. "It was a long time ago, so don't go investigating it."

"I wasn't planning on it."

"Anyway. I ended up with a bottle of ink spilled all over my hand. It didn't go away for a long time." Oscar just shrugged.

"That's it?"

"You thought it would be something more exciting?"

"I was hoping. I figured a nickname like the Hand meant that you were the most skilled thief and had quick hands."

"I am that." Oscar grinned at him. "Men don't get their name based on their choices. Look at yours. You never wanted to be called Shuffles."

"Had I stayed in the crew, I wasn't going to be called Shuffles my whole life."

"Probably not. Eventually, you would've earned another name. Everybody does over time. Eventually, you get one that you like."

"And you never minded the nickname of the Hand?"

"I figured it fit, especially as I got a little farther in my career."

"It's not as exciting as *the King*."

"Leon was stupid to call himself that. Then he bribed others to make the name stick."

"So, you *can* give yourself your own name."

"Only if you work at it. I never liked calling him the King, but when he was running the crew, it sort of fit, so I did."

"And Wolf?"

"Well, Wolf is his surname."

"So, you're saying it was a terrible name too."

"Not as bad as Shuffles." Oscar laughed, and shook his head.

Jimmel returned carrying two steins of ale and set them on the table. "Food shouldn't be too long." He pulled a chair out from the table and took a seat, looking at Oscar. "Things have been dry around here, Hand. Need a little more activity."

"Dry can be good, Jimmel. Too much excitement and you end up drawing the wrong kind of attention."

"Aw, the Archers don't much care about Brinder section. We don't have much of anything for them to be concerned about. They would much rather stay closer to the palace."

"You might be surprised," Oscar said. "Sometimes, you get people who you never would've expected who care about your section."

"Such as?"

Oscar nodded to Finn. "Take my colleague here. He has a particular interest in this section."

Jimmel looked over to Finn and regarded him. "We don't need any trouble here. I'm not sure what you think you're going to find in this section, but we don't need anybody snooping around and causing us trouble."

"Oh, you don't need to worry about him snooping around. He knows his way around the section just fine."

"Does he, now?"

"That's enough," Finn said.

Oscar smirked slightly. "See? Now he's getting a little upset."

"You don't want to upset your employer," Jimmel said.

Oscar took the stein of ale and took a long drink as he watched Finn. There was a hint of amusement glittering in his eyes, and Finn just shook his head. Oscar was doing this to play with him. "You're probably right. I need to be careful. I don't want to lose out on any jobs because I got a little ahead of myself." He turned to Finn. "You will forgive me, won't you, Mr. Jagger?"

Finn clenched his jaw, but the proprietor turned, looking at Finn in a different light. "I've heard about you." He glanced from Oscar to Finn. "You brought the executioner into my place?"

"I didn't see that was going to be a problem," Oscar said.

"You might as well have brought Archers in here," he said. Jimmel got to his feet, backing away from the table. "I don't want any difficulty. If you're going to take the Hand away, just make sure it's clear I cooperated."

Finn regarded him for a moment before nodding. "I will keep that in mind." He disappeared, and Finn turned back to Oscar. "Was that necessary?"

"I don't know about *necessary*, but it *was* entertaining."

"For you."

"Oh, he's harmless. Besides, I think he'll get a kick out of telling the story about how the Hand and the executioner came to his tavern. You know how his kind like stories."

Finn looked toward the kitchen where he had disappeared. "I just wanted to come here and talk with you a little bit. I didn't need you to taunt me."

"Come on, Finn. You know how it is."

Finn nodded. He had been away from the streets a long time now, and had forgotten about the steady teasing, the occasional taunt, and the constant desire to try to show off for others in the crew. It was a lifestyle that he no longer missed.

"How have you been?" Finn asked.

Oscar lifted his ale, taking a long drink. "You not going to give it back?"

"There's no point," Finn said.

"No point? Come on, Finn. Would it help if I called you Shuffles?"

Finn tensed, then took a drink of his ale.

Oscar started to smile again. "There he is. There is the stubbornness you take after your father with. The Goat." Oscar leaned forward. "I always saw it in you, you know. When Meyer claimed you, I knew you'd be a good fit. There wasn't any choice for you to do otherwise, and you're too damn stubborn to give up."

"Have you seen any of the others?"

"Have you?" Oscar looked over the top of his stein of ale.

"They were banished, but that doesn't always mean much." It wouldn't have were it Finn. Stay away from the Archers, and none would even know. "I thought I saw Wolf the other day. At least, someone like him."

"He's became a ghost. Left the city like he was supposed to. Not that I can blame him. He was too wrapped up in Leon and his crew, and too many people knew that he had a hand in all of that. It was better for him to go quiet for a while."

Finn took another swig of ale. If Wolf decided to resurface, that might be trouble for Finn. He was the kind of person who would get revenge, and given what had happened to the King, and how Finn had been responsible for the disruption of the crew, he could easily imagine Wolf deciding to take action against him.

Finn was in a place where he didn't have to worry about such things anymore. He was the executioner's apprentice now. He helped supervise the wardens, the iron masters, and had some role with the Archers.

"If you hear anything, let me know."

"You know that's not how it works."

"I know that, but you wouldn't do a favor for an old friend?"

"Would you?"

Finn set the mug of ale down, and he looked over to Oscar. "What do you need?" He started to wonder if his meeting Oscar was not a chance one at all. "You've got something going on."

Oscar took a drink and looked up, grinning at Jimmel as he carried a tray of food over to the table. He slid biscuits and gravy and sausage toward each of them. It smelled amazing. Finn had been eating his sister's cooking ever since staying with Meyer, and while Lena was a good cook, she tended to use less fat than Finn had eaten while running with the crew. There was something about the grease that left Finn's mouth watering.

Jimmel eyed Finn for a moment before turning and leaving.

Finn grabbed the biscuit and shoved it into the gravy

before taking a bite. The flavor burst in his mouth. There had been a part of him that had worried that Jimmel might do something to his food—and he might have—but it tasted good enough that Finn put those thoughts to rest.

Oscar finished his sausage and licked his fingers. "I figured I'd ask what you were working on these days."

Finn shrugged. "There's always something going on. Why?"

"Just curious what he has you doing. I don't know much about how the master executioner works, or what your role with him is. Just that you help him hang people." He mimed wrapping a noose around his neck and his eyes bulged. "Figured there has to be more to it since we don't have a Blood Court each day."

Finn chewed on the sausage. It was just as good as the biscuit. "I've been looking into a fire in the Jorend section." He was careful about how he said it, not wanting to give away anything to Oscar. The Hand might be able to help with the investigation, but only if he chose to do so.

Oscar looked up. "I heard about that one. Sounds like the bastard who did it left ten people dead."

"Not ten, but there were a few who died."

"Still. A whole section of the city burned."

Finn nodded. "It was pretty bad."

Oscar sniffed. "Can't imagine that's a pleasant part of the job. I don't know if I'd want to go see something like that. Too much bad luck, you know."

"I doubt any of the gods would curse you for going to look at the remains of Jorend."

"Maybe not, but I'd rather not take any chances. I know better than to anger the gods. I do enough of that as it is."

Finn laughed as he finished his sausage, following it with another swallow of ale. There was something relaxing about being there in the tavern again with Oscar, even just like this. Ever since Finn had lost his father, Oscar had been a mentor for him. This was different. This was almost friendly.

"You figure out if the bastard is guilty?" Oscar took a drink and set his ale down. "That's why you went there, isn't it?"

"I don't really know if the man is guilty. He claims he isn't, but then, he wouldn't. A crime like that isn't the kind where you go and admit your guilt. That's a sure way to hang. If you've heard anything…"

Oscar looked over at Finn. "Not so much that would be helpful for you, Shuffles."

Finn finished the plate of food and pushed it off to the side, leaving only the ale remaining. He had a feeling that when the food and drink were both gone, his conversation with Oscar would be over. He needed to figure out what Oscar wanted from him and see what he might be able to learn from Oscar in the meantime.

"You could help."

"Could I?" Oscar straightened. "I imagine you're looking for any others in that section who might have wanted it to burn," Oscar said while taking a drink. "Or do you plan to let the man you have in custody hang?"

"My job is to find out whether someone is innocent or

guilty. If they're innocent, then I can't sentence them for a crime they didn't commit."

"All men are guilty of something," Oscar said. "All you have to do is figure out what, and then you can sentence them for that. You don't need to go digging too deep into something like that."

"I guess that's why I'm the executioner's apprentice and you're the Hand."

"You weren't innocent, Finn."

"I didn't deserve to hang, either." They fell into silence, and Finn took a long drink of his ale, setting down the empty stein. He wasn't going to get anything from Oscar this visit. "You had a favor in mind. Why don't you get on with it? I have a feeling you followed me."

Oscar watched him. "And if I did? There's no crime in doing so."

"No crime," Finn agreed. "But it tells me you need something now, not just sometime in the future."

Oscar regarded him, and a debate warred behind his eyes. Finn had never been able to read Oscar and couldn't now. He got to his feet and tapped on the table.

"It really is good to see you, Finn. I know you don't want to stop by the Wenderwolf, but Annie would welcome you. The others too."

"Others?"

"The other girls."

"I don't think I can do that," Finn said, shaking his head.

"You've moved on from girls? Gods, Finn! I don't even recognize you anymore."

"It's not that. It's just..." Finn shrugged. "I'm not so sure there are too many women eager to get involved with an executioner."

"You don't have to get involved with them. The kind of girls that hang around the Wenderwolf aren't looking for marriage. At least not yet. You can have a good time."

"I'll think about it." Finn looked around but didn't see anyone watching. "What aren't you telling me?"

"What am I not telling Finn, or what am I not telling the executioner?"

"Oscar—"

"I've got this round," Oscar said, tossing a few coins on the table. "The next time, you get to buy." Oscar glanced over to the door, and his brow furrowed for a moment. "Don't be a stranger."

With that, Oscar headed out of the tavern.

Finn sat for another moment before getting to his feet and making his way out. Oscar had already disappeared, though Finn wasn't surprised by that. He had given Oscar a chance to get moving so that Finn wouldn't be able to follow.

The conversation had helped, surprisingly. He had a bit more direction with what he needed to do for his investigation, but a little less direction with what he needed to do about Oscar. It wasn't that he wanted to ignore that past, but Meyer didn't want Finn to hold on to it too tightly, either. That was how Finn had almost got into trouble before.

As he wound through the Brinder section, making his

way toward Jorend, he saw Helda in the distance. She caught sight of him and started toward him.

Finn looked down, smoothing his shirt and pants, before looking up and meeting Helda's blue eyes with a grin. "You're looking quite nice today."

"I'm surprised to see you in Brinder again. What are you doing out here?" she asked.

He straightened, trying to keep himself from looming too close to her but wanting to show confidence. It was so easy to do with the prisoners but strangely difficult when talking to Helda.

"I came out here to talk with an old friend."

Helda looked around, touching her hand to her head and tracing her fingers through her hair before turning back to him. Her pale blue dress caught the wind, revealing a bit of leg.

She looked past him, her eyes narrowing slightly. Finn was tempted to see what caught her eye, but kept his focus on her.

"Are you here on official business?" Helda asked.

"I'm always on official business," he said. Maybe she'd appreciate it that he started taking his work seriously.

"Even in Brinder?"

Finn shrugged. "I represent the king and his justice. I might not always have an active investigation, but Master Meyer has instructed me to remember how I'm viewed when I'm out in the city."

It wasn't *quite* like that. Meyer didn't want Finn to do anything that would dishonor him, though Finn didn't intend to. Now that he didn't even have a crew to go back to—and having seen Oscar, it had become quite clear that he didn't—Finn had already been fully invested in his apprenticeship, but that had only made it clearer to him.

"I see." She started to turn.

Finn knew he needed to say something to her to keep her from walking away. "Helda—"

She turned back to him, frowning.

"Now that Lena has moved in with Master Meyer, and I'm working with him"—her eyes narrowed slightly—"maybe the two of us could talk?"

He didn't know why he felt so awkward with her when he hadn't around Annie's girls.

Helda's eyes softened slightly. "I would be open to that."

Finn licked his lips and swallowed. "I haven't always been the best to Lena, but I want to help. Her and my mother. I'm doing it the only way I can."

She watched him for a moment. "Have you told her that?"

"Who? Lena? I'm sure she knows."

"You might be surprised." She looked back the way she'd come. She held his gaze, and smiled slightly. "May Heleth bless you, Finn."

He nodded as she turned and headed along the street. Finn watched her walk away before shaking his head. It was time to get back to work.

CHAPTER TEN

The stench of the fire had faded somewhat, though it still lingered in the air. Finn stood at one end of the street, arms crossed over his chest, surveying the damage. There were more people out today, although rather than sorting through the remains, many had started to load the burned sections of buildings into carts to carry away from the city. It wouldn't be long before the Jorend section was rebuilt. Given a lack of space in the city, there was every reason for it to be built quickly.

Two men were loading items onto a cart. Unlike in other parts of the street, where they were loading damaged sections of walls, these men loaded the remains of a home into a cart. Most of it was burned, but that didn't seem to matter to them. They carried it and loaded it carefully into the cart, almost delicately.

Finn approached and watched them work. They were quiet, though he had a sense of disappointment from both of them. One of them was older and balding, and the sun had tanned his forearms and face. He had a graying beard that had been stained by soot from the remains of the fire. The other was younger, of a similar build, and shared features with the older man. He had darker hair, deep brown eyes that glanced over to Finn as they worked, and a quiet intensity about him.

"What do you want?" the younger of the two asked.

"I take it you live here?"

"Lived. We don't live here any longer." He wiped an arm across his brow, glancing up at the sun before turning his attention to Finn and squinting. "Not too many people can live here now. At least on this street. Are you one of the investors?"

Finn frowned. "What investors?"

"The bastards who keep harassing us to sell our strip of land. It was small enough the way it was." He looked to the older man. "My father thought he would stay here, the same way his father did, but after the fire..."

"We can rebuild, Denlir."

Denlir let out a frustrated sigh, shaking his head. "We don't have the money to rebuild. We lost everything." He turned to Finn. "If you're not with the investors, then what are you here for?"

"I'm here to ask a few questions about what happened."

"A fire happened."

The older man stopped what he was doing, wiping his hands on his pants and shaking his head. "Don't mind my son. I'm Jamis Felter." He stuck out his hand, and Finn reached for it, shaking. "We just been through so much this week, and it's taken away all our manners." He shot his son a hard look before turning back to Finn. "You said you were here to ask questions?"

Finn nodded. "I'm tasked with investigating the fire."

Jamis waved his hand, sending his son away.

"Tasked by who?" Denlir asked, as he waded into the remains of the nearest building and started picking through a dresser that still stood, though nothing else around it did. The fire was indiscriminate. So much of this section had burned, but there were other parts that had not. Some things within the buildings had burned while others had not.

"Tasked by Master Henry Meyer, executioner for the king."

Jamis's brow furrowed. "It's about time we get some damn justice. I know David Sweth is locked up in Declan Prison. All of us know that. We just want to make sure he gets what's coming to him."

"Are you sure he's the one who did this?"

"We were too busy trying to save as much as we could. We didn't see anything. But if they say he did it, I'm sure he did it."

Finn just nodded. He wasn't going to argue with Jamis, given what the man had gone through. "What can you tell me about the people who live on this street?"

"What do you want to know?"

"I suppose I would like to know if there is any way I can find others."

"Some have stayed in this section. They're like me. Don't have much else to do, no place else to go. And many of them have lived here their whole lives, as well. Others have gone to family, but…"

"But what?"

"But not too many have family to go to. You understand this isn't the richest section of the city. Not like you."

Finn forced a smile. Not like him. He had gotten to that point already? People had started to believe that he had wealth just because he was dressed reasonably well?

"Can you tell me about some of the people who lived here?"

"Most are hard workers," Jamis said. He pointed to the building across the street. "Matthew Roday and his family there were a second generation in that house. His wife had taken up working in a tavern at the end of the street. She was a cook. Damn good one, too. She would always bring over the best-tasting sweetbreads." He glanced over to his son. "Not that I would tell his mother that. Matthew worked for the farrier and seemed to do good work, at least from everything I heard. A happy family." He shrugged. "Like most of us. At least, like most of us had been."

Finn had the sense that Jamis wanted to talk, to share stories, and while that might be beneficial, he also wondered if perhaps there might be something more useful he could get out of Jamis, though it would take asking the right type of question.

"I heard some people along the street were lost."

Jamis's eyes darkened and he turned toward Denril. "Far too many people were lost. Not just on this street, but from what I hear, five souls returned to Heleth that night."

Five? Finn knew of one, and Oscar had heard ten. What was the real count?

"Can you tell me anything about them?"

"I can't say with any certainty—anything other than rumors, at least. Most who talk about it don't want to spread rumors, especially if they still live. Might be they simply decided to get away. Not that I could blame them. Given the fire and everything that happened here, it would be for the best to just move on."

"What about you?" Finn asked. "What do you intend to do?"

"We have a developer coming through, looking to buy the land. A Benson. Says he can restore Jorend." He nodded to his son still picking through the drawers of the chest. "My son's not too thrilled with that, but we need the money. Can't rebuild without it. Might be we end up moving somewhere else, but at least we can start over."

He didn't need to say that moving somewhere else and away from this section meant moving to an even less well-off section.

Jorend wasn't the nicest section of the city, but it certainly was better than some. Better than the section where Finn had grown up.

"Anything that you can tell me will help," he said.

"I'm not so sure there's anything I can tell you that'll matter for your investigation, but if it gets us justice, then I'll do it." He took a deep breath and looked along the street. "The ones I know for certain are Lima Phar and

Bradley Aut. Lima was a wise woman, always helped us. I know she was out the night of the fire, trying to get people to safety. Got burned too badly and even the physician couldn't save her."

Finn couldn't imagine the horror of burning to death. It was a possible sentence, but it wasn't one that was enacted very often.

"What happened to Bradley?" Finn asked.

"Don't know. He was in one of the middle homes. They weren't burning that hot when the whole thing started, but when they brought him out, he was gone. Lima tried helping him but said he was too far gone, so she moved on to help the others that she could."

Maybe it was the person he hadn't been able to help.

The smoke had been too thick. As had the flames.

Meyer had taught that smoke could be just as bad as heat. It was a questioning technique, though one not used that often. Finn had never needed to do so. There were other techniques that he'd learned that were equally effective.

"Are there others you know about?"

"Isn't that enough?"

"You said you thought there were five people from the street who'd died."

Finn didn't want to push Jamis. He clearly grieved something more than just losing his home, but at the same time, he needed to keep digging.

"The others might not be gone. We haven't seen them back here, or their families. So, it might just be that they didn't want to come see what happened."

"How many people who live on this street haven't come back?" Finn asked.

Jamis shrugged. "Not many, truth be told. Most at least wanted to see what happened to their belongings and to see if there's anything they can salvage. A couple down there"—he motioned toward one end of the street— "wanted to see if their neighbors suffered as bad as they did. A bit of feuding there."

A feud could explain the fires. If one family got mad enough at another...

"We got lucky. There's a bit of our things that are still intact. Not much, you know, but enough that we can pick through it. Might even find something of value."

By that, Finn suspected, he meant something to sell.

These people had lost everything.

Most of them wouldn't have had that much to begin with, so for them to have gotten to the point where they didn't have anything remaining, and what little they did, they were trying to collect so they could sell it...

It broke his heart.

The person responsible for this truly did deserve the king's justice. As the apprentice executioner, Finn thought he could dig, and that he could find answers, and all he needed was to have the time with which to do so. Then he could report to the jurors about what he'd found. Even if it wasn't Sweth, Finn was determined to look through this and find answers.

"Thanks for your time. It was helpful."

Jamis nodded. "You make sure that bastard gets what he deserves."

Finn just nodded. "I will do what I can."

He started off before pausing and looking back to Jamis. He'd already started picking through his belongings again. "You said something about developers?"

Jamis shrugged. "They came through here looking for the owners of the properties. We don't have much, you see, but this was ours. Had been for generations. It might not have been much now, but there was a time when Jorend was something more." He closed his eyes. "Now it's a memory. Guess that's how all things are. Everything changes. You fight it and you get burned. You move with it and you can survive. That's all I can say we want. Just to survive."

Finn nodded to him again, then started along the street.

Those working at loading carts glanced briefly in his direction, but they didn't pay much attention to him or watch for long. When they returned to their work, he understood. They probably got paid based on how much of the debris they removed, not by how long they were out working in the cool air.

When he'd reached the midpoint of the street, seeing how many of the carts were already loaded, he was struck by a thought that hadn't occurred to him before. Maybe Jamis's words lingered in him, or maybe it was just his observation, but in a place of such destruction there was also the promise of something more. The section would rebuild. Probably with buildings that were nicer than what had been there before.

Someone would profit from all of this. If he could find

out who, maybe he could learn who was responsible. It might even be the developer seeking a way to get the homeowners to sell for less.

Finn lingered a bit before making his way to the end of the street and then beyond.

By the time he reached Meyer's home, it was growing darker, though it wasn't quite dark yet. It was still early for Finn to return. Most of the time when he came back to Meyer's home, it was later in the evening.

Lights glowed in the back windows of Meyer's home.

One came from Meyer's office, which suggested he was working. That didn't surprise Finn. Now that Finn worked with him, Meyer had taken to using his increased time to expand on his availability. Finn wished he would have a chance to work with Meyer more, though Meyer was typically reserved when it came to teaching Finn that aspect of his job. Finn hadn't decided whether that was because Meyer feared Finn learning enough that he wouldn't need him—so Finn could go off and set up his own apothecary business— or if it was simply that Meyer didn't feel he was ready.

The other light in the house came from the kitchen. That probably meant Lena, though it was possible his mother was downstairs in the kitchen.

Finn hurried along the path leading to the house, pushed open the door, and hung his cloak. When he reached the kitchen, he heard his mother and Lena speaking softly to each other. Finn smiled. At least his mother was up—and downstairs. After what she'd told him the other day, he hadn't known whether she would have been willing to come downstairs. She'd sounded almost as if she were ready to die. Finn wasn't ready to lose her.

He started toward the kitchen when Meyer's office door came open. The older man caught sight of Finn and motioned him into the room.

Finn started to say something but realized he wasn't alone with Meyer.

An older woman with silver hair sat on the cot along the wall. Her dress was older but well kept, with a fine embroidery around the collar. Her flat blue eyes looked at Finn for a moment before turning back to Meyer. A stoop to her back left her leaning forward, though she seemed balanced on the cot just fine.

"I hope you don't mind my apprentice joining," Master Meyer said. "Moira, this is Finn Jagger. He's been working with me for the better part of a year. He's a promising apprentice."

Moira nodded. "I heard you had someone working with you. I think most in the city have heard, given the circumstances."

Meyer smiled tightly. "You can rest assured he has turned out even better than I'd hoped."

"I trust your judgment, Henry."

She obviously knew him reasonably well. Despite her aged clothing, there was something distinguished about her. Finn couldn't quite place what it was. Perhaps it was the confident way she sat on the cot, despite her obvious discomfort.

"Would you mind sharing with Finn what you shared with me?"

Moira nodded. "I would be happy to. How can he learn otherwise, eh, Henry?"

Meyer just tipped his head, and he took a seat behind his desk, clasping his hands together in front of him. He nodded to Finn.

It was unusual for Meyer to call Finn like this. It was almost as if Meyer were testing him—though why test him like this? Finn hadn't enough time to study healing to help a woman like Moira.

He glanced over to Meyer and found him engrossed in a book folded open in front of him. Finn tried to get his attention, staring at him intensely, but Meyer ignored him.

Finn turned his attention back to Moira, and he tried to offer a reassuring smile. He didn't have any experience even starting this conversation, so he didn't know quite where to begin. It wasn't like an inquisition, not the way it was when he went to a prison, and he certainly didn't have to confront her the way that he would some of the prisoners.

Maybe that was Meyer's point.

Finn took a chair and pulled up in front of the cot, taking a seat and smiling at Moira. "What can I do to help you?"

Moira leaned forward, and with her stooped back, almost looked as if she were going to fall forward. She managed to balance in place and didn't fall off of the cot, which Finn took as a victory.

"As I explained to Henry, I've noticed significant fatigue. It's new, so I don't think it's merely my age." She laughed softly, a sparkle coming to her eyes. "Though I wouldn't be terribly surprised if age was responsible for some of it."

"How long have you felt fatigued?"

"The better part of two weeks. I've been sleeping most of the day. I can only stay awake for a few hours at a time. When I'm awake, I feel like I'm in a fog."

Finn nodded politely. "You don't seem like you're in a fog now."

"Only because of what Henry provided." She pulled a small glass jar out from alongside her, and held it up.

It was a thick, yellowish liquid, and Finn wondered if he might be able to determine what Meyer had given her. In his studies of apothecary medicine, he knew of various compounds that might offer some benefit to fatigue, primarily targeting alertness, but none of them had a yellowish coloration.

"It has been quite effective. It's given me six hours up and awake. It's still not enough. I would like to get back to my normal day. I can sleep when I'm dead, you know."

Finn found himself smiling. Moira amused him, which was probably the reason Meyer had brought him in on this one. Somebody who wouldn't mind him asking all of these personal questions, and somebody who obviously had a sense of humor about all of it.

"Have you noticed anything else? Lack of appetite? Loss of smell? Headaches?" He tried to think of other symptoms that might be tied into it, his mind going to his most recent apothecary textbook, but Gisles was difficult for him to work through.

"Nothing other than the fatigue. Well, that's not entirely true. I haven't been eating quite as much, but that's because I haven't been awake as much. When I *am* awake, there is simply so much for me to do that I don't focus on dining." She looked down at herself. "I barely keep my clothes together."

She was well-dressed, so Finn wondered what he must look like to her. "Are there any others around you suffering from a similar set of symptoms?"

"My husband is long gone, Mr. Jagger. My son no longer lives with me, and I have a cleaning woman who comes in several times a week, but she has been well. These days, she hasn't done so much cleaning. Not that there's been a need. She's been focusing on trying to make me broths and stews and other things to keep my weight up."

"I see."

"What do you suggest that I do?"

Finn glanced over to Meyer, but found him still absorbed in his book.

"May I see what Master Meyer has offered you?"

Moira handed him the jar, and he took the stopper off, bringing it to his nose and sniffing. Wella's instruction on how to analyze what another apothecary had given someone came back to him. The aroma coming from the jar had a bit of a spice to it, and he picked up a hint of gersil and rose. The rose would be mostly for flavor, but the gersil could act as a bit of a stimulant. It wasn't very aggressive. Mild, for that matter. If that was all that Master Meyer had given her, then something even more potent might be beneficial to her.

Finn wasn't entirely certain if that was all that was in the compound. He wouldn't know unless he tested. He dabbed a finger into the liquid and brought it to his tongue, tasting it.

He tensed slightly, fearing that he might suddenly have his tongue go numb the way that it had when he had been in Wella's shop, but it didn't. It had a tangy flavor, and he could taste the rose, and his heart fluttered for a moment.

His mind cleared. Even a mild stimulant worked quickly. At least this one did.

He glanced to Master Meyer and frowned. There was something more than just the gersil in the compound. It gave it the more vibrant taste, and it was the reason that everything had become more alert for him, but it seemed to Finn that perhaps it was the oil he'd used.

What oil would offer a level of alertness?

He hadn't studied enough. He didn't know enough.

Finn smiled slightly. "I could offer you more of a stimulant to see if that would help," he said to Moira. "It would give us more time to get to the bottom of what you are dealing with."

Moira glanced over to Master Meyer. "Did you hear that?" Finn's heart sank, suddenly worrying that he had said the wrong thing. This was a test, of course, and he didn't want to fail it. "He's willing to offer me another stimulant."

"We've already talked about that, Moira."

"We talked about your unwillingness to provide me with anything more than this." She leaned forward, and this time she almost fell off of the cot, but she braced herself suddenly before reaching for the jar in Finn's hands and holding it up to Meyer. "This only keeps me awake for a few hours, Henry. I'm looking for something that will buy me even more time than that."

Meyer chuckled. "Of course, Moira. I will let you and my apprentice work on that."

Finn blinked. Meyer was going to let him do this?

Moira leaned forward. "Well?"

"Why don't you stop by tomorrow and I will come up with a compound for you."

She nodded. "Of course. I don't get up too early these days. It might be in the middle of the day, or even later."

"Later might be best," Finn said. "This should get you through until I come up with something."

"Very well."

She slipped down from the cot and hurried over to the door, disappearing with a glance over to Master Meyer.

When she was gone, Finn turned to Meyer. "What's wrong with her?"

"That will be your next assignment." Meyer looked up from his book, resting his hands on either side of it and holding it open. "I want you to look into anything about the illness she describes."

"Why do I get the feeling that there's something here you're not telling me."

Meyer chuckled. "You know all I know, Finn."

Finn pulled a chair up, sitting across from Meyer. He

was going to let Finn be a part of helping heal others. That mattered to Finn. It meant that he was moving along his apprenticeship, and he might even progress far enough that he could actually earn extra coin. That was the part of serving as an executioner where the real money came in. Not that Finn was terribly concerned about wealth at this point. Meyer paid him reasonably well, but Meyer did much better than most in the city.

"I started investigating the fire in the Jorend section. There are rumors that five people died in the fire," Finn said.

"I've heard those rumors as well."

"Is there anything to it?" Finn asked.

Meyer frowned. "You want me to give you the answer?"

"All I'm looking for is how many people died. I don't need you to tell me who's guilty."

"You don't think Sweth is guilty?"

Finn shrugged, glancing down at the desk for a moment before looking back up at Meyer. "I don't know if Sweth is guilty or not, but I'm willing to keep looking."

He figured that was the answer Meyer wanted out of him. Meyer didn't want Finn to take the obvious answer, and always wanted him to keep digging.

"I can't tell you with any certainty how many people were lost in the fire. The stories shift. From one report, I have heard there were a dozen people who died in the fire. That seems high to me," Meyer said. "We've had other fires in the city, Finn. None have been that fatal."

"This one spread quite fast."

"It did. The question you need to be looking into is why."

"I'm looking into who might benefit from the fire."

Meyer regarded him. "An interesting approach."

"*Interesting* as in the wrong approach?"

"*Interesting* as in *interesting*."

Finn waited for him to share anything more. "There was a man on the street loading up some of his belongings into a cart with his son, and they had heard of five people. He only knew of two of them with any certainty. The others were missing, but he didn't know if they were gone or if they simply had gone missing."

"What do you intend to do?"

"Do you really plan to let me run with this investigation?"

"Within reason," Meyer said. He folded the book closed, and slid it off to the side of his desk. "There is a bit of a time crunch here, Finn. The jurors are looking for answers. They want to know that we are doing everything in our power to find who is responsible for the fire. The magister and the jurors believe they already have the person responsible in prison."

"Let me guess. Bellut has been saying that," Finn said, shaking his head.

Meyer forced Finn to hold his gaze. "You cannot react like that."

"You know that he's a part of this."

"We've already talked about this."

"We talked about looking into Bellut, and I've told you that I'm not going to, but—"

"We are not going to go into this any longer." Meyer took a deep breath, and then waved his hand. "Focus on the task at hand and not on your personal grudge."

Finn sat back, folding his hands in his lap and sitting quietly for a moment. He hadn't thought it was a grudge, but he wouldn't deny that he was motivated to see Bellut face justice for what he'd done. More than that, he thought he needed to face justice. He was acting against the king, regardless of what Meyer might think.

"Focus on your investigation. There will be a limit to how much time we have to complete it. If we don't find anything, then the jurors will decide based on the information they have on hand."

"Which means they'll convict Sweth."

Meyer nodded.

"Even if he isn't guilty?"

"Do you think him not guilty?"

Finn needed to get back into Declan to visit with Sweth more than he had. He didn't have the answer, but also didn't think Sweth had started the fires, even if he weren't innocent.

"I don't know."

"Then you need to find the answers. And you'd better do it quickly."

CHAPTER ELEVEN

Declan Prison produced a darkened shadow that towered over the street in the early morning. A soft but gusting wind drifted out of the north, carrying a promise of cold and a coming snow, though it still felt early for it. Finn pulled the cloak around him, clutching it tightly as he made his way toward Declan. Once inside, he wouldn't need the cloak. The prison was usually hot and humid.

When he reached the prison, he pulled the keys from his pocket and searched through them to find the right key to the prison. Coming on his own was another first for him.

Getting the door unlocked, Finn made certain to lock it again behind him and paused in the entrance. There was a strange level of freedom coming there, but it mixed with the fear and terror that he'd known when he'd been here before.

He couldn't linger too long. After his conversation with Meyer, he didn't know how much time he had. He hurried through the prison, reaching the stairs and heading down. When he reached the lower level, two of the iron masters looked over. He recognized Shiner, who nodded to him.

"You comin' here yourself these days?" He looked behind Finn as if searching for Meyer. "Not used to you coming down to ol' Declan yourself, Jags."

Finn shook his head. "Jags" *was* better than what he'd been called in the crew before. Seeing Oscar put that into perspective. "Meyer wanted me to check in on things."

"You here for the new one? Bastard came in filthy, but that's typical for his kind."

Finn frowned. Meyer hadn't said anything about a new prisoner. There wasn't any reason that he couldn't question him and report it to Meyer. It might help Finn gain a bit more experience, as well.

"We'll start with him," Finn said.

"Start?"

"I need to talk to Sweth as well. There's more I need to uncover with him."

Shiner chuckled. "You got to know he's gonna swing."

"Is that right?"

"That bastard keeps muttering to himself at night. Just talks to himself about the fire." He shook his head. "Can't think he deserves anything other than what's coming."

If the iron masters had that view, it suggested to Finn that he had even less time than what Meyer had suggested.

Maybe Sweth *was* guilty. Finn didn't know. That was the part of it that troubled him.

"I didn't get the new man's name," Finn said.

"Vol Thern. Comes from Meldran. And you *know* how filthy that place is."

Meldran?

With what Finn had seen before when chasing the figure into Meldran, he wondered if that was only a coincidence, or if there was something more to it than that. Maybe it was only chance, but that *was* where he'd seen Bellut.

What if Vol could help him find what Bellut had been up to?

"Can you bring him up to the chapel?"

"No problem, Jags. We'll bring him in there for you. You don't want to help?"

"Not if he's filthy." Finn grinned.

"Leave the mess to the iron masters. Typical." Shiner chuckled and nodded to the other iron master. "You want to give me a hand, Dem? Gotta get Jags's man to the chapel so he can poke him a bit. Probably make Vol smell better."

Dem was a shorter, solid man, with a pockmarked face. When he grinned, he revealed a mouth missing a couple teeth. A bruiser, probably. Finn wasn't the only one who'd been part of a crew around here.

"Wouldn't hurt to poke him a little. Bastard won't talk to us." Dem sounded like he had rocks in his mouth, making it difficult for Finn to understand him.

Finn headed to the chapel.

The chapel had a strange calm to it.

He turned his attention to the painted glass. As the early-morning light filtered in, giving a bit of color to the room, Finn could almost believe Heleth looked down upon him, though Finn didn't know whether she was there for *him* or for the prisoner.

The counter with the various tools for questioning was as neatly organized as Meyer preferred. Finn made a point of keeping it well organized and clean, though usually he did it while Meyer was there with him and asking questions to the prisoners.

The door to the chapel opened and Finn turned to look at Vol.

He was thin and haggard, a thick beard covering his face. Deep hollows of eyes looked around the inside of the chapel, widening when they took in Finn. Even from the doorway, Finn could tell he stank. That was unusual. Typically, the iron masters cleaned the prisoners so that whatever filth they brought into the prison wouldn't add to the stench of the place.

He nodded to Shiner. The iron master dragged Vol to the chair in the center of the room, tossed him down, and quickly started strapping him into the chair. When he was done, he wiped his hands on his pants while grimacing.

"You need anything from us?" Shiner asked.

"Keep someone outside the door. I'll let you know if I need anything."

A hint of relief swept over Shiner's face as he stepped out of the chapel, closing the door and leaving him inside with Vol.

Finn stood near the counter, moving implements around. There was a strategy to doing so. He didn't even need to say anything as he worked, shuffling tools from one side of the counter to another, saying nothing.

Vol shifted in the chair.

Finn didn't look. He could hear him sliding around, and there was a jerking on the straps. They would hold. One of Finn's other assignments was testing the straps to ensure they were firmly in place.

Finally, he headed away from the counter and stopped before Vol. "My name is Finn Jagger."

"Why should I care?"

"Because I'm the one questioning you. I'm one of the king's executioners." He let the words linger, knowing the impact they had. When Finn had been there, he hadn't known much about the Lion. Only his nickname. That and he'd seemed all too eager to torment Finn. He'd taken a measure of interest in the torture that Finn had never taken. "To begin with, why don't you tell me what happened?"

Vol looked up and spat.

Finn was far enough away that he didn't have to worry about its hitting him, but it still irritated him. "This will go easier for the two of us if you are willing to share."

"You got me in this shithole. That's what happened."

"You don't care for the hospitality?"

Vol snorted. "This is your hospitality?" He jerked on his straps, trying to pull away, but they held tightly. "No. I don't care for it."

"What happened?"

Meldran wasn't typically a place where he encountered people like this. Most of them were poor, but they kept themselves together better than it looked like Vol had.

"Nothing happened."

"The Archers brought you here for a reason."

"The wrong one. They wouldn't listen. Bastards seem to think everyone is guilty just because they find us on the edge of our section."

"You weren't in Meldran when they picked you up?"

Vol looked over. Darkness shone in his eyes as he leaned his head back. Would he spit again? Finn didn't want to deal with that from him and backed away. Vol sneered at him.

"Not in Meldran."

"Then where were you?"

"Just gonna have to ask them, aren't you?"

"I don't have any problems asking the Archers, but then when I do, you lose your opportunity to speak on your behalf."

"This is an opportunity?"

"We're talking, aren't we?"

He jerked on the leather straps again, pulling on them even harder than before. "Talking, but you're doing most of it."

"I think we're having a conversation here." Finn had a feeling from Vol that he wanted to talk. If he could get him engaged, he wouldn't need any of the other questioning implements. Finn had learned to use them all and didn't have any objection to doing so in the right circumstances, but he also knew he needed to practice a level of restraint. There were times when he simply didn't need to use all of the resources. A conversation could get him as much information as torment. "The more you share with me, the better this will go."

"For me?"

Finn nodded. "I'm here as part of my job."

"Some job."

"I help ensure the king's justice is carried out. The king wants to ensure only the guilty are condemned, so if you're not guilty, you need to speak on your behalf."

"I've told you I didn't do it."

Finn grabbed a chair and pulled it over, sitting a distance away from Vol so he couldn't spit on him. "You've said you didn't do it, but you haven't told me anything else." He forced a smile. "I've had many men tell me they were innocent when they were guilty."

"How do you know the difference?"

"You learn to tell."

"You think you can tell a man is lying just by watching him? Some justice."

He turned away and spat, though this time it wasn't at Finn.

"I'm getting better at it. Master Meyer can tell with most men."

"And if he can't?"

"If he can't, then we question."

Vol looked at him through slits of eyes. "You torment an innocent man and he's going to tell you what you want to hear."

"We question a guilty man and he's going to share what he did."

"You're no different than them," Vol said.

"Why is that?"

"Because you already think I'm guilty."

"I think you haven't shared anything with me to make me think otherwise. At this point, you have given me no choice but to assume your guilt. If you're not guilty, then tell me what I need to know to look into your innocence."

Vol glowered at him. "You're not going to look into anything. You're just trying to get me to say something that will convict me. I know better than that."

Finn weighed the options. He could begin questioning him, but doing so would disrupt any chance that he had to ask other questions without needing to resort to enhanced questioning. He had a feeling that if he played this right he might uncover something from Vol. The challenge was in figuring out just what he needed to get from him, though.

"Let's start with where you were when the Archers picked you up."

"Why does that matter?"

"Because you want me to believe in your innocence."

"And?"

"And you said you weren't in the Meldran section."

"Most people think that section is nothing but thieves anyway. With all the activity moving through there these days, they wouldn't be wrong. I'm not with that crew, no matter what most people say."

"I'm not most people," Finn said. "I recognize that it is a different kind of section. I've been there a few times."

He watched Finn. "Nobody there wants to hurt anyone," he said. "No matter what they tell you."

"What they tell me?" Finn asked.

"I've heard the stories."

"What stories are those?"

"Stories about my section. They claim we've got nothing but bruisers and killers."

"I thought you had farmers and butchers," Finn said.

"And butchers? You mean those poor bastards that work in the slaughterhouse. Brutal work. Cutting up the hogs for someone who gets to keep all the coin."

"They keep the coin because they own the business," Finn said.

"They keep the coin because they filch it from those who do the work."

Finn smiled. "You still haven't told me what section you were in."

"Because it don't matter."

"Or it does and you just don't want to share it with me."

"Anything I tell you is only going to make you believe in my guilt."

"Is that right?"

"You just go ahead and ask the Archers. I'm not telling you nothing."

He lowered his head and jerked on the bindings around his wrists and ankles, but didn't look up again.

Finn debated. He had a suspicion about what Master

Meyer would do in the same situation. He wouldn't resort to strapping on the boots quite yet. Not without knowing anything about the man or why he was there. Meyer would try to find more information, which was what Finn needed to do.

He got up, headed to the door, and pulled it open.

Shiner stood on the other side, frowning at him. "That's it?"

"I'm done with him for now. I'll return to question him later."

Shiner grinned. "Maybe I'll want to be here for that one."

"Maybe you can get him cleaned up before that time," Finn said.

Shiner chuckled. "You don't like the way he smells?"

"Not really."

"The dumb bastard ran through the slaughterhouse and one of the hog pens. Says he was running from a crew chasing him, but he was on the crew and ended up there anyway. Smells like shit, he does."

"I want to visit with the Archers who brought him in."

"Yeah?"

"Either that or I want to see their report."

Anytime one of the Archers brought a prisoner to Declan, they had to fill out a report. In this case, without knowing whether or not the Archers were even available for him to visit with, perhaps it would be better for him to see the report.

"You'll have to go to the warden. He keeps all that."

"Of course," Finn said.

"You going to go and see him?"

"You don't think I should?"

"Maybe I'd like to be there when you do."

"Why?"

"Just curiosity."

Finn nodded to Vol. "You can return him to his cell. And then if you could get Sweth, I would appreciate it."

"No problem, Jags."

Finn headed out in the hallway and paused for a moment before making his way to the warden's office. He tapped on the door, waiting for the warden to welcome him in.

When he did, Finn stepped inside the office. The warden sat behind a desk covered with papers. He was a youngish man, younger than Master Meyer, though still perhaps a decade or so older than Finn. Finn didn't know him well, though they had met a few times.

"Warden James," Finn said, nodding politely. There was no reason to push his role there, especially as Finn was only an apprentice. "I hope you don't mind the interruption, but I was hoping to take a look at the Archer report on the prisoner Vol Thern."

Warden James frowned. "Meyer has you coming on your own now, does he?"

"It's part of my training," Finn said.

"I hear you've been doing good work."

"I try to."

"Probably hard for you, considering where you came from."

Finn stood silently, refusing to be drawn into the

comment. "Doing the king's work is never difficult," Finn said.

James started to smile. "I'm not trying to antagonize you, Jagger. I just figured I'd ask you if it was hard for you."

"No harder than it is for you, I suppose."

"The kind of men we get in here can be challenging."

"They can be," Finn agreed. He swept his gaze around the inside of the office. It was filled by the desk, but there was a bookshelf next to it that seemed to have been crammed in as an afterthought. He didn't have any books on it, nothing other than figurines and small sculptures. A painting on the wall behind the warden depicted the gods, though it was an unusual scene. He suspected the eye looming in the sky represented Heleth, though he couldn't really tell. Other figures surrounded the eye, as if they were celebrating, or dancing, looking down over a city. Finn wondered if the artist had intended it to be Verendal or some other city. "The report?"

James nodded. He shuffled through some papers before handing it to Finn. "Not much to this one. Came in last night. Filthy and stinking. We tried to get him cleaned up, but when you lie in hog slop as long as he did, it ends up being difficult."

"He still stinks," Finn said.

James frowned. "If you've already talked to him, then why do you need the report?"

"I need to see all sides of the case. I need to know if he's guilty or not."

"That one? He wouldn't have been there had he not been guilty."

Finn looked down at the page. Most of the Archers in the city were only barely above literate, so their report was riddled with spelling errors, but Finn made out the necessary details. He had read enough of these reports in his time serving Master Meyer, and had come to recognize there was a certain flow to each of these reports, something he could follow.

"This says he was picked up in the Joyner section."

"That's right."

"Why would he have been there?" It was almost on the opposite side of the city from Meldran. It didn't make much sense. Vol hadn't struck him as the kind of man who would go wandering the city.

"Which is why the Archers grabbed him. No reason for them to have been over there amongst his betters."

Finn let the comment slide. "They don't report what they picked him up for."

"No?" James looked over to him. "That's surprising. I figured that they would have put that in their report." James shrugged. "They are Archers, though. Not always the brightest. Maybe they forgot it."

"Why did they grab him?"

"Came out of a merchant's home. Claims he followed someone inside. Not much more to it than that. Probably would have ended up in Volthan were he not so filthy."

Finn nodded. "Can I hold on to this?"

"You want the report?"

"I'll get it back to you. I just want to visit with the Archers who took the report."

James shrugged. "Be my guest."

Finn folded up the paper, stuffed it into his pocket, and nodded politely to James before turning and heading out of the office.

He reached the chapel and pulled open the door to see Shiner crouching down in front of Sweth, squeezing his wrists.

"I can take it from here," Finn said.

Shiner got to his feet and nodded to Finn. "Perfect." He spun, glaring at Sweth. "Now you've got Jags to deal with." He passed Finn on his way to the door, leaning close. "Don't take it easy on him, Jags. This bastard killed twenty people."

"Twenty?"

Shiner nodded seriously. "That's what I hear. Twenty lives were lost in that damn fire."

"I will do my best," Finn said.

"Knew you would, Jags."

He closed the door behind them, and Finn turned to Sweth. He looked up at Finn, glaring at him.

"Is it true?" Sweth asked. "Did you bring me here to torture me?" He glanced to the door. "That guard told me you were going to jab me with needles or pour fire on me."

"You are here to answer questions," Finn said. He pulled the chair away from the wall and took a seat across from Sweth. He still hadn't decided how aggressive he needed to be with questioning. He knew what the iron masters believed, along with the warden, and given the rumors going through the city he should be justified in digging, but it just didn't feel right to him. Something there was off. "The way in which I get those answers depends upon you."

"So, I get to decide if I'm tortured?" Sweth laughed bitterly. "I think I know the answer to that. No. I don't want to be tormented."

"I'm sure the iron masters have shared with you the rumors going around the city," Finn said. He leaned back in the chair, intending to make himself look a little bit more casual. "About the number of people who died."

"I don't know anything about that," Sweth said softly. "It was a terrible fire, and I barely got out with my belongings."

"Yours, or Master Johan's?"

"Did you talk to him?"

Finn nodded. "I told you I would."

"He probably told you I have worked with him for a long time. I've been a good scribe. I do good work."

Finn just nodded. Johan hadn't told him how long he'd worked for him. Did that even matter? "He told me about the nature of your employment. And that he let you go."

"That bastard," he said, shaking his head and looking around the inside of the chapel. He craned his neck so he could look all around him, and his gaze drifted to the table in the back of the room, his eyes widening slightly. "What is *that*?"

Finn looked behind him at the tools arranged on the

table. "Nothing to be that concerned about. Why don't you focus on me?"

It wouldn't work that way, and Finn knew it. That was part of the plan, though. The more he could get Sweth thinking about the pain that might lie before him, the more likely he would share what Finn needed.

"You *are* going to torment me. That's why you have me here." He looked toward Finn, his eyes going wide. "I've told you what I know. There's nothing more I can share with you about what happened. I went into my home, grabbed my belongings, and tried to get out. I didn't start the fire." A panicked note had entered his voice. "Please. You have to believe me!"

Finn leaned back. The problem he had was that he *did* believe Sweth.

There was something more going on between him and Johan, but that was something he could sort out at another time. The bigger issue was solving what started the fire before the magister and the jurors decided they needed to get vengeance for something Sweth may not have done.

"I need to know everything you can tell me about the people on your street." Sweth stared at him, his eyes still wide. "If I feel like you're not completely honest with me, well…"

"You don't need to know anything about the street," Sweth said, irritation starting to seep into his voice.

He was hiding something. "It helps for us to establish a rapport."

Sweth looked at Finn, then behind him for a moment,

before shaking his head. "I don't have anything that will help you. It's not me, anyway. All you've got to do is—"

"Ask you a few simple questions. That's all I have to do."

"I don't have any answers!"

This time, Finn was certain Sweth was keeping something from him.

And he didn't like it. Not when it came to trying to understand what was taking place in the city. All he needed was to understand the fire and Sweth's role in it. Then he could focus on Bellut.

Finn got to his feet and stopped at the counter, looking down at the various implements laid out on the table. There were some horrific devices he had been trained to use. Most had a specific purpose. Finn didn't take any pleasure in using them, but there were times, when the criminal wouldn't reveal enough information, that Finn didn't have much choice in the matter. As Meyer had explained to him, in order to meet the king's need for justice, there were times when extreme measures were needed.

This didn't feel like it was one of them.

Finn started moving the devices around on the table, making a point of holding some of them up, if only to draw the man's attention to them. Finn didn't need to look over his shoulder to know Sweth paid attention to what he did. He could practically feel Sweth's gaze lingering on him. That and he whimpered softly.

After holding up a few different devices and setting them back down again, he turned to Sweth. The theater was part of the torment, but at least it was the part where someone wouldn't suffer quite as much.

"Now. Let's begin."

"What are you going to do to me? I told you I don't know anything more than what I've told you!" His voice had gone from panicky to full-blown terror. It rose in pitch and intensity. Either he was a skilled actor, or he truly didn't know anything more.

"We're going to talk about everyone who lives on your street. Then I will decide if I think you're telling me everything I need to know. If I don't think you're sharing what I need…"

He forced a hard smile.

Sweth licked his lips. "I'll tell you whatever you want to know. Please. Just don't use those *things* on me!"

Finn nodded. "Go ahead, then."

CHAPTER TWELVE

Sweth sat in the chair babbling, tears streaming down his face. It was almost enough for Finn to feel a bit of remorse. Almost. After what Sweth *had* admitted to, he didn't feel quite as bad. Every man had secrets. In the chapel, all men revealed those secrets, whether or not they had anything to do with the crime they stood accused of committing.

Finn pulled open the door to the chapel. Shiner looked past him, a hint of a smile crawling across his face when he saw Sweth.

"You really gave it to him, didn't you, Jags?"

Finn nodded. "He told me everything I needed to know."

"That right? We going to get a sentencing soon?"

That would be a challenge. The warden and others who'd been around Sweth would push for a sentencing, but Finn didn't think him guilty. Still, until he had someone else he could place the crime upon, there wasn't going to be any way for him to keep Sweth from his fate. He didn't have long. Meyer had made that clear to him.

"Soon enough," he said.

"Good. Don't want a bastard like that here in Declan any longer than we have to."

"This is the place for men like him," Finn said.

"This might be, but can't guarantee nothin' will happen to him, you know?"

"For him to face his sentencing, he has to be—"

"Gods, I know. Can't have him damaged going to the gods. Not that Heleth cares all that much if we give him a few bruises."

"Bruises are one thing"—and Finn wouldn't be able to keep the iron masters from beating him a little, though he might want to—"anything more will only delay his sentencing. You know how the king feels."

"Just the king?"

Finn shrugged. "I'm less concerned about the gods than I am about the king. I serve him."

Shiner grinned. "Knew I liked you, Jags. What are you doing later? Want to meet at Treble Coat?"

"What's that?"

"Ah, just this place a few of us like to go for drinks. Figured it can't hurt to have the hangman there. Well, his apprentice, at least."

Finn figured that it couldn't hurt for him to have a little time with the iron masters outside of the prison. For him to be more effective at his job, he might need to have a relationship with them so that he could sway them more effectively. Wasn't that what Meyer wanted from him anyway?

"Sure. What time?"

"Well, a couple of us get done at eight bells, so if you'd like to meet us shortly after that, you'd be welcome to. You might have to buy a round or more, but hey, you're the hangman."

Finn chuckled. "I'll see you then."

He stepped out of the chapel and paused. When he looked back at Sweth, Finn needed to dig deeper into what Sweth had told him. He had a list of names of people who lived in the Jorend section along the same street, but he didn't have much more than that.

He still had some time, but the feeling lingered within Finn that the longer all of this took, the more likely it was he would run out of time before finding answers. If that were to happen, Sweth would be sentenced—likely to hang, or possibly even worse—and Finn wouldn't be convinced that they had the right person.

He still had things he needed to do, and headed toward the apothecary. When he saw Master Meyer near Wella's apothecary, he hurried forward, catching up to him.

Meyer turned to look at Finn. He was dressed as he often was, in his formal jacket and pants, a traveling cloak slung over his shoulders. "Finn. Were you coming for supplies?"

Finn looked around the street outside of Wella's apothecary before glancing over to it. He realized that he still hadn't completed one other assignment. For Moira, he had promised to have a concoction available for her by evening. He hadn't considered what would be needed for that. Maybe Wella might help.

It could be Meyer had come out here simply to test whether she'd been involved in helping Finn create something.

"I needed to come up with something for Moira."

Meyer nodded slowly. "I see."

"I was just at Declan. Talking to Sweth." And another prisoner—he realized he needed to tell Meyer. He needed to take more initiative, so he figured Meyer would not mind. "Have you ever had a case where you felt the prisoner was innocent but you couldn't find the right answer?"

"That happens from time to time," Meyer said.

"What did you do?"

"When the time comes for sentencing, all we can do is give the information we have to the jurors."

Finn's face soured. "I'm not completely convinced we can trust the jurors."

Meyer's face flickered with irritation. It was a measure of that irritation that he revealed as much as he did. It had been Finn's experience that Meyer only showed his frustration like this when he was truly upset. "The jurors serve the kingdom the same way you do, Finn. They might serve in a different capacity, but they still serve the king's justice. Do not forget that."

Finn looked around him, lowering his voice. "You know what happened. You know the jurors aren't completely innocent." It was more than Bellut. Finn *had* seen the King bribing another juror, though didn't know how much of an issue that was.

"Perhaps not all," Meyer said slowly. "That doesn't change that we must work with them."

He had rarely been permitted to go before the jurors ever since sentencing the King. It was Meyer's way of protecting Finn, though Finn felt Meyer continued to avoid the issue. "Even if they're complicit?"

"Finn—"

Finn shook his head. "I know you don't want to talk about this, but I feel like we need to do something. We need to have some conversation about this."

"What we need is to keep doing our jobs."

"You know who I'm talking about, Master Meyer. What if Bell—"

Meyer raised his hand, silencing Finn. "You would do well to be careful with what you say, Finn." His voice was low and dangerous, and Finn suddenly realized something.

Meyer was worried.

That was unusual enough with him, but it made a different sort of sense. This was the jurors and the magister they were talking about.

"You know what they were doing," Finn whispered.

"I'm aware," Meyer said. "This is not the time for that conversation."

Finn watched him, and he had another realization. Here he thought that Meyer had not been looking into what had happened, but from the expression on Meyer's face, the tension in his eyes, that wasn't the case at all.

Meyer had been digging into it.

What he'd found left him nervous.

"I could help," Finn said.

"No. You have your assignment. Didn't you tell me you believed Sweth to be innocent?"

"Maybe not completely innocent. He had several affairs with married women on his street, and he'd embezzled some money from Master Johan, but I don't think he started the fire."

"Then he's innocent of the crime he's accused of committing. The others can be sorted out later, but if he is presented to the jurors for sentencing of the fires, we have several minor inquisitors"—Finn didn't have much experience with the other city inquisitors, only being aware that they all reported to Meyer—"along with the warden, who have submitted their claims of his guilt. That will weigh heavily against him unless we have something more to offer them."

Something more meant an alternative person to be sentenced.

"I can help with what you're looking into," Finn said carefully. "You know that I can. I still have connections—"

"It's those connections I fear, Finn." He shook his head, glancing over to Wella's apothecary. "I seem to recall the last time you thought to use your connections, you very nearly ended with both of our lives in danger."

"You aren't in the same danger now," Finn said.

Meyer studied him. "Am I not?" He nodded to Wella's apothecary. "Go ahead and gather what you came here for. I will meet with you later."

"You don't need to go in?"

"If you intend to visit with Wella, I don't think I am needed."

He started off down the street, and Finn stared for a moment. Meyer was nervous. He hadn't said it, but Finn believed he had started investigating Bellut and the magister. Maybe he had been investigating them ever since the discovery. If only Meyer would have involved Finn in it. He thought he could offer him help, but would Meyer even accept Finn's help?

Probably not.

He sighed. He had to stick to his assignment. That didn't mean he couldn't keep digging a little bit. It was possible he might find something about what Bellut and the magister had been up to, and if he did learn anything, then he could report it to Meyer. Meyer couldn't be mad at Finn then, could he?

Knowing Meyer, he would still find some reason to be disappointed in Finn for bringing up that kind of information, though it would hopefully help with their investigation.

He pushed open the door to Wella's shop.

The smell of the apothecary struck him immediately. It was the same as it often was, though this time there was a bit more of a pungent spice to it than usual. It seemed to cover an undercurrent of rot, as if some of her supplies had started to go stale. He wrinkled his nose as he swept his gaze around, looking for Wella. Normally, the moment he came into the shop, she tottered out of the back and found him, but this time there was no sign of her.

Finn wandered along the rows of shelves, pausing in front of one jar with a thick, black-looking liquid inside it. He held it up to the dingy light in the apothecary, trying to make out what might be in this bottle. He set it back down and moved on, grabbing for another jar, this one with a pink-colored paste inside. He sniffed at it, noting a hint of cinnamon, maybe some tareth berry, but not much else that he detected without tasting it.

One shelf consisted entirely of jars of different leaves, all of them dried and all of them different sizes and shapes. Another shelf consisted of powders. Some more finely ground, like pepper; others were coarser, small pebbles. They were of different colors and smells, and seemed to battle with each other for prominence on the shelf.

A jar of fingers occupied an entire shelf. Finn didn't need to take the top off of the jar to examine the fingers inside. He could see them quite clearly. He wondered how many of them were people he had sentenced over time. Wella had other human remains.

He reached the end of the cabinets and waited.

Her shop wouldn't have been unlocked unless she were there, though maybe she was in the back doing something. Finn had never been to the back of her shop and didn't know what she did there, or what she even had stored there. Maybe there were even more exotic items in the back of her apothecary shop; things that she didn't want to keep displayed like she did out there.

He smiled at the thought. He could imagine horrific items. Complete hands or feet or even more disgusting things like condemned men's manhoods. That had value to some. Finn had heard the rumors about how people claimed the part to use for their own fertility, believing that burning it and mixing the ash into a drink would bring fertility to themselves. The idea that would make a difference in fertility seemed ridiculous to Finn. It seemed far easier—and safer—to simply go to the hegen and ask for one of their magic concoctions. It might incur a cost, but at least it wasn't as obviously disgusting.

Movement from the back of the shop caught Finn's attention, and an older man hobbled out, leaning on a cane. He had a sharply stooped back, graying hair, and flat silver eyes. They swept over the inside of the apothecary shop before settling on Finn. There was something unsettling about his gaze.

"You will come back if it is not effective," Wella said, emerging from the back.

"I will come back. You know how disappointed I will be if this does not work."

"And you know that I have done my best. Not all of my concoctions work immediately."

He grunted. "No. Too many of your kind find that you are happier making excuses for when things don't go well."

"They are not excuses, Mr. Reames." Finn recognized the hard irritated note in Wella's voice, even if Mr. Reames did not. "Seeing as how you've decided to only pay in part, I think you're lucky I haven't offered you only partial healing as well."

Reames frowned, before looking over to Finn. "What's wrong with you?"

"Don't bother the executioner," Wella said.

He grunted. "Executioner? I've seen the executioner. Tall man. Short hair. Wrinkles. You're no executioner."

"This is his apprentice. Quite skilled, from the rumors I hear."

"Is that right?" Reames eyed Finn with renewed interest. "How many men have you hanged?"

Finn glanced over to Wella, before turning back to Reames. "I've been privy to two dozen executions."

"Two dozen. What man in the city hasn't been privy to at least two dozen executions? I'm asking how many of you hanged?"

"I've participated in two dozen executions," Finn said.

Reames straightened slightly, leaning on his cane a little bit. "Two dozen, eh? Not bad. I bet the old executioner has done nearly a thousand." He glanced over to Wella. "Maybe twice that. He's been here a long time, you know. I hear he came here to hide. Not that I can blame him. Given what happened to his wife and child, after all."

"That's enough," Wella said.

"So says you. A man has a right to talk, especially if he has a chance to visit with someone who might know." Reames grinned at Finn, showing a mouthful of crooked teeth. "What do you say? Your master tell you anything about what happened to them?"

Finn held Reames's gaze. "Whatever happened is his business."

"His business," Reames scoffed. "If you ask me, it's all

of our business. He trots around the city looking like he owns it."

"No one asks you," Wella said, grabbing a short cane from behind her counter and whacking Reames on the arm. She must have struck him hard enough, as he winced and glared at her for a moment. "And you and I both know the executioner serves as the king's arm of justice."

"The king. I'd rather follow the gods's justice."

"You can follow whatever justice you want, just so long as you leave my shop. You return with my payment as well. This is the last time I'll take you in without payment."

"We both know that's not the case," Reames said, grinning at Wella. "If this don't work—"

"If it doesn't work, I have already told you to return. Now be gone."

Wella made a show of swinging her cane at him again, and Reames grunted, tapping his cane on the ground as he staggered through the rows of shelves before reaching the door and pulling it open. He paused in the doorway, looking back at Finn, something flickering in his eyes that Finn couldn't quite read, before he stepped out onto the street.

When the door closed, Wella breathed out slowly. She could be good-spirited, and she could be a little bit eccentric, but he'd never seen her frustrated like that.

"I didn't expect to see you quite so soon. You typically only come once or twice a week."

"I have a few questions," Finn said. He looked toward

the door and chuckled to himself. "Maybe more than a few questions."

"Don't you go and let him get in your head."

"He didn't get in my head."

"I can see that look in your eyes, Finn. It's the one that will end up with you asking the wrong kind of questions."

"The wrong kind?"

"The kind that leads to you upsetting Henry."

"I'm not supposed to ask questions to Master Meyer?"

Wella leaned forward on the counter, looking across it at him. "Not that kind."

"Is it true?" Finn stood behind the counter, keeping a bit of distance between him and Wella, but feeling as if even more distance had formed. Maybe pushing her about this was the wrong strategy. "I didn't realize he hadn't always been here."

"That's not how the Executioner Court works," Wella said.

Finn grabbed a jar off the shelf nearest him and tipped it up to his nose. It was a sandy substance, though it smelled almost sweet. He started to dip his finger into it when Wella smacked his other hand.

"You won't like that if you do it."

"What is it?"

"We used to call it fire ash. Probably not something you had much experience with. Comes out of the south."

"So, it's not just actual ash?"

"Gods, no."

"I haven't even heard of it," he said.

"I'm not surprised about that, either. Fire ash doesn't have too much in the way of practical uses."

"What do you mean?"

"Some think it can bring them luck. They sprinkle it over their gardens, especially if they've had a poor harvest, wanting to expunge the past. Others will sprinkle it around their homes, thinking that it might push out demons that have cursed them." Wella shook her head. "Can't say that I know if either of them are true, but the powder itself is caustic. It would burn your fingers."

"Does it have any other practical purposes?" Something that might burn like that might be beneficial for some of his questioning. Finn wondered if Meyer knew about fire ash. Using something like that in the prisons might offer them the opportunity to ask questions and get answers that they wouldn't have otherwise.

"Nothing you would be concerned about," she said softly.

She took the jar from him, stoppering it, and set it on the shelf and away from him. "Do you care to tell me why you are here?"

Finn looked back toward the door. He couldn't get past what Reames had said to him. He knew Meyer had secrets. And he knew Meyer had a family that he must have lost, but Finn would've expected that to have been something that had happened after he came to Verendal. Why else would his bedroom have been set up the way that it was?

"You really won't talk about it with me?" Finn asked, turning back to Wella.

She sighed, shaking her head slowly. "I've known Henry since the very first day he came to the city. He was just a journeyman then. Came to work with the old master executioner, a man by the name of Fortin Range. A skilled man, diligent, but nothing like Henry. Henry has proven himself not only skilled at his task but also beyond reproach. I doubt you would find anyone in the city who could claim he does not serve the king to his best ability."

In the time Finn had been serving Master Meyer, he had seen that. Meyer certainly had proven himself over time to be a man of honor, of dignity, despite the trappings of the job. It was something that had appealed to Finn when he had first apprenticed with him. Meyer had given Finn the belief that he could do and be something more, and it didn't have to be a mindless executioner.

"What happened to his family?"

"None really know. All I can say is that they were lost before he came. He spoke about them a bit more in those days, but as you can imagine, that has changed over time."

"I see."

Wella frowned at him. "Do you?"

"What is that supposed to mean?"

She cackled and slapped the counter in front of her. "How is it that you don't recognize the connection?"

"What connection is that?"

"The connection between his past and your future?" Wella grabbed a stool from behind the counter and took a seat. She clasped her hands, looking up at him. "Do you think he chose you because of your good looks?" She cackled again. "Or perhaps you think he chose you because he liked you. Or maybe you thought he chose you because he believed the jurors had your sentencing wrong."

Finn shrugged. "I suppose I did think that."

She laughed again. "Perhaps that's true. It's possible he did see a wrong had been committed, and decided to do whatever he could to right that wrong."

There was more to Finn's suspicion than just that, though. As he looked at Wella, he wondered whether or not she would even acknowledge it to him. He figured it couldn't hurt to ask, though. She might not know the answer, but if he didn't ask, he might never learn the truth.

"To be honest, I started to question whether it was tied to the hegen."

She frowned. "Why would hegen care anything about you?"

"I don't know. I thought maybe they decided to use me." He still had the most recent card, and though he didn't know what the crown on it represented, he suspected. Esmerelda wouldn't tell him, and despite him digging, he doubted that he would find those answers very easily.

"I can't say whether or not the hegen were involved, but that wasn't my impression. When he first exerted his right with you, I wondered why. All these years, and Meyer had never been one to go outside of the trappings of his office." He chuckled. "I suppose he still didn't. He simply went back in time, using an ancient right that had not been used for a long time."

"And you don't think the hegen were involved?"

"Maybe they were," she said, shrugging. "I know Meyer has rapport with them that Fortin never did. Fortin always tried to chase them away after the executions. Made me getting supplies a little bit difficult." She leveled her gaze on the jar nearest her, and Finn glanced over to see it filled with toes. "Henry arrived and must've had a different experience with the hegen. He accepted them, normalized them, to an extent."

"I don't think he completely normalized them," Finn said.

"Not for those within the city, but for those who tried to keep the hegen from collecting prizes following the execution, he most certainly did." She cackled again. "But none of that matters. I think the only thing that really matters is that he saw a little bit of himself in you. Didn't know that at first, not when I first met you, but the more I learned about your mother and sister..."

Finn frowned. Could that be it? Could it be that Meyer had only chosen him because of his family connection? Depending upon what happened to Meyer's wife and daughter, maybe that did fit. Maybe he saw in Finn an opportunity to help someone when he hadn't been able to be helped.

Perhaps it didn't even matter.

That wasn't entirely true. If the hegen were involved, Finn thought it absolutely mattered. If they were using him, and using Meyer to get to him, then it mattered to him. If there was another reason, and if it were only about what Meyer wanted, then perhaps he shouldn't push quite so hard to try to understand.

"Don't go talking to him about it," Wella said. "He hasn't spoken of them in a long time. I know that kind of grief in a man. I know what it does to them. And I know what bringing up the past can do."

"Bringing up the past can help them heal," Finn said.

"Heal? Or crack?" She got to her feet again. "None of that is the reason that you came here, though. Why don't you tell me what you're looking for and I can see if I can help you find it."

Finn let out a long sigh and tried to shake away the thoughts filling him. Wella was right. He couldn't go and question Meyer about any of this. He knew Meyer well enough to know he wouldn't take it very well. He might even get angry. It was one more question he might not ever know the truth about.

"He tasked me with helping a woman."

"Helping?" Wella leaned forward, grinning. Her breath smelled of mint. "By that, you mean *healing*. It's about time he started to introduce you to that aspect of your responsibilities."

"He's taught me other parts of healing," Finn said.

"Other parts, but they are all applicable to your responsibility in the prison. What I'm getting at is a different kind of responsibility. Not everyone can afford to go see the physician." Wella shook her head. "And I'm never going to be the one to tell you I have the same knowledge and experience as the executioner. Mine is here in the shop, mixing compounds and offering different medicinals, but Henry sees things that I don't." She tipped her head to the side. "What is it? What did he ask you to help with?"

"Fatigue," Finn said.

She chuckled. "That's an odd one to start with."

"I'm sure Master Meyer had his reasons."

"Most definitely. Knowing Henry, he must have something he intends for you to learn from it. Not just about the healing, that is. If I know him, he intends for you to gain a different lesson from it. What do you think it might be?"

Finn thought about what Moira had come to them with, the nature of her symptoms, and he realized that he didn't even know. Maybe it was about how to ask questions so that he could get to the bottom of what she needed. Or maybe it had more to do with trying to find the answers to what might work for her.

"I don't really know," Finn said, shaking his head. "I want to get this one right."

He wanted to impress Meyer with something other than his pursuit for Bellut.

Maybe with this he could even trade it for information about his father.

"You *are* taking your training seriously."

"Shouldn't I be?"

Wella laughed softly. "There were quite a few in the city who questioned whether or not you'd be able to move on from your past."

"I didn't realize there were rumors about me in the city."

"There are always rumors, Finn. The key is piecing together what is factual from the rumor. Most rumors have some basis in fact."

"This woman has suffered from fatigue for several weeks. She says that it got better when he provided her with gersil, though she is only awake now for six hours of the day and needs to sleep the rest of it."

Wella pressed her lips together frowning. She drummed her fingers together, blinking slowly. "An interesting choice. I wonder why he would have gone in that direction."

"There was rose to it as well."

"Interesting. I wonder what he mixed it with."

"I'm not sure what oil he used. I tried to taste it the way that you instructed me, but I couldn't determine what it was."

"Tasting oil when you have something as pronounced as rose in the flavoring would be challenging, even for a skilled apothecary. Did you detect the gersil?"

Finn nodded. "I have used that enough times I was able to pick that up pretty easily."

"Very good. That's also difficult. It has a distinct taste, along with an odor, but I have not had much luck in teaching people to detect it. Most the time, you have to taste it repeatedly."

"If it's a stimulant, why would that be a problem?"

"Because it doesn't fade very quickly. Those who taste it directly find they cannot sleep."

"I think Meyer has already tried that. I think he wants me to try something else."

"It can also be dangerous. What do you think stimulants do, Finn?"

"I don't know. Wake someone up?"

"And what happens when you are awake?"

Finn held his gaze on Wella. "What are you getting at?"

"I'm getting at nothing. I only seek to have you engage in critical thinking."

"I suppose your heart beats faster." Wella nodded. "Your breathing quickens." She nodded again. Finn thought about what he had experienced when he had tasted the concoction, and remembered both of those experiences. He had started sweating, as well.

"Which of those would pose a danger to someone?"

Finn started. "I get what you're saying. If I were to give somebody too much of the gersil, it's possible their heart might go too fast."

"A racing heart can be incredibly dangerous. Not always while you're young. The young have the ability to withstand many things that someone who is older would not. But I suspect this person is advanced in age?"

"Is that your polite way of saying she's older?"

"I like to think that while I might be advanced in age, I am still young at heart." Wella cackled, and she leaned forward. "I don't think I could handle my heart racing quite as well as you could, Finn. Much like I doubt this patient of yours would be able to handle the same."

"You're suggesting I need to find a stimulant that won't lead to side effects."

"I think you need to be cautious with your stimulants. Which is why I suspect Henry used a tiny amount."

"Would a higher dose make a difference?"

"It might, but there are alternatives."

"If you search well enough, you find that there are some that work more cleanly than others."

"Cleanly?"

"I realize that is a strange way of referring to it, but there are some that don't have nearly the same side effects as others. Search Gisles. I'm sure you can find what you need there."

"It would be easier if you just told me," Finn said.

She laughed again. "Easier, but what would you learn if I told you the answers you need? You would miss out on the journey." She cackled again. "When you find what you need, you can return and I can help you with whatever supplies you might need."

"The answer is in Gisles?"

"Of course. Who else but Gisles would know about some of these different techniques?"

Finn shook his head. "Thank you for your time."

"You know you're always welcome here, Finn."

"I might be welcome, but you won't always provide me with what I need."

"I've given you exactly what you need. Now go, take the journey, and learn how to help this patient."

CHAPTER THIRTEEN

E vening had fallen in full by the time Finn gave up reading through Gisles's texts, still not finding anything that would be useful to help Moira. Answers were there, but it was difficult working through the book to find them. There was something about the old style of writing that made it difficult for him, but it was more than that. Gisles referenced different medicines that Finn didn't have the background to know. It meant looking up those while reading, turning it into tedious work.

He rubbed a fist against his eyes and looked around his small room. Strange that he'd come to think of it as small, though it was that. Large enough for his bed, a dresser, and a narrow desk by the window. More than that, it was all his. Finn hadn't learned what Meyer used the room for before Finn had been given it, but maybe it didn't matter.

The lantern flickered. It needed more oil, though he didn't plan on staying in the room much longer, so there wasn't the need to refill it just yet. The stack of books on the desk was mostly untouched. Other than the Gisles book, Finn hadn't been studying as much as he had when he'd first come to work with Meyer. There wasn't time. Now that Meyer trusted him to run errands on his own and to take care of aspects of the job that didn't involve questioning, Finn didn't have the same ability to sit and study. That might be a mistake. He could imagine Meyer getting irritated if he knew that Finn hadn't devoted himself to his studies the way he wanted.

The hegen card rested on the table in front of him. It had been in his pocket, and he'd pulled it out to study it but hadn't uncovered anything more than what he'd seen about it at first. The gold crown. The king—or someone close to him. That was what the hegen wanted from him.

Finn slipped the card back into his pocket and got to his feet. He headed down the hall, knocking briefly at Meyer's office. When Meyer pulled the door open, he eyed Finn for a moment.

"What is it?"

"I don't have an answer for Moira yet."

Meyer's brow furrowed. "You had told her to return soon. Finding another stimulant wasn't all she needed, Finn."

Finn nodded. Maybe this was part of Meyer's lesson. It was possible he wanted Finn to realize that he shouldn't make promises if he wasn't going to be able to keep them. When Moira had been there, Finn had thought that it would be a simple matter of looking for a different stimulant, but it seemed that it was more than just that. The task meant looking for whatever had caused her fatigue in the first place. Finn didn't have that answer, which was probably the point Meyer had tried to make.

"I can wait for her to stop by and let her know I don't have any answers for her just yet. I will keep looking, though."

Meyer watched him for a long moment.

Finn took a deep breath. "You wanted me to uncover what was wrong with her."

Meyer watched him for a long moment before shaking his head. "Even that isn't entirely the key. Let me know when you have found what you need to know."

"I will."

Meyer closed the door, and Finn just stared at it for a moment.

"What was that about?"

Lena stood on the stairway, and Finn looked behind her, wondering how his mother had been doing. "Probably nothing."

"You two shouldn't argue."

"It wasn't arguing." Finn stared at the door for a moment. "He's always trying to teach me some lesson. The challenge I have is learning what he wants me to learn in the time frame that he wants me to learn it in."

"At least you have somebody wanting to teach you," she said.

She headed past him, moving into the kitchen, and Finn followed her. "What does that mean?"

"It feels like…" Lena shook her head, turning away from him. She placed one of the pots into the washbasin and began scrubbing it. "It just feels like we have fallen back into the same patterns as before."

"Not quite the same patterns," Finn said. He picked up a pot and offered to help, but Lena shook her head.

"Maybe not the same," she agreed. "I don't have to worry about you being picked up by the Archers now; not the way I did before."

"You worried about me?"

She looked over. "You're my brother, Finn. After what happened to Father, how could I not worry about you?"

"I had always thought myself safe with my crew," Finn said.

"You thought you were safe because Oscar convinced you that you were."

"Let me help," he said.

"No. I can do this. Besides, you have so much more you need to be doing."

"I'm having a hard time with what I need to do. I am trying to figure out how to help a woman with fatigue. Unfortunately, I haven't been able to find the answers in the text of that I've been reading."

"Which one?" Lena scrubbed at the pot, not looking up at him.

"It's an old book that I have in my room. Meyer lent it to me."

"Is that the one by Gisles?"

Finn smiled. "Have you been sneaking into my room?"

Lena paused. "I don't have a whole lot else to do. In between checking on Mother, and helping keep the kitchen neat, and baking and cooking for the two of you, I have plenty of free time."

"You could get a job."

She looked over. "I've been trying... but there's nothing for me. No one is willing to meet with me." She sighed and shook her head. "Besides, what kind of job do you think I could do? I don't have any skills. What's more, I'm not exactly sure that I want to take a job that would employ me these days."

"You can read. You can write. There are plenty of opportunities for somebody like you. I might even know somebody who could help." Master Johan would need an apprentice, and perhaps it was something Lena could do. Though Finn didn't know if Johan would even be willing to consider anybody Finn might propose.

"I can read and I can write. Two traits that men in the city love to hear." She shook her head, staring at her hands. "You can go, Finn. I know you have other responsibilities."

He frowned. "Maybe you could help me."

"I don't have any interest in—"

"Not that," Finn said. His sister had helped their mother for years. Why not help him research a way to help Moira? "If you're going to be reading the books, see if you come across any sort of stimulants."

"Is this for your questioning?"

He shook his head. "There's a woman Meyer asked me to try to help. She complains of fatigue. I thought that maybe since you were already looking through those books..."

She smiled slightly. "It *would* give me something to focus on. Only if you're sure Master Meyer won't mind."

"I don't think he'll mind. And besides, with everything else going on, having your help would be great."

Her smile widened. "I'd be honored to help."

She left, a quickness to her step that hadn't been there before. Finn understood Lena's issue. He had a job. Responsibility. He had a place in Meyer's home.

What did she have?

It was something he should talk to Meyer about. He might not be able to solve it, but at least he could offer some insight. Out in the street, Finn headed toward Declan Prison. The Treble Coat tavern would be nearby, and though he didn't know exactly where to find it, he suspected he could come across it by searching around the area.

He hadn't gone far from Meyer's home when he started to feel a strange sensation. Every time he turned a corner, a shadow behind him seemed to follow.

He wasn't alone.

Finn started to glance in either direction, looking for signs of Archers.

Finn thought he still remembered how to lose a tail, but it would involve moving quickly. He also was curious.

If somebody followed him, he wanted to know who —and why.

He ducked into an alley, moving along it until he got far enough that he didn't have to worry about getting trapped. He paused there for a moment, waiting for his pursuer to get close.

It didn't take long.

Finn darted out and lunged toward the pursuer. His time working with Meyer had strengthened him.

He grabbed the figure, throwing them behind him.

"Hey, Shuffles. Easy now."

Finn froze. He recognized the voice.

"Wolf? You aren't supposed to be in Verendal."

The figure pulled back the hood of their cloak. Wolf was an older man, with dark hair, hard eyes that flickered around him at all times, always aware, and a lean build in constant tension. Everything about him screamed *danger*.

"I just want to have a word, Shuffles."

"What are you doing here?"

"Look at you," Wolf said, taking a step toward Finn. Finn backed out of the alley, getting onto the street. "You've taken to this lifestyle quite well. The King suspected you would."

"Is that why you're here?"

"For revenge?" Wolf shook his head. "I don't need any revenge. The King knew what might happen to him. The same way all of us know." He took another step toward Finn, forcing Finn to move back. "Much like I suspect you have considered what might happen to you."

"I serve the king now."

"You served the King before."

"Not Leon."

"He'd be hurt to know."

"I doubt that," Finn said.

Wolf grinned at him. "Maybe you're right. Given that

he swung from the end of your rope, he's not going to tell us much of anything, is he?"

"What do you want?"

Finn hesitated to back up any farther. Doing so would only entice Wolf and would probably show weakness.

"What do you know about the Client?"

Finn frowned. "That's what this is about?"

"The bastard is the reason I'm running."

He looked as if he wanted to take another step toward Finn, but he didn't.

"You should leave Verendal. If the Archers catch you—"

Wolf grunted. "Them bastards can't find their pecker if it floated in front of their face. Nah. I'm not leaving this shithole of a place until I find what I want. Bad enough I had to hide out in Meldran again. Had enough of that heap when I was a kid."

Maybe Finn *had* seen Wolf when he'd been there.

"What do you know?"

Finn laughed bitterly. "If you think that you can go after the Client yourself, you're mistaken."

Wolf glared at him. "Talk, Shuffles, or you're going to learn what it's like to lose your newfound coin."

Finn recognized a true threat. "You intend to go after one of the jurors?" Finn shrugged. "Be my guest."

Wolf glowered at him. "I knew about the bastard Bellut. There's another."

"I don't know the other." Finn had suspected, though hadn't managed to find anything.

"What are you doing about this, Shuffles?"

"There's not much I can do about it. I serve as an executioner's apprentice, but I'm not able to start any investigations."

"Start? I figured that given what you knew, there shouldn't be any difficulty getting him to kick the investigation into gear."

Finn regarded Wolf for a moment. As much as he hated the idea, there might be something he and Wolf could do together. If he worked with Wolf, it was possible he might be able to get some answers from him. He might be able to help Finn figure out just what had happened. If Meyer weren't going to go digging into it, or even if he intended to, Finn might be able to help.

"What have you found out?" Finn glanced in either direction along the street, before turning his gaze back to him. "I want to bring them down the same as you."

Wolf frowned at him. "I doubt you want to bring them down the *same* as me, Shuffles."

Finn hated how he kept using his nickname, especially that one. It was as if he were doing it just to needle him, which was probably the case. Knowing Wolf the way that he did, he expected him to try to do anything and everything in his power to annoy Finn. Worse, it worked. He hated the way Wolf used the nickname, but more than that, he hated the way that Wolf had been the one to have started the nickname.

"Given what they've done, I want justice."

Wolf watched him, and there was something in his eyes that gave Finn a moment of pause. Finn wasn't sure if it was the way that he watched him or if there was more to it, but he knew better than to trust Wolf.

If he did this, Finn was going to need to pull Oscar in as well. It was the kind of thing that only somebody like Oscar would really understand, and the only other person he trusted.

"I don't give two shits about justice," Wolf said.

"If you want my help, then you should."

"You don't double-cross me and my team and get away with it. You don't make me go back to *there* after all this time. Make me beg for a place to hide." Wolf took a step toward Finn. "I don't care how protected you think you are."

Finn took a steadying breath. "This doesn't need to be complicated," he said. "We can work together. If you're not willing to do that—"

"That's not how this is going to work, Shuffles."

"How do you see this working, Felix?"

He said it a bit harder than he intended, but he was getting tired of Wolf throwing around his old nickname. He knew how much it annoyed Finn.

"Put on some fancy clothes and suddenly the boy decides he belongs here. I guess I shouldn't be too surprised. Not the first time somebody gets a little ahead of themselves after getting a taste for the high life. Trust me. I been there."

Finn had a pang of curiosity about Wolf he hadn't known before. "If you think what I've been doing is the high life, then you have no idea."

"I have some idea. Do you think this is the first time I've watched you?"

Everything within Finn went cold.

"You need to be careful, Felix. You're a known accomplice to Leon Konig, exiled from Verendal for crimes against the king."

Wolf started to smile. "Seems like Shuffles got a spine, too."

"Call me Shuffles one more time—"

Wolf darted toward him, anger flashing in his eyes. "And what? Go ahead. Finish that sentence."

"Call me Shuffles one more time, and I will make sure the Archers find you. Even in Meldran."

"Only if you get out of here alive." Wolf looked around, scanning the street. "Seems to me you're all by yourself here."

"Am I?" Finn whistled sharply twice in quick succession. "How much time do you think you have?"

Wolf watched Finn, smirking. "Long enough to shove a blade into your belly."

"Maybe. But if they find me bleeding out, guess who comes looking for you?"

"No one ever comes looking for me," Wolf said.

"I wouldn't be so sure of that. Have you heard anything about Henry Meyer, the master executioner? If you haven't, I'm happy to inform you he's known as a dedicated servant to the king. He also would be quite disappointed to learn his apprentice was slaughtered. Again. I doubt he would rest until finding what happened this time."

There was movement on the end of the street as Archers came. Finn suppressed the sigh of relief that immediately came to him. He needed to be careful with Wolf and should have been more cautious with him there than he had been.

"This isn't over, Shuffles."

"We want the same thing, Wolf."

"No. You want something different. I want to know who's responsible for what happened to my team, and you—"

"I want justice."

Wolf started. "Maybe I was wrong. Maybe you changed much more than I thought. Keep your eyes open, Shuffles. I'll be seeing you."

He slipped off down the street, disappearing.

When he reached the Archers, he ducked down an alley, and one of the Archers stood in the mouth of the alley for a moment, watching, though Finn doubted that the Archer would even go after him. He wasn't surprised when the Archer returned to the other, and they headed farther down the street. When they reached Finn, they studied him.

"I know you," one of the Archers said. "You're the hangman. You the one who whistled?"

Finn nodded. He debated how to answer. If he shared enough with them, it might push Wolf to keep from attacking Finn, though had Wolf wanted to attack, Finn had a feeling that he would've just done so.

"The man who went down the alley is a wanted criminal."

"Some Poor Bastard that you released?"

Finn shook his head. "He escaped custody. I thought he left the city. He's an accomplice of a man once known as the King."

"I know that name," the other Archer said. He was tall and thin, and had a higher voice than Finn would've expected. "He hanged a few months back. Some sort of thief who broke into the palace."

"That's him," Finn said, looking down the street after Wolf. "And the man who just got away is his accomplice." If he could put pressure on Wolf, maybe he could also put pressure on Bellut. He thought they'd gotten away, but they had thought that because they believed everybody else involved in the crime was gone. Finn had no idea where Rock had ended up, and Oscar was smart enough not to say anything, but Wolf…

He was angry.

If he were smart, he would've stayed away from the city and not returned, but his actions were anything but smart.

"Put out word to the other Archers he's back in the city."

"What do you think he's doing?" the tall Archer asked.

Finn debated. He could use this, too. All of it would help him get what he needed on Bellut. "I don't fully know. Maybe he's planning another job. He might even be here for revenge about what happened on his last job. The Archers should keep an eye on him."

"We'll spread the word," the other Archer said.

They headed off down the street, and Finn lingered for

just a moment before hurrying on. He needed to be careful, but more than that, he needed to start paying more attention to what happened around him. He couldn't have Wolf sneaking up on him again.

The problem he had was that he had fallen out of practice. During the daytime, Finn simply didn't need to sneak the way that he once had. In the evenings, either he had a destination or he was on an investigation.

Either way, with Wolf back in the city, Finn had to be careful.

He found himself looking down each alley that he passed, his gaze darting into the darkness, finding nothing. When he reached an intersection, he paused to look along it, searching for shadows that might move toward him. Other than an occasional grouping of people who were out and wandering the streets, Finn saw nothing to be concerned about.

Maybe that was Wolf's intention. He wanted to put Finn on edge, making him jumpy. A man who searched the shadows could make mistakes.

Finn had to be smarter than that.

If there was one thing Meyer had taught him, it was how to be smarter about everything. He had learned to be more calculating, mostly because it was important for questioning, along with investigations. He might not have all of the answers, but he believed that he could at least get to them.

He would use Wolf.

Finn had been searching for some way to dig into what

happened with Bellut without upsetting Meyer, and Wolf might finally provide that to him.

The King and Wolf had used Finn before. Now it was his turn.

There had to be more to why Wolf returned. It couldn't *just* be about revenge. That was what he *wanted* Finn to think... only, Wolf was a thief. He cared about the jobs. The crew had been a means to an end. And the King might have been a friend, but Wolf knew crime had consequences. That was something the King had warned Finn about when he'd been imprisoned.

Which meant Wolf was after something more.

It was another reason for the Archers to keep an eye on him.

When he reached Declan, the prison towered over him. The sound of music filtered along the street, a muted but jaunty sound, and Finn was drawn toward it. Something about the music reminded him of the Wenderwolf tavern.

He found a marking for the tavern above it. It was situated on a narrow street just outside of Declan. The sign for Treble Coat turned out to be simply that: a coat. He had no idea what the *Treble* part of the title meant.

There were other things he had to be doing, but Meyer had made it clear he needed to work with the iron masters. They knew things he would need to do his job well.

This was how he would get that information.

He pushed the door open, stepping inside. It was dark, with tables clustered close together. Several minstrels played in the center of the tavern, the tables arranged around them. A smoky haze greeted him, and a fire in the hearth glowed with a soft warmth that wasn't unpleasant, given how cool the days in Verendal had been.

He looked around the tavern, searching for a familiar face, and found Shiner sitting with several other iron masters. Cards stacked on the table, ale piled in front of them, they shouted, laughing and generally having a good time.

This was what he missed.

As he approached the table, Shiner looked up, grinning at him. "Jags! Damn, I didn't think you were actually going to come." He looked down at the others. "Make room for Jags." He looked over to Finn. "How do you feel about ale, Jags?"

Finn smiled slowly. "I'd feel better if I had one."

Shiner chuckled. "That's what I like to hear."

CHAPTER FOURTEEN

F inn sat at the table, resting his elbows on it, glancing over to his sister as she prepared lunch. Lena had on a simple gray dress, her hair covered by a kerchief, and with her back turned to him, he couldn't see her face, though when he had first come into the kitchen, he'd recognized the tension around her eyes. He had seen it from her over the last few weeks.

His stomach grumbled, though he didn't know if it was because he was hungry or whether he was unsettled after spending the night drinking ale with the iron masters and had to leave early for errands, or perhaps he was more unsettled because of the interaction he'd had with Wolf.

"You haven't said much," he said to Lena.

"There's nothing to say," she said softly.

The sausage sizzled in the pan, along with the smell of the sweet bread she made. It was a better lunch than what he would've made for himself. "Is it Mother?"

The sudden stiffness to her back told him the answer.

"I can help."

"I know that you can help," she said. "This is my responsibility."

"There are other things you can be doing."

She took a deep breath, letting it out slowly. "I have been. Like you asked. It's just that understanding the different stimulants isn't easy."

"I know. I've looked through Gisles, but haven't found any answers." They would be there, he was sure, but Finn didn't know where, and the book was difficult enough to get through that he didn't know how long it would take.

"There are a few different options you could have her try. Benel works as a stimulant, but you said she needs something long acting." Finn nodded. "There are horath and vren, but neither of those would last very long. I think the challenge is the duration."

"That was her complaint."

She frowned. "I wonder if there might be a mixture that might..." Her frown deepened. "I need to check on something."

She handed him a plate and hurried out of the kitchen, leaving him looking down at the plate. She had made an amazing lunch, the same way that she often made an amazing meals for him. He needed to be more thankful for all that she did for him, and needed to share with her just how much he appreciated it. And now she was helping him research.

He ate slowly, starting with the sausage, moving on to the sweet bread, before finishing. By the time he was done, Master Meyer had returned and come into the kitchen, looking over to the stove before flicking his gaze back to Finn. "Where is your sister?"

"She's off looking into something," Finn said, waving his hand. "It's to help with my mother's sickness," he added. What they used for Moira *might* help their mother.

"I've done all I can for her."

"I know. And I think she knows. It doesn't change that she remains disappointed."

Disappointed wasn't even the right answer. Perhaps Lena was more sad.

"I think she questions what she's going to do with her time."

"She can do whatever she chooses."

"I don't think my sister sees it like that."

He pulled the pan back out, heated it, and started preparing eggs and sausage for Meyer. It wasn't going to be quite as skillfully made as what Lena had done for him, but it was good enough.

"What do you think she needs?" Meyer asked.

Finn took a deep breath as he flipped the sausages, and then turned over to look at Master Meyer. "I don't know. She's looking for purpose, the same as most people do, I suppose. She doesn't have what she wants, though I don't even know what it is that she wants. She's been trying to find employment but has been turned away."

Meyer looked to the opening in the door, as if to see Lena through it. "I will see what I can do."

"I'm not sure that's what she wants, either. She wants to find something for herself." He handed Meyer a plate and took a seat across from him. "I ran into Wolf last night. I thought he'd stay away from the city, but Oscar thought..." Finn trailed off, wondering if he should have mentioned the man.

Meyer started to smile. "You can say it. I know who Oscar is."

"Fine. Oscar is a thief. And I don't know that he can get involved in this without drawing attention to himself. Besides, there's something of an unspoken agreement when it comes to thieves and those who work with them and against them." Oscar would never say it, but Finn suspected he wouldn't go after Bellut directly simply because he was a public figure. Instead, he would go after Bellut in a way that made sure that no one really knew that it was Oscar who had gone after him.

If it came down to it, Finn was perfectly willing to work with Oscar, and perhaps he needed to. Especially now that Wolf had returned.

"Are you sure this Wolf has been out of the city?"

Finn shook his head. "I'm not sure about anything, really. All I know is I haven't seen any sign of him since the attack on the palace. He's the kind to go after revenge, if you know what I mean."

Meyer looked over to Finn. "Only him?"

"I'm not trying to get revenge," Finn said.

"Which means that you have decided to settle for justice."

"Isn't that what you want me to do?"

Meyer settled his arms on the table, looking over to Finn. He watched him with a bright intensity in his eyes.

"I want for you to recognize you cannot seek revenge. You most of all."

"Why not me most of all?"

"That I must explain it to you is troublesome. Others watch you, and they are watching for you to fail. You might've passed the Executioner Court, and you might have proven yourself, but there are still those who would love to see you fail. You need to demonstrate integrity beyond reproach. Not just because the position demands it, which it does, but because of the circumstances of your coming to work with me demand it. Do you see that?"

Finn nodded slowly. "I see that," he said softly.

"Are you sure?"

Finn took a deep breath, letting it out. "I see that."

"Then recognize you cannot be after vengeance. You cannot side with anyone who is after vengeance. All you can do is search for the truth and let that guide what happens next. All you can do is ensure that the king's justice is carried out."

"What will you do if we find information that implicates Bellut and whoever he's working with?"

"I will do what I am tasked with doing. I will serve the king, serve his justice, and I will ensure that it is carried out in the way that it must be." He turned his attention back to the food, eating slowly, deliberately, and didn't look up at Finn.

Finn scrubbed at the pan, getting it clean, and watched Meyer.

He didn't like the idea of Bellut getting away with what he'd done. He deserved the king's justice. It was just that

Finn also recognized that what Master Meyer said was true. He did need to find a measure of peace, such as it were, if only so that he could move past what had happened.

Besides, as much as he might want to get revenge for what they'd done, perhaps that simply wasn't in the cards.

Only, it *was* in the cards. The hegen card.

He turned to Meyer. "I've been wondering about your involvement with the hegen. When did you start working with them?"

Meyer looked up. "What is there to tell?"

"I understand you helped develop that relationship."

Meyer nodded slowly. "I did."

"Why?"

"Many people fear the hegen," Meyer said. "They're found throughout the kingdom, and perhaps my feeling toward the hegen stems from my interaction with them in my previous assignment."

"Before you came to Verendal?"

"This hasn't always been my home."

Could he get Meyer to share more about himself? Wella knew quite a bit about Meyer, but Finn had never gotten the old executioner to discuss anything about himself. He was private, almost frustratingly so.

"Where did you serve before?"

"I told you about my first master. I was taken in as an apprentice when I was younger than you. My father needed money, and my family struggled, so they apprenticed me to him."

"Why?"

"Most people recognize the executioners as something almost undesirable. Not all, though. My family saw the executioners as an extension of the king's justice. I wasn't the first executioner in my family. That would've been my great-uncle, but not many had served as executioners in recent generations. But my family knew it paid well, and knew that even as an apprentice, I would earn my keep, and that it would provide for me in the years to come." He smiled tightly, turning his attention back to the food. "I was given an opportunity to have a life. My father was a laborer, poorly paid, and dependent upon jobs coming in. My mother was a baker, but again, finding work was difficult."

Hearing Master Meyer talk about his experience made Finn wonder if perhaps he had chosen to work with Finn because he reminded him of himself. Perhaps it wasn't anything more than that, nothing to do with the hegen themselves, or anything but the fact that he had seen something in Finn.

If so, then Finn should be thankful for it.

"How did you end up in Verendal?"

"I suppose this is something we should talk about, anyway. Once you move far enough in your training, you progress to journeyman status. As a journeyman, you can travel, if you so desire. It gives you the opportunity to see part of the country and to serve the king more directly, though not to be tied down to any one city. From there, eventually you can progress to master executioner, though not all executioners do so. Only those chosen by the Executioner Court can progress.

Once you do, you will be given an assignment and a location to serve."

"And you were assigned to serve in Verendal."

"I was. It suited me, and I've been happy to serve here, and happy to offer my services to the city." Master Meyer started to chuckle and then looked over. He smiled at Finn. "You have many years before you have to face that question."

"What question is that?" Finn asked.

Meyer smiled again. "I can see the look in your eye, Finn. You wonder when you will be asked to leave the city."

"Isn't that the point of all of this? You train me, pushing me further along, and eventually I'm to leave."

Meyer nodded slowly. "That is the general progression. You can't remain apprenticed to me indefinitely. You won't want to, either. Eventually, you'll decide you want and need autonomy you can't have remaining with me."

"But only when I reach journeyman status."

"That is part of the progression. As you move beyond apprentice, you move into journeyman, which grants you autonomy I cannot quite grant you."

"What would that include?"

"Other than more cases such as you have started to investigate?" He shrugged. "You would be able to carry out sentencing on your own. As you learn more about medicines, you will even be able to offer healing on your own, which means additional income."

Surprisingly, income was one thing he hadn't been concerned about during his time working with Master

Meyer. While he wanted to ensure he had enough money, Meyer had certainly not been stingy with his coin. Finn had always been paid on time, and paid well, and more than what he would have earned in any other traditional employment.

"None of this matters until you have proven yourself, Finn. You still have quite a bit of time before that occurs." Meyer got to his feet, looking around the inside of the kitchen for a moment before his gaze drifted toward the door. "You should keep working. There is much to be done."

Finn looked around the kitchen. He needed to do more than what he already had, and he needed to finish what he had started, but all of this felt like it was more complicated than what Finn had intended.

"You should be careful. If the man known as Wolf has returned to the city, you need to be cautious and alert. Someone like that has an agenda."

Finn nodded. "I know."

"The challenge is determining what agenda he has and what that has to do with you. The challenge becomes trying to decide if it's anything you want to be caught up in."

"What if I don't get to decide?" Finn asked.

"You always get to decide."

"Always?" He arched a brow, glancing over the Master Meyer. "I didn't get to decide when it came to my appointment with you."

Meyer frowned at him. "Didn't you? You were given two options."

"The other option was dying."

"Sometimes, dying is a choice."

Meyer departed, leaving Finn in the kitchen. He finished cleaning up from lunch, knowing that he still had quite a bit of work to do for the day, and needing to get everything settled. They were on a timeline that he had to meet. He couldn't delay any longer than he already had.

The problem for Finn was that he didn't entirely know what way to take the investigation. For him to prove Sweth was innocent, he figured he had to dig a little bit more and perhaps even question him a little bit more. Beyond that, if he failed to prove Sweth's innocence, then he was going to hang. Regardless of what Finn might believe about him, he didn't think Sweth was guilty of the crime.

He finished in the kitchen, then gathered whatever belongings he might need for the rest of the day, including the hegen card, which he slipped into his pocket, thinking that if nothing else, he might look down at it to see if it changed, though it never did, and headed out of the house.

Once out on the street, he paused. Wolf had found him easily. Wolf knew where he was and knew how to come across him. It meant that Wolf could be anywhere in the city. It could be that he watched him now.

He didn't like the idea that Wolf stalked him through the city, but maybe Finn could keep ahead of him. Knowing that he was out there gave Finn the opportunity to move quickly and watch for any signs of anybody trailing after him, keeping tabs on him. If he were careful, he should be able to avoid Wolf.

He found himself drawn to the Jorend section. Answers weren't there, he didn't think, but maybe if he visited the fire again, he might gain a different perspective. As he reached the street, he slowed, smelling the remains of the fire. If he hadn't known better, he would've thought that it was no different from the smells coming off of a crackling hearth. It was comforting, other than knowing how many people's lives had been destroyed. Losing their homes, belongings, everything. Some had even lost their lives.

He lingered on the street for a moment, studying the remains. There was no way for him to determine anything from this. Meyer wanted him to dig into what happened there. How could he dig into it without having any way for him to uncover just what it was that had happened?

He wandered along the street. He paused at one point where he had seen the men loading up the remains of their belongings in the wagon, piling up items out of the drawers, before heading farther along. In some of the homes, it was obvious that people had picked through it, taking what they could. Hopefully, only those who lived there had picked through the belongings, though there had been no security, so it was entirely possible looters had come through, claiming items from those who had lost everything. He stopped about midway along the street, looking at the buildings that hadn't burned.

Some of them were partially intact, as if the fire had started there, but the fire brigade had managed to make quicker work of putting out the flames. It was different from the far end of the street, where everything had burned down.

The fire must have burned in this direction.

Of course, Finn knew it had. Having seen the fire himself and been pushed back from it, he had known it had started from this end of the street, working its way forward.

What he needed to know was who lived where in this section. Not just the names of the people, but he needed to know addresses and recreate a map of the entirety of the section.

If he were to do that, he thought it would give him a better idea of how to start.

He reached the end of the street. The wooden buildings near this end the street were little more than shells, though they were shells that remained intact. There was no sign of the same complete destruction as there were otherwise. The face of most of these buildings had burned off, leaving evidence of the homes inside. Even there, they had been picked over, with very few of the people's belongings remaining.

He still didn't know who was missing.

That fact was enough that he thought it would make a difference.

As he turned in place, looking behind him again, a crew of a dozen men stopped at the far end of the street. They had two wagons, and they started loading. They were already planning and beginning to remove the burned sections of the city. Soon, all of this would be cleared. Eventually, the rebuilding would begin. Hopefully, those who had lost everything would have an opportunity to build alongside the others, though from what he had heard, he didn't know if that were going to be the case. That was where he could start.

He jogged down the street, finding the foreman. "Do you have a list of which homes you are clearing?"

The foreman was a shorter man, dark-haired and with ropy muscles. He had a tattoo on one arm in the shape of a star, as if signifying his dedication and devotion to Heleth.

"Who's asking?"

"The executioner."

His eyes widened slightly. He turned away from Finn, reaching into a box on top of the cart before handing something over to Finn. "This is what I've got. You don't need to take me in for questioning."

Finn shook his head. Several of the other workers had turned and watched. Most of them were burly men, strong-appearing, and he could easily imagine them impeding him were he to try to bring the foreman along with him.

"I'm not bringing you in for questioning," Finn said. Tension within the men began to ease, and they turned back to their work. "I'm just trying to investigate the fire."

"Thought they got the bastard who did this."

"We have a man in custody, but we're trying to ensure his guilt before we—"

"Before you hang him?" the foreman asked.

Finn nodded briefly as he turned his attention to the page.

Someone had taken the time to detail each of the buildings on the street, along with a list of the owners.

That's strange.

"Are you sure about the details of this?"

The foreman looked over to him. He'd been motioning to a couple of men, getting them to lift one of the massive charred logs and toss it into the wagon. "I got this from my boss. Can't tell you whether it's accurate or not."

"Why did you need it?"

"We are only supposed to clear most of these buildings, not all of them." He pointed to the end of the street. "Some of them think they're going to rebuild." He shook his head.

"You don't think they should rebuild?"

"I'm not in construction," he said. "They don't ask my opinion on that sort of thing. If they did, I would tell them that it isn't worth their time rebuilding burned buildings like that. Best tear it down and start over. That way, you don't have something rotting from the inside."

"Carpenters have a way of securing it," Finn said.

"Sure they do," the foreman said. "But you want to trust yourself and your family to that possibility?" He shrugged. "Might save a few coins, but not for me."

"How long will you be here?"

"We got this job to finish the street. Can't say how long it's going to take, but given something like this..." He looked up, scanning the street. "Better part of a few weeks. We're not the only crew working, though. They want to get this swept out of here as quickly as possible."

"Who are *they*?"

"Talk to my boss. He'd be the one to know."

"I take it your boss is the one listed on the top of this page?"

The foreman grinned. He was missing a few teeth, and looked like the kind to have been in a tavern brawl. It was the kind of person that Finn would've spent time with were he still in the crew. Maybe all of this was less on the up-and-up than he thought.

"I'm going to need to confiscate this."

"You take what you need. I'm sure he's got more. Besides, I'm just here to clear out the debris. Once we get that done, then we move on."

Finn pulled up the paper, stuffing it into his pocket.

He had questions for Sweth.

CHAPTER FIFTEEN

The chapel was quiet other than the soft whimpering coming from Sweth. Finn stood by the counter, looking down at the tools, trying to decide which one he wanted to use. Sweth hadn't been completely honest with him. It was time for him to push a little harder.

"Most prefer it when I avoid using the ankle braces," Finn said, carrying over the bands of metal that he could tighten around his shins. They were painful. There were ways of adding to that discomfort: he could tighten them, poke and probe, or even add a surge of heat to it as well. "I had intended to avoid using that with you, but unfortunately—"

"I didn't do it," Sweth said.

"Then help me understand the map."

He had moved a table close enough to Sweth where Finn could fold out the map, angling it so that he could see it, but not so close that Sweth could grab it and damage it. He needed to keep that map intact for him to finish his investigation. At this point, he had a few questions that still hadn't been answered. Primarily relating to why Sweth had been in that part of the section, especially as he didn't belong there.

"I can't tell you why they have it listed that way. It's wrong; that's all I can say."

"Let me tell you what I found," he said, crouching down in front of Sweth and strapping the ankle braces on. He started with the left foot, tightening it just enough that it created a little bit of pressure. It was the threat of more pressure that Finn wanted. There were ways of applying these implements where a man's mind would draw upon more information and create even more fear, which made Finn's job even easier. "You told me that you had run into your home to gather a few items for Master Johan."

"I ran into my home."

"Only, your home isn't listed here."

That should've been the very first place that Finn had started when he had begun his investigation, but even as he had begun to dig, he hadn't considered the possibility that Sweth hadn't lived on the street. The people that he had asked had not known him, and for whatever reason, that hadn't struck him as significant.

Mostly because he had experience with living on the street and not knowing any of his neighbors.

"What can I say? My home isn't listed there because I haven't been there that long."

Finn stopped, smiling at him. "That is what you told

me before. I gave some thought to it as well, and so I went to Master Johan."

His eyes widened. "You did?"

Finn nodded. "I did. Do you know what I discovered?"

He shook his head slowly.

"I discovered that you hadn't worked for him for very long, either."

Something wasn't adding up. Finn had spoken to Master Meyer about it, but there was some part of this that troubled him, and Master Meyer had been unwilling to piece it together for him.

The answers were there. Finn was certain of it, but it was a matter of figuring out just what he would have to do to separate out what he knew from what he suspected. Here, he'd gone into this thinking that Sweth was innocent, and maybe he was—but not completely.

"Did he tell you that?"

"He said that you came to him with some skills. You had experience as a scribe."

"I did have experience as a scribe. I—"

Finn finish strapping on the other ankle brace, standing and backing away from him. Right now, the braces applied just a little bit of pressure, enough that they were uncomfortable. With a few turns of the screw, that pressure would intensify and gradually begin to compress around his shins and calves, becoming ever more painful. With enough pressure, even a resistant man would cave.

If that failed, there were other ways.

Given the deadline they worked with, Finn needed to get answers. He wanted to know whether or not he was guilty. This was his investigation. If he got a confession, maybe Meyer would trust him to do more the next time. Then the next.

After his conversation with Master Meyer about the progression he expected out of him, Finn wanted to fulfill his end of the bargain, and he wanted to be able to do what Master Meyer wanted of him, proving himself to the old executioner.

"You misled me," Finn said.

"I didn't mislead you. I told you what you wanted to know."

"Not entirely," Finn said. He watched him. "When you mislead me during our questioning, you make it difficult for me to trust what you say."

He smiled tightly. Finn might not have Master Meyer's experience, and he might not have his age—which lent him a certain intimidating factor—but he had seen him enough times during questioning that he thought that he could model something similar.

"I haven't been misleading you."

Finn cocked his head to the side, frowning. He shook his head, stepping forward and beginning to apply pressure. He turned the screws a few times. It was enough that it would dig into the shins but not so much that it would cut off all circulation. There was a balance he needed to maintain, and it was a balance Master Meyer had instructed him on mastering.

Sweth cried out.

"Why don't we start from the beginning. What I'd like to know is your name."

"You know my name!"

"I know what you have told me is your name. What is your name."

"David Sweth!"

Finn nodded. He held up the map. "Did you live on this street in the Jorend section?"

"I lived there."

"How long were you there?"

"Only a few months."

Finn watched him again, still uncertain about whether or not Sweth told him the truth. "Why didn't you tell me that when I first questioned you?"

"You didn't ask."

Finn tipped his head, regarding him.

When he had come before, he'd wanted to avoid the direct questioning himself and had taken to approaching him with kindness. That had obviously been a mistake. There was no kindness to be had for somebody like Sweth, especially if he was guilty.

Of course, that was what the Lion had thought about Finn as well. He'd been quick to torment, though had he not, Finn doubted he would've said anything either. He needed to take a different approach.

"Are you working with any crews in that area?"

He blinked at Finn. "Crews?"

Finn crouched down, turning the screws a little bit further. "You've finally admitted to me that you were only there for the better part of a few months, which is different than you alluded to before." Finn stopped at the counter with the implements, glancing over to him.

"Whether or not I asked the question directly, that would have been relevant information. I would've expected you to have shared what you thought would be helpful in exonerating you."

"I don't know what that means."

Finn glanced down. There were many different items that he could choose from, and quite a few of them might be helpful in getting answers. He'd seen Meyer using different techniques, and Finn had even read about many others, though he had no experience in using them himself.

He grabbed one of the narrow metal rods with the pointed tip. He carried it over, patting it against his hand as he looked at Sweth.

Sweth's eyes drifted to the rod before looking up at Finn. "What are you going to do with that?"

"This is used to penetrate the skin. The mark it leaves is barely noticeable, which as you know is important."

"Why is it important?"

"The gods want the condemned to come to them unharmed."

"Why would the gods want that?" Sweth's eyes lingered on the rod, and Finn paused as he crouched down in front of him. Sweth couldn't move. He was restrained in bindings to his ankles and wrists, but he leaned forward, trying to see what Finn was doing. So far, he hadn't spat at Finn, which Finn considered a victory. "What do you mean?"

Sweth held Finn's gaze for a moment before shaking his head.

Something didn't fit.

Finn turned the screws again. Now there was incredible pressure on Sweth's shins, making him cry out briefly. "What were you doing the night of the fire?"

"I didn't do anything!"

"You were seen running along the street. You were seen running into a building."

"My home."

"Are you sure?"

"It was my home!"

"For only a few months, then."

"Does it matter if it was my home for a few months or if it was my home for years? Either way, it doesn't make a difference. I was trying to save items from the fire before it burned down. I knew that Master Johan would be angry if I failed." He leaned his head forward. "Do not put that into my leg!"

Finn held out the rod, bringing it close to Sweth's exposed skin. "I'm afraid I don't feel you're being completely honest with me."

"I've told you everything you want to know. You don't have to do this."

"You were only there for a few months. Where were you before you moved to that street in Jorend?"

Sweth hesitated.

Finn slid the rod into his calf.

Sweth cried out, shrieking.

He shoved the rod through the meaty part of the muscle of his calf, knowing it was painful, but there would be no permanent or disabling injury to it. Besides, anything he did on the calf to the muscle would be covered by the Sinner's Cloth.

He had learned to be careful. Injuries that were visible delayed the sentencing. Some criminals understood that, and they used the situation so that they could keep from facing their sentencing. Others feared the injury. Like Sweth.

"Where were you before you lived in that building in the Jorend section?"

Sweth rocked his head back and forth, staring at Finn.

That was the key.

Finn returned to the counter, grabbing a few more of the metal rods. They were slender, sharp, and left barely more than a drop of blood when removed.

They hurt going in. They hurt even more if coated with various substances.

There was one that Finn could try.

He didn't have any fire ash on him, but he suspected if he were to use that, he might be able to get even more answers. He wouldn't even need to pierce the skin all the way. Maybe he could even rub it on the surface of the skin. It would burn, at least according to Wella, but it wouldn't leave any permanent markings.

Finn crouched down, holding out another rod on Sweth's opposite calf. "Where were you before?"

"I didn't live in Jorend before."

"That wasn't the question," Finn said. He shoved the rod into the other calf.

Sweth cried out, shrieking just as he had with the first one.

Finn straightened, and he held one more of the slender rods. There were about a dozen of them, all of them gleaming and sharp. Finn had cleaned them many times, oiling them, as Master Meyer wanted all of the equipment well maintained, which meant keeping it oiled, though he wondered if there was any real reason to do so with something like this. "We are going to get answers. I can see that you are reluctant to provide any, so perhaps we will keep at this until you decide to tell me something different."

"I don't know what more you want me to tell you. I have told you everything. I wasn't the one to have started the fire. I was just there—"

"I know. You were just there gathering items for Master Johan." Finn shook his head. It was that part which had troubled him. He had been gathering items for Master Johan, but as far as Finn had been able to tell, there was nothing Master Johan had felt was all that important. Some things were, but nothing that Sweth would've kept on him. "Master Johan told me that you wouldn't have anything of value at your home."

"Nothing that he would've seen as of value," Sweth said. Sweat streamed down the side of his face, and he rocked his head back and forth, moving as much as possible, though he couldn't move his arms or legs. The muscles were tense as he strained against the straps. "They were important to me."

Something didn't add up, and Finn crouched down, tapping one of the other metal rods in his hand, looking up at Sweth. "We will keep at this until we have answers."

"I told you I don't know."

"Then like I told you, we will keep talking."

Shiner pulled the door open, looking over at Finn before turning his attention to Sweth. Shiner had a bruise on one cheek and a scratch on the other, looking like he'd been in a fight.

"Damn, Jags. Didn't know that you had it in you."

"You didn't know I had what in me?"

He nodded to Sweth. "Look at him. Looks like he is going to need some time to rest before you question him in the chapel again."

"He didn't tell me anything," Finn said.

"What were you hoping to find out?"

"Answers," Finn said. "I need proof if he's going to be sentenced."

Shiner stared a moment. "Before I came to work here, I didn't know you had to go so far to get justice," he said softly. "Did you figure out how many people died?"

Finn shook his head. "It's been difficult. I finally got a list of people who lived on the street, so coming up with who died is my next step." After what he'd seen during the fire, he needed to know who died. Finn doubted it would make him feel any better not saving the person he'd heard crying for help, but it was something he put upon himself regardless.

"They say it was nearly two dozen, but I bet that's too high."

"I don't think it's that many either," Finn said.

"Pretty bad fire, though. I went by there the other day. Curious, you know."

"Were you?"

He nodded. "I think all of the iron masters have gone by there. At least, all of them who took care of him. Gives us a reason to keep him confined, you know."

"I don't know if you need a reason to do that other than we have to question him."

"I suppose that's reason enough," Shiner said, smiling. "But we still like to know, you see. Hard to believe the entire street had burned. Never seen anything like it. Have you?"

"I haven't."

"I bet you see all sorts of crazy things. The old hangman brings you around everywhere, doesn't he?"

Finn looked over to Sweth. His head was bowed, and Finn had removed the metal rods, wiping them clean, and had removed the braces from around his ankles. Sweth hadn't provided any more information. As soon as Finn had started pushing on where he had lived before, Sweth had quieted.

That was the key.

There was something more to it, but Finn wasn't at all sure what or why it mattered. Only that something didn't fit.

He might have to bring Meyer in on this investigation. As much as he didn't want to, if only so that he could prove that he was capable, he also didn't want to make a mistake. The consequences were too high if he did.

"I never saw anything quite like that fire when I lived in Olam."

"I don't know that section," Finn said.

"Not a section, Jags. It's a village a couple days away from here. Not surprised that you didn't hear about it. Most people haven't heard about it. Hell, I haven't met a single person since I came to Verendal who's heard of it since I been here."

"You came to Verendal to work?"

"Not much in my village. I never took up a trade, so I wasn't of much use. Besides, there weren't much in the way of women there, if you catch my drift." He flashed a smile and started to release the bindings around Sweth's wrists. Sweth didn't move. Finn was thankful that he hadn't tried to fight, though Finn stayed just in case Sweth were to resist. "Got to Verendal a few months back, thinking I could make something of myself. You hear all the stories, you know. Men who come to the big city, strike it rich. That hasn't been my experience at all."

"Me neither."

"You've done pretty well for yourself."

"It wasn't always the case."

Shiner chuckled. "Nah, I suppose that's true. You made something of yourself here. I hear the rumors about you, though. Heard you almost hanged." Sweth looked up slightly.

"Almost," Finn said. He wanted to keep Shiner from talking about it. It was time for Finn to move on to something else, but he stayed there, troubled. There was a nagging question in the back of his mind that he felt as if he hadn't answered. He didn't know something.

Maybe the answer would be found by returning to the Jorend section, though if the men cleaning the debris worked quickly enough, there might not be much for him to investigate.

"Pretty rare that you lived," Shiner said. "I heard you hanged but survived."

Finn snorted. "Is that the rumor?"

"It's one of them."

"I suppose that's better than some of the others."

He undid Sweth's ankles. Finn helped lift him, carrying him through the halls, back down the stairs, and into his cell, where Sweth collapsed. He crawled back into the corner of his cell, pulling his knees up to his chest, and he started rocking in place.

"You did a number on him this time, Jags," Shiner said.

"I need you to tell me if he says anything."

"You know I will. Say. We had a good time drinking with you the other night. The boys wondered if you were interested in joining us again."

Finn nodded slowly. "I could be up for a mug of ale."

"Yeah. We had that impression of you. Figured it could be good for us boys to get to know the new hangman. Never got to know the old one all that well."

"I don't think he ever drinks ale," Finn said.

"Have to take the stick out of his ass first, you know."

Finn chuckled while he shook his head. "Let me know what you hear."

Finn headed out of the prison, still troubled. He

unfolded the map he'd taken from the demolition crew, steadying it again. Sweth's name wasn't on the map anywhere, which left Finn thinking that perhaps there was something else about it that he needed to figure out. Which home had Sweth lived in?

None of the names really made all that much sense to him, but he knew which one Sweth had occupied, even if the name wasn't the same. The consistency to what Sweth had claimed, the fact that he had repeated the same refrain as Finn questioned him, left Finn thinking that perhaps he actually had lived there for the last few months.

Fol.

That was all that he could see on that building.

That name didn't strike any chord with him, but maybe Meyer would know it.

He made his way over to the Jorend section. The crew had been busy over the last few days, and had already made quick work of removing the remains of one end of the street, carting them away. They were still working on the opposite side of the street, though that hadn't burned quite as badly as the other. As he headed along the street, the foreman noticed him and stiffened, but Finn continued past him, ignoring him. He paused at the building Sweth had occupied.

Not owned.

It was burned, like all of the others, though there was something about it that was a little bit different. As Finn looked in either direction of the street, he realized that his initial impression had been wrong.

He'd believed that the street had burned from one end

forward, but now as he stood there, looking along the street, he had a different impression. Maybe it was wrong. Finn wasn't a master in fires, but it seemed to him that the fire would burn hottest where it originated, and it would burn down the farther it went from there. The fire brigade had saved one end of the street, but of course they had. That end of the street was closer to the central sections of the city. It was closer to wealth.

The other end of the street was closer to the outer sections of the city and farther from those with any sort of money. Finn stood in place, looking in either direction, and began to realize that he had been wrong.

Sweth was guilty.

The fire had started there.

Why would it have started in Sweth's home?

Better yet, why would Sweth have started the fire at all?

Finn stared, troubled by not knowing, but also troubled by the fact it seemed to him there was something more taking place than what he had determined so far. Maybe it was little more than the fact that Sweth had denied having a hand in it and had misled Finn, but it seemed to him that there was something more. He needed answers.

It meant he was going to have to keep questioning Sweth.

As Finn turned, heading back along the street, he paused at the foreman.

"What now?"

Finn frowned at him. "When you get to this one," he

said, pulling out the map, and pointing to the house with the name Fol on it, "I want you to work around it."

"Why that one?"

"Because it looks to me like the fire originated there."

"That right? Didn't realize the executioner was such an expert in fire."

Finn frowned at him. "If you find anything in the buildings nearby…"

"You want me to send word?"

"That would be helpful; otherwise, I don't really want to have to bring you for questioning."

The foreman stiffened again. "I'll tell you whatever I find. Just leave my boys alone."

Finn looked over to the men cleaning up the debris. If anyone was a boy, it would've been the foreman, not the other men. They were all much larger than him, but Finn nodded nonetheless. "I'm just looking for answers. That's it. I know you're here on a job, and doing what you've been told to do, so just work with me, if you would."

The foreman nodded back.

Finn pulled up the map, stuffing it into his pocket, and he paused at the end of the street. Sweth was guilty, but now he needed to figure out why. It was past time that things started making sense.

CHAPTER SIXTEEN

Finn sat at the table in the kitchen, lantern resting next to him. He checked off the list of names. Each one represented a person who owned property on the street, and each one that he had confirmed still lived. It had taken him the better part of a day to chase down all of those leads, but thankfully there were still enough people in the Jorend section who knew where many of the people had gone. They also knew whether or not many of the people had survived.

For the most part, Finn had first- or secondhand accounts of survival. So far, he had eight names that were unaccounted for, and eight people—including Fol, the name on the house where Sweth had lived—where he still didn't know if they lived or not.

"What are you doing?"

Finn looked up to his sister. She had on a thick white cotton nightgown, her hair pulled back in a bow, and looked tired. She must've been up with Mother. "I'm trying to figure out how many people died in this fire."

"I heard it was a dozen." Lena shrugged. "You know how rumors can be, though. It's probably not nearly that many."

"I have eight names of people from the street I haven't accounted for."

"That's still quite a few," she said.

"It is," he said.

"Why are you trying to figure out how many people died?" She asked, looking down at the map and then the sheet of paper with the names listed on it. "If you have the man responsible, does it matter?"

"It's not just about having the man responsible," Finn said. "I need to understand why he did this. I need to know *who* died."

Lena watched him. "Some people like fire. I know it sounds strange, but I've known a few people who like fire. They like to see things burn."

"I never would've thought that people like to watch things burn before." He looked up, shaking his head. "Before working with Meyer, I never would've thought that people would enjoy watching others suffer like that."

"I imagine you've seen some terrible things."

"Quite a few," he said.

"How is she?" Finn asked, flicking his gaze toward the door and then up the stairs.

"She's been fine," she said softly.

"Just fine?"

Lena shrugged, rubbing both of her temples with her

middle fingers, breathing slowly. "At least I have her to care for."

"What is that supposed to mean?"

"It means that with Mother here, I have some reason to remain."

Finn started to smile, but his sister looked down at her hands, now clasp on the table. "You have a reason to be here."

"Do I? I'm here because of you. Gods, Mother is here because of you. I suppose we should be thankful to Master Meyer, but I can't help feel as if we're imposing. When is he going to demand we leave?"

Finn shook his head. He didn't know if Master Meyer would ever demand that they leave. For that matter, Master Meyer hadn't said anything about Finn leaving until after he was a journeyman.

"I'm saving up my earnings," he said.

"That's well enough for you, but what about me?"

Lena held his gaze, and there was a pained look in her eyes.

"I'm saving them for the family," he said.

"Family," she muttered, shaking her head. "I haven't found anything more for your patient. I thought if I could, then maybe it would work for Mother, but…"

Finn had shared the same thought, so he wasn't surprised Lena would as well.

"I used to think that I would find some man to marry and he would bring me out of our section. As I got older, and Mother grew sicker, I started to wonder if maybe I could just find some man." She shook her head.

"Is that sad? I stopped wanting to even leave our section."

"I don't know if it's sad or not," he said.

"*Practical*," she said. "And that's what's become of me. Practicality. I suppose that has served me well. It lets me keep Mother alive, so there is that."

"Master Meyer is helping with that, isn't he?"

Lena looked up briefly before looking back down. "He's helping."

"What is it?"

"Nothing. I don't mean to be unthankful."

"I don't think anybody claims you are."

"They don't need to claim it. I feel it. I understand what he's done for our family, Finn. If it weren't for him, I..." She shook her head. "I know what would've happened. I know what would have become of you. So, I have him to thank. And for Mother as well."

"She's going to get better," Finn said.

"Is she?" She got up, turning to the stove, and began to gather things. "I used to think she would get better, and when we first came here, she did, at least for a little while. I didn't know if that was the hegen magic, or if that was Master Meyer, but either way, I was thankful for it. Then I started to wonder. She got a little bit better but not all the way."

"It just needs time," Finn said.

"Time." Lena shook her head. "What is time but a way of saying that she's going to dwindle?"

"Lena..."

She looked over her shoulder. "When she's gone, I

don't know if I can stay here any longer. At least with her here, sick as she is, it gives me a reason to stay."

"I don't think Master Meyer intends for you to leave."

"He might not have said it, but I'm sure he doesn't want us here. He had to move so much out of the room for me to stay there. Every so often, I still find a few things from his daughter."

Finn had only caught a glimpse when Lena had taken over the room, but enough to know that Meyer's daughter had once occupied it. He'd given it up to Lena and their mother without complaint. If only he could get Master Meyer to talk about it.

"I'm sure he doesn't mind," Finn said softly.

"Did he ever tell you what happened?"

"No."

"I wondered." She paused where she had been rolling out dough, resting her hands on the counter. Flour coated her fingertips. "It looked like she was young. I wonder what happened."

"It's not the kind of thing that Meyer would talk about."

"I suppose not."

Finn got to his feet, looking down at the map again, memorizing the names. Eight more. If he could find what happened with those eight, Finn thought he might be able to get a little closer to having answers. At this point, that was what he wanted more than anything else. He wanted to know that there were answers available for this particular crime. He had no idea what extent to be concerned about Sweth's crimes. It might only be what he said. He was in the wrong place at the wrong time, but the more Finn uncovered, the more he began to fear that he actually was guilty of the crime.

"And what happens if you finish this?" Lena asked, looking over her shoulder to where Finn studied the map in the pages.

"When this one is done, I suspect there will be another one."

"Isn't there always?"

Finn smiled. "In a city the size of Verendal, there's always something taking place."

"He's been gone a lot."

"Master Meyer?" That might be why Meyer had let Finn work on finding an answer for Moira.

Lena nodded. "I don't know where he's gone, and figured he was with you, but it looks like you've been doing your own thing."

"I'm leading this investigation."

"That should make you proud."

Finn smiled slightly. "I'm not so sure if it makes me proud or if it makes me nervous." He chuckled. "I have been digging, trying to make sure I get this right. I worry that if I don't, Master Meyer will be disappointed."

"I doubt it. If you don't get it right, he's going to give you another opportunity to figure it out."

"I don't know about that," Finn said.

Everything was a progression. Meyer had made that clear. It had been that way from the very beginning. First he had to prove himself to Master Meyer. Then he had to

254 | D.K. HOLMBERG

prove himself to the king. Then he had to prove himself to the executioner court.

Now that he was a full apprentice, he was having to prove himself to Master Meyer again.

"What would happen if you failed?"

He shook his head. "To be honest, I don't really know. Maybe nothing. It might just be that he has me take more time before he gives me more responsibility."

"But you don't think that's the case."

"I don't know if that's the case," Finn said. He folded up the map, sticking into his pocket, and took the list of names and held onto it. There was something to it. He wasn't at all sure what it was, but the answer seemed close at hand. All Finn had to do was figure out how many of those names still lived. Then...

Then he had to think he could keep digging.

Only they didn't have that much time remaining.

The magister and the jurors limited how much time they had, which meant that Finn had to work quickly. That was part of the test; he was certain of it. Meyer wanted to see if Finn could work on a deadline. If he failed, it wouldn't be him swinging this time but possibly Sweth. Increasingly, Finn thought that he had the truth of the matter, and thought that Sweth was guilty of something, but he didn't know whether or not he was guilty of the crime he'd been accused of.

"I can see you're preoccupied."

"No. I'm not too preoccupied," Finn said.

Lena smiled at him. She returned to rolling out her dough. "You need to focus, and I should focus. I want to get this bread baking before Mother wakes again. Then dig through a few more of his books to see what I can find. I *will* find something, Finn."

"I could help with the baking, then we can work together."

Lena shook her head. "Not with this. Let me do that much, at least."

Finn wished there was something more that he could say to assist her, some way for him to offer her a little bit of reassurance, but he didn't think there was anything.

Besides, she was right. He *was* preoccupied.

As he stepped in the hall, Meyer's door opened, and he looked out at Finn. "Come in here."

Finn looked back to his sister before turning toward Master Meyer and following him into his office. He realized that Master Meyer wasn't alone.

There was a younger man there, maybe ten years older than Finn, with bright red hair, pale skin, and a strangely blotchy complexion. One leg rested propped up on the cot, clearly misshapen.

"What happened?" Finn asked, hurrying over to the man.

He shook his head. "I done fell from the rooftop," he said.

"What rooftop?" He glanced from the man to Master Meyer. For an obvious injury, the man managed to hold himself together fairly well. It would be incredibly painful. This kind of thing was straightforward enough that Finn knew what to do. It involved aligning the bones, stabilizing them, and making sure there wasn't any puncture through the skin. If there were, something like that would get infected quickly.

"Does it matter?"

Finn glanced over Master Meyer, and he shook his head. Was there something about what happened that he didn't want to reveal?

"What do you need my help with?"

"I need you to help me stabilize this," Meyer said.

"I'm happy to," Finn said. He took a position at the end of the cot, and he grabbed the man's foot. "Have you given him anything to ease the pain?"

Meyer held Finn's gaze. "What would you choose?"

"There are a few options. Oil of poppy might be the easiest, and certainly effective, though it might make him too sleepy."

"Nothing makes me too sleepy," the man said. "I can drink three mugs of ale and still stay on my feet."

Finn liked the man. This was the kind of person that he would've enjoyed chatting with at the Wenderwolf back when he was still in the crew.

"Only three?" Finn asked.

"You think you can do more?"

"There was a time when I could've had five mugs of ale and stayed standing," Finn said.

"Five? Maybe when I was a child, but most of the time, I tried to keep it less than eight. Gets too expensive, otherwise."

Finn started pulling on the leg as he was talking to him, noticing Master Meyer gathering supplies behind him.

"When I used to run the streets, I thought the same way. You have to just find the right place. You get in good with the tavern owner, they don't charge you quite as much."

"No. They get you in other ways."

Finn started to laugh, pulling softly on the man's leg. "I didn't catch your name."

"Seamus Sullivan."

"Seamus, I'm Finn Jagger. I work with Master Meyer here."

"I didn't know the hangman liked to drink."

"I don't think he does," Finn said without looking over to Master Meyer. "But I'm still young."

"Hey, there," Seamus said. "Did you hear that, hangman? He's calling you old."

"I *am* old," Master Meyer said.

Finn continue to pull. Seamus hadn't jumped or jerked, and having seen the vial of oil next to the cot, Finn knew that Meyer had given the man something to ease the pain. Whatever it was had taken off the edge enough that Seamus no longer struggled.

"How far did you walk to get here?"

"I made it three sections. I figured it was either the hangman or a surgeon. Damn surgeons can be tough to find. They stay in the dodgy parts of the city."

"Dodgy?" Seamus didn't strike him as high-class, especially not with him bragging about how much he had to drink, but maybe he had read him wrong.

"You know the type. You said you ran the streets?"

"It's been awhile," Finn said.

"What did you do… wait. I heard about you." Seamus looked over to Meyer. "Heard when you took an apprentice. Said he survived hanging and drowning?"

"Really?" Meyer said.

"Can't say that I believed it," Seamus said. "Only that the stories were that you survived something no man has before. Maybe having a man like you around would give me luck." He grinned, and Finn just shook his head.

"Why do you need luck?"

"Look at my damn leg," he said.

Finn continued pulling on the leg, drawing it down, but knowing he needed to work carefully and quickly in order to do so. Meyer held on to his makeshift splint, and it wouldn't be much longer before he was ready for Finn to finish with traction, and when he did, then Meyer would place the splint.

"What exactly happened to you?" Finn asked.

"Can't say that I remember. Told you I'd been drinking."

"How much had you to drink?"

"I had… ow! What was that?"

Finn pulled just enough that he had popped the leg into alignment.

"That was me finishing this," Finn said. He looked up, holding the man's gaze for a moment. "Now we just have to put a splint on."

Meyer braced the leg with the pieces of wood that he had for just such a purpose, and then began to wrap cloth around it. "You're going to need to keep this in place for the next month. If you pull it off before it heals, it's possible you'll end up losing the leg."

"That's what the damn surgeons tried to tell me," Seamus said.

"They weren't wrong," Meyer said.

"Not wrong, but they wanted to cut right away. You know surgeons. They figure they can't do anything but cut."

"I suspect they warned you that if you were to walk on this too much, you would find that you will end up losing it anyway."

"How am I supposed to get around without walking?"

"Carefully," Meyer said.

"Carefully," he scoffed, glancing over to Finn. "Says the man who don't drink. You have a few ales in you, and you can't help but stumble."

"Then stay in one place," Meyer said. He headed over to his cabinet, pulling out two wooden crutches made of a faded and twisted wood. "You may use these. I expect them back when you are finished."

"What's all of this going to cost me?"

"For the healing, supplies, medicines, I'll take two silvers."

"Gah!" Seamus waved his hand. "Two silvers. Still cheaper than the damn surgeon would've been if he had taken the leg. You know he wanted to take the thing off up to here?" He pointed to his knee. "The break was way down there."

"Just be careful with that," Meyer said. He went over to

the cabinet, grabbing a few supplies before handing it over to Seamus. "You might need this. For pain."

"Why would I need anything more for pain? Didn't you take care of me?"

"We set the bone. We straightened it. Now it's up to the injury to heal. It's usually pretty painful for the first few days. I can't promise that you'll be able to sleep well for the first few days, but in time, you'll do fine."

Seamus shuffled off to the side of the bed, and he took the crutches, wobbling for a moment. "Seems like it's going to work just fine, hangman."

Meyer guided him out of the house, out the back door, and then when he returned, he glanced over to Finn. "That was very good work."

"I didn't do much other than set the bone."

"You distracted him. That's a skill that not all learn. Too many people feel they need to be aggressive, such as it is. You do need appropriate tension, but too much and you find you can actually hurt the person you're trying to help." Meyer shrugged. "In this case, I think he probably didn't feel much anyway. He'd been drinking long before he came to me."

"I don't know if I've ever had enough to drink that I fell off a roof."

"You would have, were you sneaking around the way he had been."

"He's a thief?"

Meyer took a seat at his desk, opened a book, and began to make a note. "A thief, but not one who advertises that status very well. You noticed how he deflected anytime you asked too many questions."

"He didn't really deflect. He just chose not to answer."

"That is deflecting."

"Where was he breaking in?"

"There was a building in the Nethel section he fell from."

"Did he tell you?"

"Not so much. I got a report from one of the Archers that someone was spotted, and then about a half an hour later, he showed up." Meyer shrugged. "I figure it's too unlikely to be coincidence."

"What do you think he was up to?"

"I can't say I have the answer to that," Meyer said. "And I'm not so sure it matters. Hopefully, he'll have learned his lesson."

Finn chuckled. "If he's working for a crew, there's no lesson to be learned. He got away with whatever he was up to."

"He may have gotten away with it, but he didn't come away unscathed. There's a difference."

Finn just shrugged. He took a seat on the cot, looking over to Master Meyer. "I am starting to think Sweth is guilty."

"You're starting to think that?"

"I'm not so sure; it's just..." Finn shook his head. "It's just that I don't have any other explanation."

"Does that trouble you?"

Finn breathed out heavily, looking around the inside of the office. He hadn't spent that much time there.

Master Meyer might work with him, but he didn't often include Finn with his healing. It was a wonder that he had this time, though it wasn't the first. He had included Finn with Moira, even though Finn had not been able to help her. Yet. He was determined to find some answer for her. He had delayed her, but eventually...

"I think it troubles me I didn't see it at first."

"Why is that?" Meyer looked up at him, his hands resting on either side of the table, and he hadn't said much.

"I guess I wanted to believe him."

"What does that show you?"

"I guess it shows me I need to question more."

"One of the lessons I learned early on was that men are willing to tell you whatever they think you want to hear. The challenge we face is deciding what we need to hear. More than that, the challenge is deciding what we should pay attention to."

"I still don't even know if he's guilty or not, just that I'm starting to suspect it."

"We don't have much time remaining for you to come to terms with whether or not he is guilty, Finn."

"I know." He pulled out the slip of paper. "I have a list of names of people who've been missing." He held it out, and Master Meyer's gaze slipped along it before looking up at him. "Not that it matters. I suspect arson by itself is a punishable-enough crime for what took place, but with this..."

"You're trying to justify what needs to happen."

"I'm not even trying to justify it. I'm just trying to figure out what I think needs to happen."

Meyer smiled at him. "You do well to investigate it, but sometimes you need to know when to stop looking and to start paying attention to what you've already uncovered."

"What is that, then?"

"That will be for you to determine."

Meyer turned his attention back to the book, and Finn left him.

He headed to his room, taking a seat, and stared at the map. Between the map, the number of dead, and what Sweth had been accused of, Finn needed answers, though he felt as if the answer was just beyond his understanding.

He was going to have to question more, but how?

CHAPTER SEVENTEEN

S weth didn't cry out nearly as much today. Finn had used a little bit of fire ash that he had acquired from Wella, applying it to the end of one of the metal rods, trying to uncover answers, though Sweth was stubborn enough that he refused to provide them.

"All I need is little bit more information," Finn said. "Do you know anything about them?"

Finn had read off the names of the missing. He had narrowed it down to six that he hadn't found any answers to, including the mysterious Fol. Whoever owned that property didn't appear.

"I told you. I didn't know anybody on the street. I'd only lived there for a little while."

"You said that a few times," Finn said, nodding to him and crouching down in front of him. "Why don't you and I talk about that little bit more. What brought you to the Jorend section?"

"I needed a place to stay. It was available."

"Did you know the owner? A Mr. or Mrs. Fol?"

"Don't know who I rented from. I just needed a place to stay."

He had hesitated just a moment, long enough that Finn knew there was more to it.

"Tell me more about where you were before you came to Jorend."

"Why does it even matter?"

Finn smiled tightly at him. "Consider me curious. It matters."

"I hadn't been there long."

"Where in the city were you before?"

He hesitated, and Finn took one of the metal rods, dipped it in the fire ash, and pressed it into his leg.

Sweth screamed this time.

"I was in Yelind!"

Finn froze.

That wasn't even in the kingdom. They were to the south and had warred with the kingdom over the years, though there had been peace recently.

"What were you doing here? What brought you to Verendal?"

"I needed to get away. Is that so bad?"

"It wouldn't be if I believed you," Finn said.

"I just came for steady work. I lost…"

"You lost what?"

Sweth looked up. His eyes had a haunted expression in them that couldn't only be from what Finn did to him.

"My family."

Finn swallowed. Was he telling the truth? "You could have been a scribe anywhere. You came to Verendal for a reason."

Sweth held his gaze. "Not in Yelind. Not after…"

Finn wanted him to say more. "Are you really a scribe?"

"I worked for Johan. What do you think?" he muttered.

If he *was* a scribe, why would someone from Yelind end up in the kingdom?

There were always rumors of skirmishes between the kingdom and Yelind, fighting for land or the iron found in the south, that came with merchants who dared travel between the two lands.

"Why didn't you want me to know why you were from Yelind?"

He looked up. "I know how you people view mine."

"Did you start the fire?"

He looked down.

"It started in your home. Tell me what brought you to the city?"

"The chance to start over. That's all!"

Finn took another rod and dipped it in fire ash. Could it be some plan to attack the city?

Not with somebody like him. There was no reason for that.

He was a scribe.

Wasn't he?

Finn probed, pushing another rod through his leg, listening to Sweth scream. He tried to ignore it, but there was no ignoring the agony in his voice.

"Were you here to hurt people from the kingdom?" Finn asked. "Did you intend to kill these people?"

The scream of the person he hadn't saved came back to him. That and the memory of smoke and heat that had prevented him from doing anything.

"I didn't start the fire," Sweth said.

Finn caught the catch in his denial.

"I only wish I could believe you. Until you tell me what I need to know, I will keep at this."

Finn pulled the chair from the far side of the room over, sitting in front of Sweth. Sweat dripped down from Sweth's brow, and tears streamed from his cheeks. His jaw clenched, as if he were trying to bite back the pain Finn subjected him to.

When he had questions about Sweth's innocence, it had been harder for him to use these techniques, but learning that he might have involvement, Finn found it increasingly easy for him to carry it out.

At this point, he wanted the answer so he could end this investigation. He grew tired of digging into Sweth's involvement in the fire, but knew that he needed to wrap it up in an acceptable way that provided answers and would then provide a satisfying solution to what had taken place.

"What happened to your family?"

He shook his head.

"If that's what you want." He started to reach out with a rod when Sweth shook his head.

"They died. An accident. That's all it was. I wanted to get away."

"And you came to Verendal? There are easier places to go in Yelind." Finn didn't know Yelind, but he couldn't imagine crossing the border would be easy.

"Because that was the work," he said.

"Your work, or that of king of Yelind?"

"I told you—"

The door came open, and Finn looked over to say something to whichever of the iron masters popped their head in, but it wasn't any of them. Instead, it was Master Meyer.

He was dressed in his more formal jacket and pants, and he glanced from Finn to the jar of fire ash and to Sweth, an unreadable expression on his face. "Bring him."

"What's going on?" Finn asked.

"It's time."

"Time? I haven't gotten the information I needed."

Meyer held something out. It was a blackened object, though it looked something like a lantern, though not any lantern that Finn had ever seen before. "This was found in his home."

"What is it?" It looked something like a bucket, though it had been burned, leaving only a hint of a handle. The shape was strange, slightly oblong, and it had a terrible stench to it.

"A fire starter. At least, that's what all who have examined it feel it is. Found by the crews cleaning the city."

"So..."

"So he is to be sentenced."

"We don't know everything." Finn lowered his voice, leaning toward Meyer. "He's from Yelind."

"It doesn't matter where he's from."

"What if he's here for some nefarious reason?"

"He is to be sentenced," Meyer said.

Finn sighed. He wanted to argue, but at this point, he didn't feel as if he could even do that.

"Given the nature of the crime, and how many have perished, we are to expedite this."

"You're disappointed in me," Finn said.

"I'm not disappointed. You've done what I asked. You've done *more* than what I asked, in fact."

"But I haven't gotten a confession out of him."

"We have enough evidence to convict," Master Meyer said.

Finn was conflicted. While he agreed that they had enough evidence to convict Sweth, there was some part of it that left him unsettled. Maybe it was just his inability to get a confession out of Sweth. He felt as if he had let Master Meyer down.

He removed the cuffs from Sweth's ankles, setting them back on the counter. He pulled the rods out and cleaned them, setting them neatly into place as well. He left the fire ash, thinking that if he were to need it again in the future, at least it would be there. There didn't seem to be much other purpose in something like that, regardless of what Wella might claim. When he was done, he unstrapped Sweth and motioned for him to follow.

"What now?" Sweth asked.

"Now we're going to go."

"Who was that?"

"The master executioner."

Sweth glanced from Finn to Meyer's back. "The master executioner. What are you?"

"His apprentice."

Sweth started to laugh. "Here I thought I was dealing with the real executioner."

There was a hardness in his voice that Finn hadn't expected. It was almost as if Sweth were taunting him. Finn grabbed him, guiding him forward.

One of the iron masters was there, an older iron master by the name of Grady, with a bulbous nose, wide-set eyes, and close-cropped hair. "You need me to bring him back to his cell?" Grady asked.

"No. We're to escort him to City Hall."

Grady glared at Sweth. "Good. It's about time. Bastard killed thirty people."

"It was no more than six," Finn said.

"Still. That's enough. Bastard like that deserves to hang. Maybe worse."

Was that what they were going to have to do?

He didn't want to consider the various possibilities of what the jurors might sentence him to. Certainly not an honorable death. He wouldn't die by the sword. There had been a few of those in the time since Finn had served with Master Meyer, and he always kept the sword Justice gleaming and sharp for just that purpose, but it was rare. Most got the rope. There had been no other exotic executions, though from Finn's reading, he knew there were other sentences. He'd read about quartering, though had never even seen it in Verendal. He had once seen someone accused of witchcraft burned to death, though that was rare enough. It was strange, especially now that he knew about the hegen, but perhaps it was the form of witchcraft that mattered. And then there was the one time when somebody was sentenced to die by drowning. They used the river for it, and he remembered it only because he had been young enough that he had tried to avoid watching, but there had been a crowd near their home, and he had no other choice but to go around it, and had caught a fleeting glimpse of the drowning.

Meyer walked with Finn, each of them keeping an arm on Sweth. Given what Finn had done during his questioning, there was little chance that he was going to run. Finn remembered just how badly it hurt with the braces around the ankles, and having rods shoved through his calf made it so he would be even less likely to run.

As they approached City Hall, Sweth started to slow. Finn jerked him forward, and Meyer glanced over.

"What happens in here?" Sweth asked.

"You have an opportunity to speak on your behalf," Meyer said.

"What about you?"

"We are to present our findings to the jurors," Meyer said.

"Findings? I didn't say anything!"

"It's what you didn't say," Meyer said.

It was more than that, but even that might not matter. At this point, the only thing that mattered was getting enough information about what Sweth had done, and whatever role he might've had in the fire, and then...

Then he had to convince the jurors.

They both did.

Finn wanted more time, though he had seen the jurors push like this a few other times. It was uncommon, but in cases like this, particularly in cases where there was a question that felt like a public need, there was more of an urgency to the sentencing.

In this case, it felt like there was an incredible urgency.

They guided him into City Hall and into the jurors' chamber. Not all of the jurors had arrived. Several of them had, and Isabel, Horace, and Barth glanced from Finn and Meyer to the prisoner.

"Where's the magister?" Finn asked.

"He will be here," Isabel said.

The others came and took a seat, including Bellut. When he arrived, he glared at Finn for a long moment before settling his gaze on the prisoner. "We may begin," Bellut said.

"We should wait for the magister," Horace said.

"He sent word that he was preoccupied. He trusted the jurors to make a decision in his stead. He has made sure to provide some guidance."

Finn glanced to Bellut. In the times that he'd been coming to the jurors' chamber, this was the first time the magister hadn't been involved in a sentencing. As the leading legal scholar from the university, he was considered the representative for the king, the one person who could offer guidance as to the rule of the law.

"Begin," Bellut said.

"This is a bit unusual," Horace said.

"Unusual or not, the accused stands before us having

burned an entire section of the city to the ground. Should we wait for the magister?" Bellut swept his gaze along the line of jurors. "We have many people who've died in that fire. Rumors are that there were at least a dozen—"

"No more than six," Finn said.

Bellut turned his attention to Finn, glaring. "Six? That stands in disagreement with my reports."

Finn bit back the irritation he had. He couldn't say anything to Bellut openly, but he *could* defy him. "I can show you the map of the street, along with the people who lived there. I have taken reports from almost everyone on the street, and have accounted for all but six."

"Still," Bellut said, as if annoyed it were only that many. "Six lives. Lost because of this man."

"I didn't kill anyone," Sweth said.

Finn glanced over, shaking his head. "You should be quiet," he whispered.

"They don't have all of the information."

There was something odd about the way he said it.

Bellut chuckled. He had a narrow face and thin lips, and Finn despised looking at him. Still, as he was one of the jurors and sat at the behest of the king, serving the viscount, Finn still had an obligation to answer to him.

"Whatever information you feel we need is unnecessary." Bellut looked at the others seated at the table with him before turning his attention to Meyer. "What can you report?"

Meyer nodded. "What I can report is that we've gathered information. My apprentice will present for you."

Bellut turned his irritated gaze on Finn, and Finn

made a point of ignoring it, focusing instead on Isabel to keep from paying attention to him. She was dark-haired, older, and stern in appearance.

Finn stepped forward. "I was tasked with the investigation into the fire. I've found evidence of the fire originating in the residence of David Sweth." Finn glanced over Meyer. "There has been additional evidence of some sort of fire-starting device there." He turned to Sweth. "He had only been in the Jorend section for a few months."

"A few months?" Horace asked. "Where was he before?"

"As far as I know, he came from Yelind." There was a gentle murmuring from the others around him, and Finn looked at them. "He was reluctant to admit that."

"That seals it," Horace said.

"He must've been sent by those bastards. Yelind has been unstable recently. There have been skirmishes along the border. They've been making a play for our silver," Isabel said.

"Skirmishes?" Bellut asked.

"I received word from my caravans of the same," Horace went on. As head of the merchant guild, he would have access others didn't. "Typically, they're unrestricted, but trade has been challenging. Yelind has decided to take action."

"They wouldn't attack the kingdom," Bethany said.

She was a little bit younger than Isabel, but had just as stern an expression. Maybe she wasn't like that outside of the jurors' chamber, but she had always seemed irritable when she was here.

"Who is to say?" Horace asked. "They likely believe the kingdom is distracted, and unfortunately, we've been lately."

"The situation with the Alainsith has been settled," Bethany went on. "I have it on good authority—"

"Whose authority?" Barton asked.

"Never you mind," Bethany went on.

Finn found himself staring at Bellut, and for the first time since they came to the chamber, Bellut ignored him, looking instead at Sweth.

When Finn had dealt with Bellut as the Client, he'd known he was responsible for setting up the crimes, and attacking the palace, and trying to instigate conflict between the kingdom and the Alainsith. But not alone.

Could he have been working with Sweth?

A fire like the one in Jorend could be dangerous to the whole city.

Finn had to keep rational. Destroying the city hadn't been what Bellut had wanted. He'd gone after the king and had intended to disrupt the Alainsith treaty. Finn didn't know why, and the search for answers in Jorend had kept him away from looking deeper.

"We need to vote," Horace said.

"This one will be very straightforward," Isabel said.

"I concur. Perhaps we didn't need the magister here for that."

"Not for something like this. Of course not," Bellut said.

Finn glanced from one to the other, feeling a growing uncertainty.

Finally, they turned back, and Bellut leaned forward. "The jurors have decided. According to the laws of the city of Verendal and the demands of King Porman, we of the jurors declare you guilty of the crime of arson in the Jorend section. You are guilty of the crime of killing at least six people through the fires in the Jorend section. And you will be sentenced to die by fire."

Finn looked over to Sweth. He had an unreadable expression on his face, though it seemed to be one of acceptance, as if he had known this was coming.

The jurors all got to their feet. Meyer motioned for Finn to follow, and they guided Sweth out of the chamber. They were quiet the entire walk back to Declan, and quiet as Finn guided him into the cells, where the iron managers took possession of him again, and quiet when Finn returned, rejoining Master Meyer outside of the prison.

"Have you had many sentences like that?"

Meyer shook his head. "Not many. In this case, I suspect it's probably fitting, but that doesn't change the difficulty of it."

"Fitting?"

"This will be a bit more challenging to prepare. I will source the necessary lumber for the pyre and walk you through the process."

"I thought you said we should be after justice and not vengeance."

"That is what the law demands."

"This seems like it's vengeance."

"I think it is meant as a deterrent."

Finn could see the troubled look on Master Meyer's face.

"This is the end of this, Finn. The investigation is over. It's time to get back to your studies."

"I could—"

"No. You can't."

That was all there was to it. Despite how Finn might feel otherwise.

He couldn't keep looking.

It was like a punch to the gut. Meyer made it clear he couldn't keep at it. If he did, Finn suspected he knew what would happen. Meyer would not be pleased.

He and Meyer went separate ways, and Finn debated where he needed to go, though carrying out a sentence like this was not one he knew all of the steps involved. If he were to help build the pyre, he would have to stay with Master Meyer, making sure they had all the supplies necessary in order to carry out all steps of it.

He once again found himself drawn to the Jorend section. He caught sight of another figure dressed in a crimson cloak, the color of the king, and with a balding head and glasses.

The magister.

When he saw Finn, there was a flash of recognition.

He didn't necessarily want to chat with the magister, but at the same time, if he didn't know that Finn had seen him, it would come across as awkward.

He caught up to the magister.

"The apprentice," he said, glancing past Finn. "I understand Sweth has been sentenced. We have a man guilty, we have enough evidence to convict, and we will be carrying out his sentence. Perhaps a little harsher than I would have chosen but no more undeserved." He seemed disappointed more than anything else. "The king's law makes it clear that sentences can be determined by those affected. It's rare that we carry out such extreme sentences, but when we do so, it is typically for cases like this. You think of how many lives it disrupted, and because of that, you can only imagine how the families of the affected would feel."

"I can only imagine," Finn agreed.

"Indeed," he said. "The fire was bad enough, but seeing as how many were killed..." The magister shook his head, looking down at the ground. The section was empty today, but the air still stunk of the charred fire that had burned through here. "Such a sad way to go."

"That's the way Sweth is going to go."

"And one would say it is deserved."

"One would say."

He smiled at Finn, somehow making it look almost friendly. "Tell me, Mr. Jagger. Have you settled into your apprenticeship well?"

"I have settled in as well as I can."

"It must be quite the transition from where you started."

"A bit," Finn said.

"I myself can understand what it's like to have a transition like that. When I was younger, I transitioned away from my home."

"Oh? Where was that?"

"I wasn't always from Verendal," he said. He glanced over to the church of Heleth visible in the distance, then his gaze drifted to the palace. "But I found myself drawn to the university, where I studied. I was a historian, by training, but I also began to become something of a scholar at law, and given the king's predilection for scholars, I found a calling."

Why was he telling Finn this?

"Where were you before the university?"

"Many places." He smiled sadly. "If you don't mind, I only came to see the destruction for myself. I should have done so sooner, but..."

The magister didn't have to explain. Finn suspected he was superstitious like so many.

"I have more of my investigation to complete, anyway."

"Another investigation?"

Finn held his gaze. "I'm still not complete with this one."

"I thought we had our man and we had a conviction. The people want closure, Mr. Jagger. If you continue pushing..." Finn had to drop it or he'd anger the magister. The magister smiled sadly. "Though if you uncover anything that will be of any use to us, please pass it on."

A bit of relief swept through him. "I will do as I'm expected."

"But do not dig too deeply."

The relief faded as the magister left him.

Finn watched the street after him, no answers coming. He had to be ready. He had to finish with the task ahead of him, help Meyer with the sentencing, and he still had to deal with Wolf.

All while trying to make sure Bellut faced his own justice.

It would be easier if Master Meyer were a part of it, but he had shown no interest in participating. Which meant it truly was up to Finn.

CHAPTER EIGHTEEN

Finn was running out of time to get any more answers.

With Sweth's planned sentencing, he felt as if there remained too much unresolved.

He had a list of names. That was it. None of those living along the street were involved; Finn was certain of it. Even the feuding families had reconciled when they'd seen how much each person had lost. There was no residual anger there.

The only thing he had left was the developer.

Which was where Finn headed now.

It was unusually cool, with the wind gusting through the streets, carrying with it a hint of an early fall. Despite that, an uneasy pall hung over everything. The developer's building was in the heart of the Ghislan section, situated on the opposite edge of the river, and on Porman's Path, heading toward the palace.

All he needed was to ask a few questions.

Finn found the street the foreman had indicated, and he picked his way slowly and carefully, sweeping his gaze on either side of the street. Most of the buildings there were multiple stories tall, all of them with fresh paint, and many with walled yards. In some parts of the city, that was an impossible luxury, but there, it was common. Finn had to look for a horse surrounded by a circle, standing on a strange platform. At least, that was what the foreman had said.

When he found it, Finn knew it was the right shop.

It was a massive two-story building and took up the end of the block. Enormous arched windows let light in, and even the door was incredibly ornate, with brass worked into the outline of the developer's crest. Given that it was late enough, Finn knocked rather than just trying to enter the shop.

He stepped back, waiting.

It wasn't long before the door came open, and a mousy brown-haired woman in a black gown and pale white apron tied in front frowned at him. Thin lips pressed together, and she sniffed, leaving Finn to wonder if he was foul-smelling from his time in Declan. "May I help you?"

"I'm looking for Master Benson, the proprietor," Finn said.

"And who may I ask is calling?"

"My name is Finn Jagger, executioner for the king."

Her eyes widened, and she let go of the door, taking a step back. "No. He didn't—"

"I am not here for him. I'm here to ask a few questions

regarding the case that I am investigating."

Relief swept across her face.

Could the developer have been involved?

"You may come in, Mr. Jagger," she said.

Finn nodded and stepped into the entryway. As soon as he did, a floral fragrance filled his nose. Two massive ceramic vases set on pedestals were on either side of the hall, filled with flowers. Other decorations lined the hall, including another pair of vases with flowers filling, and portraits that looked to be older men, seeming as if they stared across the hall at each other.

"Where is Master Benson?" Finn asked.

"I will let him know you're here. He will be with you shortly," she said.

He just nodded. The woman slipped off down the hall, disappeared into a doorway, and was gone for only a few moments before a portly older man tottered out, leaning on a cane.

He had a wide face, heavy jowls, and a thin line of a beard. "May I help you?"

"Master Benson, I presume?"

The man nodded, looking up at Finn. "Are you here to question me?"

"I only have a few questions for you," Finn clarified. "I'm looking into the fires in Jorend."

The man's eyes widened. "I see. I understand they caught the one responsible."

"Possibly," Finn said.

"Only *possibly*?" He shook his head. "It was my understanding he is to be sentenced soon."

Had word already started to spread about Sweth's sentencing?

"He has been sentenced," Finn agreed.

"Then I fail to understand the reason for your visit, Mr. Jagger. I apologize for my ignorance, but I am simply trying to understand what you might need from me."

"I'm responsible for investigating all aspects of the case," he said. There was a part of Finn that worried how Meyer would react if he knew that Finn were still digging. Maybe Meyer would understand, but Finn couldn't help wonder if perhaps he would not. He had been the one to escort Sweth to the sentencing, after all, and the way that Meyer had made a point of telling Finn to let it go had been clear.

"Is there an aspect that remains unresolved?"

"Do you have someplace else that we can visit?"

Master Benson watched Finn. "Do we need to?"

"I only ask because I thought it might be more comfortable."

"If you need to question me, then question. Otherwise, I have much business that must be attended to."

Benson had already dismissed Finn. And it wasn't unreasonable for him to have done so, either. Finn couldn't do much with somebody like Benson. He was protected. Even if he were guilty, there would be very little that Finn would be able to do to get to him without evidence. It was the same as with Bellut.

It would be easier if he were to leave. Not right, but easier.

"I understand you're developing Jorend."

Benson shrugged. "I develop many parts of the city," he said. "It is a gamble, especially in a place like that," he said, opening his mouth as if to say something more before shaking his head, "but I see potential. That section of the city can be redeveloped, and I envision the Jorend section with magnificent homes lining the street."

"You envision the Jorend section filled with people of wealth," Finn said.

"I don't determine who purchases the properties," he said.

"Do you determine who you purchase from?"

Benson frowned. "I'm not sure I understand the implication."

"No implication. I'm just trying to understand. Some of the families didn't want to sell to you."

"Perhaps not, but I was in no rush. I had a good section of the street already purchased, and the others would come along."

"I imagine they would come along faster with a fire, especially when they had no place to go and needed to sell in order for them to recoup anything."

He needed to be careful with Benson. Accusing him too hard could get Finn into hot water.

"As I said," Master Benson started, "I did not feel the need to rush into the development. I had other assignments to work on, and my crews had more than enough business in order to keep us occupied." Benson frowned, and his jowls seemed to hang on the lower with the expression. "Are you thinking to accuse me of setting a fire so I could develop a neighborhood?"

Finn *had* considered it.

"There is little value in destroying a neighborhood only to build it back up," Master Benson continued. "Superstitions and all."

"I don't understand," Finn said.

"Too many people fear that neighborhood is now cursed by Volan."

The trickster god. That would be enough for some to avoid it.

"And now we'll have to wait. We can certainly start the development process, but I would have made a tidier profit had the section not burned." Benson shook his head, his jowls jiggling. "A shame, if you ask me. Worse, there were three residents who lived in the section who had wanted me to rebuild for them but now have changed their minds. That's lost income for me, Mr. Jagger. And them, when they were to resell."

"I see."

"Besides," Benson went on. "It would not serve any purpose for me to run the risk of angering the viscount. Not if I want to get in on the king's next development."

"Thank you," Finn said.

"Is that all?"

"I believe it is," he said.

He turned, pulling the door open, hesitating for a moment. He had thought that Benson was involved, at least in some way, but even that was a dead end. Now what? He didn't have any answers. Benson closed the door behind him, pulling it shut with a loud bang, and Finn stood in the street, staring for a moment, and had no answer.

Sweth was going to burn.

He hadn't gone far from Benson's home before glancing back, where he saw somebody looking out the window, as if watching him.

Finn debated what he needed to do.

Answers.

That was what he needed, and he only had a little time before Sweth burned.

He found himself heading toward Declan, and when he stopped in front of the prison, Finn looked up at it, hurrying inside and to the cells, nodding to the iron masters standing guard.

When he reached Sweth's cell, he grabbed the bars, looking inside. "We're going to talk," Finn said.

Sweth looked up. "It don't matter," Sweth said.

Finn looked down the hall, nodding to the two iron masters. One of them, Norel, was a muscular, short man, with a balding head. "Bring him to the chapel."

"He's already been sentenced," he said.

"I don't care if he's already been sentenced. I still need information from him, so bring him to the chapel."

The iron master's eyes flickered with a moment of concern, glancing to Jory, another iron master, who shrugged.

Maybe this was a mistake.

It was possible he should reconsider, but at the same time, he felt as if he needed answers, and this was going to be the only way he could get them.

Question Sweth.

Finn made his way to the chapel and stood at the counter with all the tools of his trade in front of him, waiting until the iron masters brought Sweth up. It didn't take long.

When they did, they brought him over to the chair.

"Strap him in," Finn said.

"Jags?"

He looked over to Shiner. "Just strap him in," he said.

"Are you sure about this?"

Finn's gaze hardened, and he nodded. He had to get the answers, and how could he do it without pushing the issue? How could he do it without questioning him?

Shiner strapped Sweth down. He looked up at Finn, and there was a measure of concern in his gaze.

"Leave me," Finn said.

The iron masters regarded Finn for a moment, but then they turned away.

Finn made his way around the chair, and he leaned toward Sweth. "We're going to talk."

"There isn't anything to talk about. You already got what you needed out of me."

"Maybe," Finn said. "I still don't think you've been completely honest with me."

"It don't matter." He glared at Finn. "They've already told me what's going to happen."

And they had. Finn was well aware that there would be very little that he could do that would change his fate. More than that, he didn't even want to change Sweth's fate. If he was responsible in some way, changing his fate wasn't Finn's problem. What he wanted was answers, and he didn't feel as if he fully understood them.

"Tell me about the fire starter found in your home."

"I don't know anything about it," he said.

"I think you're lying. You had it there. Why are you in Verendal?"

"Because I had to be," he whispered.

There was something about the way he said it that suggested he told the truth.

"What would your family have wanted?"

Sweth looked up. His eyes were pained. Haunted.

"To have lived."

"What happened to them?"

Sweth looked as if he wanted to say something more, before looking down at his lap. "I've already been sentenced. The rest of this doesn't matter."

Finn glanced over his shoulder, looking at the tools on the counter. They were all neatly arranged, all gleaming metal, and all cleaned by him.

Sweth had already been sentenced, so at this point, he might be taking a greater liberty with things than he should. But he was running out of time to learn more. And there *was* more. He could feel it.

He headed over to the tray of rods, studying it for a moment before changing his mind. If he left marks, he ran the risk of delaying the execution, something that would not only be upsetting to the magister and the jurors, but it would upset Meyer.

No. Finn needed something else.

There were a few different techniques he knew that wouldn't leave any marks.

That was what he had to do.

"I'm going to get answers," Finn said, turning back to Sweth. "Whatever it takes."

Finn walked away from Declan Prison. It was late, and he didn't have any further answers, nothing other than what he'd already uncovered. Sweth had refused to share anything more. Either he hadn't known anything—something that Finn had increasingly grown to think was possible—or he simply didn't care anymore. Considering that he already had been sentenced, the latter was probably true.

He had pushed Sweth harder than he had ever pushed before.

Sweth had screamed.

The more Sweth had screamed, the more Finn had pushed, and the more he had tried to find answers.

It wasn't until nearly the end when Finn began to question whether he was pushing because he wanted to know so that he could find justice for those who had been wronged in the Jorend section, or because of his frustration in Bellut and how he had escaped his justice. Either way, Finn had left the prison feeling as if some part of him had been twisted.

Word would get back to Meyer.

Finn was certain of it. He might have wanted to push,

and to get answers, but he had little doubt that Meyer would learn that he had gone back to Sweth, and little doubt that Meyer would discover that Finn had found no more answers.

He didn't feel like going home just yet.

The execution would be carried out soon. Finn would be expected to burn Sweth. In the time that he had served Meyer, Finn had never built a pyre and didn't know all that was involved. He needed to read a book Meyer had on such techniques, but at the same time, he didn't feel any interest in doing so, either.

Finn let out a long, frustrated breath, looking up at the sky. A heavy, near-full moon shone in the sky. He could imagine Esmerelda in the hegen section, studying the moon, looking for magical power within it, or perhaps using some of the power of the moon itself in order to cast her hegen magic. There was a part of him that wanted to go to her, to see what he might find, but there was no time. Even if she offered him a card, he wouldn't be able to do anything with it.

More than that, Finn didn't know if he deserved to go to the hegen. For all of their focus on death and how they used the remains of those sentenced in their magic, he didn't have the sense from Esmerelda that she enjoyed the macabre. Given the way that he had approached Sweth and how hard Finn had pushed him, Finn felt dirty.

He couldn't go back to Meyer's home, either.

Not only did Finn feel like he couldn't face Meyer, not yet, he didn't feel like he could face his sister.

Was this what he was to become?

Since serving Meyer, Finn had felt as if he were doing something honorable. This was the first time when he had started to question it.

And it wasn't anything that Meyer had forced him to do. All of that had come from Finn.

He had gone too far.

Would he do it again?

Meyer had warned him. Finn had not listened.

He found himself wandering the streets, and when he reached the Wenderwolf, watching the glowing lights inside, the music drifting from the closed door, he leaned in the shadows, watching it. There was a time when he had been welcomed into the Wenderwolf, and now he didn't think that he could ever go back. He had been a thief, but it wasn't until he had left that type of work that he had begun to feel as if he were truly dishonorable.

There was a part of him that wanted nothing more than to go inside the tavern and take a seat. Oscar would likely welcome him. But Finn didn't want Oscar to welcome him. Not with what he had done.

Instead, he stayed in the shadows, staring at the tavern, listening to the music, avoiding going anywhere else until well beyond curfew, and well beyond the time when he should return. Only when he thought Meyer and his sister would be asleep did he start to head back, and when he did, he still couldn't shake the unease he felt.

He had crossed a line.

For his sake, and for his sister and mother who needed him, and Meyer's home as a place to stay, Finn hoped he could come back from it.

CHAPTER NINETEEN

The flames crackled in front of him, and Finn forced himself to watch. As Sweth burned, the flames shifted to a darker color, taking on a bit more heat and a blacker sort of smoke. Meyer had shown him that there were accelerants to use to help the fire burn hotter and faster, and he had shown Finn how to bind Sweth's mouth, but the bindings only held for little while before the screaming began.

The pyre had been set outside of the city, away from any other structures, including the hegen section and the Raven Stone, so that it didn't run the risk of burning it.

"I've never cared for this sentence," Meyer said softly.

He'd been angry when learning how Finn had pushed Sweth after his sentencing. Angrier than Finn had seen him before. Finn still didn't feel as if he had all the answers. Despite sentencing Sweth, the investigation felt incomplete.

A priest of Heleth stood off to the side, a young man with a clean-shaven head and the hint of whiskers growing on his upper lip.

Finn look over to see the arranged jurors, along with the magister, standing in a line far enough away from the fire they wouldn't have to be subjected to its heat but close enough that they could watch. Each of them stared at the burning pyre, some with looks of horror in their eyes—Isabel, Horace, and Bethany especially—while others appeared satisfied.

"What happens when he's gone?"

"In the case of death by fire, we need to ensure the fire has burned completely out," Meyer said. "The key is to place enough accelerant around it to ensure that it burns hot and fast."

"Why?"

"Do you want to be out here any longer than necessary?"

Finn look behind him. The crowd had assembled, the same way that they assembled for every execution, though they were farther away than typical. "I suppose not."

"Tahn's store has been good about ensuring that we have the necessary supplies to burn through this quickly, but even with that, we must wait for the timbers to burn."

The pyre consisted of three massive timbers formed into a triangle, smaller logs set around the base, and an enormous pole that had been set deep into the ground in the center of it. Sweth had been strapped to the pole.

When he started screaming, he called out in Yelindish,

a bit of a harsh tone. It surprised Finn that he had never heard him speak with an accent. As he cried out, as he fell into his death throes, he defaulted to his native tongue.

"He was here for a reason," Finn said.

"Don't," Master Meyer said.

"You don't want me to look into it."

"You've done what was needed. I asked you to investigate the fires, which you have done, and I asked you to ensure that the appropriate sentence was carried out, which you have also done. Anything more than that..."

"Anything more than that would be what I should do," Finn said. "Are we not to make sure we have all of the information?"

Meyer shot him a hard stare at the idea that Finn would raise that point again. "We have all of the information. And you have gone beyond what you need to do."

"Something doesn't smell right to me." This was the last he'd push it, but he needed to say something.

"That's just the fire," Meyer said.

Finn glanced over, and he found Meyer with his jaw clenched and an uncertain look in his eyes. Finn had seen that look from him before, and he recognized the darkness in Meyer's eyes, the worry that was there.

Meyer knew what Finn was getting at, but he also knew that they didn't have anything he could necessarily do without risking angering Meyer. Possibly even the magister and the jurors.

"I could—"

"Don't," Meyer said.

Finn knew better than to argue at this point. If Master Meyer didn't want him to get involved, then he certainly could not get involved. At least, he couldn't get involved as far as Master Meyer knew. If he investigated on his own and uncovered something, maybe he could share it with Meyer. Then he could help solve what truly had happened there.

They stood there for a little while longer, watching the flames burn. It happened quickly, and for that, Finn was thankful. Neither of them wanted to be here.

The burning and the flames died out quickly. Eventually, they were left with the smoldering remains of the fire, and the crowd behind them dissipated. There were some who lingered a little bit longer, and as they did, Finn couldn't help but question whether they were like those his sister had mentioned, people who enjoyed watching fire burn for the sake of burning. He hadn't encountered anyone quite like that yet. When he had interviewed Sweth, he didn't have that impression of him. He had another reason.

Finn turned and saw that most of the jurors had started away. The magister, dressed in a velvet robe of office, holding a long, slender silver staff marking his position, stood next to Bellut. Bellut had on a deep green jacket and pants, a short sword sheathed at his side, and seemed to watch the burning of the pyre with interest.

Finn studied them, but neither man noticed him. They had turned off to the side, so that they were looking over toward the city, with the fire blazing near them. Meyer moved away, heading off to ensure that the pyre burned completely, leaving Finn alone.

The other jurors had all departed.

The magister spoke softly to Bellut, his head off to the side listening. Had Finn not approached, he might not have heard anything, but as it was, he could make out the sounds of their quiet conversation, even if he couldn't understand what they were saying.

Bellut suddenly strode away, heading back toward the city, leaving the magister standing there alone until he caught sight of Finn and made his way toward him.

"Magister," Finn said. "What were the two of you talking about?"

The magister's gaze darkened. "Official business of the king."

"The king?" Finn watched him. What would he say if he knew Finn's suspicions about Bellut?

"You understand we serve the king. As do you, now that you are apprenticed to the executioner. We all must work together, Mr. Jagger."

"I understand my responsibilities," Finn said.

Master Meyer remained near the pyre, his hands clasped behind him, as he watched the blaze burning down. There was something in his eyes Finn could not quite read.

"I was curious after the two of us talked the other night," Finn said to the magister. "You said that you hadn't always been in Verendal."

"I studied at the university," the magister said. "In order to be assigned as magister, one must devote themselves to their studies." He smiled, managing to make himself look almost endearing. "If you devote yourself to your studies in the same way, and with the same passion, you will likely do well as an executioner."

"That's what Master Meyer tells me," Finn said.

"You don't believe him?"

Finn shrugged. "I need to devote myself to my studies. That's the only way I will get what I want."

"And what is it that you want?"

Meyer turned toward him, glancing from Finn to the magister. "There was a time when I wanted nothing more than to be a part of a crew," Finn said, looking at the fire. The heat wafting off of it was not nearly as potent as it had been before, and there was nothing remaining of Sweth, just the burning timbers that lingered. "It was important to me." Finn shrugged. "I think it was about acceptance, or maybe it was about finding what I'd lost."

"What had you lost?" The magister asked.

"My father."

"Is that right? I wasn't aware you lost your father."

"My father got caught up in working with a crew," Finn said. "It changed things for him. Too many things. It changed things for the rest of the family as well. He did what he did because he thought it was necessary to protect us. Protect my family."

"You don't think he protected you?"

"I don't know what he did," Finn said. "He was caught and then taken from the city."

"Taken?"

Finn looked at the magister. "I thought he was little

more than a thief, but for him to have been taken from the city... Well, it tells me that he was involved in much more than what I knew. It tells me that maybe he was something more than just a thief."

"What was he?"

"I don't know, but from what I've understood, there's only one reason for a prisoner to have been brought from the city." Finn watched Meyer for a long moment before tearing his gaze away and looking at the magister. "Treason."

The magister smiled slightly. "Unfortunately, or perhaps fortunately in this instance, that is not exactly correct. Treason is a crime usually sentenced by death. Depending upon the person, there are reasons to question those involved in treason. Especially if they are guilty of spying for someone. The king then brings them to the capital where he can oversee the questioning."

"Spying."

"Gaining intelligence, using that against the kingdom and the king himself. A dangerous game, as you are aware, Mr. Jagger."

"I'm not aware of anything that approaches spying or treason," Finn said.

The magister nodded slowly. "Perhaps that is for the best. We try to protect the public from such crimes. They are dangerous, and most don't fully understand how insidious such crimes can become."

"I'm sure," Finn said.

"I am certain that you are."

Meyer came over to him. "Magister," he said, nodding slowly.

"Master Meyer. I was having quite the conversation with your apprentice about the legal system. You have quite the inquisitive apprentice. It's good he has such a mind, but one must be cautious. I have known far too many people with such curiosity who have suffered for it."

He smiled tightly at Finn before turning and leaving him.

Meyer stared at Finn. "What was that about?"

"I haven't really had a chance to talk with the magister before." Finn just shook his head. "He's always been pleasant with me."

"Scholars usually are," Master Meyer said. "He took the job because he is the king's lead scholar in Verendal, not because he has any interest in sentencing criminals."

"But he doesn't provide the sentencing."

"Not directly. He offers guidance and little else. Occasionally, he can intervene, but only if he feels there is a reason to do so."

Meyer motioned for him to follow. They started toward the city; now that the flames had started to die down, the Archers and the fire brigade would ensure the rest of it burned all the way down. Finn was thankful they didn't have to linger any longer to watch the rest of the fire burn out, but he doubted Meyer would permit him to do what he really wanted, which was to go after Bellut, and to try to get more information.

"You have to stop with this, Finn."

As they reached the Teller Gate, the crowd of the city

had started to ease. The festival was different from most. Typically, there was a crowd that lined the street, hawkers selling items. Today was different in that there were fewer stands, as many of them had moved outside of the city walls.

"There was another prisoner at Declan. What happened with him?"

"I—"

"As I thought." Meyer turned to him. "You neglected him. You did start with your questioning, I'll grant you that, but you got focused on Sweth and this perceived plot within the city. It's time for you to put that aside and return to your studies."

"I'm sorry."

And he was.

"Each of us find ourselves drawn into a particular case. There are always some that pull us for one reason or another. I can't say what draws you to one case more than another, but that is not on me to explain. What you need to do is find a balance."

"I have a balance," Finn said.

Meyer shook his head. "No. You do not. You have been given multiple assignments over the last week or so, and which ones have you focused on?"

"On Sweth," Finn said slowly.

"On Sweth. Now, it's understandable given that you believed the time commitment was necessary. Unfortunately, by doing that, you abandon other parts of your responsibility. Have you found an elixir to help Moira?"

Finn shook his head. "I've been looking but none of the

combinations has made a difference for her." Lena had helped, but neither of them had found anything.

"Of course you haven't. Let me tell you what you've refused to learn about her. She is wasting. The same as your mother. There is no cure." The words were harsh. "Any number of stimulants might work, but all have the same temporizing effect, and all will eventually fail. As you've no doubt found with Moira."

Finn swallowed. He and Lena had just thought they hadn't found the right compound.

"That was the lesson I wanted you to learn."

Finn had seen his mother suffering, wasting, but there had always been a part of him that assumed she would eventually improve. What if she wouldn't?

"It's time you dedicate yourself to the reason you're here." Finn nodded carefully. "Now that we have that completed, I would like for you to gather some supplies. Visit the general store, the apothecary, and if you have any need to stop at Declan, you certainly can, but you will meet with me this evening. It's time for us to regroup and work together once again."

Meyer started away from Finn, and Finn breathed out slowly. Meyer wasn't wrong.

Worse, Finn felt as if he'd suffered a setback. Meyer was upset with him, and having had a measure of independence, having it snatched away from him again felt as if he were moving backward rather than forward in his training.

Finn had to be careful.

He was close to Wella's shop and decided to start there.

If he had errands to run, it was time for him to finish what he needed to gather and then be done with it.

He was approaching the shop when he caught sight of Bellut.

He was standing near an alleyway, talking to somebody within it.

For a moment, Finn debated what to do, but his irritation and his curiosity overrode any rational thought. He made his way to the far side of the street and stood, trying to look as inconspicuous as possible, but dressed in his executioner leathers, it was difficult for him to conceal himself in the shadows altogether. He couldn't see who Bellut talked to, but he found it odd that he would be there in this section.

Finn needed to get closer. He needed to know who Bellut was talking to. He crept across the street, moving a little bit closer and listening. He didn't hear anything.

He looked in either direction but didn't see anything.

Bellut moved on, leaving the alleyway empty.

Finn looked over to Wella's shop before looking back to Bellut. He moved along the street, and Finn considered what he should do. He could still run his errands, and maybe he would put off going to Declan for another day, but having an opportunity to follow Bellut...

It was too good of an opportunity to pass up.

Meyer would have to understand.

Finn stayed behind him, moving slowly and carefully, but he didn't do anything that exciting. Bellut made his way down the streets, pausing at some stores but never going in. At one point, he reached another alleyway, and he didn't step down it, the same way he hadn't before, but he paused and looked as if he were talking to someone.

Finn couldn't see anything. Bellut blocked him.

If he had any idea how long Bellut was going to be there, he could loop around and come up behind. The alleys in this part of the city were easy enough to navigate, and Finn knew them fairly well. He still remembered the interconnecting alleys from when he had crept through the streets working for the crew, and so it wouldn't have been a challenge for him to use that knowledge now.

Bellut moved off.

Gods, but he had to stay with him.

Finn hurried forward, slipping along the street, creeping along with Bellut.

Where was he going?

He wasn't heading back toward City Hall, and he certainly wasn't going toward Bellut's home. Finn had seen his home one other time and knew that while he lived in a nicer section of the city, it wasn't overly ornate, and certainly not what one would consider wealthy.

He stayed in the outer sections.

Surprisingly, he made what appeared to be a circuit around the outer sections of the city. Every so often, he paused in alleys, speaking to someone, but Finn never caught sight of any of them.

The day grew long, and Finn continued following out of curiosity more than anything else. He never got close enough to see who Bellut followed, and could not make out anything other than the fact that he was standing in the mouth of the alley, as if somebody anticipated his arrival.

At one point, Finn tried to sneak up behind and get into the alley, but he almost lost sight of Bellut, so he stopped that, and he returned to just following him.

As the day went on, Bellut finally turned to the center of the city.

Whatever he had been up to was done.

Finn tore himself away. It was time for him to get back to his tasks.

He'd probably upset Meyer anyway.

He hurried to the general store, collecting oils and rope and other items that they might need, before stopping at an apothecary—not Wella's, since he had moved far enough away from it, but Dorphene had quality stock as well—and past Declan Prison on his way back to Meyer's home, deciding that he didn't have time to visit.

When he reached Meyer's home, darkness had fallen in full. Finn approached, looking around him, a bit nervous that Wolf might be out there and spring up on him the way that he had surprised him before, but he didn't see any movement on the street. If nothing else, having Wolf track him had put Finn on edge again, which couldn't be a bad thing. He needed to keep that edge. It was necessary to ensure his safety.

He pulled open the door, stepped inside, and headed down the hall to deliver the apothecary supplies to Master Meyer. When he knocked, Meyer was there quickly, pulling the door open, an irritated frown on his face.

"I was expecting you earlier than this."

"You told me to gather supplies."

Meyer watched him. "Gather supplies." He glanced down. "You went to Geralt's general store, and to Dorphene. Not that I have any issue with either of them, but neither were close to where we were."

"I..."

"You will tell me what you did, and you will tell me the truth."

Finn took a deep breath. "I was going into Wella's store when I caught sight of Bellut. Now, Master Meyer, I know what you're going to say, but I saw him making his way around the city, stopping in alleys, and speaking to—"

"Enough. You have got to move past this. We have spoken about this at length. I know what you believe about him, but it is not about what you believe."

"I know what I heard."

"And what can you prove?"

Finn stared. Nothing. That was the problem.

It *was* about what he believed—and that wasn't how their position operated.

"I'm trying to understand what happened."

"Following one of the jurors to the city is not your way of investigating the fire, at least, no way of investigating the fire the way that you told me you were. And any investigation of Bellut needs to be done correctly." His tone said something more: *if at all.* Meyer turned away, headed over to his desk. He picked up a slip of paper. "I think it's time for the two of us to approach our responsibilities differently." Meyer looked up, holding Finn's gaze. "You and I are going to take a trip. Be ready to leave in the morning." He nodded to Finn. "And close the door."

Finn expected him to say something more, but Master Meyer didn't. He took a seat at his desk, pulled the book that he always had closer to him, and sat, leaving Finn wondering what had happened.

He'd upset Master Meyer.

Worse, he didn't even know if he might have lost his position.

Was that why they were leaving the city?

Finn pulled the door closed, and he headed to the kitchen, taking a seat at the table. Lena was there, and Finn had barely even noticed her. "I heard some of your conversation. Not all of it, but I gather that Master Meyer is upset with you."

"I think he's upset I continue to look into what happened to me."

"With a juror?"

Finn looked over to his sister. Her eyes were reddened, and he could tell that she'd been crying. "What is it?"

"It doesn't matter."

"Is it Mother?"

"I said it doesn't matter."

"I'm sorry, Lena."

Once again, Finn had been away when she needed him. Once again, he had found himself caught up in some other aspect of his responsibility and had abandoned what his sister needed.

He needed to be better.

And he needed to prove it to Lena.

Not only to Lena but to Master Meyer.

"I will do better for you," he said, looking up at his sister.

"It sounds like you have to be better for yourself," she said. She laughed softly. "Don't anger him."

"I'm not trying to. It's just…"

"It's just what?"

Finn turned so that he could look toward the closed door to Master Meyer's office. "It's just that I'm not sure that he's right about this."

"You think you know something more than he does?"

Meyer was gifted. Finn knew that he was not only intelligent but calm and rational, and he had a clear way of thinking through problems. Finn had seen that every time they had performed investigation together. In this case, though, maybe what they needed wasn't a clear mind.

Maybe they needed somebody willing to look and dig, somebody like Finn.

If Meyer didn't ship him out of the city, Finn was determined to get to the bottom of this, regardless of what Master Meyer wanted.

"I don't know if I know something more than he does, but I might be willing to look into something he is not."

"You don't think he's willing to look into this?"

Finn turned back to look at his sister. "Either he's not willing or he's not able. Either way, I think it has to be me."

"I'm worried about you, Finn."

"Why are you worried about me?"

"Because you look almost eager. I think that's dangerous. Whatever you're doing has to be equally dangerous."

He took a deep breath, letting it out as he stared at the
tabletop. He traced his fingers along the faded wood, and
then looked up. "It might be dangerous, but I think it also
might be necessary."

CHAPTER TWENTY

Finn had been given a little time to gather supplies before they departed. He knew better than to take too long. At the same time, if he would be leaving the city for Meyer to demonstrate whatever responsibilities he had outside of the city, then Finn wanted the opportunity to learn what else he could before they departed. He remained convinced there was more taking place than what Meyer believed. The problem was that Finn might be the only one who believed it.

He ended up near Declan prison, and he glanced up to it.

He still had some time, though he worried that if he lingered too much longer, he would find Meyer angry with him again. Considering what had happened the night before when Finn had shown up late, he didn't want to risk that.

Something still troubled Finn.

Vol Thern.

That was what troubled him.

Finn debated, glancing up at the sky, cocking his head as he tried to count out how many bells had already rung before deciding.

He hurried into the prison, nodding to the iron master standing guard, and made his way down to the cells. Shiner was there. He started to grin at Finn, but Finn shook his head.

"I need to meet with Thern."

Shiner nodded, and Finn hurried to the chapel. He didn't have much time, so he needed to work quickly.

He arranged the implements on the counter, but even with that, Finn wasn't entirely sure that he would be able to use them.

He started pacing, waiting for Shiner to arrive, and when the door came open, he looked up to see him guiding in Thern.

He'd been cleaned and dressed in the prison garb. He looked no different than so many others who were imprisoned within Declan. A thick wild beard matched his eyes. Shiner strapped him into the chair, securing the leather straps around his wrists and ankles, before looking up at Finn, as if waiting for him to nod his approval.

"You can leave me," Finn said.

Shiner shrugged, and he pulled the door closed.

Finn made his way around to face Thern. "We need to talk about what happened."

He looked up at him, shaggy hair hanging down in

front of his eyes. "I told you what I know. And I know you don't care."

"I care. I need to know what you were doing when you were caught."

He looked up at Finn, and for a moment, it looked as if hope flickered in his eyes, but then it faded.

"You don't care. You're like the others. You already have me condemned. Probably have me swinging."

"You're not going to swing for breaking into some merchant's home."

"They always make up some excuse to hang a man like me. I'm sure you'll be complicit."

"I'm not going to make up any accusation," Finn said.

Thern glared at him.

"Just tell me where you were."

"I wasn't nowhere. Isn't that what I'm supposed to say?"

"You've already admitted that you had gone into a merchant's home. What I'm trying to figure out is why." Finn flickered his gaze to the tray of implements and decided against them. There was no point in reaching for any of the torture tools. Besides, he really didn't have much time before he had to get back to Meyer. "All I need is to know what you were after."

"It wasn't after anything," he said.

"You don't go breaking into a merchant's home unless you're after something."

"Is that right? And what do you know about breaking into a merchant's home?"

"I know enough. I used to run with a crew."

Something shifted on Thern's face, and he blinked. "What do you mean used to?"

"I'm sure you've heard the rumors. And if you haven't, then it doesn't take much for you to ask around to find out what that means."

He studied Finn. "You really him? The thief whose neck wouldn't break?"

That was a new one, but Finn wasn't at all surprised that rumors had spread about him. "I just need to know what you are doing there."

"I saw a crew break their way in. Is that what you wanted to hear?"

"And you followed the crew? Were you working with them?"

"No," Thern said. "It…"

He cut himself off, looking back down.

"Who was it? Somebody you know. Maybe a brother. A friend." Finn studied him for another moment. "A son." Thern tensed, and Finn knew that he had the right of it. "You wanted to find out what he was after?"

"I've been trying to keep him from getting in too deep." He shrugged. "Said he wasn't taking anything, only delivering something. Nobody delivers something to a house like that in the middle of the night." He looked back down, shaking his head. "So do with me what you need."

Finn took a step back.

As he stared at him, he couldn't shake the feeling that Thern had been telling him the truth.

Something about it didn't feel quite right, and if he didn't need to leave the city with Meyer, he would have known what he needed to do next. Go and investigate what had happened.

He had the report, and he knew which house Thern had targeted, and which house his son's crew had targeted, but he didn't have the time.

And maybe it didn't matter.

"A sentence for breaking into a home like that will likely involve flogging," Finn said, backing toward the door. "I will speak on your behalf, though. I'll advise the magister to offer leniency."

Thern looked up, holding his gaze. "Why?"

"Because I believe you."

He pulled the door open, nodding to Shiner. "Bring him back to the cell."

Shiner flashed a quick grin. "Got it, Jags. You plan on joining us again tonight?"

The idea that he could have someone to share a drink with appealed to Finn. "Maybe when I return."

"You going somewhere?"

"Apparently."

"You don't sound too eager."

"That's because I'm not."

He strode out of the chapel, through Declan prison, and back out into the street. It was time for him to join Meyer and time to leave the city. The only problem was that Finn felt increasingly sure that he had much more he needed to be doing now.

Finn felt as if he were close to an answer—and leaving the city now took him from that chance. There *was* something more to Sweth, but he just had to find it. There was what Thern had told him, but he hadn't the chance to investigate.

One more task that would wait while they were out of the city.

Too many things were left undone.

And Meyer didn't seem troubled by it.

With as much work as Finn felt like he had to do, leaving the city now left him thinking that perhaps it wasn't the right time, and that perhaps this journey could have waited, but he wasn't about to argue with Master Meyer over it. He sat atop a horse, feeling completely uncomfortable because he had very little experience riding on horseback. Meyer straddled the other horse, swaying easily with each move of the massive creature, looking as if he had done it every day for his entire life.

"How far do we have to go?" His backside already had started throbbing.

Meyer glanced over to him. "Logard isn't far from here. If you weren't so concerned about figuring out some way to get to Bellut, you'd enjoy this opportunity."

Meyer grunted, shifting in his saddle so that he could look around more easily. They'd ridden only a short ways from the city, though even there, Finn could make out the hegen section. There was a vibrancy to it, almost an energy, and more than that, it felt like someone within that section were watching him.

Maybe they were.

He wouldn't put it past Esmeralda to have some arrangement with Meyer even outside of the city. She obviously used that connection for her magic, though Finn really wanted to better understand the nature of the magic and how she used it. He tore his gaze away, looking at Master Meyer's back, the sword Justice strapped to it, and frowned.

"How often do you leave the city on trips like this?"

"Before you, I had a journeyman who worked with me, so I would send him out of the city to handle sentencing within the nearby villages."

"I'm sure the people you sent the Lion to loved that."

Meyer chuckled softly. "You're probably right. He had a tendency to be cruel, which is something I'm trying to keep you from developing."

"So, you haven't left the city on these journeys in a while?"

"My service is to Verendal, but that doesn't mean I can't serve the king in other ways."

"You're not answering the question."

Meyer looked over to him, frowning. "Am I not?"

Finn sighed. "You haven't left the city in quite a while, have you?"

"Not often," Meyer agreed. "When you reach journeyman status, you'll be given the opportunity to leave the city without me. It's a good way for you to make a few extra coins, to hone your skill, and to feel a measure of independence."

"Even while I'm still serving you."

"It's the journeymen who do most of the work outside of the cities."

They rode in relative silence, following the hard-packed path as it headed off to the north and the east, until Meyer took a sharp right, veering off the main road. It was wide, with remnants of cobblestones that looked to have been grown over with time, the trees bounding the road on either side arching overhead and shielding them from the sunlight.

Finn looked everywhere. Everything felt so *open*.

It was more than the trees spaced around him. It was the lack of walls—and the lack of other people. Then there was the threat of Alainsith. They controlled the forest outside the city.

Not along the King's Road.

That was what he had to tell himself.

"I don't know if I would've seen this had I been by myself," Finn said.

"Which is part of the reason you will start to study maps," he said. "In time, you will come to know how to navigate the lands around Verendal just as well as you once learned to navigate the alleys throughout the city."

"I see."

"It's not a punishment, Finn."

It might not be, but there was something more reassuring about the city than there was outside of the borders of the city. "Do you ever worry about highwaymen?"

"There are always those who think to abuse others. Even outside of the city, and while traveling on the king's road. We are relatively well protected, but more than that, we aren't traveling anyplace where crime is likely."

"You don't think we'll encounter anyone here?"

He shifted, trying to get comfortable on the horse, and failing. Everything seemed so *high* here. He had grown better with guiding the horse, but he still didn't know if he was supposed to talk to him while riding or not.

"We might, but anyone we come across will see two men, one of them wearing a sword, and might think twice before deciding to attack."

They continued onward, and Master Meyer led him along the path, guiding the horses through the forest. The canopy arched overhead, sealing off the sky, leaving darkness hovering overhead. Finn looked up, glancing to the sky for a moment before turning his attention back to Master Meyer, who remained silent.

It was late in the day before the trees started to open up. He didn't notice it quite at first, but gradually the forest thinned, before parting as a larger clearing appeared. The village in front of them was small and quaint, and it looked comfortable. Homes were made of wood, and many of them were single-story, though there were two-story homes that had tall, arched roofs, and most of them were painted with browns and whites, colors that blended in with the countryside. It was nestled in the forest, with a small hill rising up behind it, and a stream running around the south edge. The burbling water carried to his ears.

"What kind of crime do they have here? It doesn't

strike me as the kind of place where I would expect to see enough violence that would necessitate our presence."

Meyer grunted. "You will see."

"What happened here?"

Meyer shrugged, gripping the reins of the horse and jerking them softly. "Perhaps what was reported, but there's also the chance that the reason we're here may not be reason enough to warrant the king's justice."

That wouldn't be all bad.

Finn wanted—or was it needed?—to get back and continue looking into Sweth.

More than that, Bellut *was* up to something.

He had to figure that out, as well.

"If they've already sentenced him—"

"Things work differently outside of the city. Within Verendal, we are subject to the decision of the jurors and the magister, but outside of the city, we serve a dual purpose . Not only do we carry out the sentence, but we also help with passing judgment and suggesting an appropriate sentence."

"What if they've already sentenced the person here?" He could hope that was the case.

"If they have, then we will investigate and decide if we agree." Meyer nodded to the city. "It is no different than what you would do in Verendal."

"It's a little different. We don't have the same resources here as we have in Verendal."

"Because it should be easier for you to find the answers. This should not be a difficult challenge, Finn. A village like Logard should be straightforward for us to work through, ask the questions needed to get the information we need, and move on."

They rode forward, and as they neared the outskirts of the village, Meyer climbed down from his saddle, and Finn followed. The village had several dozen buildings, a few farms on the outskirts, and plenty of green space between buildings, unlike Verendal. Finn trailed after Meyer.

"Do you know where we are supposed to go?"

"All places like this have someone in charge. In the case of Logard, we are to head to the village hall, and we will meet with the town leader."

"Do you know him?"

Meyer shook his head. "There was a time when I did, but I haven't spent much time in Logard in many years. As far as I know, things have turned over since then."

"Will we be staying here tonight?"

"Unless you want to travel through the forest in the dark, we will."

"Why do you say that as if it would be dangerous?"

"There are some dangers traveling at night, especially in this forest. It's more than just a worry about highwaymen. There are other things to fear."

Finn started to smile, laughing softly. "Such as what?"

"Such as other things," Meyer said softly.

Finn wanted to press the question more, but he had a feeling that doing so would not yield him any further information. Instead, he let the question drop.

They reached a slightly larger building in the center of

the village, and Meyer handed Finn the reins to his horse. "Hold them."

Meyer wasn't gone very long before he finally returned, walking alongside an older woman with graying hair, dressed in a faded green gown. She glanced over to Finn, her frown deepening.

"We only agreed to pay for your services," she said.

Meyer nodded. "You won't be responsible for paying for my apprentice. I brought him here for his benefit." Meyer turned to her. "I think you could make arrangements to offer him a place to stay for the night."

"It will reduce your fee."

"I don't expect it to reduce my fee very much," Meyer said carefully.

"He can have the room next to yours. You will clean up after yourselves."

"Very well," Meyer said. "Is there any place we can get a meal at this time of day?"

"It'll cost you. We didn't agree to pay for your food."

Meyer chuckled again. "I understand."

"There's a place on the southern edge of town. You can't miss it."

She turned and headed back into the building, leaving Finn watching after her.

"What was that about?"

"A reminder of my negotiation skills," Meyer said softly. He took the reins of his horse again, and motioned for Finn to follow. "One of the things that you will come to learn when you are a journeyman and on your own is that everything is negotiable, including your fee, and whatever ancillary benefits that might be required."

"Ancillary benefits?"

"Typically a room. Food. In this case, I neglected to consider you." He laughed softly. "There was a time when I pushed for many different things, and most of the time, I got them."

"What sort of things?"

"When I was your age, I enjoyed having a mug of ale the same way as you do, I suppose. I would often negotiate that into the price of my service. Typically, places like this charge exorbitant amounts for a simple mug of ale, and I could link my usual fee and add in a couple of extra mugs of ale, and come out farther ahead than I would have otherwise."

Finn found himself laughing, surprised by that.

"She didn't seem to care very much for you."

"You will find there are quite a few places outside of the city that are like that," Meyer said. They meandered through the village, taking a narrow road where they couldn't even walk side by side. At one point, they passed a row of shops, which likely served as the village center, before moving onward while leading their horses.

"Our presence is tolerated within the city. Perhaps honored, as we serve the king directly." He glanced back toward the village center. "Out here, it's a little bit different. We might be tolerated, but we certainly aren't appreciated."

"That makes sense," Finn said. "Why would they want us out here, especially if it means that something happened in their city or town or village that requires the presence of an executioner?"

"I think you're right," Meyer said. He motioned to a small stable and handed the reins of his horse to Finn. "Take care of the horses, feed them, and join me inside."

"They don't have a stable boy for that?"

"I'm sure they do, but it's something else I didn't negotiate for."

Finn took the horses into the stable and found empty stalls for each of them, figuring out how to unbuckle the saddles off of them and pulling them down. He had seen others brush down the horses, though he didn't know if that even mattered. He closed the stall, found a bale of hay, and carried it over to the horses, splitting the bale in half, and dumping half in one stall and half in the other. He had no idea if what he had done was the right way of caring for a horse, but he was a city boy at heart, and this was very much not a city activity.

When he was done, he looked around the inside of the small barn. It was illuminated by a single lantern, carefully hung with no hay around it. That would burn, and he imagined that whoever owned the stable was at least smart enough to know that they needed to keep that away. He saw one of their horses in the stable, and looked over and realized that they hadn't put the bale of hay in the same way that he had. Maybe he had done it wrong.

What about water?

He didn't see anything and would have to ask Meyer if he was expected to bring a bucket to the horses or if they would be fine for the night. That was what Meyer got for entrusting something like this to someone who had no experience with it.

He closed up the stable, headed back into the building were Meyer had disappeared, and found him sitting at a table in what looked to be a small tavern. He had a tray of food in front of him, and another tray rested where Finn assumed he could sit. A mug of ale had been placed there as well.

Finn took a seat, grunting. "I have no idea if we'll find those horses alive in the morning."

"Then we're walking back."

"That's not my choice, but you might have wanted to pay for somebody to provide a little better care for them."

Meyer looked up from in between bites. "I figured it was something you could manage."

"Well, seeing as how this is one of the few times in my life I have ever sat on a horse, let alone ridden for more than an hour, I think expecting me to know how to take care of the beast is a bit of a reach. Now, I did give the horses some hay, but I couldn't find any water, so if we need to go out and get a bucket or something like that, then I'm happy to do that, or maybe we just offer somebody from this place a copper to go and check on them."

"They'd charge us for that. I guess we have no choice but to pay. So eat. You can eat now, maybe in the morning, but after that…"

"You don't think we will get to eat much after that?"

"It depends upon how long we stay here."

"Are we returning tomorrow?"

"Maybe," Master Meyer said.

Maybe meant *probably not.* That surprised Finn.

Where else did Meyer intend to lead him?

He didn't think that they were going to stay outside of the city all that long, but perhaps Meyer had more in mind than Finn knew.

How many other jobs like this did they need to do?

Finn started eating. The venison was dry, a bit bland, but his stomach rumbled and he ate quickly, hungry from the day on the road and from not having anything since they left early this morning. He glanced over to Meyer every so often as he ate, but the old executioner remained silent, saying nothing to Finn.

After he was finished, Meyer rapped his knuckles on the table and got to his feet. "Get some rest, Finn. Tomorrow we will carry out the sentencing. You should be well rested before we do."

He headed to the back of the room, where a small doorway led out and up to a loft above the tavern. Finn just sat there.

When the server came by the table again, he leaned close. "Another mug of ale?"

Finn looked toward the door. Meyer would want him to get his rest, but troubled thoughts plagued him. They were the kind of thoughts that he needed the ale to help him contemplate. It wouldn't solve any problems, but it might make him feel better about the answers he came up with. Besides, he was young, and he could get up early despite how much he might drink.

"Why not?"

CHAPTER TWENTY-ONE

The morning sunlight drifted through the window of the small room. It really was little more than a closet, but at least they hadn't needed to sleep out in the open. When Meyer had proposed the journey, Finn had feared that was what Meyer would intend for them. The lumpy bed would normally make sleep difficult, but with drinking as he had the night before, he hadn't paid much attention to it. Now that he was awake, it was all he could think about.

He sat up slowly. His head throbbed a little, though he didn't know if that was because of the ale he'd drank the night before or because he'd had a long day traveling. Either way, he needed to get moving.

A knock sounded at the door and Finn hurriedly pulled on his pants and jacket, running his hand through his shaggy brown hair to smooth it flat, and opened it to see Meyer already dressed and waiting for him.

"I figured you'd be ready by now," Meyer said.

"I overslept," Finn said.

"The ale you had last night will do that to you."

Finn sniffed, then winced, resisting the urge to grab his head. "I didn't have that much ale." Meyer arched a brow and Finn shrugged. "Fine. I might have had another mug after you left. I had things to think about."

"It's been my experience the best thinking is done without the influence of ale. Especially bad ale."

"It wasn't that bad."

Meyer grunted softly. "We need to introduce you to some better ales. You're not living in the Brinder section anymore. Get moving. We've got a prisoner to visit."

"Any word on them?"

Meyer smiled tightly. "Had you not spent your night 'thinking,' you might have considered asking a few questions. I'm sure you would have found anyone in the village more than happy to share with you details about the prisoner."

"You can't just tell me?"

"You're the apprentice. You're supposed to tell me."

Meyer turned away and Finn hurriedly grabbed his belongings from the room. He had only a single pack with a change of clothes, nothing that would have made it difficult to gather everything together. When he had everything, he hurried through the narrow hallway and down the stairs leading to the tavern.

The tavern was quieter than it had been the night before, though it had been quiet compared to most of the taverns in Verendal. There had been no music and no shouting, just the occasional murmuring from nearby tables along with the whispers of the server when he'd come by to bring Finn his drink.

Meyer waited for him at one of the tables, though not the same table as the night before. He rested his hands on the table, sitting patiently.

Finn settled down in the chair across from him, rubbing sleep from his eyes. He tossed his pack off to the side and stared at Meyer. "Now are you willing to tell me anything about our prisoner?"

"Not ours," Meyer said.

"Fine. Are you willing to tell me anything about the village's prisoner?"

The server came by, a different man from the night before. This one was balding and had on a heavily stained brown apron, and his pudgy cheeks were ruddy, as if he'd already been deep into drink. He bobbed his head, his gaze darting nervously to the sword resting next to Meyer before turning his attention back to the two of them.

"Master Meyer, I presume?" When Meyer nodded, the server's eyes widened slightly. "I have been instructed to make sure that you have everything that you need."

Meyer's eyes narrowed slightly. "Is that right?"

"Can I offer you anything?"

"Coffee. Food."

"Of course. And for you?"

"I'll have the same," Finn said.

The server hurried away, pausing at the door leading back to the kitchen, his gaze lingering once again on the sword resting next to Meyer.

"Is it like that every time you leave the city?" Finn asked.

"Most of the time," Meyer said. "There aren't too many people excited to see us. We are a necessary evil, much like I told you."

"I would have expected that we would have gotten a better reception than this. Aren't we taking care of a problem for them?"

"We aren't taking care of any problem." He paused when the server swung by, setting down two mugs of steaming coffee. Meyer tipped his head politely, but the server hurried off without saying anything more. "We are serving the king. The sooner you come to realize that, the sooner this becomes easier for you."

"I recognize serving the king; it's just that—"

"It's just that nothing. You are here on behalf of the king. No other reason than that. We're ensuring his justice is carried out. If we weren't to come, think of what I've told you about how the families of the victims wanted justice before."

Finn nodded. "I can see that."

"I would hope so. The issue is complicated. If we were to leave these people to their own devices, they would pursue their own sort of justice. While it might make them feel better about what they have done and might give them a sense of closure, it is not justice, and it only furthers the likelihood that others will take justice into their own hands in the future."

Finn glanced down at the sword. "Do you really antic-ipate you will need to offer somebody an honorable death?" He said it softly and glanced up, smiling as he did.

"What is an honorable death?" Meyer took a sip of his coffee, breathing it in, and set down the mug. "You will come to find that things are different outside of the city. Expectations are different. Your decisions are different. You aren't beholden to those who believe there are more or less honorable deaths. A clean death is all that matters."

"You use the sword more often outside of the city?"

"I use whatever technique I feel is appropriate. It is much more my decision than it is anywhere else."

The server carried out two plates laden with eggs and sausage and toasted bread. Meyer dug in immediately, and Finn picked at his food, his stomach churning a little bit, before starting to work at breakfast. If he were to be the one to carry out the sentencing today, he wanted his stomach settled, and it wouldn't do for him to have an empty stomach, especially after a night drinking, but he couldn't deny the nausea rolling through him. It threatened to overwhelm him.

They ate in silence, neither of them saying that much. There wasn't much for Finn to say at this point. When they were done, Meyer finished his coffee and got to his feet.

"Come," he said.

Finn hurriedly finished, and he got up, grabbing his pack, leaving half of his plate uneaten. He followed Meyer out of the door and paused. It was still early morning, but the sun was shining down, a bit of warmth in an otherwise crisp day. A breeze gusted out of the north, carrying some of the smells of the nearby forest, mingling with a hint of lilac, but also an earthy odor. He breathed it in slowly.

Meyer glanced over, shaking his head. "I thought you were a city boy."

"I am."

"Not when you breathe in like that, you aren't."

"It smells so different here."

"Not the same filth as in Verendal," Meyer said.

"I suppose so." Finn took another deep breath, looking at the buildings lining the narrow road. When they'd come in the night before, Finn hadn't paid that much attention to the village itself. It was simple. Many of the homes were taller than he would've expected, stretching two stories high, with steep roofs, lining the narrow road in front of him. Many had lawns around them, something unthinkable in Verendal. The stream burbled nearby, and he listened to it for a moment before turning his attention back to Meyer. "Where now?"

"They keep a prison on the edge of the village."

He motioned for Finn to follow, and he did so, walking past one townsperson, who eyed him strangely, before hurrying after Meyer. They neared the stream, and Finn paused in front of it, listening to the sound of the water as it rushed past the stones, the steady splashing of the stream carrying out into the early morning. Meyer crouched down next to the stream for a moment, resting his hand in the water.

"What is it?"

Meyer shook his head. "Nothing."

He got up, shaking his hand and wiping it on his pants as his gaze drifted out into the forest, looking toward the trees. What did he see? Finn stared but didn't know just what Meyer was paying attention to. He looked back to the village, noting the small central church, its spire rising higher than any other building in the village. That was unusual in Verendal. The palace strained to be of equal height to any church there, putting the king on equal footing as the gods.

Meyer guided them farther along the stream, heading gradually around the outskirts of the village. It wasn't until they curved around a little bit farther that Finn began to get a sense of where they were heading.

A stone building, so different from most of the others in the village, came into view. The building itself was small, situated on the edge of the stream, and nestled near the outskirts of the village, close to the forest. Meyer nodded to the building.

"Why there?" Finn asked.

"This is one of the oldest buildings in the village," Meyer said. "The people have converted it over time into various different purposes, and now it serves as something of a prison, though it hasn't always done so."

"It seems like a strange place for it."

Meyer swept his gaze around the inside of the village. "All of this used to be different. These lands were different."

"By different, I presume you mean Alainsith?"

"All of this once was their land," he said.

Finn stared at the brick building with renewed interest. "You're saying the building itself was Alainsith?"

"It is one of the oldest," Master Meyer said.

As they approached, Finn studied the building itself. Most of the buildings within Verendal were old, many of them a hundred years or more old, but there were some that were even older, built long before the men in Verendal claimed the city, building it to the massive scale that it was now. The city had grown and prospered over the years, spreading beyond its initial borders, reaching even greater scale over time. He had grown up knowing that about Verendal but never really thinking much about it otherwise. There wasn't much to think about when he was a thief simply trying to navigate the streets of the city, attempting to survive. There were other buildings, though, that had been repurposed. City Hall was one such building, and it shared some features with this. Made of a pale white stone, it looked as if it blended into the forest, or perhaps it had been grown there, some god having pulled the stone free of the riverbed, piling it into the shape of the building. The edges of the building were curved and it gave it something of a smooth, almost natural appearance.

Meyer fished a key out of his pocket and carried it over to the main door.

"No guards here?"

Meyer glanced over to him. "What do they need to guard?"

"The prisoner."

"The prisoner isn't going anywhere. The building itself is stout enough they wouldn't be able to run."

Strange writing was etched into the stone over the doorway, and Finn regarded it for a moment, trying to make out the words and failing. Meyer pushed the curved door open and stepped inside.

A lantern glowed with a soft light, hanging on one of the stone walls. Finn had to duck his head to go into the door, and he had to stay slightly stooped over as he moved through the hallway, following Meyer. The building was made of the same pale white stone as the outside of the building. Even the floor was covered in that same stone. Meyer took the lantern off the hook near the door and guided Finn along the hallway. They reached a point where the hall opened up, and he motioned off to their left. Once they stepped beyond the stone hall, it opened, but then there were wooden walls that were built, and they seemed so out of place considering the stone. One of the walls had rows of bars worked into it.

Meyer approached, glancing at the person in the cell, and it took Finn a moment to see through the shadows in the back of the cell, but when he did, he frowned.

It was a woman.

"What did she do?" Finn whispered.

"She stands accused of killing a man," Meyer said.

Finn had seen killers many times since he began serving Master Meyer and had started to feel there was a general type to them. Not all of them looked the same, but there was a hardness to someone willing to kill. A dark-ness in their eyes, and something more, something Finn had never managed to put his finger quite on. Killers had a seething sort of anger deep within them. Not all of them, certainly, but enough.

There were other killers harder for him to identify. They were those who got caught up in the crimes of passion, anger or rage flaring within them briefly but then fading. Many of them never knew they had the potential for violence, or if they did, it was deeply buried within them. It was something that could be elicited during questioning, though, and Meyer had trained him on drawing that anger and violence out, though often it took days and weeks in order to do so. Those were some of the more challenging interrogations but necessary. Mostly necessary so that he could understand whether or not a person truly had the capacity for violence.

Then there were people who looked completely innocent and possibly were.

That was what he thought of this woman.

She had dark hair and couldn't be much older than Finn. Her face was dirty, and her hair was little ragged, but still Finn could tell that she would be a great beauty were she clean and dressed as she probably normally was. She cowered in the back of the cell, leaning back against the wall, her knees drawn up to her chest, her eyes darting around, and said nothing when they approached.

A tray of food looked to be untouched, resting on the ground not far from her feet. She barely looked up as they approached.

"Jasmine Melth?" Meyer asked.

She didn't respond.

"My name is Henry Meyer; I'm the king's executioner. I'm here to ask you questions."

"They've already asked me all their questions," she said, her voice little more than a whisper.

"I'm here to ask a few more," Meyer said.

"I don't have any answers."

"I'm not certain that's true," Meyer said. "You know what they have accused you of doing?"

"Killing Matthew Avard."

"Did you do it?"

For the first time, Jasmine looked up, and something within her demeanor shifted. It might have been the intensity in her eyes, or it might have been simply the fact that she looked up and met Meyer's gaze, but in that moment, Finn suddenly doubted. There was something about the way that she looked at Meyer, a defiance, that he had seen in other, similar criminals.

"I didn't do what they accused me of," she said.

"What did you do?"

"I didn't kill Matthew," she said.

She lowered her gaze, staring at the ground in front of her. She still hadn't moved otherwise, her knees drawn up to her chest, her arms wrapped around them, though now she started to rock a little bit.

"What evidence do they have against her?" Finn asked.

"They claim to have found her in the victim's home," Meyer said.

"Just that?"

Meyer turned to Finn. "You don't think that's enough?"

"Finding somebody in a home isn't enough reason to accuse them of killing someone."

"It is when they're covered in their blood," Meyer said.

"I tried to help him," Jasmine said. "I did everything that I could, but he was already gone. They had taken him."

"Who do you think took him?" Master Meyer said.

Jasmine looked up briefly, a hint of panic in her eyes that faded. "I... I don't know."

There was enough hesitation that suggested she had something in mind.

"Who do you think were responsible?" Finn asked.

Meyer had been pushing Finn to take an increased role, and regardless of what happened with Sweth, Finn still felt as if he needed to keep digging and pushing, looking for answers. In this case, maybe it was more about Jasmine than it was about the crime itself.

"I don't know."

There was no hesitation this time. If she truly didn't know, then pushing wouldn't accomplish anything other than to coax her into coming up with an answer to try to appease them. If she were guilty, then he would've expected her to have come up with her own explanation already.

"Did you know him?"

"We were close. Once."

Meyer regarded Jasmine for a long moment before turning to Finn. "What would you do next?"

He considered what Meyer would do if he were the one investigating. Finn thought about what he would do if they were still in Verendal, and investigating a crime that had happened there. He knew exactly what he would do at that point. "I'd like to see where the crime was committed," Finn said.

"Very well."

Meyer watched her for another moment before shaking his head and turning away.

When they were back outside, Meyer secured the door, locking it again.

"What did the townspeople tell you?" Finn asked.

Meyer pulled out a folded paper that he handed to Finn. It was thick parchment paper with a jerky sort of handwriting, barely legible, detailing the crimes that Jasmine had been accused of. Murder of this Matthew Avard. Found covered in his blood. A dagger resting near her. And a history between them.

Finn glanced back to the door of the prison, frowning. "It would've been helpful to have known about the history between them."

"She told you the history."

Finn shook his head. "She said they'd been close."

"What does that mean to you?"

"I don't know. They were friends? Lovers?" Finn looked back behind him.

"Probably," Meyer said.

"How long have they held her there?"

"We received word earlier this week, so no more than that," Master Meyer said.

"Do you think they would have cleaned up the crime?"

"It's difficult to know. Within Verendal, we have a

tradition of waiting until the investigation is complete and sentencing has been carried out before anything is removed, but in the outside towns and villages, you will find different traditions."

"You know how to find it?"

Meyer nodded, guiding Finn along the outskirts of the village again before taking a cobbled street. There were more people out now as the morning grew later, and all of them looked at Master Meyer and Finn with suspicion in their eyes. None paid much attention to them otherwise.

"Have you ever not carried out a sentencing when you were summoned to do so?"

"It's infrequent, but it does happen," Meyer said.

"What happens then?"

"The townspeople typically rebel."

"Even if you find evidence that the accused was innocent?"

"There's a measure of pride within these places, Finn."

They stopped at a two-story home not far into the village. Meyer glanced along the street, looking in either direction, before settling his hand on the door.

"This is the place?"

He nodded. "This is the place."

Meyer tested the handle and pushed the door open. Once inside, he paused. Finn stayed just outside, giving Meyer a chance to look around before motioning for Finn to join him.

Finn did so, stepping a little farther into the home, then pausing.

The air stank.

He had investigated several crimes with Master Meyer before, and he had come to know the stench of death. This had a very distinct odor to it, and he wrinkled his nose, wishing for a face covering to keep from having to smell the foulness of death.

"It doesn't smell like they cleaned anything here," Finn said.

"No. It does not," Master Meyer said.

A light blazed inside the home, and Master Meyer was illuminated. He held a lantern, resting it above a small table just inside the entryway. He turned the lantern, sweeping around, and Finn stepped inside, resisting the stench there.

He followed Meyer.

There was a small trail of blood along the inside of the home, but it wasn't until they got into the hearth room that there was even more blood. It pooled on the stone, splattered on the walls, and covered a table nearby.

"What do you see here?" Meyer asked.

"Besides the blood?"

Meyer shot him a look. "Besides the blood."

"There is considerable splatter."

"There is. What does that suggest to you?"

"Typically with that much splatter, it means the crime was violent," he said.

There was a difference between violent crime and the violence of crime. He had seen criminals wanting to remove a threat to their success, and typically those were quiet crimes, little more than bloodless affairs. It was sort of how the Lion had been killed, his body dumped into the river, left with no way of tracking who might be responsible. When there were crimes like this, they were typically different, wrapped up in the passion of the crime, the anger and violence of it, and were less likely to be someone who had calculated or planned for the event.

Finn paused in front of the largest pool of blood before moving onward, looking at the table, even the hearth itself, splatters of blood everywhere.

"All of this from a knife?" Finn asked.

"You don't think a knife could do it?"

Finn pressed his mouth together, considering. "I suppose if they were to strike one of the arteries, the force from that might lead to this, but..."

None of it gave him enough answers to believe in Jasmine's innocence.

"There's not enough here," Finn said.

"No," Meyer said.

"What now?"

"Now we ask those who were involved."

"What do you think they will say?"

Meyer shrugged. "It's possible they won't say anything at all, but it's also possible that they have more information for us."

"Why go through all of that?" Finn frowned at Master Meyer. "If she's guilty, why would you go through so many steps?"

Meyer cocked his head to the side, watching Finn. "Do you believe her to be guilty?"

Finn took a deep breath, letting it out slowly. "I don't really know. I look at this, and I see a crime of passion, which suggests to me somebody like her could have committed it. Without an alternative explanation, it is difficult to know whether she is guilty or innocent."

"Without having enough proof, do you think we should sentence her?"

"No, but I think you're going to have a hard time convincing the townspeople of that."

"I agree. Which is why we must make sure we are doing everything in our power to find the answer before we carry out a sentence that might lead to a potentially innocent woman dying."

"What if she's not innocent?"

A flicker of concern cross Master Meyer's face. "It's possible that she did it, but..."

"You don't think she did."

"Do you?" Meyer asked.

"There was a moment when she was looking at you where I thought she could be guilty of it, but only that moment."

"I've told you how many people I have sentenced," Master Meyer said.

"You have." It was an enormous number, and with that level of experience, Meyer would obviously know whether someone was guilty or innocent fairly quickly, so for him to have any measure of hesitation was reason for Finn to share in it. "I don't know that your experience is going to sway them, either."

"Perhaps not," Master Meyer said. He looked around the room again before heading out, carrying the lantern with him. Finn joined him outside, and Meyer closed the door behind them, pulling it tight. "If she is guilty, I will carry out the sentence as requested, but I need to be convinced of her guilt."

"And if you're not? What would you do then?"

Meyer didn't answer. Instead, he headed along the cobbled road, deeper into the village.

CHAPTER TWENTY-TWO

The town hall was a simple structure and almost cozy, situated as it was in the center of the village, with the nearby church rising toward the sky. This was the place where they had encountered the woman, though in the daylight, the bright sun shining down, there was a little bit less of a feeling of unwelcome.

"Why here?"

He understood Meyer wanted to be thorough, but he wanted to get back to Verendal.

It felt like things were happening there while he was away—and he needed answers.

"We need to question those involved," Meyer said. "I figure it's best to do that here rather than on the outskirts of the village. Certainly not near the prison, such as it is."

"You want them to be comfortable."

Meyer nodded.

He raised his hand to knock, but the door came open, and the old woman poked her head out. "So?"

"Mistress Elaine. I have a few questions I'd like to ask before we move forward with our sentencing."

"Questions? All the questions have been answered. You are here to perform a task, hangman. I don't need for you to be questioning my people."

Meyer bowed his head slightly. "I understand why you've summoned me here, but the purpose of my visit is more than simply to carry out the sentence your people have requested. As you can well understand, I'm tasked by the king—"

"I understand who you are tasked by. That's the only reason I sent word. Otherwise, we would have been done with this ourselves. I have no trouble tying a rope."

"Be that as it may," Meyer said, "my responsibility is such that I need to question all who might have involvement in this case. I would like to speak to the ones who found the body, along with a few people who knew Jasmine Melth the best."

"You can't tell me that you want to get to know the girl. She was trouble from the very beginning."

"How so?"

"Trouble, hangman. Do I need to be any clearer than that?"

"I'm afraid you do," Master Meyer said.

"Fine. She got herself caught up in far too many situations like the one with Matthew. He wasn't the first boy that she tussled with."

"Is that right?" Master Meyer said.

"A little bit of a trollop, if you ask me. Going around and slipping into a man's bed."

"That is no crime," Master Meyer said.

"No crime, but the gods certainly don't care for it." She glanced over to the church nearby, her gaze drifting all the way to the top. Finn suspected that it was a church of Heleth, but he didn't really know. Within Verendal, there was a church for each of the gods, but here there seemed to be only the one church. It might celebrate all of the gods, though such a thing would be difficult. Each of the gods had their own forms of celebrations, and he couldn't imagine the priests working together like that. Heleth looked over all of the gods, though, so would be the most logical one for the people in this village to celebrate. "You can't tell me that a girl like that can go running around without any repercussions."

"I can't say I would expect there to be repercussions," Meyer said.

"No repercussions? Let me tell you, when I was young, a woman waited for man to woo her. He did so delicately and with the gods' approval."

Meyer smiled tightly. "I understand the tradition."

She arched her brow at him. "Do you? I didn't know a hangman could marry."

"There are no laws against it."

"No? Maybe there should be. Maybe you shouldn't have the opportunity to take a wife, especially since you are so quick to take a life."

Meyer tensed, though nothing in his expression changed. "I would like to visit with those who found her, along with those who accused her. Additionally, I would like to speak to whoever might know her best."

Mistress Elaine sneered at Master Meyer. "Do what you think is necessary."

"And I will be using the village hall as I question," he said.

"That wasn't the agreement."

"I am on official business," he said.

She frowned. "I suppose you are, but that doesn't mean I have to like it."

Meyer smiled slightly. "I'm not asking you to like it."

He strode forward, into the village hall, and Mistress Elaine watched him before stomping off along the road. Finn followed Meyer into the hall and joined him at a table. It was a simple space, a long table running the length of it, and several rooms off to the side. Meyer had set his pack and the sword Justice up against the table, leaning it there, and he took a few shallow breaths.

"Did you take anything from what she said?" Meyer asked.

"Other than the fact that we might have alternative explanations as to who killed Matthew?"

"Very good."

"It's going to be difficult proving that," Finn said.

"Difficult but not impossible. And it's something they should've considered."

"Should they, though?" Meyer frowned at him, and Finn just shrugged. "You said it yourself. You've carried out over a thousand sentences, which means you've carried out at least that many investigations. Possibly more." Meyer nodded. "You have experience looking for alternative explanations and trying to find those who might be guilty but have not yet revealed themselves." Finn shrugged. "It looked to be a crime of passion, and it means either the lover or a spurned lover."

The door to the village hall came open, and an older man came in. He looked to have once been muscular, but muscle had turned a bit to flab, and he limped, his knee or ankle, or possibly even his hip, bothering him as he stepped into the room. His hands were clasped behind him, and he glanced from Finn to Meyer nervously, taking up a position at the end of the table as he watched them. "I understand you wanted to meet with me, master executioner?"

Meyer nodded. "Your name?"

"My name is Bester Holanth."

"And your role?"

"Well, I heard the wailing, and I went to take a look. I suppose you'd say I found the poor man. Avard didn't deserve nothing like that. Skilled carpenter and all as he was. Up and coming, you would say."

"I'm sure," Master Meyer said.

"Never seen anything like that before." He rubbed his eyes, shaking his head. "So much blood." He widened his eyes, looking at Meyer. "Not that blood's a bad thing. I'm sure you get to see that often enough, and I'm sure that it doesn't—"

"Take it easy," Master Meyer said, smiling slightly. "I'm not here for you. I'm here for information."

The man breathed out. "The girl was sitting there,

holding on to that knife. Couldn't believe she would do it. Always so sweet, you know. Said hello to everybody in the town. Of course, she was known to flirt and all. Use it to get things."

"Did she?" Master Meyer asked.

"Not that she… oh. I was just trying to say that I didn't think it was the kind of thing she would do, but she just sat there with the knife, staring at Avard."

"Is anything else you can tell us?" Meyer asked.

"Just that we can't have a killer like that in our village. Glad you're here, master executioner. We've never had to call for your kind before, and it's just so hard on us."

Meyer nodded. "Thank you for your report."

He turned, hurrying away, and Finn frowned. "You said that you had been here before."

"I suspect it was before his time," Meyer said softly.

"That long ago?"

"Long enough."

"He didn't think she was likely to have done it."

"He didn't, and I think if Mistress Elaine were to be honest, she would have said the same thing."

"But?"

"But we still don't have somebody else to accuse," Meyer said.

The door came open again, and this time a woman entered. She was a few years older than Finn, blonde, curvy, and he flashed a grin at her before remembering why he was there and suppressing it. She rocked from foot to foot nervously, her fingers twisting the fabric of her pale blue dress as she looked at Master Meyer, ignoring Finn altogether.

"You wanted to see me?"

"What is your name?" Master Meyer asked.

"Wendy Rithen."

"What is your relationship to this?"

"Mistress Elaine said you wanted to talk to Jasmine's friends and family."

"And you are?"

"She was my friend. *Is* my friend." Wendy shook her head, finally seeming to see Finn, and flushing slightly. "I've known her since I was a little girl. Since we both were, really. At least, since she came to the village."

"Do you think she could have done this?"

Wendy still rocked from place to place, clutching the fabric of her dress now.

"Wendy?" Meyer pressed.

"I don't know," she said. "I would have said no, but lately, she's been a bit different."

"Different in what way?"

"I am not even sure how to explain it. She has so many different men she's been involved with, and it's been hard for me to keep track. I feel like I don't even know her anymore."

"Do you think she could have killed Matthew?"

Wendy's eyes softened. "She wouldn't have done that, would she?"

"That's what I'm asking," Master Meyer said.

"I... well, I just don't know. I would tell you she

wouldn't, but she didn't like anyone getting in her way, you see."

"Is that right?"

"When she wanted something, that is. She made a point of getting what she wanted, regardless of who might be hurt."

"Did she ever hurt you?" Finn asked.

Wendy glanced over to him, the flush working through her cheeks again. "She was my friend."

"Friends hurt each other sometimes," Finn said softly.

Wendy shook her head. "No. Jasmine would never do that. She and I were friends."

"Is there anything else that you can tell us about your friendship with her?"

"Just that I don't want to lose her," she said.

Meyer nodded. "Thank you for speaking with me."

Wendy sucked in a sharp breath, gripping tightly to her dress. "Is that it?"

"Were you expecting more?"

"When Mistress Elaine told me that the hangman wanted to speak with me..."

"That's it," Master Meyer said.

Wendy scurried toward the door, closing it almost too loudly.

Finn looked after her. "She's not telling us everything," he said.

"She told us enough," Meyer said.

"She did?"

"They were friends but rivals."

"You think she might have been the one to have killed

him?"

"I doubt it. Maybe jealousy, but killing? Unless she had a relationship with this man, it doesn't strike me as something she would have been capable of doing."

The door came open again, and an old man hobbled in, leaning on a cane. He had thinning hair, deeply tanned skin, and heavy wrinkles at the corners of his eyes looked to have deepened recently. He glanced from Master Meyer to Finn, turning from one to the other, and nodded to both.

Another person? How many did Meyer plan to interrogate?

"I'm Krell Divs. Hear you wanted to speak to me."

"We are speaking with anyone who had a relationship with the accused."

"Relationship?"

"Did you not?"

"She was my granddaughter. Can't say that we had much of a relationship."

"Why not?"

"Well, her mother and father died when she was young, and I was forced to take her in." He shook his head. "Didn't care much for it, but also didn't have much of a choice."

"She wasn't from here?"

"She been raised here since she was little more than knee-high," Krell said. "Been nothing but trouble."

"I've heard that from Mistress Elaine."

Krell glanced toward the door, his brow furrowing. "She say that too? That blasted woman."

"What else can you tell me about her?"

"I told you everything I can," Krell said. "What more do you think I need to say?"

"How about you start with whether or not you think she could have done this."

"Killed him? Nah. She been trouble, but not that kind of trouble. She wants to be a good girl, you see; it's just she gets a little bit of the fire of Volan into her, and you know what that does to a person."

The trickster god was often blamed for crimes, but Finn had never heard of anybody accusing him of crimes of seduction. He might have to try that sometime.

"You don't think that she could have done this, then?" Meyer asked.

"I done say that, didn't I?" Krell shook his head, glancing over to Finn. "Is he always this dense?"

Finn suppressed a grin. "We are just trying to determine whether or not Jasmine could be responsible for what took place," Finn said, choosing his words carefully. "We have been interviewing anybody who might have been involved with her, along with the man who discovered the crime."

"If you're trying to find anyone who's been involved with her, then maybe you need to talk to Joseph Malloy."

"Why him?" Finn asked.

"Well, he and Jasmine were a thing for little while, but…" He shrugged. "Can't say I blame her for wandering. Joseph wasn't always the best for her."

"Why was that?"

"He wanted her to stay here. Figured that was the best

way to hold on to her. Jasmine, well, she wanted to be like her parents and figured she could wander."

"Is that right?" Master Meyer said.

"Not saying that she was ever going to leave, but you know how kids are."

Finn smiled. Krell was older, but he wouldn't have considered Jasmine to be a kid.

Meyer nodded to him. "Thank you for visiting with us. Would you mind letting Mistress Elaine know we would like to speak with her next?"

Krell grinned. "You think she has something to do with this?"

"I don't, but I would like to have a few words with her," Master Meyer said.

"You let her know that if she had anything to do with what happened to my granddaughter, I'm going to..." He shrugged. "Anyway. I will let her know."

He hobbled out, tapping his cane on the ground, and was gone only a moment before Mistress Elaine came in, standing in the doorway. "You want to question me now?"

"No. I would like to speak with a Joseph Malloy," Master Meyer said.

"Malloy? That boy hasn't done anything. He's too simple."

"Maybe," Master Meyer said. "But I'd still like to speak with him."

Elaine turned, slamming the door closed behind her.

"I will say one thing about investigations outside of the city: it sure is a lot easier to get people together," Finn said.

"Easier, but in some ways a bit more complicated as well." Meyer stared at the door where Elaine had departed. "You find a few more tempers than you do elsewhere. Along with a bit more to carry out your investigation."

"Of course we're going to have disagreement," Finn said. "She likely has already convicted Jasmine of the crime."

"She has," Meyer said, nodding slowly. "I have not."

They sat quietly, and Master Meyer jotted down a few notes in a small notebook he carried with him. "I need to check something with Mistress Elaine. You question the next man and we will discuss."

He stepped out and Finn waited for only a few moments before the door opened again. This was a younger man, dark hair, strong chin, a hint of a beard lining his face. He swaggered into the village hall, his gaze drifting to Finn. "I hear you want to talk with me?" he said.

Finn nodded. "You are Joseph Malloy?" He didn't look simple. Arrogant, maybe, especially with the way he held his head cocked to the side while watching Finn.

"I am. I didn't do anything to Avard."

"No?"

"That's why you brought me here, isn't it? You wanted to see if I could have done it."

"We're trying to gather information about whether or not Jasmine could have done it," Finn said.

"Knowing Jasmine the way I do, I wouldn't put it past her," he said. "She gets a bit fiery."

Finn frowned. He'd been getting annoyed by how long they had been here questioning, but this comment caught him and made him take a second look at him. "What do you mean, *fiery?*"

Joseph was sneering at Finn. "You know the type. Likes to throw herself around. Didn't pay too much attention to running off when she had the opportunity with him."

Something Jasmine's grandfather had said triggered a different question for Finn. "I understand you wanted to keep her in the village," Finn said.

Joseph frowned. "What does that have to do with anything?"

Finn just shrugged. "I'm trying to get as full of a picture as I can of her."

"She was found covered in his blood. Holding a knife. Can't be anyone else other than her, could it?" Joseph Malloy asked.

"You would think it would be so obvious," Finn said, smiling slightly.

"Yeah, well, I told her that I wanted to stay in the village, and she wasn't interested in it. Said she wanted to go and see the world. Planned to go to Vur, even to the capital, but I didn't want to do that."

"Did she end it with you?" Finn asked.

Joseph frowned. "Did she? I've never had a woman end anything with me."

"Is that right?" Finn asked.

"You can ask anyone."

"Do you have a woman now?" Finn asked.

"I thought you already knew, seeing as how you questioned her."

"I just wanted to confirm," Finn said.

"Yeah, well, Jasmine got what she deserved."

"And what is that?" Finn asked.

"She killed him, now she's sitting in that cell. That's what she deserves."

"Do you think she deserves to die?" Finn asked.

"Deserves? For what she did to him? Of course she deserves to die," he practically spat.

Finn frowned.

Joseph just shook his head. "Craziness, if you ask me. All of this business calling in somebody from Verendal. We could take care of this ourselves. Especially after what she did... Anyway. I've had enough of this." He got to his feet.

Joseph had started to turn away when Finn stepped in front of him. Hopefully, Meyer would back him on this. It wasn't how he expected this to go, but maybe that was a lesson Meyer wanted him to learn. "Joseph Malloy, I will be detaining you for additional questioning."

"Questioning?" He shook his head. "What do you mean, you're questioning me? You got the person responsible. You need to question anyone else."

"I have the person responsible. Now."

Finn grabbed for Joseph's arm, and Joseph jerked away.

Finn grabbed his other arm and slammed one knee into the back of Malloy's knee, dropping him to the ground. He crumpled, and Finn pressed down on him, holding him in place.

"What is this?"

Finn glanced over his shoulder to see Mistress Elaine standing in the doorway.

Where was Meyer?

"Mistress Elaine. Good. We need members of your town council to help escort Joseph Malloy to your prison."

"To our prison? What do you think you're doing? He isn't—"

"Innocent," Finn said. "Now, I expect you to bring your council to me."

She stood in the doorway for a long moment before turning and disappearing.

Joseph tried to fight, but with Finn on his back, he wasn't able to fight very well.

Finn looked down at Joseph. His comments came together, making a certain sort of sense. He thought he knew what happened, and could even piece it together.

"I didn't do anything," Joseph shouted.

"Let me tell you what I think happened," Finn said, leaning close to him. "I think you were upset with Jasmine. You wanted her for yourself, and when you couldn't have her, you took revenge on the man she chose over you."

"That's not how it went. I'm with Wendy."

"You are, but you still wanted Jasmine," Finn said.

Joseph tried to roll, and he was strong enough that Finn struggled against his movements and worried that Joseph would eventually fight his way free.

"I moved on. I told you."

"Moved on, but you still pined for her."

"I told you—"

"You told me that you cared for her. You told me that she was going to get what she deserved."

"She will," he sneered.

Finn leaned closer to him, whispering in his ear. "No. You will."

"No one's going to believe you. They don't care about nothing but what they know. They saw what happened. You ask old Bester Holanth."

"We did," Finn said, starting to piece things together. "He heard wailing." There was movement behind him, and Finn suspected others from the council had entered, though he couldn't see them, not with where he sat on Joseph's back, keeping him pinned to the ground. "She mourned his loss. She was in shock because of it."

"She was in shock because she did it," Joseph said.

"She was in shock because she found him. You'd killed him." It fit. By all reports that they had, Matthew was a large and muscular man, and he would've taken somebody of a reasonable build to overpower. "I imagine you tried to talk with him first. You tried to tell him that you were still in love with her. He tried to tell him that she should leave him and return to you. Maybe you even tried to tell her that she was better off staying in the village."

"She would be better off staying in the village!"

"When he refused you, you attacked."

"I did what I had to do!" Joseph shouted.

"You stabbed him, killing him, and then you left. When Jasmine found him, you had your alibi. Now she was definitely going to get what she deserved. Either way, she was guilty."

Joseph just shook his head. "She deserves what's coming to her."

"Like Matthew Avard deserved what was coming to him?"

"Yes," Joseph spat.

Finn looked behind him. The council stood arranged there, Mistress Elaine standing amongst them, saying nothing. Meyer remained off to the side, mouth pressed into a tight frown.

"Take him," Finn said.

Two men hurried forward; they grabbed Joseph. As soon they did, he tried again to fight, and two more joined, grabbing his legs, and they dragged him from the village hall.

Meyer approached, watching Finn. "Unconventional but effective."

"I'm sorry," Finn said.

Meyer shook his head. "Don't be. An innocent woman will be released."

"Innocent?" Mistress Elaine said. "I've already told you that she—"

"Didn't kill anyone," Master Meyer said. "Regardless of your feelings about her sexual proclivities, she was not guilty of the crime."

She sniffed. "She will have a hard time here."

"Yes. I'm sure she will," Master Meyer said.

He took a deep breath, let it out, and turned to Finn. "Now that we have the guilty party, it's time for the sentencing."

CHAPTER TWENTY-THREE

Situated outside of Verendal and nestled into the forest as the village was, there wasn't a formal gallows. There was a part of Finn that wondered whether or not Meyer would offer Malloy the sword, giving him an honorable death.

Meyer looked up at the massive branch with the rope now hanging from it, nodding to himself. "This will do."

"It seems so… simple."

Meyer chuckled. "Not all sentencing needs to be quite as formal as what we do in Verendal."

"Still," Finn said.

A procession started toward them, and it seemed that the entirety of the village came with them, marching through the cobbled streets, along the narrow stream, toward the makeshift gallows situated just outside of the village. Perhaps it was fitting that they not carry out the sentencing inside the village itself. Even in Verendal, they didn't carry out sentencing within the city.

A brown-robed priest led Joseph Malloy forward, his wrists tied behind him and a length of rope stretched between his legs, giving him something of a shuffling gait as he staggered toward them. The crowd surrounded him, and many of them shouted at Malloy.

Finn glanced over to the tree, to the noose, ensuring that it was set correctly, before turning his attention back to Meyer. "What do you think?"

"I think he has underestimated the will of the village."

The priest murmured a soft prayer to Joseph Malloy as they marched forward, and when they reached them, the priest looked up at Meyer, turned to Finn briefly, and nodded. "I have spoken the words of Heleth and have prayed with him during his march."

"Thank you," Master Meyer said.

Meyer strode forward, grabbing Malloy by the wrists. One of the other council members carried a short ladder, and Finn hurried over, taking it. He situated it in front of the rope, and together with Meyer, they forced Malloy up the ladder.

"Do you have anything to say for yourself?" Master Meyer asked.

"You call this justice?"

"I do."

When he was situated, both Finn and Meyer needed to work to get the rope around his neck, and once secured, they climbed down the ladder, and with very little ceremony, they jerked the ladder back.

It was a sliding noose, meant to snap his neck, but Malloy was either even stronger than he looked or simply unlucky. He dangled, suffocating slowly. He kicked, his eyes bulging and arms flailing, though he was bound and could not move. Villagers shouted at him, throwing rubbish at him as he died. It was over in a few minutes.

"Not a clean death," Finn muttered. "That is on me."

"You intended to make it clean?"

"I was hoping to make it quick."

Meyer nodded. "Then perhaps the gods gave him what he deserved."

He spoke a few words to the priest, then to the town council, before stopping in front of Mistress Elaine, and he held his hand out. She pulled a small pouch from within her dress, tears welling in her eyes, and slammed it into his palm, before turning and storming away.

"She still doesn't care for all of that," Finn said.

"I think it's more than just not caring for that," Meyer said. "That was her grandson, after all."

Finn looked back at Malloy. "He was?"

Meyer nodded. "I discovered that while trying to find more information, and when you learned of his guilt, I realized we were going to have a little bit of trouble." Meyer looked down at his hand and slipped the pouch of coins into his pocket. "At least she paid. I wasn't sure if she would."

"What would you have done then?"

Meyer shook his head. "Probably not have pushed the issue. There was no point in doing so. They had already convicted Jasmine Melth by the time we arrived, so we were starting off in the wrong place."

"What now? Are we returning?"

"I think it's time," Meyer said.

They made their way through the still-gathered crowd. Many of the villagers were talking to each other, every so often looking over to Malloy, some of them shaking their heads. One older woman had tears streaming down her face, and Finn passed Wendy standing off to the side and sobbing violently. He felt a twinge of guilt, but it was better that she know what kind of man Malloy was, and better that she not stay bound to him. Eventually, her grief would fade.

"It's not always the families of the victims who suffer," Meyer said.

"I see that," Finn said.

"Sometimes, you find it's the families of those who are left behind, both the victim and the guilty. Both must come to terms with what happened and their place within it."

"He was willing to destroy one life for the betterment of his own," Finn said.

"He was young. Arrogant. Foolish. And violent. A dangerous combination."

"I think anytime someone kills is a dangerous combination."

"Even more so when they are calm and collected, and unmindful of the consequences. I suspect Joseph Malloy was lucky more than anything else."

"Lucky?" Finn turned and looked back at where

Malloy still dangled from the tree. He doubted there would be any hegen who came to collect his remains, but perhaps they would come. Finn didn't know how far outside of Verendal the hegen reached. "Why would you call it *lucky?*"

"Lucky in that he had a moment where he probably thought he had escaped consequences. It made him arrogant."

"Do you think Mistress Elaine knew?"

Meyer frowned, looking through the village. He smiled slightly. "That is an interesting question. Perhaps we should go and visit with her."

"I didn't mean to ask it to cause more trouble in the village."

"No. It's a good question." Meyer sniffed. "And one I should have considered. She was quite disappointed when we uncovered his guilt."

"It could be just that she's his grandmother."

"It could be."

"What if she was complicit?"

"If she is a part of it, then the council will take action. That won't be upon us."

"What if they ask us to be involved?"

"Then I would suggest they send word to the king." Meyer glanced back at Malloy. "We were hired to sentence the party guilty of killing Matthew Avard. Nothing more than that." By the time they made it back to the village hall, Meyer had a determined step to his gait. He handed Finn his pack, along with the sword Justice, and nodded. "This might be something you should be a part of," Meyer said.

Finn just nodded, thankful that Meyer intended to include him.

As they entered, Mistress Elaine looked over to them, a dark expression on her face. "The terms of the agreement are over, hangman."

Meyer nodded, motioning to the table. "I would like to visit with you, if you don't mind."

"I have nothing to say to you, master executioner."

"I'm afraid this is under official business."

Her brow furrowed. "You just carried out your execution. I think your official business is over in Logard."

"Not quite."

Meyer nodded again and motioned toward the table, and Mistress Elaine reluctantly headed to it, pulling out a chair and leaning on the back of it for a moment before taking a seat and slamming her fist down on the table. "What is this about?"

Meyer pulled out his chair, taking a seat. Finn debated whether or not to join him but thought that it would be best if he stood.

"You never shared with us that Malloy was your grandson," Meyer said.

"It was of little added value."

"I didn't know until I had a conversation with Krell."

"That old fool. There isn't much he can share with you. Look what happened with his daughter."

"What exactly happened with his daughter?"

"Got caught up with those people. *Witches.*" She

sneered, waving her hand. "And then she disappeared. Figures something like that would happen to her. No different than her daughter."

"You didn't like Jasmine very much," Meyer said. "It's more than about her interest in the men of the village."

"Interest?" Elaine looked up, shaking her head. "If it was just about interest, it wouldn't be a problem, but that girl—"

"Woman," Meyer corrected.

"Fine. That woman," she spat, "was a corruption. Like all of her kind."

"You thought she was getting what she deserved, as well."

"I... what?"

"You knew your grandson was the one who had killed Matthew Avard."

"I wouldn't have called you here if I intended to sentence my grandson," she said.

"No, but you did hope you could push through Ms. Melth's guilt. You were hopeful that by forcing through the conviction, the sentencing, your grandson would stay free."

She said nothing. The darkness in her eyes answered the question for Finn, though. She *had* known. What would happen in the city if others were to learn?

"How long have you led the village?" Finn asked.

She looked over to Finn, disdain sweeping across her brow. "Who are you to ask me any questions?"

"This is Finn Jagger, as you already know. He is my

apprentice, and in that role, he serves the king, much like I do. You will answer the question."

She glared at Finn. "I've led the village for the better part of twenty years. Long enough to know what kind of people are good for our kind."

"And you didn't care much for Ms. Melth."

"Care for her? She was fine as a child, but the woman she became was undesirable."

"I have a feeling you don't have to worry about that any longer," Meyer said.

"What is that supposed to mean?"

"Had you paid any attention to your villagers, you would've known the young woman intended to leave. All you had to do was permit it."

"I didn't stop anything."

"No?" Meyer leaned forward, holding her gaze. "What about your grandson?"

"I didn't stop him from leaving either."

"I wonder what you would have said had he come to you, telling you he intended to leave the village and to go with her."

Elaine said nothing.

Meyer leaned back, crossing his arms over his chest. "The full report of my findings will be submitted to the king," Master Meyer said. "As is the nature of all such convictions. Now, I can include all aspects of the report, or if you were to prefer, I could leave out certain details."

"What details do you intend to leave out?"

"That depends on if you no longer lead the council."

"The king has no authority within the village."

"The king doesn't need authority over your council. The only thing that matters is that you step down." Meyer leaned toward her. "Otherwise, not only will the king learn of what you did, the others in your village will."

There was a hint of danger in his tone, more than what Finn expected from Meyer. Finn began to wonder if perhaps Meyer allowed himself to dip down into a bit of vengeance.

"I suppose I have gotten up there in years. Perhaps it's time I no longer serve." She took a deep breath, drawing herself taller as if making some grand decision.

"Perhaps," Meyer agreed. He nodded to her, getting to his feet, and motioned for Finn to follow him. "I will be checking in with your village."

She said nothing.

Back outside, Finn looked over to Meyer. "Is that justice?" he asked softly.

"That is as much justice as we will find in a place like this," Meyer said. "Unfortunately, that is as far as I can push it."

"You don't have to file a report with the king," Finn said.

Meyer shook his head. "No. That would go unread."

"You were counting on her not knowing."

"I'm counting on her to step down. Someone willing to convict an innocent woman should not lead her village." He glanced over to Finn.

"What now?"

Meyer looked up at the sky. "I suppose we could stay

another night, but given everything we've seen and experienced here, I'm not so sure I want to do so."

"I'm not so sure I want to, either," Finn said.

"Gather the horses. We will be on our way. I intend to push through the night."

"Is it safe? The horses could get injured."

"I didn't say we would ride hard. I only said we would ride through the night."

There was a small road leading out of the village, and once they reached the king's road, it would be a much easier journey, so perhaps Meyer counted on that. They stopped at the stable, and Finn gathered the horses, brushed by one of the stable hands and looking better than when Finn had left them before, strapping saddles to them, before guiding them back out. It seemed amazing to Finn that they had only arrived the night before, and even though it was late in the day, he didn't blame Master Meyer for not wanting to linger any longer than they needed to.

They started toward the edge of the village, and once they reached it, a dark-haired woman came running up to them.

Jasmine looked quite a bit different from the last time Finn had seen her. Her eyes were ringed with tears, reddened, but she had washed and changed and now looked at them with a mixture of relief and something else Finn couldn't quite place.

"Master executioner?" she asked, coming up to them and bowing politely. She tipped her head to Finn as well. "I was hoping that perhaps I might accompany you."

THE EXECUTIONER'S APPRENTICE | 371

"We are heading to Verendal," Meyer said.

"That's fine," Jasmine said, looking over her shoulder to the village. "I... well, I can't stay here."

Finn fully expected Meyer to tell her no, but there was a part of him that questioned whether or not he would. Meyer had a soft spot for those he thought he could help. Maybe he would see something in Jasmine he wanted to help.

"You may accompany us to Verendal, but are you sure you want to?"

"All I have is my grandfather here. He doesn't think I should stay either. Given what I've gone through, I'm inclined to agree with him. I don't think it's safe for me to be here anymore."

Finn couldn't imagine what it would be like for somebody like her to remain in a village where they had been so close to killing her. It was hard enough for him in Verendal, having gone through something similar. He wasn't innocent, not the way that Jasmine was, but he had nearly suffered a similar fate.

"We should help her," Finn said.

Meyer shot him a look to silence him. "Gather what you need. We will be leaving."

"Thank you, master executioner."

She hurried off, and Meyer breathed out heavily.

"What will happen to her in Verendal?"

"I don't know," Meyer said.

"It's not going to be all that much safer for her there."

"Perhaps not," Meyer agreed.

"Do you know of anybody who might be able to help?"

He glanced over. "I can't take another in."

"It wasn't getting at that," Finn said. "It's just that…" He didn't even know what it was. His sister struggled enough having a place for her to call her own, and he suspected that Jasmine would find the same difficulty. What training and education would she have received in a village like this that would allow her to succeed within Verendal?

Jasmine wasn't gone long before she came running over to them, carrying a pack. Finn looked behind her and saw Wendy watching, saying nothing, along with Krell rubbing his fist into his eyes as he looked to be fighting off tears.

"Is that all?"

Jasmine looked at her pack, shrugging. "I didn't have much I cared about bringing. I just want to be gone from here."

They started off, and the trees around them quickly swallowed them, casting them into darkness. The sun had already fallen quite low in the sky, and Meyer took a quick pace along the road, guiding the horses, letting Finn and Jasmine ride. After a while, Finn climbed down and motioned for Meyer to take his horse.

"I can manage," Master Meyer said.

"I know, but let me walk. Either that or we ride double."

Meyer smirked slightly.

Finn shot him a look, and as they marched along the road, Finn looked up to Jasmine. "I understand you weren't always from Logard," he said after they had walked while in silence.

Insects buzzed in the forest, their sound building as night grew deeper. Until they stepped out on the king's road, they would not be able to see much light, no starlight, and no moonlight.

"I came when I was young," she said.

"What happened with your parents?" As soon as he asked, Finn immediately regretted it. She had been through a traumatic episode, and he certainly didn't need to keep pressing. This was somebody who had suffered, and she didn't need to suffer more indignity just because of his curiosity.

"I don't really remember. My grandfather brought me to the village, saying he had to help me. Save me, I think he said." She shook her head. "I wonder what it would've been like had I been able to stay in Norasn."

It was a much larger city, nearly the same size as Verendal, and more to the north and west. "Do you remember anything about it?"

"Only the towers," she said softly. "I have dreams of them, though I don't even know if they are real or if they are imagined."

"What sort of towers?"

"My grandfather says the towers I remember are the church spires, but it seems to me I remember something else. These were gleaming white stone towers, stretching high into the sky, almost impossibly so." Her voice took on a faraway quality. "Maybe that's just the child memories, a recollection of something that never was or never could be." She smiled, shaking her head. "Or perhaps they are real memories."

"I've never been there."

"Are you from Verendal?"

Finn nodded. "Born and raised."

She glanced behind her at Master Meyer before turning her attention back down to Finn. Even in the fading daylight, the darkness swirling around her, she was quite lovely. Her dark hair seemed to catch the shadows, and so did her full lips. When she looked at him, Finn could almost imagine her kissing him with those lips.

He had to be careful. That was what Meyer had warned him of. She was pretty enough, but she had been through quite a bit. She didn't need him leering at her like that. She deserved better.

"And you are like him? An executioner?"

"I'm his apprentice."

"Oh."

"I didn't have much choice," he said softly, staring off into the trees.

"Why not?"

"I was a thief." He chuckled. "Made a few mistakes, and by the time I first met Master Meyer, I had been sentenced by the jurors in Verendal to die."

"You were innocent too?"

Finn let out a long sigh. "Not innocent at all, but I didn't deserve to die. Master Meyer agreed, and he saved me."

"I didn't realize the executioners could save people who were convicted," she said.

Finn looked over to her before shaking his head. "Normally, they can't. He made an exception with me."

"Why?"

"I'm still trying to learn the answer to that."

They walked on in silence, though Finn would look over to Jasmine every so often before focusing ahead of him again. She remained silent, and yet she stayed awake. They walked until they reached the king's road, and then moved off to the west, heading toward Verendal. Now that the road opened up, their path was easier to navigate.

They traveled until they reached a small side road, where Meyer guided them off.

"What are you doing?" Finn asked.

Meyer grunted. "I'm of no mind to ride through the dark. There's a tavern up ahead, and I intend for us to get some rest. We can return to the city in the morning."

They didn't have to go far off the road before the tavern appeared in a small clearing. It was a simple wooden structure. Lights blazed in windows, and there came the sound of jaunty music from inside. Finn and Meyer secured the horses to a post outside before Finn helped Jasmine down from the saddle, and together, they went into the tavern.

Finn and Jasmine stood in the doorway for just a moment while Meyer went off, speaking to a short, rotund man for a few moments, passing him several coins, before making his way back to Finn and Jasmine.

"I secured us several rooms for the night. Why don't we leave our belongings behind, and we can get some food?"

Finn followed Meyer through the tavern. It was only somewhat like the Wenderwolf. A massive hearth in a

stone wall near the back of the tavern cast a warm glow.
Three minstrels stomped their feet while singing in the
corner. Tables were set all around, and a smattering of
people sat at them, most on their own, though there were
a few groups of two or three.

"Where do all these people come from?" Finn asked
Meyer as they trudged up a narrow staircase to the upper
level.

Meyer grunted. "Do you think we're the only travelers
out on the King's Road?"

"I suppose not."

Meyer shook his head. "We aren't. A place like this gets
people from all over. You find these all throughout the
kingdom. This one is a little nicer than most." They
stopped at the top of the stair, and Meyer handed Finn
and Jasmine a key each. "You take the room at the end. I'll
take this one," Meyer said, nodding to a narrow door
nearest them. "And Jasmine can have the room in between
us." He held her gaze for a moment. "You pound on the
wall if you have any problems."

She nodded and flashed a careful smile.

"You can leave your belongings, and we can head
down. He said he still had food. Can't speak to the quality
here, but food is food."

"And ale is ale," Finn said.

Meyer grunted. "That's not *quite* the same."

Meyer unlocked his door and stepped into the room.

It left Finn alone with Jasmine. They made their way
along the hallway, and she paused at the door. She

unlocked it, pushing it open, and stood there for a moment.

"It's going to feel like my cell," she said softly.

"We're just out here if you need us," Finn said.

She looked over to him. "It's strange. I never would have thought that the people of Logard would've treated me like that. I knew I was an outsider. Of course I knew. They made sure of that. But my grandfather was there, and he had always been kind to me, and had always looked out for me."

"I'm sorry about what happened to you."

She forced a smile. "I suppose this is my chance for a new beginning, isn't it?"

There was uncertainty to her, and Finn wasn't sure what he could say to help. Only that he wanted to say something. "Sometimes new beginnings are exactly what we need. It gives you a chance to have a clean break and to find something you didn't know you needed."

She watched him. "You say that almost as if you have some experience with it."

Finn nodded. "I might have a little."

"Thank you. For everything."

"You don't have to thank me."

She shook her head. "I do. I have you to thank for discovering Joseph's guilt." She looked down. "I never would have imagined him capable of killing someone. He had an edge of darkness inside of him, but most men I've met have that."

"Not all do," Finn said. He realized the irony of him

saying that given his line of work, but he didn't want Jasmine to think there were people like that in the world.

"I think… I think I'm going to get some rest. I will see you in the morning."

"If you want to talk more, I'll be down in the tavern."

She nodded and stepped inside her room, closing the door.

Finn sighed before heading down the hall to his room, unlocking the door and dropping his pack. After closing the door, he headed back down to the tavern, where he found Meyer already seated at a table.

Meyer flagged down the server, a middle-aged man with a graying ponytail. He pointed to the mug of ale, and the man nodded, hurrying over to the kitchen before returning with two mugs of ale. Meyer raised his, nodding to Finn. "To your apprenticeship."

"To my apprenticeship." Finn took a long drink, and Meyer did as well.

Finn took the mug of ale and took a long drink. It was a little bitter and warmer than he preferred, but there simply was something about having a mug of ale at the end of the day.

"You have served well," Meyer said. "You should be proud of it."

"Thank you," Finn said. "I don't know what would've happened to me had you not saved me."

Meyer arched a brow. "You don't know?"

Finn shrugged. "Well, I do know what would've happened to me."

"Do you ever regret it?"

It was interesting, having a more contemplative Meyer. "I don't regret working with you."

"We all have regrets," Master Meyer said.

"What about you?"

"Mine are my own."

They sat quietly for a little while. The inside of the tavern was relatively empty, though there were a few other people. They gave Finn and Master Meyer space and didn't intrude, something Finn appreciated.

"What happened to your family?"

Meyer looked up, and for a moment, Finn worried that he had posed the question at the wrong time, or he had pushed too much.

"What have you heard?" He asked the question softly, in between taking drinks of ale, and looked over the mug at Finn. There was a hardness to his eyes.

"Rumors, mostly. I don't even know what to make of those rumors, though," Finn said.

"Rumors are like weeds. They love to spread."

"I know you had a daughter," Finn said.

"I did," Master Meyer said.

"What happened to her?"

"I couldn't save her." Meyer tipped back the mug, downing the rest of the ale before setting it on the table. "I thought I knew enough, but I didn't. Arrogance, I suppose some would say, or perhaps misguided confidence. Either way, I didn't know enough."

"Was she sick?"

Meyer nodded. "Sick."

"What was it?"

"I still don't know. It took her quickly, and she wasn't the only one."

"Was that when you first met the hegen?"

Meyer breathed out slowly. "The hegen might have helped, had I known enough. At the time, I didn't. I think that's why I've had a soft spot for them and their methods. I recognize they can help, although whether or not they will is another matter."

"If you're willing to pay the cost," Finn said.

Meyer nodded. "All things have a price."

"What about your wife?"

"Simpler. An accident."

"I'm sorry."

Meyer looked up. "I'm not looking for sympathy. You asked the question. I provided an answer." He rested his arms on the table. Holding Finn's gaze, he leaned forward. "Your turn. What do you know of your father?"

The sudden change of topic jarred Finn. He hadn't expected Meyer to be the one to bring up his father. "He was a thief. Worked with the crew, primarily with Oscar, but I don't know much about it. Why?"

"Curiosity." Meyer leaned back. "You probably wonder if I know anything about your father, including what happened to him."

Finn nodded tightly.

"Unfortunately, I'm not able to help you there. Even if I knew, I'm not sure it's appropriate for me to share that with you."

"It's not like I'm going to break him out of prison."

"I doubt you could," Master Meyer said. "I remember

your father's case. He was caught pulling a job. I don't remember all the details of it, mostly because he was imprisoned in Declan for only a few days before they escorted him out."

"Where?"

Meyer shrugged. "I can't answer that."

"You can't, or you won't?"

Meyer leveled his gaze on Finn. "Can't. You serve the king now, Finn. It would be best if you remember that."

"How is it that they took him from the city without you knowing?"

"It's not so much that I didn't know. It's that I could do nothing about it. There's a difference. We serve the king, but there are limits to our role. You need to come to terms with that."

"And if I don't?"

Meyer shook his head. "If you don't, you might find yourself drawn in ways that end up with you violating your oath."

"I didn't make an oath."

"You made an oath to me. You made an oath that promised to serve the king."

Finn finished his ale, setting it down on the table. "If you don't know, then who does?"

"Perhaps the king," Meyer said. "There aren't many reasons for a prisoner to be removed from the city. The crime would have to be significant."

"Significant?" He suspected he knew, given what he'd heard already, but it didn't fit.

Meyer nodded. "Treason."

"My father wasn't the treasonous type," Finn said.

"Not many men start that way, but perhaps he was swayed. Could he have been coerced?"

Finn didn't know. He didn't know his father well enough anymore. The man he thought his father to have been was something else. "I suppose I could ask Oscar."

"Do you think he would tell you?"

"Probably not," Finn said.

"You could still ask, but even if he answers, it may not provide you with the answer you want."

"Do you think I could ask the king?"

Meyer started to smile. "You certainly may try."

"You don't think he would answer."

Meyer shrugged. "The king may answer, but I don't know if you will have the opportunity to question."

Finn laughed. "The king doesn't come to Verendal often enough for me to question him?"

"Not often. When he does, he doesn't always choose to meet with executioners. The only reason I met with him the last time he visited was because I exerted the right."

"I see."

"That's not to say you can't ask him. The issue will be whether he chooses to answer."

Finn stared at the empty mug of ale. "Thank you," Finn said.

Meyer frowned at him. "For what?"

Finn looked up, shrugging. "For telling me the truth."

Meyer nodded. "You don't need to hesitate asking me questions."

"I didn't want to offend you. Wella warned me that—"

Meyer cut him off by laughing softly. "Wella? She's a skilled apothecary, and I won't deny that she's observant, but I wouldn't advise you taking advice on interpersonal relationships with her."

"Why not?"

"There aren't too many who call her friend. Typically for good reason, though I doubt she would ever acknowledge that."

"I can't trust her?"

Meyer chuckled, and he pushed the tray and the empty mug off to the side of the table, leaning forward. "You can trust her, but you should also question. That's the lesson she seeks to teach."

Finn thought about his experiences with Wella. She hadn't been forthright with him, unless it was about various herbs and medicinals. Even in that, she had referred him back to various textbooks, not giving him a direct answer.

"Still. Thank you."

"Does it change anything for you?"

Finn hesitated. There was still one other question he wanted to ask, and given Meyer's willingness to answer questions, he felt as if he should push. "Why me?"

"You don't think that you were worthy?"

"The person I was?" Finn shook his head. "I don't know if I was any more worthy than some of the people we've interviewed and sentenced."

Meyer smiled tightly. "Do you know how many sentences I've carried out?"

"I don't."

"Over my career, there have been over a thousand. It's brutal work. Bloody at times. There was a time when I was not much older than you and I questioned if it was what I wanted for myself for the entirety of my career. I didn't know if that was what I wanted for myself, but then I saw something."

"What?"

"It was in one of my earliest apprentices. He didn't make it very far. I saw a hint of anger within him. He took too much joy in carrying out his responsibilities. Much like the man you call the Lion did. It's dangerous, and it violates the intention of the king's justice. It's why I have taken my role as seriously as I have, and why I try to instill that in you. Anger—vengeance, if you want another term for it—is not the answer. Justice. That is what we serve."

Finn leaned back in the chair, watching Meyer. The old executioner had a troubled expression in his pale blue eyes, and the wrinkles across his brow seem to have deepened more than they normally were. Was it the conversation that troubled him so much?

"That doesn't answer my question."

Meyer smiled. "I suppose it doesn't. Maybe it's nothing more than seeing something within you. Potential. Maybe it's something else."

Meyer finished his ale, and he frowned, looking past Finn.

Finn swiveled in his chair, and he saw Jasmine stepping out of the doorway.

"She's going to have a hard time, isn't she?" Finn asked.

"Maybe," Meyer said. "I have to hope we can get her help."

Finn turned back, looking at Meyer. "What sort of help do you think you can get her?"

"The kind she needs." He got to his feet, tapping on the table. "Don't stay up too late."

He headed away and nodded to Jasmine, whispering something to her briefly before making his way to the staircase and up.

Jasmine joined Finn at the table. "Does your offer still stand?"

It took Finn a moment to realize what offer she referred to before nodding. "Of course. Do you like ale?"

Her nose wrinkled. "I suppose. I'd rather have wine, but after everything I've been through, maybe a mug of ale would do."

CHAPTER TWENTY-FOUR

Morning came quickly, and Finn was still tired.
He hadn't slept well. Dreams had been filled
with screams and flames, leaving him tossing and turning,
wishing he could find a way to settle in and get the rest he
needed. At several points, Finn had considered heading
back down to the tavern, but he'd rolled over and started
counting in his head, wanting sleep that never truly came.

After they had the horses ready and back on the King's
Road, he looked over to Meyer with weary eyes. Meyer
looked well rested, his walk quick, leading his horse with
Jasmine atop it. A bit of a spark had started to come to her
eyes, as if leaving her village had ignited it within her.

"What's your plan when we reach the city?" Finn asked
after they'd gone for a while.

"No plan. Not really," Meyer said.

"What about her?"

"She will be fine," Meyer said.

Finn sighed. There might not be a plan, but perhaps Meyer could have one of his contacts help her. He certainly knew enough people in the city, and Finn had to hope that he could use that to assist her. She deserved something more. She'd been through trauma and then more trauma again. It seemed to him that it was time for her to find a measure of peace.

He wasn't at all sure how she would be fine. Given what she'd been through, and the fact that she was coming to a strange city, knowing no one other than the two of them, Finn didn't know at all how she could be fine. If the situation were reversed, Finn wasn't even sure that he would have been able to leave the village.

She was strong. He had seen that. There was that flash that was now in her eyes that told him she had some measure of strength.

It wasn't long before they reached the city, then passed through the Teller Gate. Jasmine had drifted off during the ride, which had surprised Finn at first, but he knew what she'd been through. It shouldn't surprise him that she'd be exhausted from all of it.

When they reached the stables inside the city, Meyer climbed down, and jostled Jasmine until she came awake. "Take the horses and stable them," Meyer said.

"What about you?"

"I'm taking her with me for a moment."

"A moment?"

Meyer shot him a look, and it was one that told Finn not to argue.

He had seen that expression from Meyer before; he

knew better than to push too hard, but still, Finn felt a little obligation. He had been the reason that she had escaped sentencing. Had he not uncovered the truth...

Meyer likely would have.

Either way, she wouldn't have suffered.

Still, Finn felt as if he needed to make sure that she was safe.

"I'll get the horses stabled."

"Then rest," Meyer said.

Finn just nodded.

Jasmine climbed out of the saddle, and she glanced from Meyer to Finn, and for the first time, there was a measure of concern in her eyes. "Will I see you again?" she asked Finn.

"If you want to."

"I would like that."

Meyer nodded to Finn and waited while Finn guided the horses into the stables. Finn cast a glance over his shoulder and found Master Meyer speaking quietly to her, though he wondered what he was saying and where he intended to bring her.

He was tired, and after a long night awake, he wanted nothing more than to fall into his bed, sleep, but first he would do this. When Finn returned the horses, he paid a silver to the stable boy, found Meyer gone, and then started toward Meyer's home.

He hadn't gone very far when he had an unsettled sensation in his belly.

Someone was following him.

Finn struggled to surge into alertness. He needed to

clear his mind, but after having slept poorly the night before, he struggled. Worse, he was sore from the time that he had spent in the saddle, and even more sore from the time that he'd been walking along the road. He needed to take his boots off, take his jacket and pants off, climb into bed and…

There.

It was movement off to his left.

He made a point of ignoring it, hurrying along, trying to pretend as if he had not paid any attention to it.

But he had to be careful.

Memories of Oscar's lessons came back to him, though far more slowly than they should have. If one person followed him, there was a possibility another did. Occasionally, when pursuing somebody, there was value in letting them know they were pursued, while another followed from the shadows.

He looked around the city. He was close enough to Meyer's home that he didn't have to go very far to make sure that he was safe, but he also wanted to know who was after him. He wouldn't learn that by running.

It was better for him to keep moving along the street, and he could even loop around, head back to Meyer's home, or even slip along the alley.

That might be the best solution.

If he hurried ahead, he could make it look like he had headed into Meyer's home and then back and around, searching for whoever had followed him.

He sneaked toward the house, and as soon as he

reached the fence, he glanced all around him before darting down the street.

When he reached the end of the street, he poked his head around and saw the figure turning the corner, trying to look casual, but there was no question now that somebody had followed him.

Finn circled around the block, looping back and finding an alley that trailed through, and using that to navigate closer to Meyer's home. Having been outside of the city, the stench of the alley drifted to him, unpleasant and foul, but he had to ignore it.

He lingered in the mouth of the alley, looking along the street. Meyer's home was only a few hundred yards away, close enough he could jog over were it necessary, but not so close that he would have to fear someone approaching without him knowing.

He made a point of looking in either direction but didn't see anything.

As tired as he was, he wasn't going to be able to watch very carefully or closely, but he also needed to be certain that he had seen someone. Given how easily Wolf had caught him before, Finn needed to ensure it didn't happen again.

"You've gotten soft."

He spun, reaching for the knife he had at his belt before realizing it was Oscar. "Dammit, Oscar. Was that you following me?"

"Not following you, but I saw you darting along the street. You looked like you'd seen a ghost, so I figured you were concerned about something. These days, you don't move like that very often."

"What do you mean, *these days?*"

Oscar didn't answer.

"Have you been watching me?"

"I keep my eye on you, Finn. I told your father I would."

"Did you, now?"

"You know I did," Oscar said.

He was dressed in a black cloak, the hood drawn, and he stood casually behind Finn, though there was a tension within his posture, something that suggested to Finn he would be able to run at the slightest provocation.

"You've been gone for a little while," Oscar said.

"Meyer took me out of the city. Apparently, that will be one of my tasks as I progress."

"To leave the city on behalf of the king?"

"To carry out sentences in nearby villages."

"I didn't realize the executioners traveled so much."

"Neither did I," Finn said. "There was a murder, though probably more exciting than we expected."

"Why is that?"

Finn shook his head. "I'm not so sure you really need to know."

"It's like that, is it?"

"I'm not trying to keep anything from you, Oscar; it's just that—"

Oscar started laughing. "You don't have to explain, Finn. You're a busy man. You're becoming respectable."

Finn debated arguing with him about how respectable he might be, but decided against it. "I saw Wolf."

"I know." Oscar shrugged, stepping deeper into the shadows of the alley. It forced Finn to take a step back, and when he did, he realized that a pair of Archers marched along the street. Somehow, Oscar had known.

Finn had not. It might just be his fatigue, or it might be a lack of training, or it could simply be that Oscar was just that skilled.

"I've been keeping an eye on you, Finn."

"You kept an eye on me up until the point where I ended up in prison," Finn said. "And it took Master Meyer to get me out."

Oscar stared at him.

Finn considered pushing. There was a question that he had not yet managed to get answered, one that left him feeling as if things might be all connected. His fate. Oscar. The hegen.

All of them had seemed connected to him in some way, but unfortunately, Finn had not managed to get to the bottom of it. It was possible he never would.

The hegen had given him a card for Oscar, and he knew the hegen had a relationship with Meyer, which left him curious more than anything else. Not concerned.

"Did you have a hand in it?" Finn asked.

"Did I have a hand in what?" Oscar shifted, and it looked like he was twisting to run, but he pressed back against the alley, shielding himself. There was movement at the other end of the alley.

Damn, but he was skilled.

It was a wonder Oscar had ever been captured before.

"Master Meyer using his right?"

"I think you're reading too much into what happened," Oscar said.

"Maybe." He glanced behind him. Several people had moved along the street, though none had paid much attention to them. When he turned back to Oscar, Finn had expected him to have disappeared, but he was still there. "So, you knew Wolf was still in the city."

Oscar nodded. "Back in the city. Wolf. Rock. The other two bastards that were involved."

"Bellut and the other," Finn said. Maybe Sweth, though he didn't know. "I suppose you know what Wolf and Rock are up to?"

"I figured it was the same thing you were up to. Figuring out who set us up."

"I'm doing my best," Finn said. "There's only so much I can uncover."

"You have a little more respectability than I do. You can get places I can't."

"I can get places you can't when Master Meyer permits it, but he's made a point of telling me I'm not allowed to dig. I think he's trying to teach me a lesson," Finn said.

"What lesson is that?"

"The distinction between vengeance and justice."

"It sounds to me like they work pretty well together. You get vengeance, and justice is served."

"Not according to Master Meyer," Finn said. He rubbed his eyes, trying to get more alert. "And I'm starting to think that maybe he's right."

"Are you, now?"

"That's not to say that I don't want justice served. Bellut deserves what justice he gets; it's just that—"

"It's just you aren't able to bring that justice to bear."

"That's not what I'm saying," Finn said.

"What are you saying, then?" Oscar stepped away from the wall, turning totally toward Finn. "It's because of them I nearly got caught. You know what would've happened then, don't you, Finn?"

"I know what might've happened," Finn said, nodding slowly.

"What would you have done?"

"I wouldn't have been able to question you."

"Wouldn't have been able to, or wouldn't have been allowed to?"

"Both," Finn said.

Oscar grunted. "You can't forget where you came from, Finn."

"I don't forget where I came from. And you can't forget what I went through."

"I was there, when no one else was."

"I know. You still didn't get me out," Finn said.

"There was no getting out. Not from that place. I did what I could, though, and I was ready to..." Oscar shook his head.

"What were you ready to do?"

"I told you, Finn, it doesn't matter."

Had Oscar been there the day that he had walked along the Blood Court, making his way toward the gallows? Finn barely remembered anything from that day.

He remembered getting dressed in the Sinner's Cloth, and he remembered walking with the priest, speaking the words of Heleth, and he remembered climbing the Stone. Beyond that, everything was a blur of sunlight shining down, a bright, warm sun that should not have been. There was the shouting around him, the sound of the crowd, but no distinct voice in it. There was the fear he had felt as Master Meyer had come toward him, asking him one last time to speak on his behalf.

Oscar hadn't been there for any of it. Even if he had somehow intervened, what could he have done? Meyer was not easily swayed. He wanted justice, not vengeance, and Finn sincerely doubted Meyer would have been convinced by the hegen to help him, though maybe he wouldn't have needed to.

The hegen had magic. Could the hegen have used their magic to somehow coax Meyer into demanding his right? He was so tired, he couldn't think through things.

"It matters, Oscar. All of this matters."

Oscar eyed him before taking a step back. "I just want you to be careful, Finn."

"Careful. Does that mean you're worried about Wolf?"

"It means he's up to something. You need to be careful with him. Wolf is in a difficult spot. It changes things for a man. It makes him desperate. You know what they say about desperation in crime."

That was a lesson Finn did remember. "It makes a man dangerous."

"And a dangerous man deadly."

"I'll be careful. Listen, if there's anything that you learn about what Bellut is up to or who he's working with, I need you to share it with me."

"Sharing information with an executioner isn't good for my kind of business." Oscar studied him, saying nothing for a moment. "Be safe, Finn."

"Come on, Oscar. It doesn't have to be like that."

"What do you think it should be like?"

Finn took a deep breath and looked behind him. He couldn't see anything, couldn't even hear anything. Whatever had upset Oscar had been enough that Finn wasn't even aware of it. That wasn't surprising to him. Oscar *had* been the one to teach him, though Finn had never been the best student, anyway.

"We can still be friends, can't we?"

Oscar tilted his head to the side slightly. "Can we?"

"Why couldn't we?" Finn knew what Meyer would say were he to ask him about maintaining friends from his past, especially friends who were like Oscar, but having seen what Jasmine had gone through, he'd realized that maybe he needed to find connections. The iron masters might be one such connection, and he'd started to find a way to connect to them, but what he needed were those like Oscar who still knew him and knew where he'd come from to keep him from changing too much.

"Seems to me friends would spend a little time around each other. Do you know the last time I saw you?" Oscar asked.

"When we had drinks."

"When I had to chase you to have even a few words

with you." Oscar shook his head. "When you took on this job, I thought maybe it was for the best. Probably still is, but I can't help think there's something I'm missing out on."

"So, you just want me to do what? Come down to the Wenderwolf?" Finn asked.

"Would that be so bad?"

"I…" Finn had not been willing to return to the tavern since he'd betrayed the crew, but maybe that was his issue and not one that he had to deal with when it came to the crew itself. If it was as Oscar said and Annie had moved on, there was no reason for Finn to avoid it—and that was exactly what he'd been doing. Whether or not they welcomed him was a different matter. "I'll try to do better."

"Don't try. You can't move forward and forget your past." He smiled at Finn. "At least, not all of your past."

"Fine. I'll do better. Is that what you want?"

Oscar shook his head, backing down the alley. "What I want don't matter. Just be safe. The crew isn't *all* gone."

"Wolf is around, but I haven't seen Rock."

"That bastard is probably still roaming the streets, but Rock isn't going to be your issue, Finn. You know that. He was a bruiser, that's it. It's Wolf I worry about."

"The King trusted him as more than a bruiser," Finn said.

"Maybe, but should he have?"

Finn didn't know. When he'd been working in the crew, Rock had never really fit in quite the way that a bruiser should. The King had treated him differently, though maybe there was a reason for that. Finn would have to look into it. "If you hear anything…"

"If I hear anything, I'll think about sending word to you."

"Just think about it?"

"You got your commitments these days, and I've got mine."

Finn frowned at him. "I don't want you getting involved in anything too dangerous."

Oscar chuckled. "That's the life on a crew, Finn. You know that."

"I imagine you could do something else, though."

Oscar backed another step away from him. "Could I? Not much I know how to do. That's the one problem with living in the streets the way I have my entire life. You get to learn one kind of work and can't do much else." He shrugged. "I know you think I'm disappointed in what happened with you, but that's not it at all. You got out. That matters. You don't have to worry about getting chased down by Archers, getting pinched, or even losing members of your crew while you're taking jobs. All you have to worry about is—"

"Hanging someone," Finn said.

"Not all bad. Probably not the way you envisioned your life going, but could be worse. Could be you on the end of that rope."

Oscar started backing away and slipped into the shadows of the alley. It wasn't long before he reached the end of the alley and then darted away, disappearing from sight.

Finn stood watching where Oscar had disappeared. Maybe Oscar was right. He'd avoided anything that had bound him to that world before. Not only because he had taken up his apprenticeship, but there was a measure of fear as well. With the King gone, why should Finn fear, anyway?

Wolf could harm him, but only so much. Finn had measures of protection he didn't have before, and he should take advantage of those protections, which meant using the Archers, using his ties to the executioner, and using whatever connections he had within the city.

It was time for Finn to stop being worried.

He took a deep breath and turned. Fatigue still threatened to knock him over. He was exhausted and could barely even stand, but he plunged ahead, hurrying across the street, toward Meyer's home.

When he reached the small wall surrounding the home, Finn paused. As before, he could have sworn there was motion behind a line of wagons on the street, but Finn wasn't at all certain what it was that he'd seen. Maybe it really was just his imagination. With as tired as he was, everything seemed to come together strangely.

Meyer might not even have returned yet. Finn would have to figure out what had happened with Jasmine and where Meyer had brought her. She had wanted to see him again. There weren't too many people in the city who felt that way, so he should take advantage of the few who did. The few who weren't concerned about his line of work.

Finn stepped into the yard, up to the door, and then inside. A strange smell hit him immediately. There was something about the smell that reminded him of Wella's shop, but it wasn't quite as pure. Everything within Wella's shop was more clean apothecary medicine, as if the medicinals Wella had were harvested and purified, but what he detected now was a strange odor that drifted over everything, hanging in his nostrils and making him uncomfortable. It irritated him.

Finn paused in his room, dropping his bag on the floor next to his bed, and realized the books stacked on his table had been moved. It meant Lena, or possibly his mother, had been there.

Finn stepped back out of his room, heading along the hall, and paused in the kitchen. There was no activity, and he was glancing up the stairs to where Lena and his mother had their rooms when he heard a voice in Meyer's office.

He paused before knocking.

The door was cracked just a little bit, and Finn poked his head inside to see his sister bent over a cot resting along the wall. She looked up and over to him, relief sweeping across her brow. "Finn. Thank the gods you're here."

"What are you doing, Lena?"

"It's Mother, Finn. I found something that worked for Moira, so I tried it on Mother."

"You found something that helped her?" Meyer had believed there was no help for her.

Lena waved her hand. "I don't know what happened, and I've been doing all I can to try to help her, but when you and Master Meyer were gone, I..."

Finn hurried across the room and realized the strange medicinal odor came from what Lena had mixed. It wasn't anything Finn was familiar with.

"What did you give her?"

Lena shook her head. "I've been trying to help her. When the two of you left, she was fine at first, but then she started getting sicker throughout the day. I tried finding help, but no one was willing to come here."

"What do you mean, you tried finding help?"

Lena straightened, wiping her hands down the front of her deep green dress. The heavy cotton was stiff but clean. "When the mixture I made didn't work, I tried finding an apothecary, and then a surgeon, and when neither of them were willing to come, I went to the physician—"

"Oh, Lena."

"None of them were willing to come, Finn."

"Because it was Meyer," he said.

"But he purchases from them."

Finn stopped next to his mother and found her lying motionless, the way that she had when she'd been sick before. Her eyes were closed, her face thin, her hair disheveled. Lena had covered her with a thin sheet, but sweat had soaked through it, making it nearly transparent.

"Why would that matter if he purchases from them?"

"Not all of the apothecaries view what Master Meyer does the same way. The surgeons, either," Finn said.

"They don't like the competition?"

"I don't think so," Finn said.

"What about the physician?"

"I doubt you had enough money."

"I told him I could pay."

"I'm sure you did."

Lena turned to Meyer's desk, and she looked down at a book she had folded open on the table. "I've been reading through everything as quickly as I could, trying to find answers, but I haven't found anything. I thought about going back to the hegen—"

"You didn't, did you?"

She shook her head. "I remembered what they told me the last time. They didn't think they'd be able to help me again. If she survived, their magic wouldn't work another time."

That surprised Finn. What reason would there be for the hegen magic to have limitations? It seemed to him that there should be none. It seemed to Finn that the hegen magic should work regardless of whether they'd healed someone before.

"What have you been trying?"

Lena just shook her head. "I thought I found an answer in the books Master Meyer has, and looked through the ones that he had lent you." She looked up at Finn. "They're complicated, but I've been reading quite a few of his other books, and I thought I found an answer by merging the two."

Finn lifted a jar of oil resting next to his mother, tipping it to the side and sniffing it. That was the strange and pungent aroma that he had detected before. "What is it? I'm not familiar with this one."

"That's the one I made up on my own," Lena said.

Finn's eyes widened.

"I've used what I found in this book," she said, holding up the Gisles book, "and I borrowed from this one," she said, holding up another, a massive book on apothecary medicine that Finn had not even bothered to start. He was still struggling to work through the other one. "They're similar but different enough I hoped I might find answers mixing the information from the two of them."

"Why would you even think to do that?"

"I want to save her," Lena said.

Finn pulled a stool out, taking a seat next to his mother. "I don't know that she wanted us to save her," he said.

"You can't say that," Lena told him.

Finn looked up. "I don't know what else to tell you. She was tired, Lena. When I spoke to her last"—could it really be the last time that he'd spoken to his mother?—"she made it clear she didn't want anything more. She was ready to go."

"I'm not ready for her to go," Lena said softly.

"That is not our choice to make."

Finn turned to see Master Meyer standing in the doorway. His eyes were weary, and he had set down his pack and the sword Justice.

"I'm sorry," Meyer said. "Sometimes, the gods take loved ones from us before we are ready, but it's not always before *they* are ready." He grabbed the jar from Finn, tipping it to his nose and sniffing. He touched the thick oil with his finger, dabbing it on his tongue. "Veler root?" Lena nodded. "Nipsom powder. Ginger. A hint of rustil." He looked up at Lena. "An interesting combination."

"There's horfan in it as well. I wanted something that would help her wake up but wouldn't be too potent of a stimulant."

"I think that would work under normal circumstances, but in this case, unfortunately, I think it might have been too far along for your compound to be effective." Meyer made his way over to the cot, and he looked down at their mother. "I'm sorry I couldn't do more for you," he said softly.

"Is she really gone?" Lena asked.

Meyer glanced over to Lena. "Not yet, but I don't think there's much that can be done for her at this point. We can certainly keep trying, but—"

"It worked for Moira when I gave it to her while you were out of the city."

Finn had almost forgotten that he'd asked for Lena's help finding a treatment for Moira.

Meyer held Lena's gaze a moment. "I'm sorry. There comes a time when providing care to someone when you have to begin to wonder if you're doing it for yourself or for them. If you know their wishes, then you owe it to them to ensure those wishes are honored."

"She didn't want to be treated again," Finn said.

Lena shot him a look. "You can't just give up on her."

Finn looked down at his mother, seeing her for what felt like the first time. Resting the way that she was, she looked almost peaceful. Her eyes were closed, her breathing slightly erratic, but she was thin. Gaunt. She had wasted away.

"I'm not the one giving up," Finn said. "Mother didn't want to go on like this. She said it was no way to live."

"She's all I have," Lena said.

Finn swallowed, glancing over to Master Meyer for a moment before turning his attention back to Lena. "We could try—"

"No," Master Meyer said firmly but as gently as Finn knew he could. "There is nothing more that can be done for her. You have done more than I think anyone would've expected," Master Meyer said, tipping the concoction off to the side, swirling it in the jar. "More than I might have been able to do."

"It's not right. It's not fair!" Lena's voice raised a moment, and she clasped a hand over her mouth.

"Lena..."

She stared at their mother for a moment before spinning and running from the room.

Finn heard the front door close, and he was getting to his feet when Meyer shook his head.

"Let her be."

"She might go to the hegen."

"The hegen won't be able to help," Master Meyer said.

"I know."

"Do you?"

"I think she's fading quickly," Finn said.

Master Meyer nodded. "She is."

Finn took his mother's hand, sitting with her. "Lena worries she won't have anything to do once our mother is gone," Finn said without looking over.

"She need not worry. I will not ask that she leave."

"I don't think that's her concern," Finn said.

He looked up to Master Meyer for a moment and found him swirling the liquid for a little bit before he finally set it down on the table next to him.

"What did you do with Jasmine?"

"Do?"

"You stayed outside the city. What happened with her?"

"I brought her someplace safe."

Finn looked over, frowning deeply for a moment, and waited for him to elaborate, but he did not.

"What place is that?"

"It doesn't matter," Master Meyer said.

"What now?"

Meyer glanced from Finn to where his mother lay on the cot. "Now you wait with her."

Lena returned late in the evening, crying. Her hair had been pulled free of the ribbon she'd tied it back in and now hung loose around her shoulders. Her eyes were red and damp, and her cheeks a bit rosy, and when she came into Meyer's office, taking a seat alongside Finn and sitting next to their mother, she said nothing for a long time.

Finn had remained in place for the better part of the day. He was exhausted, but he hadn't wanted to go anywhere. If these were going to be his mother's remaining moments, he wanted to be there with her.

"Has she come around?" Lena asked.

Finn shook his head. "No. Meyer has given her some of the concoction you mixed, but it hasn't changed her much."

Finn squeezed his mother's hand for a moment. There was almost a sense that she squeezed back, though Finn didn't know if he had imagined it.

Lena leaned forward, taking their mother's hand, holding on to it with Finn. "I went to see if the hegen might be able to help."

"Even though you knew they likely weren't going to be able to?"

"I knew it wasn't likely, but I had to ask."

"What did you find?"

"They aren't able to help." She looked over to Finn. "*You* could go. You could ask. They'd help you. I know they would."

"I could ask," Finn agreed.

"But you won't." Lena looked down. "Is it because you're scared of them?"

Finn breathed out slowly, thinking about the hegen card in his pocket. He still felt as if he had an obligation to them, though he had no idea what obligation that was or what they would ask of him. Only that the card signified something to him, a connection that he now had to them, and it signified some request they would make of him. While he believed it was tied to removing the threat of Bellut and whoever he worked with, Finn no longer knew if that were the case. The card had not changed, and he was unable to get any closer to either of them.

"It's not that."

"If it's not that, then what?" She leaned back, releasing their mother's hand, and she looked over to Finn for a moment. "If you're scared, then why won't you go to the hegen? They can help her, you know."

"Don't," a soft voice said.

His mother had started to open her eyes. Could it be that Lena's concoction would work? He couldn't imagine it actually being effective, but maybe there was something in the combination that had worked for her.

"Mother?" Lena said. She took her hand again, holding onto it softly, and she glanced over to Finn, a mixture of panic and sadness ringing her eyes. "We just want to help you."

"Don't. Help. *Please*." She said the last with a long, pleading note.

"I can't lose you," Lena said, tears streaming down her cheeks.

"Always. With. You."

Her eyes fell shut, and her breathing slowed.

Finn slipped his arm around Lena, holding on to his sister, taking his mother's hand, and saying nothing. They rocked in place, holding onto her, until long after she had passed.

CHAPTER TWENTY-FIVE

F inn found it hard to sleep.

He kept waking up, realizing that his mother was gone, knowing that his father was beyond his ability to reach, and thinking of Lena up in her room, sobbing. She had been crying when Finn had left her for the evening, descending back down to his small room, knowing that there was only so much he could do or say to comfort her. Unfortunately, he hadn't known anything that would make a difference. He wanted to offer her a measure of comfort, but what could he say when he mourned as well?

Early morning daylight streamed in through his window, a faint trickle of color. Lying in bed wasn't going to benefit him any longer, and Finn sat up, rubbing the sleep from his eyes. He felt exhausted.

Ever since returning from outside of the city, he had felt exhausted.

There was much to prepare before the funeral. Lena

had offered to make the arrangements, and Finn had protested, but Meyer had suggested that he let her. His work would not rest now that he was back in the city.

The only problem for Finn was that he wasn't entirely sure what responsibilities he had. Meyer hadn't been clear about anything else. His assignment with Sweth had concluded, and other than Vol Thern still imprisoned in Declan, Finn didn't have any new prisoners that Meyer had assigned to him. He still had his usual errands, so that was what Finn intended to do.

After getting dressed, he made his way to the kitchen, preparing a mug of tea. His stomach was unsettled, and he didn't have much of an appetite, so he didn't make anything. He sat there, staring at the steaming liquid, his tired mind churning.

He felt as if he had failed.

At the same time, maybe he hadn't.

His mother had been ready. Finn knew that she had been ready, but that didn't make it any easier on him. He had wanted to help her. He had wanted to do whatever it would take to save her.

As had Lena.

"I can make breakfast," Lena said, standing in the doorway.

Finn shook his head. "I'm not hungry."

She trudged into the kitchen and sank down into one of the chairs, resting her elbows on the table and looking across at Finn. "Me neither."

"I'm sorry I wasn't here when you needed me."

"You've been here far more than you ever used to be.

I'm not upset with you. I'm just..." Lena shook her head, pushing her messy hair back and out of her eyes. "I guess I'm just mad at myself."

"Why?"

"I thought that I might be able to help her."

"It's not a reason to be mad at yourself. You did help her."

"That's not it. Master Meyer has all of these books, and he hasn't minded me reading and studying, but despite having access to this knowledge, I haven't found anything."

"You came closer than I did," Finn said.

"Only because you have other assignments. I imagine that if you could have devoted your time to it, you would have come up with answers."

Finn sniffed, and he took a drink of his tea. It wasn't nearly as refreshing as the hegen tea, and his mind didn't clear how it did when he drank the tea Esmerelda offered him. "You helped Moira. I couldn't do that."

"Only because I wanted to help Mother."

"Still."

Lena leaned back and straightened. "I'll go to the church this morning and make arrangements for her service. Do you have a priest that you prefer?"

There was a time when such a question would've been surprising, but that was only because Finn had never been religious. He had come to know many of the priests of Heleth, but he wasn't particularly close to any of them.

"It doesn't really matter," he said. "I could help."

"You said that last night."

"It doesn't change my offer."

"Do what Master Meyer needs of you."

He nodded, finishing his tea and getting to his feet. He lingered for a moment before heading out. It was still early, but hopefully not so early that the general store wouldn't be open. That was where he would start first.

He hadn't gone far when he heard somebody calling his name.

At first, he thought Lena was shouting at him, waving to him, but then he realized that wasn't who it was.

He moved carefully toward the figure.

"Jasmine?" Finn asked.

She had cleaned up, her hair shiny, glowing in the early morning light, and she had on a bright blue dress that reminded him of the hegen. A pale silver chain hung around her neck, and she ran her fingers along it while stopping in front of him.

"Finn. I was hoping I would find you. I didn't expect you to be up and out so early. I was told how to find Master Meyer's home and... well, the streets of the city are a little bit more difficult to navigate than those in Logard."

Finn forced a smile. "You were coming to see me?"

Jasmine nodded. She seemed to realize that something was amiss, and she took a step back regarding him. "What is it?"

"It's..." He wasn't entirely sure how much to share with her. He didn't really know Jasmine, though they had spent a pleasant evening chatting after Meyer had left them. He knew what she had gone through, though, and didn't want to burden her any more than necessary. "I have some errands I need to complete. We were out of the city for a few days, and Meyer expects me to get back at my assignment now that we have returned."

Jasmine's brow furrowed briefly. "If that's all it is…" He forced a smile. "Maybe I could come with you? I haven't seen much of the city. I've been trying to get settled and wanted to give Master Meyer my thanks, but I also needed help."

"With what?"

"I wanted to get word to my grandfather. I was told that Master Meyer would know a place to send a message."

She needed a scribe.

Finn wondered if Esmerelda or one of the other hegen had known that Finn had a contact, or if it was something they had seen with their cards.

Regardless, Finn doubted that he would ever learn.

"I know a place that can help."

"You do? Will you bring me there?"

There were other things that he needed to do and other things that were on his mind, but maybe taking some time with her would keep him from thinking about his mother, and about what his sister would do now that she was gone.

Besides, he figured that she would require somebody with some influence for Jasmine to get the level of service she needed. In this case, it was something Finn thought he might be able to assist with.

"I know someone who would likely take the job."

"Is it expensive?" she shrugged. "I don't have much money. I want to pay what the service is worth, but I can't afford too much."

"I should be able to help with that."

They started through the city.

When one of the bells rang, she paused, and she looked up.

"That's just the Giver's Tower," Finn said. When she frowned, he smiled. "It serves as a reminder for people in the city to contribute to the church."

"That rings every day?"

"Twice a day, actually. The church tends to be greedy." Jasmine started to smile. "I shouldn't say that," Finn added hastily.

She shook her head. "You don't have to worry about offending me, Finn."

"You're not concerned about upsetting the gods?"

"My grandfather wasn't particularly religious. He was a practical man and felt that if he couldn't see something, well, that probably meant it didn't exist." She shook her head slightly, a soft smile curling her lips. "I'm going to miss him."

"He could visit. Verendal isn't far from Logard."

"He could, but I know him. He probably won't ever take the time. And I doubt that I could go back." They walked for a little while longer, and she still looked up to the Giver's Tower. "When I was sitting in the cell, waiting for you and Master Meyer to come, I tried praying, but there was no answer."

"Or maybe there was," Finn said.

"I prayed the gods would take me," she said softly.

He realized something that he hadn't before.

He and Jasmine had both been condemned.

Finn might have come closer to his own death than Jasmine had, but both had believed they were going to die for their crimes. She was innocent of hers, whereas Finn was most definitely not innocent of breaking into the viscount's manor, but even now, after serving for the period that he had, Finn still didn't feel remorse for what he had done.

"Maybe they saved you instead," he said.

"Maybe." Her eyes remained dark, and for a moment before she shook her head. "Now I'm here. With you." She smiled.

"Most people aren't excited to be walking in the city with an executioner."

"Is it hard?"

"Sometimes," Finn admitted.

They reached the river, and they paused on the bridge, looking down. Vinlen River flowed through the city, creating a half-circle that separated the poorer sections from the richer sections and set off the palace on the city's far side. It burbled loudly here, rushing past unseen rocks, sweeping along the shoreline.

"When I was younger, I wanted to find a raft, throw it in the stream running near the village, and float all the way to the capital."

"Why to the capital?"

"I wanted to see the world. I figured that floating

might give me a better perspective than I could otherwise."

Finn started to smile. "I never wanted to leave the city."

"Never?"

Finn shrugged. "I didn't really think there was much for me outside of the walls of the city. Growing up the way that I did, I thought that I would never travel very far."

"Have you?"

He shook his head. "Not yet." But now that he served as an executioner, he wondered if perhaps his responsibility would carry him further and further away from Verendal.

Meyer had mentioned that eventually he would be a journeyman. That meant that he would be the one to make the trips out of the city. It meant that he would travel the countryside, serving the king's justice.

And eventually, Finn would be assigned elsewhere.

What would happen to his sister then?

It was a distant concern, but maybe it was something Finn should start planning for.

Another bell rang, and Finn pointed. "That's the Tower of Fell."

She nodded. "We don't have any way of celebrating Fell in Logard."

"You probably didn't have enough money, either," he said.

"The gods don't care about money."

"Apparently Fell does."

They stood there for a few more moments, and then

Finn sighed. "We should keep moving."

Jasmine smiled. "I'm sorry. I don't need to keep you from what you need to get done."

"I don't mind. I enjoy your company."

She looked up at him for a moment before turning away.

Finn felt a brief flash of foolishness. He had to be careful here. Jasmine was new to the city, had suffered, and had nearly been sentenced to die. He needed to be a friend to her, and nothing more.

A friend wouldn't be all bad for him, either.

These days, Finn had precious few of them.

"I could show you a few places while we walk."

"That would be nice," she said.

They passed a few familiar shops that he pointed to, an old temple, then neared City Hall.

"I've seen a building like that outside of Logard," she said.

"Rumor is that building is an old Alainsith structure," Finn said. "The writing on the outside of it makes that likely, but the size feels off."

She looked over, a hint of a smile on her face. "The size?"

Finn shrugged. "There's something about the building that feels larger than it should. I don't know how to explain it otherwise. The size of the rooms, maybe. The doorways always make me think they were made for a larger person."

City Hall sat in the middle of a small square with space all around it, as if the buildings didn't want to press too close into the ancient structure. There were a few shops, a stable, and an old stone building Finn also thought had to be Alainsith and was currently used as a home for one of the city administrators.

She shivered to herself and looked off into the distance. "I don't like the building. I... I don't know how to explain it."

"We can go. I'll show you some other places."

They started off, and she cast a glance back toward City Hall as they passed. "Is this all part of your errands?"

"Not usually, though I end up at City Hall often enough. Performing my job is how I met the scribe. There are probably others closer to the gate, but this one is more likely to do it quickly."

"I don't need it done quickly. I just want the message to get to my grandfather."

"I—"

Finn didn't have a chance to finish.

They turned a corner, and he nearly collided with somebody.

He backed up, offering a quick apology, before realizing who it was.

Bellut stared at him, anger flashing on his narrow face for a moment, before it faded, twisting into something else. Arrogance.

It took all of Finn's concentration for him to keep from saying something that he knew he would regret.

Meyer would be angry if Finn snapped at Bellut.

He didn't have proof of anything. He knew Bellut was guilty, but the problem was that Finn had no way of proving what he was guilty of doing, short of his own testimony. And his testimony wouldn't be enough to convince the jurors.

"Mr. Jagger," Bellut sneered. There was no attempt to hide the arrogance from his face this time. Why would there be, though? Finn wasn't with Master Meyer, and there were no others around besides Jasmine. "Aren't you in the wrong part of the city?"

"I'm on official business," Finn said.

Bellut flicked his gaze to Jasmine, sweeping it from head to toe, lingering in a way that made Finn's skin crawl. He couldn't imagine how it made Jasmine feel. They shouldn't have come so close to City Hall and he wouldn't have run into Bellut.

"As am I," Bellut said, turning back to him. "Though, given the way I serve the viscount, I am always on official business of the king."

"I serve the king as well."

"I suppose you do in your own little way. How are the prisons these days?"

"I could take you for a tour of them if you would like."

A warning flared in Finn's mind. He was getting dangerously close to saying something that he should not.

Bellut chuckled. "I'm sure you would enjoy that."

"Maybe the jurors should all take the opportunity to see the prisons. It might be enlightening."

"Perhaps."

Bellut waved his hand, as if to force Finn to move.

Finn might have to be careful with what he said to Bellut, but there was no way he was stepping off to the side to let Bellut pass. He wasn't going to show any fear or weakness.

Bellut leaned close, and he lowered his voice. "You had better be careful."

"Is that how you want to do this?" Finn asked. He resisted the urge to glance in Jasmine's direction but thankfully had the sense that she had stepped off to the side, giving them space. "I know what you did."

"Do you?" Bellut said carefully. "And what, exactly, do you think you know?"

"I know enough. You will make a mistake. I will be there when you do."

"And what do you think will happen when you make a mistake?" Bellut said each word low and soft. There was still a threat laced within them. "And what of people you care about? Do you really want to be the reason they suffer?"

Finn frowned. He hadn't considered what Bellut might do to people he cared about.

There were some, like Meyer, that Finn doubted Bellut could torment. Meyer had the king's ear, as well as his respect, so there was no reason for Meyer to fear. But who else could Bellut torment on Finn's behalf?

"How has your sister been doing? I hear she has been looking for employment." He flashed a dark grin at Finn.

Finn blinked.

Lena's comments came back to him.

She'd been looking, and failing, to find employment.

Could Bellut have been responsible?

Finn would have said no, but maybe he was responsible for it.

"It would be a shame if something were to happen to her the same way as it happened to your mother."

Finn's insides went cold.

"What do you know?"

Bellut snorted, and then he straightened. "Just make sure the reward is worth the risk." With that, he pushed past Finn and strode down the street.

Finn turned, watching him go, and wanted to chase him, but knew that if he were to do so, it would only lead to the kind of trouble that Meyer had warned him to avoid.

He felt a hand on his arm, and he spun quickly.

Jasmine looked up at him. "What was that about?"

Finn breathed out, trying to settle himself. "That is someone I don't care for."

Jasmine laughed. "I gathered that, but who is it?"

He took a few more breaths. He would have to investigate Bellut for a different reason now. More than that, he was going to have to watch out for Lena.

It was time to get Meyer involved. Somehow, Finn would have to convince him that Bellut was more dangerous than Meyer had believed.

"He is somebody that I will be dealing with sooner than later." He forced a smile. "Why don't we get going?"

They headed along the street, and Finn looked back, searching to see if there was any sign of Bellut, but didn't find anything. He didn't even know if Bellut had been leaving City Hall or heading toward it. Finn found that he wanted to know.

By the time they reached Master Johan's shop, he had finally settled down. He'd half-heartedly pointed out other sites, but Jasmine seemed to sense his distraction. Walking through the city with Jasmine had helped him relax more than he had expected, but seeing Bellut had changed it, tormenting him once again.

"I'm going to get you set up with Master Johan, and then I'm going to have to get back to my responsibilities. I'm sorry that I can't stay here longer with you, but Master Johan will take good care of you. You can ask him how to find your way back through the city."

She nodded carefully. "I could meet up with you when you are finished."

Finn wished that he could but didn't feel as if this were the right time for that. "How about another time?"

"I'd like that."

They stepped into Master Johan's shop, and when Johan looked at him with eyes filled with suspicion, Finn found himself smiling. If nothing else, getting Johan to help Jasmine might help him feel a little better about everything.

The problem was that he couldn't shake the unsettled feeling that filled him after running into Bellut.

Finn doubted that he would shake that feeling until he managed to unearth Bellut's guilt.

Maybe Finn couldn't be comfortable in the city until then.

Meyer would have to understand—and this time, he would have to help.

CHAPTER TWENTY-SIX

The bright day felt off, considering the sadness he felt, though perhaps it should not. Maybe the sunshine was Heleth's way of telling him that she would watch over his mother.

He chided himself for the thought. Here, he liked to convince himself he was not a faithful follower of any of the gods, but when it came down to it, there was some part of him that still found him reciting the old stories of the gods and believing that perhaps the gods were there, watching over him. Watching over all of them.

There was still much he needed to do. Meyer probably wouldn't push for him to get back involved in other aspects of his responsibilities, but Finn didn't want to avoid it for too long. He felt as if he needed to keep working with Meyer. Other than the pleasant morning spent with Jasmine, it was the only thing that he had.

Unlike Lena.

Finn would have to help her. Maybe not now, but he would have to start working with Lena to help her find a place, much like he had found a place. He didn't want her to commit herself to the church if she didn't want to, and he certainly didn't want her returning to the slums where she took on jobs that she didn't deserve and were beneath her. Lena was smart—smarter than Finn. She deserved something that would challenge her. Maybe Meyer would have something in mind that she could do.

He glanced down at the blank card he'd found in his room.

The hegen called him.

Maybe it was nothing more than Esmerelda's irritation that he'd spent time with Jasmine, or maybe it was time they called in whatever debt, either way, the timing annoyed him.

When the bells rang, he paused. He still had an hour until the funeral, but he didn't want to be late. Lena would be even more annoyed with him.

After passing through the Teller Gate, he turned to the Raven Stone, looking out at the massive gleaming stone situated on the outskirts of the city. It was a place of death, but it was a place of power as well. He'd seen how the hegen collected their items.

Finn made his way toward the hegen section, and when he reached the Raven Stone, he looked up at the gallows, instinctively already starting to check to ensure the wood hadn't cracked, that there were no faults to the actual gallows itself, before sweeping his gaze along the top of the Raven Stone. He found nothing more to it.

The last execution within Verendal had been Sweth, but the last on the Stone was long enough past that he knew there was no reason for there to be anything atop the Stone, and there wasn't.

He turned away, heading toward the hegen section, and as he approached he slowed, though he thought that perhaps he should not. Showing hesitation as he approached the hegen ran the risk of drawing their notice. Instead, he plunged ahead, following the twisty street, nodding politely to two older hegen, both dressed in colorful clothing, and smiling as a child saw him before turning and running the opposite direction. By the time he reached the red-painted door of Esmerelda's home, he had already started to come up with multiple questions.

Finn knocked and waited. He glanced toward the rest of the city, tapping his foot.

He didn't have time to wait.

When Esmerelda's door opened, he was ready for his questions. What he wasn't ready for was Jasmine.

"Finn?" She smiled at him. "I thought you were busy with errands."

Finn swallowed. "I was busy. Am. But Esmerelda sent word to me."

Before she had a chance to say anything more, Esmerelda came to the door. "You may return to your studies," Esmerelda said.

Jasmine nodded to her before turning to Finn. "Will you stop by again? I had a nice walk with you this morning and don't know many people in the city."

"You don't mind that one of the people you know is an executioner?"

"It can't be all bad. One of the men I dated was a murderer." She flashed a smile before heading into Esmerelda's home.

"I think you will find that one to be trouble for you," Esmerelda said.

Finn turned his attention to her. Esmerelda looked lovely in her deep blue dress, a shawl covering her shoulders. Her bright red lips were pressed in a frown.

He held her gaze. "Why would she be trouble for me?"

"She's been through quite a bit, Finn Jagger. She doesn't know what she wants. It has been my experience that women like her often struggle with understanding their place."

Finn looked past her, into her home, but Esmerelda shifted so that Finn couldn't see very much. "Why did Meyer bring her to you?"

"Master Meyer and I have an agreement that he would return our people if they are found," Esmerelda said.

She hadn't said anything in their time together, but now that she did, it made a certain sense. "I didn't know."

"Her mother was one of the people. Her father was not. She wandered, married, and was lost."

"Did she know?"

"Do you mean did she know before Master Meyer brought her here?"

Finn nodded. He noticed movement next to him and saw several people making their way along the street. One of them was singing, another dancing, and still another clapping their hands. There was a general energy within the hegen section that Finn always found intriguing.

"She knew, but she didn't know."

"And she's willing to stay here?"

"We take care of our own," Esmerelda said. She looked over her shoulder.

Finn shifted, looking around him again before turning his attention back to Esmerelda. He needed to get on with the reason that he had come in the first place, and ask the question that had brought him there. Why the summons now?

What he said was not what he intended, though. "My mother is gone."

Esmerelda nodded slowly. "Your sister came to visit one of the people."

"They weren't able to help."

"Unfortunately, there was nothing that could be done."

"Would *you* have helped?"

"There are times when even our abilities are limited, Finn."

"That's not an answer."

"I would've offered whatever assistance I could have, but there wouldn't have been anything we could have done to help her."

"Why not?"

She watched him, and he nearly took a step back. She had a vibrancy to her gaze, but it was something more than just that. She had a darkness there as well. "Had you spoken to your mother?"

"I spoke to her."

"Then you know there was nothing we could have done."

He looked over to her, and as much as he wished there was another possibility, he knew that Esmerelda was right. There wasn't anything that could have been done— or that his mother had wanted to be done.

Finn regarded Esmerelda for a moment. "Did you know my father?"

"I'm afraid I don't understand the question."

Finn regarded her for another moment before shaking his head. It wasn't fair to Esmerelda to challenge her about this.

Finn let out a long sigh, shaking his head as he looked around. This wasn't the time for the question, but his mother's death made him more introspective. "It's probably nothing. I just thought that maybe the hegen were involved with my life before I got caught up with Master Meyer."

"What would give you that impression?"

"Knowing that my father would have done everything in his power to help her. Thinking that perhaps you had some other reason to draw me in."

"Did we draw you in?"

Finn smiled at her. "You didn't?" He reached into his pocket, pulling out the card, flipping it. "You sent for me."

Esmerelda looked behind her for a moment before turning her attention back to Finn. "Only because I thought you may benefit from this." She reached into her pocket, pulling a card out, and holding it to Finn. "No obligation, just information."

"Why do I feel like you're trying to still manipulate me?"

"Because you have been taught to distrust the hegen. Consider this an offer of help."

"Why would you help me?"

"We pay our debts." She handed him the card and closed the door.

Finn stared at it, and as he looked down, understanding washed over him.

The people pay their debts.

He had helped Jasmine. That was why she offered help now.

Now Finn had to use what he had learned.

This card was the easiest of the ones Esmerelda had given him but also one that left him curious. As he stared at the card, seeing what looked to be a splinted leg, the ink a bright red though not a blood red, Finn knew that there was only one explanation.

Seamus.

Why would she have sent Finn after him?

Another bell tolled distantly in the city. It was past time he return.

The priest spoke the words from the Book of Heleth, and Finn mouthed along with him, feeling comfort in hearing the words spoken in such a way. It was unusual for him, especially given that he had grown accustomed to hearing them spoken to one of the condemned.

The church of Heleth was a simple structure. The center part of the church was a tall stone room, the walls bare, leading to an open chamber high overhead from where Heleth was rumored to watch over her followers. Candles glowed throughout, illuminating the inside of the church, though not all that well. Shadows still drifted through the church, keeping everything shrouded in a dim light. Incense burned, giving off a soothing aroma, though Finn didn't know if the incense was for the funeral or it was part of the typical services. He hadn't been to the church in a long time to celebrate.

The priest was dressed in his ceremonial robes, the brown fabric draped around him, flowing to the ground. A simple silver chain hung around his neck, a star for the symbol of Heleth visible. He was an older man, with thick glasses and a neatly trimmed beard. Not any priest that Finn had ever seen while marching along with the Blood Court. Typically, those priests were younger, as if they were punished as well by ministering to the condemned.

There weren't many people in the church. Master Meyer, Lena, and Finn. Two other priests stood near the back of the church, situated on the hard wooden pews, and the head priest, an older man Meyer seemed to know quite well, presided over the service.

A shroud covered their mother, and even covered like that, she still looked thin and frail, leaving Finn thinking that she had faded long before she had died.

He glanced over to his sister, taking her hand, and found her speaking the words of Heleth along with him. After returning from the hegen section, he'd almost been late. The service went quickly, and when the priest was done, he bowed politely to Finn and then Lena, and finally to Master Meyer.

Meyer left Finn, heading to the back of the church and then out. It left Finn and Lena standing together, with their mother, one last time.

"Father won't even know," Lena said.

"I know," Finn said.

She looked over to him. "Do you think Master Meyer would have any way of sending word to him?"

"He doesn't have the answers either."

"How can he not have the answers? I thought he was in charge of all prisoners within the city."

Finn looked around the inside of the church. The walls stretched high overhead, and though they kept their voices hushed, it still felt uncomfortable having a conversation like this in a place of worship. He wasn't even a faithful servant of Heleth, but he didn't feel as if he needed to question whether or not he should be speaking about such things in this place.

"Father was moved out of the city," Finn said. "That's all I've been able to find about him. I will keep looking, but I don't know if Master Meyer will be able to help."

Lena turned her attention back to their mother, and she reached forward, touching her forehead for a moment, and then took a step back. "It's wrong."

"I know it is," Finn said.

She looked over to him. "All of this is wrong."

"I know it is," Finn said.

She looked over to the altar before glancing to the

back of the church. "I don't know what I'm going to do. Maybe I should join the church. Heleth would have a place for me."

"Do you want to?"

Lena took a deep breath, letting it out slowly, before shaking her head. "I don't think I have the right faith." She looked over to Finn, her brow furrowed. "Isn't that terrible? Here we are, in this place, and knowing what I know, and I'm questioning whether I have the right faith. It's just that..."

"I don't have the right faith either," Finn admitted. "And I've escorted several dozen men to their deaths."

"Is it hard?"

"Not having faith?"

"I know how that is. And it's not that I don't have any faith," Lena said, looking back to the altar. "It's just that I question. I wonder which of the gods I should follow, if any of them. I wonder if the gods even pay any attention to us." She shook her head, looking back to Finn. "Not that I question the existence of gods. I know some do."

Finn was one of them.

"It's just that I start to wonder about my place. Maybe I should just start to follow the Church of Fell."

"I don't know if you have enough money to do so," Finn said.

Lena's eyes widened slightly, and then she started to smile. "They do prefer those with money, don't they? I was invited once, but I never took the opportunity."

They fell into a silence, looking to their mother, up at the altar, and finally Finn inhaled deeply. "It's time."

"I know."

As they headed through the church, a darkened figure near the back of the church stepped forward.

"Oscar," Finn said. He glanced around but saw no other priests. Oscar had dressed in one of the priests' robes and had likely been there the entire time. "How did you hear that she was gone?"

"I'm sorry." Oscar looked over to Lena. "I know how much you did for her. I know how much it meant to her. Your father cared very much for her."

"I know," Finn said.

Lena remained silent next to him, and Finn didn't know if it was because she didn't care for Oscar or that she was mourning. He knew that she didn't necessarily love Oscar, and she blamed him somewhat for what happened to Finn, but at the same time, what happened to Finn had actually helped their family in some regards.

"I just came to pay my respects. I didn't come to get in the middle of the two of you."

Finn glanced over to Lena, worried that she might snap at Oscar, but he needn't have worried. "Thank you."

She pulled away from Finn, stepping out of the church, leaving Finn with Oscar. Finn wanted to stay with Lena to comfort her, but felt he had to talk to Oscar.

"I wish that I could've helped her more," Oscar said, looking after Lena. "After your father was pinched, there wasn't much that could be done. I tried, but…"

"Are you talking about my mother or Lena?"

"Both, I suppose. The only thing I knew how to do was

help you. I figured you would do the right thing and take care of your family."

"I tried," Finn said.

"You did more than just try," Oscar said.

Finn inhaled deeply. "Thank you for stopping by."

"That's all you want to say?"

"What do you think I need to say? That I appreciate all that you did for my family after my father was caught stealing with you?" There was more he had to do, anyway. Get back to Lena, figure out why Esmerelda had given him a card indicating Seamus, *and* make sure Bellut didn't harm anyone he cared about.

"Finn—"

"I know it wasn't your fault. And I know I got caught up in the same thing, following in his footsteps, but I can't help but wonder what might've happened had he not gotten caught."

"Why do you think your father started taking the jobs in the first place, Finn? He wasn't always a thief. He might not have always paid for everything, but he didn't pull jobs. Not until he had to."

Oscar kept his voice low, and in the confines of the church, it felt as if the building itself swallowed the sound. Or perhaps Heleth scooped up what Oscar said, keeping it for herself. Either way, the words were muted.

"She was sick all that time?"

Finn had very few memories of his father from that time. Finn knew that he had been stealing, and Finn had even watched him get followed by the Archers, knowing the danger in it, but he had never really understood why his father had done so. As he had grown, and trapped as they were in the section of the city that they were, Finn had believed that it was simply a matter of trying to get an advantage. They were poor, and who wouldn't have wanted to have a chance to earn more?

"It was something simple. At least at first," Oscar said. "She had a cough. She was tired. Nothing more than that. When it lingered, they tried to get her more help."

"What kind of help?"

"First they went to surgeons, but they didn't know what to do. They were cheaper, of course, and your father still grumbled about the expense, but the surgeons couldn't do anything. He tried going to several different apothecaries after that, but none of them were helpful."

"I didn't know." He looked back to where his mother rested. She would remain there for the rest of the day before the priests removed the body. From there, Finn would never know what happened. It was part of the celebration of Heleth, something that those outside of the priesthood never had an opportunity to see.

"He didn't want you to know. He didn't want your sister to know. He thought he could get enough money. He tried everything that he could think of, but nothing worked."

"She wasn't that sick when he disappeared."

"No. Not that sick, but getting sicker. He knew that. She knew that. And the two of them did everything that they could to try to get her help."

"Did they go to Meyer?"

Oscar shrugged. "I don't know. I don't know if they

went to him, or if they went to a physician. Regardless, they knew they needed something more."

"Which was why he started stealing," Finn said.

"Maybe not started. When she was getting sick, she couldn't work, so your father had needed to pick up some of the slack. He started taking small jobs to begin with, and those jobs turned into bigger jobs and then bigger jobs. Before he was pinched, he had started getting involved in increasingly significant jobs."

"You were there with him. What was the job?"

"Finn..." He looked as if he wanted to say something more, but shook his head. "None of that matters. When I learned he was moved. It was too late for me to do anything about it."

"What would you have done?"

"I would've tried to break him out." Oscar shrugged. "I can't say I would've been successful. Same reason I wasn't able to break you out of Declan. I would've tried."

"I need to go."

Finn looked toward the door. Meyer and Lena were out there, probably waiting for him. Lena likely would've told Meyer about Oscar coming to the church, and Finn had no idea what Meyer might even say, if anything.

Oscar grabbed his wrist. "I understand. Listen. I didn't come only to pay my respects. There's something else you need to know about."

"Really?"

Oscar looked around, as if concerned about who might be listening in. Finn doubted that anyone within the church of Heleth would be spying on them. What would the priests care about what they said to each other?

"I'm not exactly sure what's going on. Crews have been active. Really active. Not exactly sure what's going on, but they've been up to something."

"What about *your* crew?"

Oscar held his gaze, saying nothing.

"You don't want to tell me?"

"I've had some difficulty with jobs recently," Oscar said carefully.

"The Hand? How is that even possible?"

"I imagine the Client has made things a little more difficult for me."

Bellut *had* threatened those Finn cared about. "Why would he be able to?"

"Same way that he hired the King. Don't you go fretting about that, Finn. I can take care of my own business. I'm just letting you know that something is up. Something big."

And it had to be, especially considering Oscar had been willing to say something. It spoke to his level of concern.

"You really don't know anything?"

"I'm not in on this one, Finn. The Mistress has seen to that. Tried to figure out more but haven't been able to get anywhere."

Finn didn't know much about the Mistress, other than she often controlled jobs in the city.

"That's why you came to me."

"I came to you because it might help both of us."

Finn grunted. "Now I get it."

Oscar shook his head. "There's nothing wrong with both of us benefiting here."

"I suppose not." He frowned. "Say. Do you know a man who runs in a crew by the name of Seamus?"

"Why?" Oscar asked.

The way that he said it suggested to Finn that Oscar did know him. "He's involved in something. He came to Meyer for healing a while back. And now the hegen want me to find him."

As soon as he said hegen, Oscar's eyes twitched slightly. "You need to be careful."

"I don't owe them anything for this," Finn said.

"Are you sure about that?"

"This time, I am."

Oscar looked around the church before settling his gaze on Finn. "I know him. He will be in the Nethel section. That's where his crew likes to run. Pretty distinctive man, so he shouldn't be too hard for you to find."

Finn nodded slowly. He knew the section.

"I can see you need to go," Oscar said. "Just remember that I'm trying to help."

Finn grunted. "Now you want to call in a favor?"

"It can work both ways."

Was that the way their friendship was going to go now?

At least it *was* a friendship.

If Finn saw Rock again, he had no idea how he might be received. No, that wasn't entirely true. He had a pretty good idea how he would be received.

"And be careful. I don't know what's going on, but whatever it is strikes me as dangerous."

"The same kind of dangerous we had with the King?"

"Close enough to make me worry."

He clasped Finn on the shoulder, holding his gaze for a moment, and then nodded to him.

Finn shuffled off to the side, looking out of the door leading into the church, and didn't see any sign of Meyer. Or Lena, for that matter.

Where would she have gone?

Finn paused and found Oscar making his way toward the altar, moving slowly, and when he reached the altar, he paused there for a moment, looking down at Finn's mother. He stood for a long time in front of her. Dressed as he was in the priest's robes, Finn could almost feel as if Oscar were praying over her, though that might only be his imagination.

He stepped out into the sunlight. Meyer and Lena were gone.

CHAPTER TWENTY-SEVEN

He hurried through the streets. It was late enough that he didn't encounter much of a crowd, and when he passed a pair of Archers, he nodded to them. Dressed as he was, he didn't attract much notice. Not only was he dressed well, and still for the funeral, but he moved with a determined step.

He had to get answers.

The moon was out, fat and full, and a hint of starlight glittered in the sky. A gentle north breeze blew in, carrying with it the smells of the forest, along with a hint of what must be a coming rain. The air had turned crisper, and Finn knew that they wouldn't have much time before the season shifted and winter came in full.

Finn wasn't sure that he was ready for winter yet. Working the streets in the winter was not easy. People dressed differently, which meant stealing from them was harder, and it was also harder to sneak around late at night. There weren't darks for winter. Either you suffered the cold or you simply didn't pull the same jobs. He wasn't sure what it would be like working with Meyer in the winter.

He had to focus on the job at hand. Find Seamus.

That was where Esmerelda had guided him.

Now he had to figure out why.

Finn moved carefully, and when he reached the Nethel section, he slowed. Oscar suggested he'd find him here, but where to look?

Finn paused, pulling out the card, flipping it in his hand as he stared at it for a long moment, before finally putting it away. When he looked up, there were shadows moving in the distance.

Darks.

Seamus shouldn't be able to pull any jobs these days, not with a broken leg, but why was it that one of the figures looked to be moving differently? There was a strange hobbling sort of motion. That had to be Seamus.

The fool thought to pull a job while using crutches?

What kind of person did that?

The same kind of person who fell off of a roof, Finn knew.

And it was the kind of thing that Finn actually understood. Having worked with crews before, and knowing how hard it was to take up a position in a crew, there was the pressing desire to hold that position. If you lost it, if you were replaced, then it was incredibly difficult to claw your way back into the crew and prove your worth. That had to be part of the reason that Seamus would be willing to come out there in this way.

Finn stayed along the shadows, though he wasn't dressed nearly right to conceal himself. He moved carefully and quietly, staying concealed as much as he could, and when he caught up to where the crew had disappeared, he paused.

Oscar—and Wolf, for that matter—had made a point of telling him just how out of practice he was. He'd lost a step. He wasn't dressed right for this.

He turned the corner and came face-to-face with a tall man dressed in all dark clothing. He had a large forehead and narrow eyes, and clutched a knife that he brought back.

Finn immediately danced back and crashed into someone else.

Damn.

This was a mistake.

"What are you doing, following us?" the bruiser asked.

There was something about his voice that was familiar. Finn looked up, but he couldn't see his face. "I'm not following you. I'm looking for Seamus."

"We don't know a Seamus."

"I don't know what you call him, but he's got red hair. Broken leg."

Finn tried to get up, but someone kicked him from the side. He braced himself, managing to ignore most of the brunt of the kick, but it still hurt.

He debated whistling for the Archers, but he might just

as well end with a knife in his belly as he would with any answers.

"I just need to ask him a few questions."

"We're not letting some upper-class cunt ask him any questions."

Finn chuckled. "I'm not upper-class."

He could feel movement near him, and he knew that somebody was getting close enough to kick again, and he braced, pushing out his hands, preparing to block.

Finn had never been a fighter, and certainly not a bruiser, but he had trained enough with Master Meyer that he'd grown stronger. When the kick came, Finn pushed, shoving the person staggering down the street.

It wasn't the bruiser. If it had been, he doubted he would have been successful. He got to his feet, looking around and slipped his gaze at the others. "I'm just looking to have a few words with Seamus."

"Hey there, boys," a familiar voice said. It was Seamus. Finn recognized the strange lilting accent to his words. "You don't need to protect me from him. He helped bandage me up. Worked with the old hangman, he did. Sounds like he likes to have a few mugs of ale, this one."

"That one can't handle any mugs of ale."

It came from the bruiser, and once again, Finn thought he recognized his voice.

"Rock?" The bruiser stepped closer, and Finn's eyes widened. "Damn, it is you. It's good…" The hurt on Rock's face made Finn cut off. There was no warmth there, not like there once had been. "What are you doing with this crew?"

"You shouldn't be out here, Shuffles."

"Shuffles?" Seamus asked, laughing. "Here, I thought mine was bad."

"What's yours?"

"Fish."

"I don't get it," Finn said.

"I don't either, but they liked it better than *Red*."

Seamus glanced from Finn to the others before tipping his head in a slight nod.

They drifted off to the side of the street, leaving Finn with Seamus and Rock.

"I'm not going to do anything to him," Finn said.

"Can't trust you, Shuffles. Not no more."

"That's how it's going to be with us?"

Rock glowered at him. "There is no us."

Finn breathed out slowly. "I'm just here to ask him a few questions. He's not under investigation."

Rock snorted. "Like I wasn't?"

Finn rounded on him. Rock was much taller than Finn, more muscular, and intimidating, but Finn knew him. They were friends. Maybe not anymore, but he didn't think Rock would hurt him.

"You know what happened as well as I do, Rock. Don't go running around, blaming me for that. I did what I had to."

Rock frowned. "What you had to?"

"The same way you did what you had to." Finn took a step toward him, looking up. "Leon got what he deserved. I'm not going to feel one bit bad about it."

"Wait," Seamus said, glancing from Finn to Rock. "You

were on the King's crew? I can't believe it," Seamus said, laughing. He brought his hands together as if to clap, but then caught himself before he lost his balance with his crutches and fell forward. He chuckled, shaking his head. "Damn. I knew you had some crazy story."

"He's not in the crew," Rock said.

Seamus just chuckled. "You can leave us alone, big guy. He's not going to do anything to hurt me. Gods, if it weren't for him, I might've had one of those damn cutters take my leg all the way off."

Rock backed away, giving Finn and Seamus a chance to talk. Seamus leaned forward on the crutches, keeping his injured leg bent up, though the bandages looked quite a bit dirtier than they had when Finn had been with him last time.

"You should keep that clean," Finn suggested.

"It's not always easy to keep it clean with the kind of work I do," he said.

"Then maybe you shouldn't be doing that kind of work," Finn said.

Seamus shrugged. "What can I say? I have jobs to run."

"You're the crew leader."

Seamus just shrugged again.

Finn wouldn't have guessed it from his time with Seamus, but having seen the way Rock protected him and the way Seamus instructed them, he should have known better.

Had he only known, maybe he would have thought of a different set of questions. Maybe he would have asked Oscar for help. At least Seamus seemed to be the crew leader. Rock couldn't hurt Finn unless Seamus decided he should.

"What do you want to know? You obviously have something on your mind, Shuffles."

Finn glanced over to where Rock loomed in the shadows. If Finn were to take any action, he had little doubt that Rock would be there and prevent him from getting too close to Seamus.

"I have a few more things now."

Seamus frowned. "I'm not going to turn any of my team in."

"It's not about your team." He looked along the street, trying to figure out just what it was that he needed to understand. There was something there, Finn was certain of it, but he didn't have any idea what it was that the hegen wanted him to find. "Can we talk somewhere else?"

"You don't like talking out here in the street?"

Finn shrugged. "I thought you boasted about how much ale you could drink."

Seamus glanced at the others within his crew, shaking his head. "Can't report any of my crew, you see."

"I'm not asking you to report any of your crew. I'm asking for a few answers. And I'm not investigating you."

Seamus sniffed. "I've seen how those things go. I'm sure you have, too. You start looking into one person, it leads you to another, then another, and pretty soon everybody is lined up in prison, all of them trying to keep from getting their lashes or facing banishment from the city. I think it's probably for the best if I just thank you for setting my leg and letting me keep it."

"I could—"

"You could nothing," Seamus said. There was a dark and dangerous edge to his words.

It reminded him of the King. Mostly humor but an undercurrent of something else. There was a danger to him, the same way that the King had a danger. Without it, they wouldn't be able to run the crew quite as well.

He needed to figure out just what Seamus knew. And Finn was convinced he knew something.

There was only one way he could get answers. He pulled the hegen card out and handed it to Seamus.

He took it slowly, frowning. "What is this…"

"This is the reason I came to talk to you."

Seamus glanced over to the others in his crew, nodding slowly. "I see. Maybe we could get a drink," Seamus grinned. "I know a place."

The Wandering Hog was very little different than the Wenderwolf. Music played, though the musicians weren't quite as skilled as were found in the Wenderwolf. Ale flowed, served by women revealing quite a bit of cleavage, and couples danced, bouncing around the inside of the tavern, voices and boots on the wooden floor, giving a low-level noise to everything.

Finn sat at one of the back tables, near the door, looking across at Seamus. A mug of ale sat in front of him, barely touched. Seamus had already gone through half of his mug.

Rock stood off to the side, watching. He hadn't taken a seat, but he wasn't the only one. There was a dark-haired woman with a long dagger sheathed at her side, and she watched Finn, a deadly look in her eyes.

"It looks like your crew is keeping tabs on you closely," Finn said.

"What can I say? They care about me."

Finn took a sip of ale. It wasn't quite as good as was found in the Wenderwolf, either. It was better than what he had found outside of the city. These days, Finn didn't get the opportunity to enjoy ale quite as often as he once did.

"I think I need to know about the job you were on when you fell."

Seamus took a drink, glancing over to Rock and then the woman before looking across his mug at Finn. "Not sure there's much I can tell you."

Seamus looked down at the card resting on the table between them. He hadn't let it go, and given that Finn had come specifically because of the hegen card, he understood the uncertainty he saw in Seamus's eyes.

"Where did you get that?" Seamus asked, looking up from the card and meeting Finn's eyes. "I know where you got it, but where did you *get* it?"

"There's one of the hegen named Esmerelda—"

"Shit," Seamus said, shaking his head. "That one?" He glanced over to the others, and leaned toward Finn, lowering his voice. "How did you get involved with *her*?"

"It's a long story. You obviously know the hegen too."

Seamus took a deep breath, then downed the rest of

his ale before setting the empty mug on the table. Some-body was there within moments, giving him a new mug. Seamus didn't even look up. "I know them. Not that I want to talk about why."

"Then tell me how you got hurt."

Seamus sniffed. "We took on a job. Didn't know the employer, so you don't need to ask. Somebody willing to pay quite a bit. Not from around here, you see."

Finn took a sip of his ale. "What did they sound like?"

"Heavy accent. Said we needed to place these items in a dozen buildings around the city." He shrugged. "Paid well, especially since we weren't asked to take anything like we normally are. This was placing something."

"What were you putting in these buildings?"

"Don't really know. It wasn't hard work. Most of the buildings weren't heavily guarded."

"How much did they pay?"

Seamus shook his head. "No, that's not how it works, Shuffles."

"I'm not trying to ask so I can take your money. I'm asking so I can figure out how valuable the job might have been."

Seamus glanced over to the others in his crew, pausing as he looked over to Rock, before leaning forward and lowering his voice even more. "We got ten silver drebs for each one we placed," he whispered. "I kept half, split the rest with the crew."

"Just to sneak in and put something into these buildings?"

He nodded.

"What were they?"

"Can't say I even know. Really strange-looking things, they were. Look like a little bucket with a strange tail on it. They had a handle, and I was told not to shake them. Dangerous, you see."

Finn closed his eyes. "Could you draw a picture of one?"

"I'm no artist, Shuffles."

"Could you?" Finn asked, opening his eyes.

"Maybe I could. I suppose if it's that important to you. Not like I can go and do much about it now. All of them have been delivered. We were on the last one when I slipped. The crew took care of the rest of it. I hobbled over to your place, though I stopped at a few surgeons along the way. Hell, had I known better, maybe I would've gone straight to the old hangman myself."

Seamus raised his hand, and the dark-haired woman came over, keeping her gaze on Finn as she did. She leaned close to Seamus, and he whispered something in her ear, her brow furrowing. She nodded once, slipping away before returning only a few moments later with a piece of paper and a bottle of ink along with a pen.

"You're well supplied here," Finn said.

"You know how crews run," Seamus said. He looked up at Finn for a moment. "Well, maybe you don't. Anyway, I've got to keep everybody working together. That's the key to the job, you know."

He started drawing, and it wasn't long before he finished. He slipped the paper over the table to Finn, who took it and studied it.

Finn had only seen the item once, and it had been damaged at that time, but not so damaged that he didn't recognize it.

It was the same thing that had been found in Sweth's home. The same item that had started the fire that had burned an entire section of the city.

"You said you put a dozen of these all throughout the city?"

"Yeah. I tried to get more work. Pretty easy job, you see, but there were others involved too. I tried to corner the market on this but didn't nail it down in time."

Finn just stared at it. How many of these items were in the city? How much of the city was going to burn?

"I need to know everything you can about the man who hired you."

"Listen, Shuffles. I like you. I think you're an interesting guy. You got a story, and that's something I like. But I can't really tell you too much. Got a reputation to uphold and all."

"I'm sure you do," Finn said softly.

"And I wouldn't have said as much as I did were it not for that card. I didn't make the arrangements for the job. Somebody else pulled my crew in. They were coordinating the whole thing."

"I need to know where you placed them."

Seamus leaned back, crossing his arms over his chest. He flicked his gaze to the woman, who took a step toward Finn. Rock stood off to the side, saying nothing.

"I'm afraid I can't do that, Shuffles."

"I need those names. If you don't, then—"

The woman was there at the table in little more than a blink of an eye. She was quick, but Finn had been ready for her, and he scooted off to the side, jumping to his feet. He had the table between him and Rock, and the door just at his back. He didn't want it to go down this way.

"This thing..." Finn said, pointing to the piece of paper on the table. Finn had dragged it toward the end of the table as he got to his feet. If nothing else, it was coming with him. "... is responsible for the fire in Jorend." He looked from Seamus to the woman and finally to Rock. There were a few others in the tavern looking in his direction, so Finn suspected they all worked with Seamus as well. "And you placed a dozen of them. We need to find them before the entire city burns."

Seamus started to grin before laughing. "Damn, Shuffles. That's a bit dramatic, don't you think? Who's going to pay to have somebody place items like that throughout the city?"

"Somebody who wants to see it burn," Finn said.

"Nah. Now, I don't know everything that you been involved in, but from the way I hear it, the bastard you lit on fire started that fire. Everybody said he likes to see the flames."

"I don't think that's what happened," Finn said.

He thought about the things that he had learned from Sweth. He had focused on his role as scribe, but that wasn't even the key. Sweth wasn't from the city. He hadn't owned the home. That had been Fol.

He was the key.

Finn looked across the table, getting Rock's attention. "Was it the Client?"

Seamus started to laugh, glancing from Finn to Rock. "What are you going on about now?"

"Was it the same person?" Finn asked, but Rock ignored him. "I need to know, Rock."

Rock took a step toward him, leaning on the table, lowering at Finn. "You're the reason the King died. You're damn near the reason that I almost hanged. You think I'm going to tell you anything?"

"You will if it means saving the city."

Rock grunted. "Why would I care about saving the city?"

Finn looked at the others and realized that he wasn't going to get any answers from them. He backed toward the door. "I'm going to need those names," he said to Seamus. "You can deliver them to the executioner's home. If you don't..."

Seamus leaned forward, locking eyes with Finn. "What happens if I don't?"

Finn just shook his head. He had to play this differently. A man like Seamus needed him to lose the friendly act. That wasn't going to get the answers Finn needed. It was time for him to be the executioner. If he didn't, the city would suffer.

"People are going to die."

"People die all the time. An executioner would know that."

Finn thought about discussing the hegen card, but he had a feeling Seamus wasn't going to be swayed that way.

There wasn't any way for him to get through to him but authority.

It was time he accepted that.

He'd been trying to strike a different balance, wanting to have friends, relationships, but maybe that wasn't in *his* cards.

Finn had to be the executioner.

"If you don't, then your enterprise here is going to be severely impeded. I will make sure the Archers investigate every single bit of what's taking place in the Wandering Hog, along with following you constantly." He glanced to the crutches leaned up against the table. "You won't be hard to keep track of. And maybe we bring you in for questioning. You can ask Rock what it's like when we bring you in for questioning. I can guarantee you that you will give me those names." He backed toward the door. "You have until morning."

Finn pulled the door open, stepped outside, and slipped across the street to a darkened alleyway, where he lingered, watching.

He didn't have to wait for long.

Half a dozen people slipped out of the tavern, heading down the street, including the dark-haired woman and Rock. They all went in different directions, but Finn followed Rock. He was easy enough to follow, and Finn didn't even have to stay that close to him.

It wasn't until he turned a corner, stopping at a darkened building where he tapped on the door that Finn slowed. When the door came open, Wolf poked his head out.

Finn stayed pressed up against the darkness, hoping that he hid himself as well as possible. Rock might not see him, but he had little doubt that Wolf would be alert and looking for others. There was something about the building that struck Finn as odd.

It was small, at least compared to the others in this part of the section. The front of it was painted with dark colors that didn't stand out very well in the night. The air had a strange odor to it, almost one of smoke, and reminded him a little bit of fire ash. Wolf made a motion to Rock, and he slipped along the street with Wolf, disappearing.

Finn was tempted to follow but worried about doing so. Following Wolf was more dangerous than following Rock. Instead, he hurried up to the door and glanced along the street before pulling it open only a crack.

The bitter scent of something burning drifted out of the inside of the building. He'd smelled it before. Finn breathed it in slowly, his eyes adjusting to the darkness. There was no light other than a soft glow somewhere deep in the building. He looked to see if there was anyone inside.

At first, he thought the room empty.

Finn pulled the door open and stepped inside.

A shadow moved at the end of a narrow hallway.

Finn tensed, leaning against the wall, wishing he had his old darks for concealment. This was the kind of job Oscar had always been good at, not Finn, but he needed to know what Wolf had been doing. Still, the sensible thing to do would be to gather several Archers to investigate.

The shadow disappeared.

Finn's heart started again.

He stepped forward.

A thudding in the distance caught his attention. He waited, but it seemed to be at the end of the hall and behind another door. There was one more door along the hall, but he couldn't tell where either led.

Finn couldn't stay here long.

Still, there was the smell he'd detected. As he breathed it in, he realized what it was.

Fire ash.

He looked around the inside of the room and made out a table along one wall with something resting on top of it. Finn hurried over to the table, sneaking as carefully as he could to avoid the others discovering his presence.

When he reach the table, his eyes widened.

It was the same device Seamus had just drawn for him.

The sound of thudding feet came from the back of the building.

It was time to leave before he *couldn't* get away.

Finn looked behind him. There was no sign of Wolf. Not yet.

He grabbed the item and raced toward the door he'd entered. Finn started out when he saw movement along the street. He couldn't get out that way.

Finn closed the door, backing quietly into the room. He had to find another way out.

Then back to Meyer's house.

The door at the end of the hall came open.

Finn raced toward the other door along the hall and

reached it just in time. A small kitchen opened up. A lantern rested on a narrow counter. A small stove radiated heat. Another door on the opposite side of the room caught his attention.

The thudding of footsteps came toward him.

He hurried across the kitchen and yanked the door open quickly, stepping out of the door and into an alley as the door behind him came open.

He ignored the shout behind him and clutched the strange object to himself as he raced along the alley, his heart pounding rapidly and a cold sweat on his forehead.

Finn had to get back. Meyer had to know about this.

CHAPTER TWENTY-EIGHT

He didn't stop running until he reached Master Meyer's house, his heart pounding in his chest and sweat pouring down his brow. Wolf was involved. Rock was involved.

And it was all tied to the fire.

Not just tied to the fire. It was an attack on the city.

He'd known Wolf hadn't just been interested in figuring out how to get revenge for what happened to the King. There had to be another angle. He just hadn't thought *this* would be it.

When he reached the gate leading into Master Meyer's home, Finn paused, looking along the street before stepping inside. He hurried into the home, pulling the door closed and racing down the hall. Everything was dark. He knocked on the door to Master Meyer's office but found it darkened and empty.

This couldn't wait.

He hurried up the stairs. When he reached the door to Master Meyer's room, he knocked.

Lena's room was not closed. "Finn? Where did you go? You just left—"

"I know. I'll explain later. Go back to sleep," he whispered.

"What is it?"

He shook his head. "You should go back to sleep."

"I haven't been able to sleep that well. I've been trying." She stood in the doorway wearing a thick robe, her arms crossed over her chest. Her jaw held an angry tilt Finn was all too familiar with seeing. As she opened the door, a hint of lantern light glowed from inside the room. It was just enough that he could see that she had not slept, fatigue burning in her eyes. Lena had been awake. "Ever since Mother—"

"What is it?" Meyer asked, pulling the door open.

Finn glanced over to his sister before turning to Meyer. "I need to talk to you. It's urgent."

"What can be urgent in the middle of the night? There is no aspect to our job that is—" Meyer cut off as Finn held the device out in front of him. "Where did you get that?"

"Apparently, crews were hired all throughout the city to place these in different buildings. You remember Seamus?" Meyer frowned. "You do remember him. Broken leg. He'd fallen off a roof while his team was placing one of these items inside of a building."

"I don't understand," Master Meyer said.

Lena leaned over Finn's shoulder. "That smells funny. What is it?"

"I'm not exactly sure," Finn said. "It's an explosive of some sort. It's responsible for burning the Jorend section of the city down."

Meyer stepped back into his room, closing the door. Finn stared for a moment.

Could he really not see what was going on?

Finn turned to his sister when Meyer's door came back open. He'd gotten dressed, and he motioned for Finn to follow. "Downstairs."

They headed down the stairs, into Master Meyer's office, and Lena went to light the lantern when Master Meyer shook his head.

"Don't."

"What's wrong?"

Meyer nodded toward the device Finn held. "Until we know what it is and how to counter it, we have to be careful we don't unintentionally ignite it."

"We have to have some light to examine it," Finn said. He looked around the room. "We could put a lantern on either end of the room, far enough away that we could examine it in the center of the room."

Meyer took a deep breath before nodding. "That might work."

He and Lena placed the lanterns, keeping them dimly lit but offering enough illumination into the room where they could see things better. Meyer had placed the device on a small table in the center of the room, and he pushed everything else out of the way.

Finn approached slowly before realizing that wasn't necessary. He'd already carried the damn thing through the city, going so far as to have run with it. If it were going to explode on him, it would've done so by now.

It was made of a coppery metal, and it looked something like a teakettle with a handle on one side, a spout coming off the other, and swirls leading along the top, heading down the sides. A lid of sorts had been fashioned onto the top, and while Finn had run, that lid had not come free.

"I've never seen anything like this," Lena said.

"I think it's from Yelind," Finn said.

Meyer looked up, frowning. "Finn…"

Finn shook his head. "You can discount my idea, but at least let me say it. Think about what we knew about Sweth, Master Meyer. He'd come from Yelind. He hadn't been here all that long. And he'd been living in a rented home."

All of it fit in Finn's mind. Yelind intended to attack the kingdom, starting with Verendal.

"That doesn't point to Yelind."

"No, but a device just like this had been found inside the remains."

"And there are rumors about Yelind attacking," Lena said.

Finn and Master Meyer looked over to her. "I haven't heard any rumors," Meyer said.

Finn had.

One of the jurors had mentioned something, but what was it?

"I don't know what to make of them, but Helda was talking to a man she's been seeing." Finn started to smirk, and Lena shot him a hard look. "He's a farrier, and had been warned to be ready. Apparently, there has been activity to the south with Yelind. Soldiers gathering. From what he heard, King Porman planned responding by sending troops that way."

"That's nothing but rumors," Master Meyer said.

"Sometimes, rumors have a way of being true," Finn said.

Meyer shook his head. "And most of the time, rumors have a way of being wrong. If they were true, you would have died a dozen different times before you came and served me."

Finn snorted as he turned his attention back to the device. "Fine. Maybe they are nothing but rumors, but this isn't from Verendal." He pointed to a series of symbols made on the top of it. They were worked into the metal on the lid, strange letters or markings that Finn didn't recognize. "Have you seen anything like that before?"

Meyer frowned. "No. I have not."

"Hear me out. I know you don't want to believe it, but what if there is some plot on the city? If a dozen of these have been placed, and if what Seamus said was true and he wasn't even the only one to have been hired to place these"—which meant there might be many times more than that—"we could have explosions throughout the city, fires just like we had encountered in Jorend."

"We don't know that this will even lead to any sort of fire," Meyer said.

"But if it does?"

Meyer took a deep breath as he shook his head. "We need to open it."

At least he was willing to investigate. Finn should be thankful of that.

"Once we open it, then what?"

Meyer looked up at him. "Then we will decide what comes next. One step at a time, Finn."

Finn knew better than to argue, especially at this point when he suspected there was much more taking place than what Master Meyer wanted to believe.

"You should be cautious. If this has some sort of explosive powder inside of it, any movement might trigger the explosion," Lena said.

Finn glanced over to his sister. "How do you know about that?"

She shrugged. "I've been studying. I told you. One of your books has a discussion on particular types of powder." She glanced over to Meyer, flushing slightly. "None of them really talk about explosions, but it can be inferred. Then when you combine what is written in Gisles with what I found in the book by Tradler, the combination makes that suggestion."

Meyer simply watched Lena. "Perhaps the two of us need to speak."

"I'm sorry, Master Meyer. If I'm not supposed to be using those books—"

"Do you think I'm displeased?"

Lena paled. "I didn't know if you were upset I was reading Finn's books."

"They are not his books. They are mine, and they are for anyone who has a desire to learn." He regarded her for a long moment. "Perhaps I have not given you the appropriate opportunities. It's time that changed."

"Opportunities?" Lena asked, glancing over to Finn with worry etched in her eyes.

"If you would be interested, I would work with you."

The rest of the color drained from Lena's face. "I don't think I can do what Finn does."

Meyer shook his head. "Not that aspect. With medicine. As an apothecary. I could train you."

For the first time in a while, Finn noticed a light burning in his sister's eyes.

"You would do that?" Lena asked.

"I think I should have started a long time ago." He took a deep breath. "First, we need to finish with this." Meyer stood in front of the strange device, holding it closely, frowning at it. "Unfortunately, seeing as how I have no idea what they used on this, I am concerned that we will not be able to open it safely."

"There's someone who might be able to help us," Finn said. "She had fire ash and I know you don't approve of it, but I think it might be similar."

Meyer's frown faded. "Wella," Meyer said.

Finn nodded.

"Go get her. Tell her what you told me. Make her listen."

Finn looked to his sister before looking to Master Meyer, nodding. He didn't want to leave them there with something that might explode on them, but there was one person in the city who might be able to help them.

He gathered his cloak from the closet, stepping out into the night.

It was late, and a time of night when he normally wouldn't even be out. He would likely startle Wella, but it wouldn't be the first time. He suspected she had been startled awake more than once in her time serving as an apothecary. After he stepped through the gate, out onto the street, he darted along the street, heading toward Wella's home.

He hadn't gone very far when he felt something off.

Movement.

Finn slowed just enough to look around him. He needed to be more careful. Especially given what he had just done and how he had taken the device from Wolf, but at the same time, he also wanted to move as quickly as possible.

He ducked down a side street, waiting for a moment, testing for any sign of additional movement, but there was none.

He looked again, turning down another side street, and still found no movement. By the time he turned a third corner, Finn had started to feel a bit more relaxed.

Shadows moved away from the wall nearby.

"There you are, Shuffles."

Finn recognized Wolf's voice. He was still quite a ways from Wella's shop, and though he was still in Meyer's section, this wasn't one of the nicer sections of the city. "I know what you're up to, Wolf. Not so much about trying to get revenge for the King, is it?"

Wolf started toward him, a wide sneer on his face. "Revenge would have been fine, but I'd rather have the coin."

He nodded, and another shadow slipped forward.

Rock.

Wolf sneered at him. "Do you think you're the first executioner's apprentice I took care of? The other one was easy. The King and I had very little difficulty removing him when he posed a danger to our operations. Got a little too close, you know?"

Could the Lion have been investigating some of the same things I had been?

Maybe he'd end up the same way. Drowned in the river.

"You won't be quite as challenging," Wolf went on, "but you certainly will be more fun."

He had to buy time. "Why are you so eager to destroy the city?"

Rock and Wolf converged on him, and Finn glanced in either direction along the street, knowing that he would either have to run—and he didn't know if he could run fast enough to get away from both of them—or he had to try to get the Archers' attention.

They were well past the city curfew, so any noise should draw attention of the Archers. Finn could whistle and call for them, but he suspected Wolf and Rock would react quickly in dealing with him definitively.

"It's not my city," Wolf said.

Finn frowned. "You're from here."

Wolf glared at him. "I might have been from here, but it's not my city. If it were, it would've taken care of me. No. All the city wants to do is punish people like me. Take from people like me."

"People like you? You mean thieves."

"You were once a thief," Wolf said. "Could've brought you in on this. Still could."

There was the threat of violence in the offer. Finn either agreed or suffered.

Finn backed along the street, trying to keep his attention on Rock, but he also had to focus on Wolf. If either of them got too close, he had to fight.

"I was once a thief, but I was never one like you. I never betrayed my crew." Finn glanced over to Rock. "You know that, don't you? You've been working with Wolf and the King long enough. You do realize that they were more than happy to betray everybody on the crew. And now you betrayed the King by choosing coin over vengeance."

Justice wouldn't appeal to Wolf. Vengeance might.

"You aren't going to try to convince me," Wolf said.

He reached an intersection. At least there, out in the open, there was a bit more opportunity for Archers to see them. Lantern lights shone down, giving him a slight advantage when it came time for either running or fighting. He had to be careful there.

"And now you've taken up working for Yelind?" Finn asked.

"That's all you think it is?" Wolf laughed darkly. "It won't matter pretty soon. You caught on to this too late.

Just a little longer, and you're going to start to see other places exploding."

"Like what happened in Jorend section."

Wolf frowned. "That stupid bastard. He nearly ruined us. Damn apothecary. All he was supposed to do was write down what he mixed. At least he managed to do that much before he got himself pinched."

That didn't fit with what Finn had known of Sweth. It just didn't feel quite right.

"You used him?'

"Way I hear it, he blasted a hole through half of his village," Wolf said. "Didn't have much choice but to come here."

It explained why Sweth was here, but not why he served.

"Who forced him to help?"

"A man will do almost anything for those he's got left. Until he's got none left. Right, Shuffles?"

Wolf nodded to Rock, who darted forward, grabbing Finn before he could even react.

He wrapped his arms around Finn and squeezed. "I'm going to enjoy this, Shuffles."

"You would destroy the city, Rock? I've seen Jorend. I was there when it burned. If that's what you want for your city—"

"It's not my city, either," Rock said.

"Fine. Then it's going to be on you when all of those people die."

"All of them?" Rock chuckled. "It don't matter. Not anymore. Not with what's coming."

"What's coming?" Finn asked.

He glanced along the street, raising his voice as he spoke. He needed to draw attention to him, but he also had to do it in a way that wouldn't alarm the other two. He kept his voice loud, anxious, agitated.

"War," Wolf said.

He nodded, and they started dragging Finn through the street.

"Meyer knows about it," Finn said.

"It don't matter," Wolf said. "The device you took from me was going to be the last. Why shouldn't it explode in the hangman's house?"

If it did, it meant Lena would be there. Meyer.

Finn whistled.

He used a sharp and shrill sound, belting out three quick trills, and the suddenness of it caught Rock off guard.

He loosened his grip just a little bit, and Finn spun quickly, punching him in the midsection, though it did nothing. He brought his knee up, connecting with Rock's groin. Rock groaned, dropping to the ground.

Wolf started toward him, slipping a knife out of his belt. "You're going to regret that."

Movement along the street suddenly appeared in either direction. Archers.

"You see, now that I'm the executioner's apprentice, I can move freely. I don't have to fear curfew the way you do. And I don't have to be dressed in darks to conceal my movement. I've got plenty of reason to detain you. And Rock." Finn nodded to Rock, kicking him in the face to keep him on the ground. "And you're going to tell me where the other devices were placed."

Wolf just sneered at him. "This isn't over, Shuffles.

He spun, racing off.

Three Archers appeared, and Finn motioned down the street. "My name is Finn Jagger, apprenticed to Master Meyer, executioner of the city!" He hated needing to slow down chasing after Wolf, but at the same time, the Archers needed to know who he was and why he was out. "We need to detain the man who just ran down the street."

Two of the Archers took off, racing after Wolf, though Finn had a feeling they weren't going to be fast enough.

The other Archer motioned and two more hurried toward them along the street. They grabbed for Rock. "What about this one?" one of the Archers asked.

"Bring him to Declan. He and I are going to have words."

Rock tried to fight, and he got so far as to knock one of the Archers down, but the other two unsheathed their swords, and Rock fell still.

"Either tell me now or tell me later, but I will know how many devices you placed throughout the city," he said.

Rock sneered at him. "I'm not telling you nothing."

"So, you just want to see the city burn. What will that accomplish? Revenge?" Vengeance wasn't the answer. This had to be about justice, not about vengeance. "If you tell what you know, I'll make sure you have a more lenient sentence."

Rock glared at him. "Lenient. You don't know anything about that."

"I know that you will hang—or worse. If those devices explode and fires burn throughout the city, who do you think they're going to blame? The ones we have in custody. The same way we've had to blame Sweth. So, if you want to go out the way he did…"

Rock said nothing.

Finn waved the Archers away. "Bring him to Declan. Have him strapped into the chapel. I will be there shortly."

He hurried off. When he reached Wella's shop, he pounded on the door, and was surprised when she pulled it open quickly.

"Finn Jagger," she said, frowning at him as she looked along the street. "It is quite late for you to be out here."

"Meyer needs your help. We discovered a plot against the city. Explosives have been placed throughout it. We need your help learning how we can counter it."

Wella's eyes widened. "I will be right there."

"I'll wait."

She shook her head. "Don't wait. I need to gather some supplies, and then I will meet you at Henry's home. You get back there to help him as much as you can."

Everything felt like it was happening so quickly now. He raced back, seeing no signs of movement. When he reached Master Meyer's home, he hurried inside, taking off his cloak, and moving to the back office.

There was one more person in the room.

The dark-haired woman that he had seen at Seamus's tavern.

"What are you doing here?" Finn snapped.

She turned, looking at him. She had on a dark cloak, with the hood pulled up over her head, but she hadn't unsheathed her knife, which he figured meant they were safe.

For now.

"I was to bring this to you," she said. She reached into her pocket, and Finn tensed immediately.

When she pulled the slip of paper out of her pocket, Finn let out a relaxed breath.

"Seamus?"

She nodded. "He's found the location of all he can. The items we were to deliver, along with the four other crews hired for the job. There are about fifty of them in total. I can't say if there are more than that, though I don't think so. We would have heard."

"He did it that quickly?"

Her gaze drifted over to the device resting on the table. "Will it truly destroy the city?"

"Did you see Jorend?"

She looked over, nodding. "We can help."

Finn frowned. "You would help?"

"We will do what we can to remove them. All of them. But..."

"But what?"

"But we need immunity."

Finn looked over Master Meyer. He had pulled a chair over and sat in front of the small table, staring at the device. "What do you think?"

"We don't have the resources to get these items that

quickly," Meyer got to his feet, looking at the woman. "If the only thing taken out of the places where you delivered these devices is the device itself, I will promise you immunity."

The woman nodded. "We will have them delivered to the southern forest. I will personally keep an eye on them until you notify us of what you want done with them."

She slipped out of the office, and then out of the home, leaving Finn staring after her.

"Who is she?" Lena asked.

"She's known as the Mistress," Master Meyer said.

"*That's* the Mistress?" Finn asked.

Meyer nodded. "She has been known to be complicit in crime throughout the city, but we haven't been able to catch her."

"You don't want to try now?"

Meyer sighed, shaking his head. "I suppose it fits."

"What fits?"

"Relying upon the underworld of the city to help resolve this particular dilemma." He looked up at Finn.

"Fol. That's what this is all about. He's the one person we haven't found."

Meyer frowned.

"Do you really have authority to grant immunity?" Finn asked. There were times when that might be useful in the future.

"In a crisis, I would be able to sway the king, so yes."

The door came open, and Wella slipped in, glancing from Lena to Master Meyer before finally turning to consider Finn. "This is it?" She hurried over to the device.

Her eyes widened. "Yelind," she muttered. "Someone had knowledge. They should not have used it like this."

Sweth. There had been more to him than Finn had managed to uncover.

If only he had the time.

"You recognize it?" Meyer asked.

"I recognize the writing. Dangerous, this is."

"Do you know how to neutralize it?"

"As well as I can. I'm afraid we don't have much time."

"Why is that?"

"Do you remember the fire ash?"

Finn nodded. "I remember it."

"The substance inside of this would be similar, I suspect. It will gradually burn through one layer, combining with another substance, and when the two mix, you get an explosion. A dangerous and deadly explosion."

"How long does it take?"

"It can be anywhere from a few hours to a few weeks. It all depends upon the purpose of the explosion and how the device was fabricated."

She held her hands up from it. She frowned. "It's growing warm. I don't know if we have much time." She hurriedly pried open the top of the device, ignoring Meyer's sudden protestations, and reached into a pouch strapped to her side, pouring in a grayish powder. "I have to hope that will be enough," she said.

"You have to hope?"

The device took on a fiery glow, and she stepped back. "Oh. This might have expedited it."

"Wait." Lena hurried behind Master Meyer's counter, and she grabbed for a vial of liquid. She brought it over to the device and tipped a single drop into it.

"You have a reaction taking place between the two powders. You need to have more of a contrasting reaction than what you're adding to it," Lena said. "I read about something like that in Kessel, though I don't think it related to this."

Wella watched her. "You need to start working with this one," she said to Master Meyer.

"I know."

"Or I will."

Meyer glanced over, nodding slowly. "I know."

They stood back, and the glow coming from the pot started to ease until it dissipated altogether.

"Well. That is that."

"Not quite."

Wella frowned, looking at him. "What do you mean?"

"Because there are somewhere near fifty of these devices still in the city."

"Oh," Wella said, her eyes wide. "I think I will need to gather more supplies."

CHAPTER TWENTY-NINE

A knock came at the door as Finn prepared to head over to Declan Prison and interrogate Rock. He glanced down the hall to where Lena and Master Meyer were visiting softly inside of his office, neither of them speaking very loudly, before pulling the door open and frowning.

It was one of the Archers. He was tall, dark-haired, and little bit older. The sigil on his left shoulder implied rank.

"Is the hangman here?"

Finn nodded. "What is it?"

"Dozens of men moving in the city. We detained one, and he claimed he was working on behalf of him?"

"He was," Finn said. "We discovered devices in the city. We are removing them so they don't explode and lead to fires like occurred in the Jorend section."

The Archer's eyes widened. "I lost an uncle there. Devlin. He was a cobbler. Burned."

Finn nodded slowly. He recognized the name. He would have been one of the six who had not been found again after the fire. "I'm sorry for your loss. The master executioner has granted immunity to those involved in removing the devices." Finn frowned. "The Archers should help. Offer them a measure of protection."

"You want us to work with these thieves?"

"Not *work* with them, but make sure that they're protected against anybody who might attack while they're removing them."

"This is most unusual," the Archer said.

"It *is* most unusual," Master Meyer said, striding down the hall. "And I trust you will ensure that my wishes are carried out, Thelen."

"I'm sure the magister and the jurors will hear of this," he said.

"I'm sure."

"And if the king does?"

Meyer took a deep breath, letting it out slowly. "If the king does, then I will accept whatever responsibility is necessary. This needs to happen."

The Archer nodded. "So be it. Care to tell me what these things look like?"

Meyer raised a hand, hurried down the hall and he returned with the device. "This."

The Archer frowned. "I've seen something like that somewhere."

"When?"

He shook his head. "I don't quite remember. It's just familiar, is all."

"It's dangerous, is what it is. We need to gather them. These crews are removing these items as quickly as they can, bringing them out of the city. When this is done, we will neutralize them so they don't explode."

The Archer mouthed the word *explode*.

He hurried off.

Finn looked over to Master Meyer. "Even if they get all of these devices, we still don't know who in the city is responsible for placing them. We know Yelind sent them," Finn said. "Had Sweth not been convicted, we would have had an opportunity to learn what he knew."

"You have someone you can question, though."

"You would trust me to do this?"

Meyer regarded him. "I think you are the only person I should trust. I didn't recognize the true threat to the kingdom. Not the way that you did, Finn. I didn't acknowledge that more was taking place than just an arsonist. I should have listened. Now, I will work with Wella to acquire the supplies necessary to neutralize all of these devices, but I think it's important you be the one to proceed with questioning."

Finn took a deep breath. Meyer would trust him with something so critically important? He needed to honor that.

Finn grabbed his cloak, slipped it on, and looked over to Master Meyer. "I will get the answers we need."

"I'm afraid we won't have much time. You will have to push, Finn. If you aren't comfortable with that yet, I understand."

"It needs to be done."

"Be careful."

"I know. I'm not after vengeance. I need to be after justice."

"No," Meyer said, but tipped his head, nodding slightly. "Be careful navigating through the streets. It seems there's another out there. We will neutralize these fire starters."

"We?"

He looked behind him. "Myself, Wella, and Lena."

"Please be careful," he said softly.

"I don't think your sister will give us any other choice."

He hurried out of Meyer's home and along the street, and reached Declan Prison without any issues. He fished the keys out of his pocket, twisting one in the lock, stepped into the prison and closed the door, locking it behind him. Once inside, he took a deep breath, letting it out slowly. He had never been to Declan at this time of night before, and he certainly had never performed any questioning at this time of night, but it seemed crucial to do so.

Finn paused and looked around the inside of the prison, taking in the narrow hall, the dimly lit lantern set into the wall, and the stale, almost foul odor that permeated everything. He reached the row of cells and motioned to the iron master standing guard.

"He's in the chapel," the iron master said.

Finn started to turn.

"The Hunter comes! All will quake—"

"Not now, Hector," Finn snapped at him.

He hurried along the hall, up a flight of stairs and to the chapel. One of the iron masters—a younger man named Cor who he had spent some time drinking with in the tavern—stood guard.

"Heard you were coming. This one must be a particular bastard," Cor said to Finn.

"He is," Finn said. He glanced to the door. "Do you have him strapped?"

"We did it right away. We didn't wait. I can go inside with you, if you prefer."

Finn looked over to the closed door, shaking his head. "That's not necessary. He isn't going to cause me much trouble now."

"If you need anything…"

Finn just nodded. "If I need anything, I will be sure to let you know."

He pushed the door open and looked over to Rock. He was large enough that he filled the chair, though he was strapped down, still in his darks. He jerked against the leather straps but couldn't get free.

"I remember the last time you were here like this," Finn said.

"I bet this makes you pleased," Rock said.

"None of this pleases me. We were friends, Rock."

"Were. Can't be friends with the hangman."

Finn sighed. He'd wondered what he would do were his friends to come before him, but hadn't known. Not really. Even now, Finn didn't know if he could do it. This was Rock.

He stopped at the counter, looking at the implements. He needed answers. He needed them quickly.

"I'm going to give you an opportunity to tell me what I

need to know." Finn turned back to him. "I'm not going to go into great detail describing the technique I would use to draw the questions out of you."

Rock sneered at him. "You don't have the stones, Shuffles."

"Perhaps not." And he didn't know. This *was* Rock, after all. Regardless of anything else, this was—or had been—a friend. "All I need is to know who hired Wolf. Tell me that, and this can be over. As I told you, I will offer you leniency." Finn forced a smile. "*Leniency* doesn't mean *no punishment*. You were involved, and given your past crimes, I can't guarantee there won't be a punishment involved, but I can guarantee it won't be death."

"I'm not afraid of death."

"All men fear death," Finn said. "Especially thieves." Finn regarded Rock. "What would your niece think if they were to know that you refuse to answer? Do you think she wants to lose you like she lost her father?"

"Don't you dare threaten my family, Shuffles."

"So, they wouldn't be pleased. I can't believe you'd do that to them."

"They were safe."

Finn frowned. "So you got them out."

Rock shook in the bindings. "When I get out of here, I swear to you—"

"You swear to me that you will do what? Hurt me?" Finn shook his head. "Haven't you heard the stories? I've died and come back. I've been hanged and survived. I've been burned and walked out of the fires."

Rock grunted, shaking his head. "Can't believe you started to believe the bullshit spread about you."

"And what is that?"

"Like you're some sort of god."

"Now, I know those are the stories spread about me," Finn said. "But that doesn't matter. The stories I care about are the ones that offer me a measure of protection. As you've seen, the Archers work with me now. Not against me. Besides, if you don't answer the questions the way I need, we both know how this is going to turn out for you. You have already been implicated in the placement of these devices. Seeing what happened with Sweth…"

"You don't have the stones," he repeated.

"I tried to give you the opportunity to answer questions without me taking the next, more aggressive step, but seeing as how you have no desire to do so, perhaps you and I will have to go into a different line of questioning."

Finn grabbed for the ankle braces. Meyer had used them on Rock before, and they had been ineffective against him at that time, but he hadn't used fire ash then. Finn didn't necessarily want to use that on him now, but for him to get the answers he needed he was willing to take whatever measures necessary.

He strapped on one of the braces, quickly tightening it. He watched Rock as did so, securing it to his leg until he stopped kicking. He reached for another and tightened that one down as well.

"We will proceed until you provide the answers I need.

At this point, I am afraid I won't be able to take any leniency on you until I have a few more answers. Who hired Wolf?" Finn looked up at Rock. "It's a very simple question."

"I'm not telling you shit."

"That's unfortunate."

Can I do this?

It was Rock.

And he was willing to destroy the city.

People Finn cared about would die.

Finn grabbed a fistful of the slender metal rods, carrying them over to Rock along with the jar of fire ash. Finn dipped one of the metal rods into the fire ash. "This compound is very similar to the one used in the device that you and Wolf decided to spread throughout the city." Finn cocked his head. "Did I tell you we obtained a list?"

"Fish is too stubborn to give you that."

"It wasn't Fish. It was the Mistress."

Rock said nothing.

"I see I have your attention. Yes. She had a list of all of the crews involved. As we speak, the devices have been picked up, and we know how to neutralize them. They will be carried out of the city, where they won't pose any more threat."

"Then you don't need me," Rock said.

"Unfortunately for you, I do. I need to know who hired Wolf."

Rock didn't say anything.

Finn pressed the metal rod up against his calf. "You

will feel a little burning here. This is called fire ash. It's quite unpleasant."

Rock started to shout.

"Now, as I said, all I need is for you to tell me who hired Wolf."

"I'm not telling you shit!"

Finn pressed the slender rod into his calf, sliding it all the way through.

He hadn't known if he could do this with someone he had once called a friend.

But Finn had changed.

"Who hired you?"

"You can do whatever you want, but I'm not telling you a thing."

Finn dipped another rod into the fire ash. "Then we will keep working."

Tears streamed down Rock's face. He had a dozen different metal rods slid into his calves, and he still hadn't given up the information Finn needed. He was tough, though most bruisers were. Finn wasn't surprised that Rock wouldn't reveal anything, but he had hoped that he could at least get through to him enough for him to provide some answer. It was that answer he needed.

He been working for the better part of the night. Finn had lost track of time, though he suspected it had been several hours. By now, hopefully, the crews led by the Mistress and working with the Archers had managed to secure each of the devices and get them out of the city and Meyer, Wella, and Lena had managed to disarm them. If they hadn't, Finn wouldn't even know. For all he knew, the city burned while he was in there interrogating Rock.

"Just tell me who hired you. Once you do, all of this can be over."

Rock looked up at him. "Didn't think you had it in you," Rock said.

"I don't enjoy this," Finn said.

Rock chuckled. "You could've fooled me, Shuffles."

"Who hired you? I'm not able to stop until I get the answer. We've only begun with the techniques I have available to me. If you don't share what I need now, then we move on to other, worse questioning techniques."

Rock grunted, shaking his head. "Worse?"

"I realize you think this is terrible, and it is, but there are worse things I can do."

"This isn't so bad."

"Do you want to hang? Worse, do you want to burn the same way that Sweth burned? I was there. The smell was terrible, but the screams were worse." Finn grabbed a chair, pulling it close so that he could sit across from Rock. "I don't want to do this. We were friends." He made a point of emphasizing 'were.' "I know you're a strong man, Rock. Even strong men have limits. Tie you to the pyre, get the flames working around you, and you would burn. I wonder if Master Meyer would even use as much accelerant as he had with Sweth. Given your role in all of this, he might choose to take it slowly."

Rock hung his head, shaking it slowly. "I tell you, and I'm dead. My family is dead."

It was almost enough to give Finn pause. "Do you really think that's true? Wolf isn't going to be able to work in the city again. If the Mistress is involved, there's no way he's pulling another job. He might not even survive."

"I'm not telling you anything."

"Then the city's going to burn."

"You told me it wasn't going to burn."

"Do you really think this is the last attempt on the city?" Finn shook his head. "Whoever is involved is not going to stop. They will keep trying. They want war with Yelind."

"What do I care?"

"Maybe you don't. Maybe you are telling me the truth that you don't care what happens to the city. If your family left, then it's possible you've got no reason to care. But I care, Rock."

"Why?"

"Because I don't want you to die."

At this point, Rock hadn't done anything that couldn't be undone.

"It don't matter," Rock said.

"It matters to me."

He looked up at Finn. "Wolf isn't going to let this slide."

"I know."

"He's going to come for you."

"I know."

"And eventually, he's going to catch you."

"No. He won't. He's going to get caught by the Archers. He is going to be sentenced. And he's going to die. That will be justice for what he's done."

"Justice," Rock said, shaking his head. "You talk about that as if you know what it means."

"I know what it's not. Vengeance. That's what it's not. And I don't want revenge for what happened to me. I want justice for what was done. I want justice for those who have been lost. I want justice for those who still might lose."

Rock breathed out slowly. "You can make sure I don't hang?"

"I will do everything in my power to make sure you won't."

"You don't have any power."

"Maybe not. But I have more than I did before, and I have Master Meyer backing me." As he said it, Finn realize that was true. If Finn were to recommend the sentence be more lenient with Rock, he had a strong suspicion that Master Meyer would go along with it. "I just need a name."

Rock snorted. "I can't believe you didn't know."

"I didn't know what?"

"Wolf never stopped working for the Client."

"Bellut," he whispered.

Rock grunted. "Sure, if that's his name."

"I have his name."

"Yeah? Well, did you know Wolf never stopped working for him? Pay was too good, you see. Didn't matter that he'd gotten pinched or nearly so. Didn't matter that the King got pinched and hanged. All that mattered was that he got paid. The coin was always good. The Client is the one who had us moving those things."

Bellut *was* involved.

And the only other name he had was Fol, though he didn't know much about it.

"Who is he working with?"

"The Client? Can't say I know that. He's never really said. Wolf don't bring me along, either." Rock leaned forward. "I told you what you wanted. Now you have to go along with what you promised."

Finn nodded slowly. He knew where he had to go and what he had to do.

"You going to do that, Shuffles?"

Finn looked over. "It's Finn."

Rock grunted. "Can't even use a name, can you?"

"I'm not in the crew anymore. I don't need a name." He got to his feet. "I'm an executioner now."

He pulled the rods out of Rock's legs and carried them over to the counter, setting them down. When he was done, Finn headed to the door, pulling it open. He nodded to Cor. "Bring him to his cell."

Finn headed out of the prison, into the early morning light. He was tired, but his mind raced, his heart pounding.

Of course they would be tied together.

He hurried through the streets. He remembered how to find Bellut's home. When he reached it, he paused on the street, staring at the simple wooden door. He needed proof. That was the only way this would end.

Bellut's home was in a nicer section of the city. He should wait for the Archers to arrive, and should have this done more formally, but the desire for answers—and, if he were honest with himself, maybe a measure of vengeance —stayed with him.

Here, Finn thought that he was beyond wanting vengeance.

It was one thing to feel compassion when it came to Rock, but Bellut was something altogether different. He had convicted Finn. He was the reason that Finn had nearly hung. He was the reason that others had suffered.

He knocked.

There was no answer.

Finn looked along the street, then tested the door. When he found it locked, that didn't slow him. He employed his old skills to pick the lock and pushed it open.

It was empty.

The air was musty, but it had a slight stench of ash mixed within it.

One of the devices.

Maybe Bellut had been part of building them.

Finn headed into the home, sweeping through it, searching on the main level and then upstairs for any signs of Bellut, but he wasn't there.

When he reached the bedroom, he found it empty. The wardrobe was empty. The desk empty. Bellut had cleaned out everything.

Bellut was gone.

Finn headed back down the stairs, pausing in the main

room. The strange items that he'd seen when he'd been here with Meyer were still there. The entire home was almost decorated in them.

Bellut had a table with a stack of papers on it. He flipped through the papers. There was nothing obviously incriminating there, certainly nothing that would implicate him in this plot. Without knowing who Bellut's partner was, Finn wouldn't have answers that he wanted.

Rock *could* testify against Bellut, but Meyer had made it clear they needed something more than testimony.

He reached a formal-looking paper near the bottom of the stack. It was a large parchment, folded in half, and sealed with a bit of wax marked with the king's sigil.

That was odd.

Finn flipped it open. As he skimmed the page, it was a note from the king, much like Finn had suspected. It discussed his pending arrival to the city.

He looked up. The timing fit.

Why not cause destruction when the king came to the city?

Meyer never knew when the king came, and these days, the king would come in and out of the city without any warning, typically to help secure the peace treaty with the Alainsith. That was the reason that he had been in the city the last time.

Bellut and his accomplice had known.

Bellut worked for the viscount.

The viscount wouldn't have betrayed the king. He was an appointee, but he also served the king.

Why would he have wanted to kill him?

Perhaps there was money in it.

This was tied to Yelind, though.

Something about it didn't quite fit.

Finn kept sorting through the papers. As he did, he came across another official-looking paper, and he swept his gaze along it.

This one was a sentence.

Not just any sentence, but Sweth's sentence. It discussed the accusations against him, using Finn's testimony, and then the sentencing that was to be carried out.

Why would Bellut have this there?

Something caught Finn's eye.

He stared at it for a long moment, his mind working through things more slowly than it should have, given his fatigue.

It was a simple statement. Only three words: *Sentenced to die.*

A signature at the bottom of the page, one made in a tight, flowing scrawl, carrying with it a flourish that obviously came from university training.

Magister Teller Fol.

Fol.

Everything clicked together.

Sweth. Bellut. Even knowing that King Porman visited Verendal.

The magister was Bellut's silent partner.

Another paper written in the same hand detailed the location of the fire starters.

There was no doubt.

Bellut and Fol.

Sweth had helped, but he had only designed the fire starters, nothing more.

Then they'd trained Wolf. Used the crews to place them throughout the city.

It would look nothing like an attack.

But it was.

Light suddenly exploded near him, and Finn looked up to see flames shooting from the hearth.

The air took on a sudden stench. It was something that reminded him of fire ash.

That was why he hadn't taken any of these papers out of there. The fire crept up the wall, getting hotter and hotter, forcing Finn back.

He grabbed the papers and then darted out of the home.

Once outside, he shouted, "Fire!"

It got the desired reaction.

Archers appeared, but that wasn't what Finn needed. He needed the fire brigade. By the time they arrived, the flames had engulfed the lower level of the home, but thankfully it hadn't spread beyond that. He waited there until he was confident that the flames had been completely put out, and then grabbed a pair of Archers and said, "I need your help. It's time for us to detain Teller Fol."

CHAPTER THIRTY

Finn approached the home slowly, with three Archers trailing along behind him, giving him support, but he needed more than just a little help for what he was going to do. His heart hammered. It had less to do with taking a man into custody—an action he wasn't entirely sure Master Meyer would support—than with needing to do this before the magister managed to escape the same way that Bellut had.

This part of the city was much nicer than his section. It was even nicer than Bellut's section. It was home to families of wealth. The buildings were all multiple stories tall, all with large lawns on either side, and many had walls surrounding them. Quite a bit of wasted space.

He slowed. "Are you sure this is the place?" Finn asked, glancing back to one of the city Archers who had come along with him.

"I sent word ahead to City Hall. Figured that you

wanted to know," the Archer said. He had a pinched frown on his wide face and wrinkles forming at the corners of his eyes. He hadn't shaven in the last few days, leaving a bit of a haggard appearance. Most of the iron masters within the prisons kept themselves clean-shaven, a distinct difference from the prisoners that were within their care. The Archers didn't seem to feel the same way. "Why? Do you think it's the wrong place?"

Finn shook his head. "I don't really know."

He reached the iron gate and pushed it open, pausing for a moment before heading along the path leading to the entryway. He would do this. He was the king's executioner, and he was tasked with ensuring justice was served.

Even when it had to do with the magister.

When he reached the door, it came open before Finn even had a chance to knock.

The magister had a look of confusion on his soft face.

Finn tried to look past him. *Could Bellut be within?*

"Teller Fol. I am here to question you in the matter of David Sweth and the fires that have raged throughout Verendal."

"Mr. Jagger?"

He still managed to sound confused, and yet there was a hint of something else beneath it.

Was it fear?

Finn had gotten better at identifying emotions in the people that he questioned, and he had certainly gotten better at identifying those who were guilty, though he still wasn't as skilled as Master Meyer. If he had been, he would've known that David Sweth had a hand in the fire that had raged throughout the Jorend section. Unfortunately, Finn had not. He had allowed himself to be too cautious with Sweth.

It was a lesson that Master Meyer had wanted him to learn, though perhaps not quite in that way.

"I'm here to ensure you come quietly."

That wasn't at all true. Finn didn't need him to come quietly, though he did want to be there for the magister's arrest. He wanted to know just what the magister might have been involved in and how much of it had been his responsibility.

If he were right—and as everything that had happened came together in his mind, Finn suspected he was—the magister had been the one pulling the strings all along. Bellut had been a part of it, and accomplice, and maybe even a co-conspirator, but he had not been leading it.

That had been the magister.

"Come where?"

"It's over, Fol."

"I'm afraid I'm a bit confused, Mr. Jagger. What is over?" The magister looked past Finn. "And why do you have four Archers with you? What is taking place?"

"We've uncovered your plot against the city. We've found your fire starters, removed them, and captured those involved with you."

Not entirely, but knowing Wolf and Rock were involved and having Rock in custody gave Finn the confidence that they would find any others who were involved.

Even Bellut.

He no longer had to worry that Bellut would escape his punishment.

They just had to find him first.

"You found what?"

"We found the fire starters. Tell me, magister, where you came from before you came to Verendal."

"I'm afraid that has no bearing. If you would like, we can take this up with the king. I'm sure he will be here soon."

Finn smiled tightly. "The king *will* be here soon. I saw the note in Bellut's home. A note with your signature on it. A note that tells me that the two of you were working together." Finn frowned at him. "I'm sure you intended for his home to burn, as did he, but unfortunately, he did not coax the fire starter fast enough. I recovered documents from his home and have removed them, and all implicated both you and him in the plot against the kingdom."

Not just documents, but after going through the documents, papers that detailed where each of the fire starters were to be placed. Everything fit together.

The only question he had was why.

The magister's demeanor suddenly changed. "And what do you know about it?"

Finn fished the folded document with the location of the fire starters out of his pocket, holding it up. The magister's eyes widened.

"What I know is that there is a scribe in the city who can certainly attest to the fact that these signatures are the same. And I know what I've seen. And heard. You and Bellut have worked together."

When he had been sentenced to hang, the magister had advised the jurors.

"You were responsible for what happened to me," Finn said.

Finn stepped aside. The Archers stepped forward, grabbing him. They marched him through the street, and Finn said nothing.

"I am the magister, serving directly under King Porman! I demand you bring me to the palace!"

"I will bring you to Declan for questioning, as I would any prisoner like you."

The inside of Declan Prison was quiet and dark, and Finn had more nervousness as he approached the chapel more than he usually did.

Shiner stood at the door, a more serious expression on his face than he'd worn the last few times Finn had come.

"Is he ready?" Finn asked.

"He's ready, Jags. You sure you want to do this?"

"No," Finn said. He held his hand on the door, taking a deep breath, and he tapped his pocket, feeling the papers he'd confiscated from Bellut's home. He needed confirmation.

And then what?

Finn pushed those thoughts away. He opened the door, stepped inside, and looked at the magister. Sitting in the prison grays, his thin, wispy hair hanging in front of his eyes, and strapped to the chair the way that he was, he didn't look as imposing as he did outside of the prison. Then again, the magister had never looked terribly imposing. Kindly, perhaps; scholarly, definitely. Never imposing.

And perhaps that was the problem.

"You're making a mistake," the magister said. "It's not too late for you to rectify this."

"I don't know that I am," Finn said.

He grabbed the stool and set it down in front of the magister, sitting far enough away that the man couldn't spit on him, but Finn wasn't as concerned the magister would do that.

"You claim you found something in Bellut's home. How can you be sure that it wasn't a way of incriminating me?"

"I can't," Finn said. "Which is why you and I are going to have a conversation." At least, they were going to have a conversation until Meyer showed up. Once he did, then Finn would be taken out of the conversation. It would be the last chance Finn had to understand what happened. "Tell me your name."

"My name?"

"Yes. We're starting with something you can answer simply."

"You know my name."

"Actually, I only knew you as the magister."

"That's my title. And I serve at the behest of the king. Much like yourself. Or rather, much like you *had*."

Finn ignored the not-so-veiled threat. "Your name."

He tried to straighten. The restraints held him. "I am Magister Teller Fol."

Finn nodded. "Very good. I'm glad that we have that out of the way."

"That's all?"

"Tell me about your time at the university."

"What is there to tell?"

"This can go however I choose it to go," Finn said, scooting the chair closer. He looked at the magister, watching him, trying to read his expression and decide how the magister might answer, but couldn't tell anything more. "Perhaps you are unfamiliar with the type of questioning we use here. If you are, then let me reassure you that Master Meyer has trained me well."

"I am quite familiar with the kind of barbaric things you do here."

Finn shook his head. "There is nothing barbaric about what we do to find answers."

"The work you do is barbaric," he said. "Once King Porman arrives in the city—"

"Once the king arrives in the city, I will be getting my report to him," Finn said.

"The king will not welcome you."

"That would be unfortunate," Finn said. "Almost as unfortunate as the documentation that I found at Bellut's home."

The magister looked at Finn, and for the first time, a hint of doubt crept into his gaze.

"I don't know what you think you uncovered, but it is likely insignificant."

"Can you tell me why Bellut would have this paper?" Finn flashed a page at him briefly before folding it back up and tucking it into his pocket.

"What paper is that?"

"A paper detailing your connection to Mr. Sweth."

He watched the magister. He had no idea what the magister would do—or say. Maybe nothing, but all he needed was to coax a confession out of him, and then he could present him to the king for treason.

"Sweth was the one responsible for burning the Jorend section," the magister said.

"And Bellut's letter to you states there is even more of a connection." He wasn't about to reveal to him what the letter really said.

"I have tried to be patient with you, Mr. Jagger. Truly I have, but if you continue this farce for much longer, my patience will wear thin. I can grant you clemency for this mistake, seeing as how you are acting on behalf of the city, but if you feel it necessary to continue this line of questioning, then you are going to have to face the consequences. This time, I don't think that even Master Meyer will be able to save you."

Finn wasn't going to get many opportunities to question the magister. In this case, Meyer would almost certainly give him a very short leash, but Finn wasn't sure that he even needed to use the more aggressive approach.

The magister had an arrogance to him.

Finn hadn't seen it before, but he recognized that arrogance. He might even be able to use it.

"Tell me about your and Bellut's plan," Finn said.

"There was no plan. There was no Bellut and me."

"And why does this letter to you say anything about it?"

"Because I'm sure that Mr. Bellut has decided to implicate me. I can understand why you would be so upset with Mr. Bellut. He was responsible for your fate."

"He wasn't alone," Finn said.

"Perhaps not," the magister said. He tried to take on a warm smile, but Finn saw through it. "And I don't know why he would claim my involvement."

"He claimed more than your involvement. He claimed you planned it."

"Did he?"

"The papers in his home prove it."

"And what papers did you find?"

"Enough for you to be sentenced," Finn said.

"I'm afraid there isn't anything that will implicate me," the magister said, his voice getting firmer. "I'm afraid all you have is a letter with my signature on it. Probably an official letter of office, seeing as how the two of us corresponded in that way often because of my position as magister and his position as juror." The magister leaned forward, his brow furrowing. "Now. If you have nothing more, I think it's about time you release these restraints, return me to my home, and we can get on with dealing with the consequences of your actions."

Finn stood. He headed over to the cabinet and began to move the tools around. "That's not going to happen," he said. "You and I are going to have a much different conversation than you might have expected."

"You're making a mistake," he said.

Finn picked up a large hook and carried it over, sitting in front of the magister. The magister glanced at it, and his brow furrowed, his eyes tightened.

Finn had to be careful now. Either he used it and he risked being wrong even though he didn't think that he was, or he didn't use it and the magister would realize he had nothing but empty threats.

"This is a toenail hook. It's used to... Well, I suppose you understand what it's used for," Finn said. He grabbed for the magister's boot and pulled off, peeling down his sock as well. "At first, it begins to bite, but then the pain sets in." Finn brought it closer.

"You are making a mistake, Mr. Jagger. The moment you do that, you will find I lose all tolerance for this."

"The pain is quite exquisite," Finn went on. "And most unpleasant. It burns." He looked up. "Now, all you need to do is explain away the documentation that Bellut had."

The magister glared at Finn.

Finn started to press the hook up against the magister's toenail. He was going to have to go through with this. His heart hammered.

The magister tried to kick, but Finn pressed forward.

"I can't tell you why he would have that documentation. I can't tell you why he would have saved those letters. And I can't tell you why he had something to imply I knew the location of the fire starters throughout the city. He must have decided to accuse me, and—"

Finn scooted back and sat up.

Finn blinked. "I didn't tell you anything about the paper documenting the location of the fire starters."

"You must have. When you first came to my home."

"No. I did not." He got to his feet and carried the hook back over to the counter.

Finn headed to the door, and as he pulled it open, the magister started yelling at him. "You are going to finally hang for this, Mr. Jagger."

"Why Sweth?" Finn asked. "That's what I need to know. He'd lost his family. You coerced him into helping with this plan."

"I did nothing."

Finn crouched in front of him. "He was an apothecary." That much Finn believed. He would have to have been. "And you turned him into a killer."

"He was always a killer."

"Because of the accident that claimed his family?"

The magister sneered at him. "Be careful where you dig."

"I've heard that warning before. Who did you threaten?"

The magister chuckled. "All men have weaknesses. Even you, Mr. Jagger."

Maybe Finn wouldn't learn who the magister had threatened to force Sweth into helping. All that mattered was that he had. And now he was gone, all to hide the magister's crime.

Finn pulled the door open. Shiner stood outside, but so too did Master Meyer, his face covered in ash.

Finn swallowed, letting out a relieved sigh that he was

still alive. Hopefully that meant Lena and Wella had survived disarming the fire starters. Finn glanced over to Shiner. "Return him to his cell."

Shiner nodded and headed into the chapel.

Meyer looked at Finn, who held out the papers. A look of concern crossed Meyer's face as he took them, but Meyer scanned them briefly before nodding. "You got a confession?"

"Essentially." Finn hoped it would be enough. And that Meyer would believe him.

"This is going to be difficult," Master Meyer said.

"He's guilty. Bellut as well."

"That doesn't change that this will be difficult."

"Does it mean that we shouldn't do it?"

"You know it doesn't," Meyer said. "I'm just warning you that there will be consequences. I doubt we can hold him here. Not for long. Prisoners like him often get held in the palace, where they have cells for men of his station. I would advise you to finish questioning him quickly, if that's your intention."

"You would permit it?"

"You don't need my permission for this." Meyer sighed. "I wish you had been wrong."

They approached the palace slowly, and Finn glanced over at Master Meyer every so often, waiting. It had been a long day. After questioning the magister in Declan, they had returned home in silence. It was much later in the day when the letter had come from the king, demanding their presence. Meyer had taken it in stride, but Finn remained apprehensive. The magister had committed treason, and in Finn's mind, he knew what *should* happen. Men like the magister, those who were as well connected as he was, rarely faced punishment.

In this case, Finn struggled with whether he wanted vengeance or justice. When it came to Bellut, he wanted vengeance as much as he wanted justice. The magister... He was someone who had masterminded the crime, but Finn didn't feel as strongly about him. Given his role in what had happened, Finn wanted justice, but he also feared they wouldn't have the opportunity to see it carried out.

"You know why he summoned us here?"

The street was darkened, with little lantern light illuminating it, and other than a few of the Archers patrolling, it was only them out in the city at this time of night.

"We are here because he requested our presence."

"He hasn't been here since—"

"I know the last time he came," Master Meyer said.

As they neared the entrance to the palace gates, Finn looked over to the Archers, hesitating there for a moment before nodding to them. The palace Archers were much more skilled than those of the city, trained to protect the king and everything he owned from threats within the city and outside. From men like Bellut and the magister.

"What if he pardons them?"

"Then he pardons them," Master Meyer said.

"You would just allow it?"

Master Meyer looked over to Finn, holding his gaze. "I think we need to make sure that you understand that whatever else happens, the king decides. You will not question."

"I won't question, but—"

"You won't question. You serve on his behalf. That is the only reason we are here."

They headed along the path leading up to the palace, and Master Meyer walked quickly, though Finn was a little bit slower. More reluctant. Though that might only be because of what he had experienced the last time that he'd been there.

Meyer glanced over to him. "Are you ready?"

Finn just nodded.

When they reached the main doors of the palace, another pair of Archers waited. They pushed the door open and Finn stepped inside. He had last been there months before, and when he had, everything had been different. He had come to seek approval to serve as the executioner, and he had come hoping that the king would grant him that permission, though not knowing whether he would.

Now he was there, and now he no longer felt as if he were still trying to be a part of a crew and struggling with his role as executioner. He felt more confident in his role, but he also had questions about it.

Master Meyer stared straight ahead.

A balding man greeted them. He was dressed in the crimson colors of the king, a yellow stripe down the right lapel, and a sigil worked into his left lapel. His gaze lingered on Finn for a moment before turning to Master Meyer and tipping his head. "Master executioner. It is good to see you again."

"And you," Master Meyer said.

"If you will follow me..."

He turned away and headed straight down the hall.

Master Meyer joined him, moving quickly along the hallway. Finn followed, his gaze sweeping all around, darting to the ceiling, before looking to the walls, the portraits of past Kings, swords crisscrossed along them, and statues and sculptures and other such artifacts that adorned them.

Finn was guided forward by Master Meyer and the servant.

They reached a grand doorway, and the servant held one door open, waiting for Master Meyer and Finn to step inside.

Finn followed Meyer inside, and it took a moment for his eyes to adjust. The lights inside the room were bright, candles blazing, lanterns glowing, and a thick carpet spread across the floor. It was nothing like the throne room where he had visited the king before. This was almost comfortable, were it not for the ornately decorated chairs surrounding a heavy oak table in the center of the room. A hearth blazed with a bright fire along one wall, and two statues rested on either side of it, the shape strange.

King Porman was a dark-haired man in a long velvet robe standing off to the side of the room, swirling a glass of wine as he watched them enter. Meyer bowed deeply to him before looking up.

Finn hurriedly bowed. He hadn't expected the king to be there without anyone else. There were other servants, no guards standing watch, no one other than the three of them.

"Would you like something to drink?" King Porman asked.

Meyer shook his head. "That isn't necessary, sire."

"I find a glass of wine in the evenings helps me sleep, especially after traveling as far as I have. The road gets long, but it is necessary to visit all of the kingdom."

It was more than just visiting the kingdom. The crown jewels were stored in Verendal, though Finn suspected there were other reasons for the king to come.

"I received your summons," Master Meyer said.

The king turned to Finn. "And you? I remember you from when I was here the last time."

"You do?"

The king smiled slightly. He had a wide face, but there was a hardness to it, along with an air of authority. Finn was accustomed to trying to read the people he encountered, but with the king, he found himself struggling. "My dear Master Meyer decided to follow a tradition of his brethren. It took me aback, but from what I understand, you have progressed nicely."

"Thank you," Finn said carefully.

"I understand I have you to thank for the current predicament."

"Predicament?"

"He won't be charged with treason. I can't have others thinking the city vulnerable," the king said, glancing from Finn to Master Meyer. "The death of my citizens is enough to sentence him. From what I understand, he was implicated in the fires in the city. Anywhere from one to two dozen people died, depending upon the reports. That will be grounds enough to prosecute him."

"As far as Finn discovered, it was five who died," Master Meyer said. "He was diligent in his research, looking to ensure he had all of the information needed so we had the right man."

"Very well. You have both served well."

"What's going to happen to him?" Finn asked.

Meyer shot him a hard look, and Finn realized that maybe he shouldn't have spoken so freely.

"I will leave that to the jurors to decide."

"He was not the only one guilty," Master Meyer said.

The king's brow darkened. "Unfortunately, that one has disappeared. He's gone south, I suspect, to rejoin Yelind. They had a spy among us all that time." King Porman stepped forward, handing a glass to Finn. He took it, too startled to do anything else. "You have served well," the king repeated. He glanced to Master Meyer. "Enjoy the drink."

With that, he strode out of the room, leaving Finn and Master Meyer alone.

"That's it?" Finn asked, looking around.

"Were you expecting something more?"

"I guess I..." Finn shook his head. "I don't know what I expected."

He hadn't even the chance to ask the king about his father.

Finn took a sip of the wine. He was more of an ale kind of person, but he couldn't deny the wine tasted delicious, slightly sweet, with a hint of oak and an earthy note buried within it. It was probably incredibly expensive. When he finished the glass, he looked over to see that the bottle remained resting there.

"I would not steal from the king," Master Meyer said.

"Is it stealing if he let me have it?"

"He let you have a glass. He didn't let you have the bottle."

Finn just chuckled. "Now what?"

"Now we prepare."

"For what? We don't know when the jurors are going to sentence him, and we don't even know what they will sentence him to." There was a part of Finn that feared they might decide to simply punish him, which might involve jailing him indefinitely within the palace. While it was still prison, it wasn't nearly as hard a sentence as what Finn thought he deserved.

"We don't know what they will do, but we must be ready."

"What happens if they choose not to sentence him?"

Meyer looked over to the hearth, shaking his head. "That is for the jurors to decide. We have prepared enough evidence that he should be convicted."

They left the palace, making their way quickly to the wall surrounding it, and from there back into the city. As they headed through the streets, Finn slowed.

"There's something I need to do. What are you going to do?"

"I told your sister that I would begin her lessons. I think it's time for her to train, don't you?"

Finn didn't necessarily love some of the aspects of his lessons, but he suspected Lena would enjoy every bit of it. She would thrill at the idea of learning how to heal, learning what it took to become an apothecary. Perhaps more. She didn't have the extra baggage Finn did with his job. She could simply enjoy what she was asked to learn and study, and from there...

From there, Finn didn't know. She had possibilities, though. For the first time in a long time, Lena could be whoever she chose.

As he made his way across the river, he headed toward the Olin section. It had been a long time since he'd been there. Long enough that the streets were familiar, but they weren't comfortable the way they once had been. When he reached the Wenderwolf, Finn paused. There was the same energy around it that there always had been. He could hear the music drifting out of the tavern, and could feel the energy of the tavern itself, even if he weren't there. He was tempted to rush inside, take a seat at his old table, order a mug of ale from Annie, and see if he could find a sense of normalcy, though Finn doubted there was normalcy for him.

"You can go in," a voice said out of the darkness.

Finn turned to see Oscar standing behind him. "I was just trying to decide what to do."

"You don't think you should enter?"

"I don't know if I would necessarily be welcome."

"The crew is gone, Finn."

"It's not the crew. It's more about Wolf. He's still out there. The Archers have been looking for him, but we haven't found him yet."

"And the others?"

"Bellut is missing. The magister"—Finn shrugged— "he's going to get what he deserves."

"And what is that?" Oscar stepped into the light, shadows darting along his face. "I only ask because he is someone of status, and given what I've seen in the city, people with status tend to get an exemption when it comes to following the king's laws."

"Not this time."

Oscar smiled bitterly. "Are you sure about that?"

"I just met with the king."

"Seeing as how Leon is dead, I presume this is Porman?"

Finn nodded. "He gave me a glass of wine."

Oscar started laughing. "That's not what I was expecting you to say. How was the wine?"

"Amazing, in fact."

"Well, lookie here. Finn Jagger has decided to join the upper class of society."

"I doubt I get to join any upper class," Finn said. "I might be honorable, or as honorable as I will ever be, but that doesn't mean I'm accepted."

"And that's what you're after?"

"Shouldn't I be after acceptance?"

"There are lots of ways to be accepted," Oscar said.

"Such as?"

"You're concerned about being accepted in the city, and I think you are accepted. You can travel freely, both in the city and outside of it. You have a measure of authority, which gives you even greater privilege. What does it matter if you aren't beloved by everybody?"

"I guess I was thinking of something else."

"What? Women?" Oscar shrugged. "You've got time, boy."

"That's reassuring, coming from you."

Oscar started to smile. "What's that supposed to mean?"

"I've known you a long time, Oscar. You've never been with anyone."

"Only by choice." He glanced over to the Wenderwolf. "There's another kind of acceptance, though. It's the most important, especially for you, Finn."

"What is that?"

"You need to accept yourself. You might not be the person you thought you were going to be, you might not have the life you thought you were going to lead, but from where I stand, I think you have quite a bit to be thankful for. Proud of, even." He shrugged. "I didn't get to talk to your mother much over the last few months, though I did visit once."

That was news to Finn. "I didn't know that."

"I didn't make much of a deal of it. I snuck in one night."

"Let me guess. I slept through it?"

Oscar shrugged. "Can't say I know whether you were

even there. It was late enough that you probably were. I think you're on the lower level, aren't you?"

"In the room in front. Why did you stop to visit my mother?"

"I wanted to see how she was doing. I did everything I could to help your father," Oscar said.

"I know."

"I don't know if you do or not, but I don't want you to think that I abandoned your mother when she needed help. I was trying to bring you along, knowing the King had jobs where you could get the money you needed. I figured..." Oscar shook his head. "I suppose that don't matter now. I tried. Didn't always do the right thing, but I tried."

"I suppose I should thank you for doing everything that you did for my family, anyway."

"I don't need thanks," Oscar said.

"We'll be fine now. Both Lena and me. Lena is going to train with Master Meyer."

Oscar frowned. "Is that right? I didn't think she had the makings of an executioner."

Finn smiled at the idea of his sister taking part in questioning, or even doing more. She could never be a part of sentencing. "Not an executioner. A healer."

"An apothecary?"

Finn shook his head. "I don't even think she's going to be an apothecary. Meyer intends to work with her, and Lena has a quick mind, so she's probably going to be better at it than I ever could be."

"Don't sell yourself short," Oscar said.

"It's not selling myself short. I know my strengths."

"And what are those?"

"Stubbornness, I suppose. Like my father."

Oscar laughed. "The old Goat. Stupidity, if you ask me."

Finn regarded Oscar, trying to come up with the question that had been bothering him. "What job were you and my father pulling when he got pinched?"

Oscar inhaled slowly. "You don't need to talk about that kind of thing, Finn."

"That's just it. I think I do. There aren't many reasons for a man to be moved to a different prison."

Oscar stared at him a moment, saying nothing. Finally, he sighed. "Your father didn't tell me. Now I know what you're going to say, but it's true. Said I had to trust him. It was one last score, and something that paid more than any we'd ever tried. Then he planned on getting out."

"How much?" Finn asked, his voice a whisper.

Treason.

That was what sat with him, though he had no idea what his father could have done.

The idea that they'd have been paid more than on any other job...

That was too much like what had happened with the King.

"Fifty crowns."

That would have been enough to pay for a physician. Healing for Finn's mother. Even to move them out of the Brinder section for good. They could have had a life.

"Was it him? Bellut?"

Oscar shook his head. "When the King started pulling those jobs, I wondered. Didn't find anything."

"Bellut served Yelind."

Oscar grunted. "So?"

"So my father was convicted of treason. That's the reason he was moved."

"Is that your concern?" Oscar asked, and Finn shrugged. "What's treason to men like us? We didn't care where the coin came from, so long as it spent. With what your father wanted..."

Maybe that was all it was.

Or maybe there was more.

"You could get the hangman to find out more," Oscar said.

"He tried. There's nothing more he can learn."

"I see. You hoped I might know something."

Finn nodded slowly. "I just want answers. With my mother gone, that's all I want."

"Does it matter?"

Finn started to tell him that it did, but maybe Oscar's practicality was right.

Did it matter?

He wanted to know what happened to his father, but learning wouldn't change anything for him. Not at this point. He'd been gone long enough. Chances were good that Finn would never learn unless Porman decided to share.

They fell into a comfortable silence for a little bit. "Can you do something for me?"

"Not so sure you want to be asking favors of me."

"This isn't any sort of favor. At least, not one that is going to cause trouble for you. I need to get word to the Mistress. I need you to—"

"I can't do it, Finn."

"I'm not trying to get you in trouble with her. I just want you to send my thanks."

Oscar frowned. "Your thanks?"

Finn nodded again. "Were it not for her, all of this would have exploded. She forced crews to help gather the devices so Meyer could disarm them." Having seen the fires raging firsthand, and having seen how quickly the device led to a building burning, Finn knew that it wouldn't have taken long before the city burned. With as many of those devices as they had discovered in the city, it would have been all too easy for there to have been even more destruction.

"I'll pass word. She's a dangerous one, you know."

"I'm sure there are stories."

"When it comes to that one, those stories have a way of being true." Oscar held Finn's gaze. "You don't have to worry about Wolf, either. *She* made sure of it."

"Oscar..."

"Told you she's taken charge in the city. The crews took care of this one, Finn. I'm not going to feel bad about what happened to him, either. He used them."

"Rock is going to be banished from the city," Finn said.

"Still only exile?"

"He provided information. Had he not, I wouldn't have uncovered the depths of the plot against the kingdom. I think this time, he'll stay gone." He had his family to look out for. Now that they were out of Verendal, Finn had to hope Rock could start fresh. It might be misguided hope, but it was still hope.

Oscar frowned. "You've changed, Finn."

"Have I?"

"Not a bad thing. Not at all." He glanced over to the Wenderwolf. "Are you going to come in?"

It was late, and they had been through so much, but perhaps he could have one drink.

"I can't stay late. I have a busy day tomorrow."

"An executioner never rests, eh?"

"Not until I find who's guilty."

"I hope I never have you chasing after me."

"Don't give me reason to."

Oscar regarded Finn for a long moment, slapped him on the shoulder, and guided him into the Wenderwolf.

CHAPTER THIRTY-ONE

Finn stood outside of the palace, looking up at the massive walls. The wind carried out of the north, bringing the scent of rain mixed with a gust of cool air, a combination Finn found comforting. Better than the smell of the city burning.

He glanced over to Master Meyer dressed in his gray leathers and swallowed tightly. "I felt nervous before executions before, but this one is different."

"This one is different," Master Meyer said. They stood before the gate, awaiting the prisoner, neither of them heading through the gate or into the palace itself. There was no purpose in doing so. Much like with any other execution, they would await the prisoner, and only when the prisoner came would they begin the procession. Unlike with other prisoners, there had been no visitation the morning of the execution. There had been nothing other than him and Master Meyer waiting.

The palace Archers stood just on either side of the gate, though they paid little mind to Finn and Master Meyer. It was the first time he had come to the palace without the trepidation he had had each time before.

"Do you think the king will pardon him?" Finn asked.

"There are very few crimes that require immediate sentencing. Treason is but one," Master Meyer said. "Even if that's not his sentence."

There was that word again. *Treason.*

It weighed heavy on Finn.

Finn had always felt like he was a part of Verendal but never truly a part of it. He had lived in the city his entire life and had known nothing other than city life, going so far as to even tell Master Meyer that he was a city person at heart. Still…

It was different, being asked to serve the kingdom.

As he looked over to Master Meyer, he couldn't help feel as if maybe he were more of an integral part than he had ever given himself credit for.

The wind shifted, gusting slightly out of the northwest now, and the smells shifted with it, carrying a hint of the forest, a fragrance from flowers, along with a bit of a familiar aroma Finn couldn't quite place. It smelled similar to one of the medicinals Wella stocked in her apothecary, though he wasn't entirely sure what it was or why it should be so familiar to him.

He turned, looking toward the rest of the city. The Gallows Festival would be different today as well. Finn didn't remember the last time anyone of any note had been sentenced, which meant that the city itself wouldn't have remembered either. Everything changed when the sentencing had more meaning to it.

Porman's Path leading away from the palace twisted and turned, giving no direct look from there toward the Teller Gate, but the march would be the same. The walk along the road would be no different from what it was in any other sentencing. The only thing different would be the duration of the march. Unlike in Declan Prison, where most of the prisoners were sentenced and left the city, coming through the city from there would be a long walk.

Finn was prepared.

"How do you feel?" Master Meyer asked.

Finn turned his attention back to Meyer, shaking his head. "How am I supposed to feel?"

Meyer nodded to the palace. "That is what I'm trying to determine. Do you feel vindicated?"

"I knew he was guilty," Finn said.

"Knowing his guilt and proving guilt are different matters altogether."

"You want to know if I am looking for vengeance or justice."

Meyer just shrugged. "Perhaps."

"Can it be both?"

"We've talked about that."

"No. We talked about your belief, but I wonder if I have a different one. I'm not angry. I don't want to carry out his sentencing to exact revenge by any means. So, I suppose that means I'm not after vengeance?"

"Perhaps," Master Meyer said.

Finn looked over to the palace. "I would have liked to have been able to sentence Bellut and Wolf as well."

"Does it matter that you were not able to?"

"It matters. They didn't face the king's justice."

Meyer watched him before nodding.

"In this case, I can't help but feel as if the vengeance is for more than just me. It's for the city. It's for the king. It's for all of us and anyone who might have suffered because of the magister."

"Perhaps in this case, vengeance and justice are served simultaneously," he said.

Finn smiled. "Would that be so wrong?"

"I don't know," Master Meyer said. "But I'm willing to question."

The doors to the palace opened, and four palace Archers strode forward, with the magister, dressed in the crimson of the king—a benefit no other prisoner would be permitted—marching between them. He had his head held high, and he stared straight ahead. Four more palace Archers marched behind him.

Finn smiled slightly.

"Are you thinking of the sentencing?" Master Meyer whispered.

Finn chuckled as the Archers approached along the path to the palace entrance. "Actually, I was thinking we have more Archers than are needed for him."

The palace Archers stopped in front of him and Meyer.

Meyer waited, and Finn hesitated, mostly because they

hadn't discussed who was going to lead, though Finn had assumed that it would be Master Meyer. When he didn't step forward, Finn did.

"Magister Teller Fol," Finn said, standing straight and meeting his gaze. "Do you have anything to say for yourself?"

The magister turned to him, and the once-gentle expression Finn had often seen on his face was gone. In its place was an angry sneer, an expression that didn't really suit him, though maybe it did.

"Do you really think this farce will be permitted?"

Finn glanced to the palace before turning to the magister. "The king has permitted you to come this far. If he were to intervene…"

He glanced over to Meyer, who just nodded slightly.

They stepped off to the side of the road, and the Archers started forward. One of the priests of Heleth marched along with him, the head priest who had presided over Finn's mother's funeral services. It was the only time Finn had seen him involved in a sentencing, though for someone who served directly under the king, perhaps such a privilege was warranted.

He spoke softly, and the words of Heleth rose against the backdrop of the city. Finn and Master Meyer took up a position behind the last of the Archers, letting the others lead the procession.

"It surprises me," Finn said, glancing over to Master Meyer. "That he is still permitted some of the trappings of his office."

"He was permitted an honorable death," Master Meyer said.

"That despite treason?"

"He was not sentenced for his treason," Meyer reminded.

Finn glanced over to Master Meyer before turning his attention to the Archers and to the magister as they marched along the streets. It seemed wrong, but at the same time, he couldn't deny that the king's justice was being served. There was nothing wrong with that, so perhaps he should find it within him to accept what was to follow.

They crossed over the river and passed into some of the poorer sections of the city. The crowds were denser than they often were, though given the nature of the crimes the magister was convicted of, along with the fact that he was a high-ranking official within the city, there was much more public interest than there usually was for such things.

Finn used Master Meyer to model how to behave and react. As they reached the Teller Gate, the crowd opened up, and thousands upon thousands of people packed the space outside of the wall, all trying to get a look at the Raven Stone.

Finn watched for a reaction out of the magister, but there was none.

He grunted. "The bastard actually thinks the king will pardon him," he muttered.

Master Meyer glanced over. "Perhaps he does."

"Do you think he will?"

"He would not have let him come this far."

They approached the jurors, now down a member along with the magister who oversaw the jurors, leading the jurors through the legal proceedings. Things would change with the new magister, and perhaps it would even give Finn an opportunity for a fresh start. Maybe with a new juror and a new magister Finn might finally have a measure of freedom.

They paused for a moment in front of the jurors, and when none of the jurors paid any attention to the magister, Finn and Master Meyer took up position on either side of him.

"Climb," Master Meyer said.

He started up the steps of the Raven Stone, moving slowly at first. Finn and Master Meyer each held on to an arm. They reached the top of the Raven Stone. Finn looked out over the sea of people, thousands gathered to watch the execution. In the distance, he noticed activity in the hegen section but could barely make out the sounds of music; the joyous, jaunty tunes that they played while the festival went on.

They took a space in the middle of the Raven Stone, and the priest stood behind the magister. He spoke the words of Heleth, his voice rising in intensity, carrying out, up, and there was actually something in the way that he spoke those words that called to Finn. He could almost believe that the god was out there, looking down upon him, offering him guidance.

On Finn, not the magister.

They looked out over the gathered assembly. Master Meyer remained near the magister, saying nothing. Finn knew what he needed to do.

He took a step forward, bowing to the assembled jurors. Meyer was going to allow him to carry out the execution.

A dozen different thoughts went through his head. *Was it vengeance or justice?* That was the first one that struck him, and even with that thought, Finn didn't know the answer. Perhaps it truly was both.

And it would be the first time he would wield the sword Justice in any official capacity.

He took a deep breath, holding the jurors' gaze. "I, Finn Jagger, present to you the prisoner Teller Fol, accused of fires in the Jorend section leading to the death of five souls of Verendal." Within Finn's mind, he named off the magister's other crimes. Treason was among them, but there were others. "By the order of the jurors of Verendal, following the guidance of King Porman, he is sentenced to die by the sword."

There was no response.

Shouts rang out from the crowd, as they often did during executions. People cried out, some seeking more vengeance, others wailing, wanting compassion, but Finn had learned to ignore them. There was the occasional fruit or vegetable tossed onto the Raven Stone, but even that Finn had learned to ignore.

When none of the others spoke, he turned back to face the magister.

"Do have any final words?"

"The king will pardon me."

"No. He won't." Finn glanced at Master Meyer, who turned, and Finn pulled the sword Justice free of the sheath strapped to Master Meyer's back.

He had held the sword many times during his training with Master Meyer, not only cleaning it, but wielding it while practicing, carving through pumpkins designed to mimic the very same activity he was about to perform. None of them had prepared him for this moment.

Hanging a man had become easier. Not easy. Thankfully, Finn still struggled enough to tell him he had a soul and a measure of compassion, but still easier. He could tie a knot ahead of time, and slipping the noose around the condemned person's neck was a simple matter to do while thousands of people watched. And then removing the stool took little more than a push. There was no strength. No real skill other than tying the knot.

Using the sword, though, was something else altogether.

In the time that he had served Master Meyer, there had been several people who had died by the sword, but Master Meyer had carried out those executions. It was those where they were sentenced to die by hanging where he had permitted Finn to get involved. As he held on to the sword Justice, he couldn't help but wonder why Meyer had permitted Finn to use this as his opportunity to wield the sword Justice the first time.

It was a test, the same way many things with Master Meyer were a test.

It was also a greater punishment for the magister to have the apprentice executioner carry out his sentencing.

The magister didn't kneel, staring defiantly out at the jurors, ignoring the gathered crowd. "He will pardon me! You have made a mistake. All of you will face—"

Master Meyer shoved his knee into the back of the magister's knee. The man dropped to his knees.

Finn took up a position, stabilizing himself, taking a deep breath, letting it out slowly, and he raised the sword as Master Meyer had taught him. He let out the breath slowly, then held it.

The magister turned toward him, as if only now realizing that Finn were the one to carry out the sentence.

Finn swept the blade in a rapid arc. His aim was true.

The magister's eyes widened slightly in the moment right before the blade cleaved through his neck.

Then he dropped.

Finn took a step back, looking over to Master Meyer and then finally out at the jurors. Several of them had already started turning away, including Isabel and Noren, but a few lingered, looking up at the Raven Stone, as if unable to believe that they had actually carried out the sentence.

It was then that Finn understood.

The sentence was not truly for the rest of the people gathered. The sentencing was for the jurors and anyone who thought that they might attempt something similar.

Finn looked over to Master Meyer. "You did well," Meyer said.

"I don't know how to feel about it."

"Then you feel the right way."

Finn reached into his pouch, pulling out the rag to clean off the blade, along with a small vial of oil. After he cleaned Justice, he held it out, waiting for Master Meyer to turn so that Finn could slip the blade back into the sheath.

"What now?"

"Now I believe you can finally get on with your training. You've been delayed. It's understandable, given everything that you had gone through, but now I think it's time for you to focus on emerging from the shadow of what took place and to find your focus back upon your training."

Finn looked over to see that the palace Archers had remained and taken up positions around the Raven Stone. "Why are they here?"

"They have remained so that they might ensure the hegen do not claim a prize."

"Why would they be concerned about that now?"

"Superstition," Master Meyer said. He looked over to the gathered Archers, shaking his head. "They likely feel that given his treasonous background, he is a danger for spreading that to others."

Finn smiled. "They can't be serious."

"Unfortunately, there are many superstitions that linger. That is but one of them." Finn looked over to the Archers and remained there for a moment. After a while, he climbed down the steps of the Raven Stone, waiting for Master Meyer to join him.

When he did, he looked back at the Raven Stone. "I feel like I'm beginning all over again."

Meyer nodded. "I'm not surprised you would feel that way. Take whatever time you need this afternoon, and meet me this evening to discuss your study plan going forward."

Finn just nodded. He had not had a dedicated study plan since he had started working with Master Meyer, and it surprised him that the man would suddenly decide to do so.

Perhaps it shouldn't, though.

Finn had started away from the Raven Stone when a familiar figure strode toward him through the thinning crowd.

Finn waited for Esmerelda. Her white dress flowed as she moved, almost shimmery. She flashed a wide smile at him. "I understand this is the first time you wielded Justice."

"You knew?"

She smiled at him. "I know many things, Finn Jagger. Did you enjoy it?"

It was a strange question, but it was appropriate as well. "I don't know that I would say that I enjoyed it so much as I understood the necessity of it, if that makes any sense."

"It makes perfect sense. You did what was needed for your people." Esmerelda smiled.

"I haven't thanked you for the card."

"There was no need to thank me for it."

"It helped."

"I suspected it would," she said.

"How is Jasmine?"

Esmerelda cocked her head to the side, smiling slightly. "Would you like to pursue her?"

It was a strange question, but at the same time, Finn wasn't exactly sure that he had an answer. "I don't know. Should I?"

"She would be receptive to it, I imagine, but I don't know if she is a suitable match for you. A man like yourself needs to be challenged, Finn Jagger."

"I don't know that I need to be challenged so much as to find somebody who would be willing to spend time with an executioner."

"Perhaps that's it. If you would like me to make the arrangement, I am happy to do so. Now that she's settled in with the people, she would be permitted to spend time with others."

"You have to permit it?"

"Only if she wants the necessary time."

Finn looked over toward the hegen section. "I think I would like that." It was about time that he have an opportunity to spend time with someone. There was something about Jasmine that helped take his mind off what he had to do. Maybe it was her lack of concern at his responsibilities, or how she managed to find a glimmer of hope in everything, despite what she'd gone through. Either way, he wanted a chance to know her better.

Esmerelda watched him, and he couldn't read the expression in her eyes, though it seemed to him she hesitated a bit. "I will have her visit you," she said.

He nodded to himself. It had been a while since he had spent any time with a woman. The last time had been when he had been in the Wenderwolf, and even then, most of those women were paid by Annie to ensure her clients stayed in the tavern, occupied, and perhaps more than that.

"Thank you," he said again.

"Of course."

She eyed the Raven Stone for a moment, and Finn could practically see the question in her eyes, a desire to make her way toward the Raven Stone and perhaps claim whatever prize the hegen wanted.

The Archers remained, blocking access.

"They won't be able to stay for long," Finn said.

Esmerelda glanced over. "I'm not so sure that is a prize my people would claim."

"What part do you need?" He paused, frowning. "Is that not the right way to describe it?"

"I suppose you could call it a part," she said, smiling slightly. "We would prefer to refer it as one aspect of the power of life."

"I don't know that I would call it the power of life so much as I would call it the power of death."

"You are not one of the people." She glanced over to the hegen section before turning her attention back to Finn. "I will speak with Jasmine. I suspect she will be quite pleased to have an opportunity to visit the city. Perhaps you will have someplace you could show her. I imagine you know many such places of interest." She smiled at him again and started away.

"Will you help me again if I need it?"

She gave him a sly look. "I think we can agree that our arrangement will be as needed."

As needed. He had no idea what it would take for him to need her services again, but he began to wonder if perhaps he would. *At what point will I be able to do my job on my own?*

He thought he was getting closer. When they had been outside of the city in the village, that had been him. Master Meyer had facilitated it, and because of Master Meyer, he had removed Mistress Elaine from her role in the village, but Finn had been the one to find the guilty party, and Finn had been the one to carry out the execution.

Maybe Master Meyer was right. Having an opportunity to travel outside of the city, to experience places beyond Verendal, simplified his job. The role of executioner was more complicated than he had ever imagined, and in a place like Verendal, situated as they were on the edge of the kingdom, it became even more complicated.

Finn could do it, though.

Not only could he do it, but he wanted to do it.

Maybe that was the most important part of all.

He started back toward the city, passing through the Teller Gate and back to his responsibilities. As Master Meyer had said, now that the threat of the magister and Bellut no longer hung over him, he truly could resume his responsibilities. And he truly could progress as an executioner. Finn was no longer the thief with the threat of execution hanging over him.

Now he could be an executioner.

Read the next book in The Executioner's Song: The Executioner's Blade.

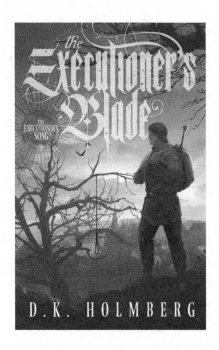

Sign up to my newsletter to get the free novella, The Fading Lion, set in the world of The Executioner Song!

SERIES BY D.K. HOLMBERG

The Chain Breaker Series

The Chain Breaker

The Dragonwalkers Series

The Dragonwalker

The Dragon Misfits

The Dragon Thief

Elemental Warrior Series:

The Endless War

The Cloud Warrior Saga

Elemental Academy

The Elemental Warrior

The Dark Ability Series

The Shadow Accords

The Collector Chronicles

The Dark Ability

The Sighted Assassin

The Elder Stones Saga

The Lost Prophecy Series

The Teralin Sword

The Lost Prophecy

The Volatar Saga Series

The Volatar Saga

The Book of Maladies Series

The Book of Maladies

The Lost Garden Series

The Lost Garden

Made in the USA
Las Vegas, NV
18 March 2021